REAGAN'S QUEST

Invaded

Virginia Tomlinson

Acknowledgements

Sometimes it is unexpected, but when a story is demanding to be told, so it will be!

Thank you, Right Cheek, without you I'd have never found my meatball!

Thank you to Elaine for your insights and helping me through the process. And thank you for a referral to the best cover artist ever!

Also I would like to extend my thanks to Mama Dean for your thoughts and encouragement.

This version is for Lauren.

CONTENTS

INVADED

CHAPTER 1 DAYDREAM

I have been here before; I know I have. I look around at the trees with their odd shades of greenish-black, the ground covered in dead leaves, littered with tree branches and stumps. Even the large jagged rocks jutting out in strange patterns on the ground are familiar, but different somehow. I know I have been here before, but it has definitely changed; something dark and ominous lives here now. I am hesitant, but I slowly make my way down the path before me as quietly as possible. I don't know what lives here, but all of my senses tell me it is something I do not want to disturb.

As I wander, I am starting to recognize where I am; it is a place I visited when I was a child. I take my next step then feel the hairs on the back of my neck stand up in warning. Behind me, I hear a heavy footfall and a twig break. Turning cautiously I see a figure in the shadows. I feel as though I am expecting this figure, like I knew it was coming. By the features of the shape, I think it is a man, though he is concealed in the shadows of a large pine tree. I feel the urge to run. Why am I not running?

"Reagan...Reagan...REAGAN!" I jerk back to reality with a start. As I look around, I take in my surroundings. I am back in Browning's Burger Palace's break room, the local burger joint where Marnie and I have worked for the past two years. The breakroom's gray drab walls are littered with various work safe and instructional posters mixed with handwritten notes from other employees. I am currently staring at a for sale poster for a 2020 Ford Escape; runs great it claims, but the photo shows it is an unfortunate shade of putrid green.

I shift my gaze to the mirror next to the bank of boring brown lockers; my brown eyes look even more dreary, very tired, too much school and work I suppose. I have not slept well since this daydream now creeps into my dreams at night. My strawberry red hair is a tattered mess, the frizz leaking out of my messy bun on the back of my head. My hair has massive natural volume, as my mom calls it. I call it frizz. When I was a little girl it hung in beautiful ringlets; if it still did I'd be thrilled, but now it just frizzes everywhere. My hair is hard to tame on a good day; these days, the local store has been out of my favorite shampoo for over a month. Let's face it, there is no help in sight for this mess. I ignore Marnie a minute more, continuing to stare in the mirror considering my reflection critically, my conclusion...I need a vacation.

"Sorry Marnie, it's that same daydream. It doesn't help it happens so frequently now I'm starting to mix fiction and reality in my mind. I try to dig deeper and see if I can understand it, but no luck. I am fairly sure I recognize the place from my childhood. This time there was a guy there, at least I think it was a guy, I couldn't see him very well. I don't think I've ever seen anyone like him before. You snapped me back to reality before I could get a good look at him, but there was definitely something weird about his appearance."

"Rae, you have got to let this go. It's just a daydream, a fantasy; you're becoming wholly consumed," Marnie protests. "There's an entire world thriving around you that you are missing out on spending so much time dwelling on a silly daydream." Marnie continues, looking at me with a mix of concern and agitation. It is the 'I think you've lost your damn mind look,' not the first time I've gotten 'the look,' I've come to recognize it.

"It seems SO real though, quite frankly, it's disturbing," I rebut with a bit of a pout on my face.

"Are you showing this weekend?" Marnie asks, abruptly

changing the subject. When I go off about how real this day-dream feels, it makes her uncomfortable.

"No, Dixon is lame. Again." I say with a huge sigh. Dixon is my new horse; we've owned him about seven months now; he's been on stall rest for almost 4 entire months of that time. He was supposed to be the one on which I win the World Championship Titles that have eluded me thus far, but he is never sound. This will be my last year as a youth competitor since I turned 18 last December. It is my last shot at winning the Horsemanship and Trail classes at the world show. Last year I was reserve in the horsemanship and third in the trail, the closest I've come yet. I love Dixon; he is a huge bay gelding with puppy dog eyes and a bushy forelock that makes him a bit dorky looking. He is so easy to get along with and has such a great personality, but he has definitely not turned out to be what he was supposed to be. I sigh out loud at these thoughts. "I thought about going to help out, but it is so depressing to watch everyone else show while I sit on the sidelines."

"I couldn't help notice neither of us is on the schedule for this weekend; let's go to the Quarry. It'll be just the break you need. The weatherman promises high seventies this week-end," suggests Marnie, hopefully.

"So, are we going to the Quarry to be teenagers or are you going to do more research?" I ask with a bit of sarcasm coloring my voice. I love Marnie, but she is such a nerd. I do not get her obsession with Geology. But, going to The Quarry and blowing off some steam sounds appealing. The reality is, Marnie and I are both nerds. By blowing off steam, I mean drinking one or two spiked seltzer drinks, then falling asleep staring out of the tent looking at stars, while talking about boys and college.

She pushes her silky caramel brown hair behind her ears so it is out of her face and responds, "why can't it be both? Besides, I heard Connor, Isaac, and AJ talking about going as

3

well." Marnie adds a devious grin. Ah, Connor, my current and longest obsession. I never thought I'd find a guy in this Podunk town worth my time but I really think he might be. His mom and dad divorced quite some time ago, his mom had a brief relationship that gave him a half-sister, but it didn't last long; apparently, the jerk didn't want to be a dad.

About two or three years ago they moved up here from somewhere in Texas for his mom's job. His dad stayed in Texas, where I believe he runs a cattle ranch. He has spent about two months the past two summers in Texas; I hear that is where he is planning to go to school, convenient for me as I will as well. His dad has remarried, he has two younger siblings in Texas he adores and would like to spend more time with them. All of this I've learned from my mom, who occasionally works with his mom on work projects.

Most girls would not say he is hot, but they wouldn't find him unattractive. He is just not the usual standout pretty boy. He is thin like me, but unlike me, he does have a lot of muscles. He is also a ginger like me, though his hair is soft and falls nicely around his face. To me, he is perfect. More than once, he has busted me staring at him in Chemistry. He has to be one of the school's politest guys, and that southern drawl when he says ma'am about undoes me every time. He doesn't have a girlfriend, but we are too shy to progress towards a relationship. Each day I watch him walk by in his starched jeans and square toe boots, cultivating a much more pleasant, downright steamy daydream I wish I could spend more time with.

"Well, I will have to check with mom, but I think you're right; this is just the change I need to break out of this funk." I concede.

"So..." Marnie says, changing the subject yet again, "does your brother have any leave coming up?"

Marnie has been obsessed with my brother Ethan since we

were in junior high. I see it; he's super polite, has street smarts, and is very handy. Ethan can fix anything. He's my brother, so I am not sure if he is cute or not. His hair is a darker red than mine, more auburn, and his features are reasonably proportionate. When he was little, his head and ears were big, but I suppose he grew into them nicely. Ethan has been obsessed with planes and flying for as long as I can remember. When he graduated high school, he couldn't wait to join the air force and fly the 'fast jets' as he called them. Now, three years later, he is part of an elite squadron of fighter pilots. I know it scares mom to death, but others say he is exceptionally good at what he does. He is one of, if not the youngest, air force pilots to make the squadron. I got to go up with him once on a visit to the base, by far the scariest experience of my life to date. "I don't know," I say, "I think he's been in Europe for the past month or so. I am not sure how long the deployment is for, but usually they do get some time off after a deployment."

"Europe? What is going on over there that would require the US Air Force?" Marnie inquires.

"Not sure, he just said 'they've had some strange occurrences, and I can't share the details,'" I say, imitating my brother's matter of fact voice. "But" I continue, "they were requesting help from the US military, so that is something. It was sudden, not something he was expecting." I continue. "We've been watching the news to try and figure it out. I'm not sure if you've noticed or not but coverage of anything outside the US has been severely lacking lately."

Marnie looks at me, genuinely concerned, so I add, "we get an email or text from him every couple of days saying he is okay."

My brother has never wanted a girlfriend; he has been way too focused on flying, much to Marnie's dismay. Once he had his place in the Air Force secured, he started to show interest in Marnie, but I think Ethan drew back knowing he'd be gone a lot. He thought it would be unfair to tie her down during her senior year to someone who was never around. I don't think she would've minded. I still think they will be together someday, but who knows when that day will be, they don't have a lot of opportunity to date with him always away. When he is home, or at least on US soil, he is stationed at a base only an hour and a half south of the house, so we see him more frequently than when he was in training 18 hours away.

Marnie does not look consoled at this news but more agitated. "What if he meets a hot French girl over there?"

"I doubt that Mar. I don't think he gets a lot of time off. Besides, isn't it the French who don't shave their armpits?" I say jokingly; Marnie snickers. "Anyway, I think he is in Germany; big Bavarian gals never appealed to him. We've got enough of those genes in our family tree," I say, enviously eyeing Marnie's slight frame. Though I am skinny, I still have a large bone structure, a size zero I will never be. "Come on, breaks over; we've got to get back to work."

The rest of the shift does little to hold my attention. I almost spilled Mr. Johnson's water on him while I was lost in thought about how to convince my mom to let me go to the Quarry. All thoughts of the daydream have been forgotten as I plan for the weekend. Connor was going to be at the Quarry; I had to get mom to let me go. She was typically easy to convince, but since Ethan's latest deployment she's been a bit weird about things. Perhaps she could come along for a weekend in the Lodge and get in some spa time.

I bump into Marnie at the drink station, "Hey, pay attention, you!" she exclaimed, "you nearly knocked my drink tray out of my hands."

"Sorry Mar, just thinking about this weekend, planning out every potential argument mom might throw my way," I apologize.

"Hey, I'm all for getting out of town this weekend, but we've got four days to get through without spilling our customers' drinks in their laps," she says with a wink. She must have seen the incident with Mr. Johnson, oops, I don't think he even noticed. I mean, nothing actually spilled on him.

Finally, nine o'clock rolls around, time to head home. I hit the breakroom; Marnie is already there, having deposited her apron in the bin, trading out her drab black sneakers for a pair of strappy sandals. I walk over, fumble with the lock on my locker, taking three tries to finally get it open. I grab my purse and backpack, change out of my sneakers for my slip-on loafers. I personally think it is still way too cold for sandals, but Marnie doesn't seem to notice. However, that girl's metabolism is so high I'm surprised she ever wears a jacket.

As we head out to Marnie's 2023 white Crossover SUV, I take in a deep breath of the spring air. It is a bit cold for a trip to the Quarry now. I'm hoping the weekend really is warmer. The air is refreshing; it smells clean, which always reminds me of spring, bringing a smile to my face. "The air smells like spring," I say, speaking my thoughts out loud.

"Yes, it does. I hope it hits eighty this weekend, though it rarely does in March," she adds, "I can't wait!"

"Don't get too excited yet. I've still got to convince mom," I remind her.

"Thanks for the ride M, see you at school tomorrow," I tell Marnie as she drops me at home. I have a car; it's just not as nice or reliable as Marnie's, so she tends to drive us everywhere. I've offered gas money, but she typically refuses; I'm not going to lie, I'm glad. Ever since dad died it has been challenging for my mom and me. Ethan was already in the air force when dad passed, so while he feels the engulfing loss, he doesn't quite feel the pinch at home. He and dad were extremely close; the loss is more than enough pain for him to endure without having to worry about finances as well.

Mom does her best to help me continue to chase my horse show dreams, but it is not always easy. Even though an unknown benefactor helps by paying off a training bill, vet bill, or horseshoeing bill when we are behind, it's still all we can do to keep up. I don't know who it is that pays these things; no one will tell us. These occasional gifts are the only reason I've managed to attain my ultimate goal; just last month, I officially signed to ride on the western equestrian team at the University of Brooksburg in Aleferado, Texas. The full tuition and board scholarship made the struggles, the sacrifices of the past two years worthwhile for sure. Despite this, things are still tight. I will have to pay for my books, travel from Ohio to Texas and other incidentals, which I am saving for now.

Even with the challenges to keep up with the bills and maintenance of a mini-farm, mom has been determined to keep us from having to leave the only home we have ever known. I am hoping once I leave for school, she finally sees reason and moves to a condo. I do think the memories hold her here as much as anything.

My mom and dad were truly in love; they had had their share of hard times and heartaches but only came through each stronger and more dedicated to each other. They were each other's firsts and lasts, though mom is incredibly young still, at 51 she has a lot of life left to live. No matter, she holds tight that there is no one in this world for her other than my dad.

The car wreck that claimed my father's life left us all devastated. Mom's always been strong though, she bottles her grief turning it into a drive. She says to 'do more, and do better for him and his memory.' I say he'd have wanted her to have an easier go of things, but there is no convincing her of that. Dad worshipped the ground she walked on; he always wanted her to have more than he could provide. Don't get me wrong, life was good, we never wanted for a thing, but he always wanted her to have the finer things in life. Truth be told, she thought late nights around a bonfire with a cold beer, snuggles from our dogs, and the horses' nickers in the barn early in the morning were the finer things.

When I get into the house, mom is in the dining room sitting at her computer as usual. "Work work or side work, I ask?"

"Oh, a little bit of both as usual. How was your day sweetie?" mom asks, standing up from her work and stretching.

She keeps her hair longer than most women her age, usually tied back in a ponytail, but not sloppy, very polished looking. She has not colored her hair, but the mixed light blond and brown tones keep her gray from standing out. She sets her glasses down at her desk and walks over to give me a gentle kiss on the cheek.

"Much of the same. I think I might start sleepwalking if this semester never ends. I'm so tired, and I still have hours of studying to do tonight." I complain.

Mom gives me a sympathetic look. "You have to keep your grades up Rae, you have to maintain that scholarship. You've worked far too hard to risk it now. I think you need to cut back at work. You're only going to have your senior year once, and there are only a few months left of that. Take some time off and enjoy life. You have your scholarship; with the money we were saving 'just in case' we should be okay without your work income."

"I don't know. I still need to get my car worked on." I hedge.

"I just heard from Ethan a few hours ago; he'll be home at the end of next week. He can look at it." She says with relief evident in her voice.

"Wow, that's great, is whatever that was going on over there handled?" I inquire.

"Not sure," she says a bit distantly, "he sounded stressed but said it was nothing to worry about now."

"That's odd" is all I can think to say.

I wander into the kitchen and start picking through the cabinets. I'm not really hungry but want something to munch on while doing my Calculus homework. I settle on a bag of trail mix, gather a soda from the fridge, and set up at the kitchen table. My mind is drifting between Calculus and convincing my mom to let me go to the Quarry this weekend. I turned eighteen in December, but I respect my mom and her opinion; she is the picture of determination, self-sacrifice, and hard work. I want her to be on board.

Spreading out my books on the table I hear sounds of the evening news drifting in from the living room. "Satellites and communications systems over much of Europe, and now parts of Asia continue to be down today, prolonging the blackout from European nations and beginning a silence from much of Asia as well. Many complain they are unable to reach friends and relatives who live or are traveling in those regions. We've been unable to get any information regarding the cause or when communication is expected to be restored. In other news…" Well, that doesn't sound good. How is it that Ethan is coming home when they obviously have not resolved the issues over there?

Since calculus is doing little to hold my attention I drift to this weekend, imagining what I will say to Connor. My vision is clear; we're sitting in the circle around the campfire, a little closer than casual friends might sit. It is getting late, I lean my head on his shoulder. He is a bit hesitant at first, a first for him too I suspect; then he slowly wraps one arm around my back, pulling me in just a bit closer. I lean tighter to his side catching the faint scent of cologne, "Rae," he says, looking down at me with careful but passionate eyes.

"RAE" my mom yells. Oops, mixing daydreams and real-life again, at least this is a pleasant daydream. "Didn't you eat at work? If not I can fix you something quick" mom's question jerks me from my thoughts.

"What, oh, no need, I did eat, just wanted something to munch on to keep me awake while working on Calculus," I respond.

"First off, doesn't seem to be working; second ick, I managed to avoid Calc in my high school days...I do not regret it." She answers with a smile.

"Hey mom, Marnie wants to go to the Quarry and camp this weekend. I was wondering if you were interested in a weekend at the Lodge. Maybe some spa time?" I ask, hopefully.

"While that sounds absolutely delightful, I've got a big report due out next week. I'll be working all weekend," she responds.

"Oh," is all I say.

She considers me thoughtfully for a moment, then asks, "who is going, just you and Marnie? What about Michela, Jen, and Rachel?

"Jennifer, Michela, and Rachel are out of town until next week touring colleges with their parents," I answer.

"All together?" She asks skeptically.

"No, I don't think they are even in the same states. Anyhow, we were planning on just Marnie and myself, but I've heard some others from school are planning to go; first really nice weather weekend and all." I hedge.

"Who are these others? Might a certain boy be planning to go?" she asks with a hint of knowing to her voice. Crap, she must have worked with Connor's mom today. She knows what I was going to ask before I asked it, great, walked right into that one. At least I didn't lie; I would never be able to recover from that!

"I've heard that potentially Connor, Isaac, and AJ might be there." Darn it, I hope this doesn't ruin things for this trip.

"Let me think about it sweetie. I know you are responsible, and I actually feel better knowing there's others around; that you and Marnie won't be out there alone. But there is still a lot to consider."

Well...that is not a no. I'll play the eighteen and an adult card if I have to, but it sounds like she will cave. Mom trusts me. She knows I won't do anything to jeopardize my scholarship; I've been working towards that goal since I was ten. I can see why she'd be happier with more folks around, particularly strong guys, versus us girls camping out there alone.

The Quarry is a pretty safe place, a camping resort built up around an old rock quarry in Indiana. It is about two hours from our home in a distant rural suburb Northeast of Cincinnati. The Quarry used to be just a dirty lake, created when an abandoned limestone mine was filled with water. For a while, people would go there to get certified for scuba diving, sinking into the murky depths to explore junk cars and other oddities found at the bottom of the lake.

A few years back, the Carter family, a wealthy family escaping from the city of Chicago's hustle and bustle, bought the property and turned it into a top-notch resort. The lake has been cleared and cleaned for swimming, boating, and fishing; then they put up a lovely rustic looking lodge complete with a full spa. Down closer to the lake, they have a camping resort. You can rent a space to pitch your tent or rent a platform tent with cots they have ready to go. The camping area is set up in 'wheels.' There is a shared fire pit at the center of each site, with spokes going out to 5-10 tent sites depending on the spot.

Many church groups, families, and school friends camp there, claiming a 'wheel' for their entire party. There are about 15 or so of these wheels spaced around the lake. Each tent site is separate from the others, but the shared fire pit makes for great socializing in a very relaxed atmosphere.

I give up on Calculus, it is NOT going to happen tonight, and head up to bed. The assignment is not due for two more days and even though I hate putting things off this is just going to have to wait. After climbing the stairs I turn right and head down the short hallway to my room. When I look inside, I see my dog Willis has already gone to bed without me; this makes me smile. He is small for a Boston Terrier, but those big brindle ears stick out from under the blankets giving away his location.

"Uh-huh," I protest, "getting lazy in your old age, didn't even come to greet me" I chide him...he doesn't seem to care... oh, the life of a dog. I changed into my favorite giant ratty T-Shirt that belonged to my father and crawl into bed. Willis gives me a snarl as I push him over to make room, but I am soon forgiven as he curls up against my side in his regular spot. Willis has been my companion since I was 12, so he isn't really that old, only 6, but he acts like an old man. He's been there through all of my major life events and so far has never complained. I lie there stroking his soft little head and drift off into an exhausted sleep. I really may not survive this semester.

CHAPTER 2 LONG WEEK

I try to be patient and not bug mom every day to see if she is on board with the Quarry trip, and quite frankly, it is making me crazy. I make it one day, just one lousy day, Wednesday morning, I cannot take it anymore, I have got to ask. I head down to breakfast, running late as always but determined to have this conversation with mom. She already has my breakfast laid out for me, waiting on the table. This has been the routine for as long as I can remember. She knows that if she does not do this, I would never get breakfast because I would never get up in time to do it myself. Just another unspoken way she lets me know she loves me.

"So," I begin, "have you given any thought to this weekend?" I look at her expectantly.

"I don't know Rae, I don't like you girls being out there unsupervised," she hedges.

"Mom, seriously, you know I've got goals. I will NEVER do anything to jeopardize my scholarship. I know the speech: 'if you screw up it'll be community college and student loan debt, blah de blah blah blah'" I counter.

"I know you won't plan to honey, but sometimes teenagers do stupid things when they are given too much freedom," she says with a wink. I am left wondering exactly what she did as an eighteen-year-old. I will not be distracted.

"Mom," I groan, "please, I need a few days off from life."

"I know, it's just hard for me to let go," she says wistfully.

"Mom, I leave for Texas in about four months; you're going

to have to put some faith in me some time," I say with a bit of hurt.

"Rae, you know I have faith in you, but you know I've always been a bit of an overprotective mom," well, she has that right. "I've got to get downtown; we've got meetings with the product managers today." She kisses me lightly on the forehead and heads out the door. The last look she gave me leads me to think she'll say yes.

Slipping college in there was a way to play the eighteen-year-old card without actually having to blatantly lay it out there. Saying 'I'm eighteen, an adult, I can do what I want' has never not ended in a fight for anyone, anywhere, in the history of teenage kind.

I finish snarfing down my microwaved biscuit sandwich and race out the door myself, yep, going to be late again. I get to school with no time to spare. The final bell is buzzing as I race in the classroom. "Late again," Marnie whispers quietly under her breath. "Of course," is the only response I can give.

The morning drags on for an eternity. Finally, the bell buzzes for lunch. I head out of my level 3 Spanish class for the cafeteria. I see Marnie at our usual table towards the back near the soda machines. The cafeteria is rather dull. The walls are painted in our school colors, a hideous orange with a white border painted at the top. The words "Go Eagles" repeatedly painted around the room in the white border, separated by poorly drawn birds I think are supposed to be eagles.

This time of year, the walls plastred with various posters, anti-bullying, join this club or that, graduation announcements, and order forms. The tables are round with about 8-10 hard plastic orange chairs each. The tables are scattered around the room with no identifiable pattern

There are usually five of us girls at the table, but today three of our friends are all on college visits with their folks. I am grateful I have college locked down already. I grab a slice of pizza, salad, and a bottle of water, check out, and head to the table with Marnie. We have not had a chance to talk all day, and I know she'll want to know if mom approved the trip or not.

As I sit down, she has just taken a bite of her hamburger, she swallows hastily and begins choking. "Mar, you may want to slow down. I know you're dying to ask, but we can't go to the Quarry if you choke to death before then." This makes her laugh, which brings on a whole other round of choking coughs turning her usually tanned complexion bright red.

I laugh hard, looking at the table; when I look up, I about choke myself. Connor is standing by our table looking at us questioningly. "Marnie, Reagan," he tips his head as if he's tipping the brim of his imaginary hat and starts to walk away.

"Rae," I call out to him.

"What was that?" He asks politely.

"Most people just call me Rae," I say with a very sheepish smile.

"Rae," he says with an answering smile.

I cannot even speak. This is the first real, albeit small exchange I have ever had with Connor. I am sure my face is beet red with the blush I can feel there.

"Well," Marnie says with a gasp, finally able to recover at least some air, "that was something. Which brings us to; is your mom going to let you go this weekend?"

"Is yours?" I counter.

"Of course," she retorts. "I just told her I am going to work on a mineral research project and you'd be staying with me as my mighty protector. Besides, I think she and my dad were planning a date night or something like that. My little sisters are going to Grandmas."

Marnie is 18 like me, but she was a surprise in life. Her mom and dad didn't add sisters until she was 12, so her oldest sibling is now 6, the others are 4 and 2. She has spent a lot of time at my house, away from 'the babies.'

"Well, she said we'd talk about it tonight, but the look in her eye tells me she's caving. I subtly played the adult card by reminding her I'd be off to Texas in just four short months." I answer.

"Well played, way to lay it out there without starting a fight!" she praises me.

"I hope so. I'll shoot you a text tonight and let you know. Are you working tonight?" I finish.

"Nope, I've got to study for that chemistry test, or I am going to be in deep doo-doo. Josh is taking my shift," she says with a laugh. We continue chatting about anything and everything through the entirety of our lunch period. The giddiness of the upcoming weekend, and Connor actually speaking to me, leaking into our moods. We are so lost in conversation it is a surprise when the bell rings. We realize we really didn't eat much of our lunch. Oh well, hopefully, my stomach doesn't growl too loudly.

The last bell finally rings. I close my history book and cram it into my backpack. I walk into the hallway just as Connor is passing moving toward the stairs. He tips his head again, giving me a big smile. For just a moment, I forget how to walk. Thankfully, Marnie runs up beside me pinching me hard on the butt cheek, bringing me back to reality. "Well now, the flirting is just getting out of control," she says in a fake Southern accent while mock fanning herself. I just roll my eyes and head off to my locker, fumbling with the lock once again. What is it with me and combination locks? Four years of this, and I still can't get it on the first try.

I'm preoccupied driving home from school, planning for this weekend, I almost run a stoplight. Fortunately, I break at the last moment because the most unfriendly town cop, Davis Everly, is sitting in the oncoming position. Once the light turns green, and we move, I shoot him a smile, he returns a scowl. Oh well, I didn't really expect anything different.

I begin to think through the day's events, starting this morning with my conversation with mom. The exchanges today with Connor, I am not sure what has finally made him so brave. Still, I am glad. I finish by wrapping up my thoughts with his smile and nod in the hallway. Despite my distractions, I manage pull into my long gravel driveway without incident.

I pull into my usual parking spot in the garage, and I see mom is not home yet. Since I have a light homework load tonight, thanks to the industrious use of my study hall this afternoon, I decide to make dinner. I am hoping this will set up the right mood for the evening. I stop at the freezer in the garage and remove a package of chicken before heading into the house.

I go about my tasks in my preoccupied state of mind envisioning every possible scenario that could happen this weekend. Maybe Connor and I will hold hands, perhaps he will seductively ask me to walk with him, we will maybe even kiss. When mom gets home forty-five minutes later, I am taking the spaghetti squash out of the oven. My homemade chicken marinara is simmering on the stove, filling the house with the smell of sautéed onion, garlic, and basil. "That smells amazing," mom says as she comes into the kitchen; walking up behind me she gives my shoulder a squeeze.

"Thanks, I have a light load tonight, I got calc done in study hall, so I thought I'd get ahead of dinner. How were your meetings today?"

"Good, we've made some progress. The latest numbers show we're getting much closer to a launchable product. The product team is of course miffed they missed the mark so badly. The research we did last spring should have told them that but I guess they didn't like what it had to say. So they did what they usually do and disregarded it." She says with a sigh, "sometimes I wonder why they even bother to go through the motions."

"Well, you tried to tell them, it is not your fault if they wouldn't listen," I counter.

"True, but they've wasted hundreds of thousands of dollars going down the wrong path. If they had gone ahead with the launch, it would've been in the multiple of millions lost," she pauses for a moment then continues. "On another topic, while I was in their offices today I had lunch with Ms. Tipton."

"Oh?" I say curiously.

"Yes, she seems to think her son fancies a certain redhead at school." She says with a wink.

"He said hi today at lunch and smiled at me in the hallway," I say with a bit of a swoon.

"Really, well, that's progress at a snail's pace, but progress none-the-less I suppose." She considers me carefully for a moment before adding, "you and Marnie go have fun this weekend."

"Seriously? Mom, THANK YOU. I need this so much," I respond, maybe a little too enthusiastically, but I want to show my gratitude. Not sure what Ms. Tipton said to her today to convince her, but I will have to do something nice for that lady in the future.

"You're an adult now, Rae. As much as I don't want to admit it to myself, my last baby is about the fly the nest." She looks so sad it breaks my heart. "But, I know you are a good, hardworking kid. I know you've poured your life into your goals and you'll make good choices." She says it almost like a challenge or maybe an order, potentially a preemptive guilt trip, but we both know it is an order I will follow.

Dinner goes by quickly with mom and me chit-chatting about our days. I complain about my European history test on Friday. She complains about the marketing director she is working with who keeps trying to blame her and her company for the product miss. Once dinner is over, I rinse our plates in the sink, then mom and I head into the living room to watch TV.

The late evening news is on. "In the latest news the communications blackout from Europe continues and has now expanded to include all of Asia. Satellites are down, and non-responsive across England, France, Germany and have become spotty in Russia, and Sweden. Experts are unsure when the communications systems will be back online. All flights in and out of these regions have been suspended pending the re-instatement of these vital systems..."

"Wow, that's odd. Have you heard from Ethan," I ask mom?

"Yes, just yesterday, whatever is happening, he seems to be able to communicate with us," she says, concern filling her eyes. We watch a bit more of the news. I stifle a big yawn and decide it is time to head up to bed. Once in my room, I shoot Marnie a quick text: 'Yo Mar, we're going' is my message to her; 'Sweet, can't wait' is her only reply. She must be studying; typically, she is much chattier.

Much to his displeasure, I move Willis over to the edge of my bed. I spread out my European history notes and begin the tedious process of memorizing names and dates of events

I simply do not care about. After about a half an hour of this, I'm so bored I move on to study European geography. As I look at the maps, I can't help but wonder where Ethan is. Is he in a place on this map I am currently looking at? I can't wait for him to be home at the end of next week. This deployment was sudden and has an ominous feel to it. I lay back on my side; Willis moves around and snuggles against the back of my knees while I pick up another map to study.

It's dark in the forest, but the air still smells so crisp and fresh. Suddenly the sound of pursuit breaks into my aware-ness. I've got to go and go now. I take off racing through the forest. I travel up a slope, and continue on a path to my right. After running another minute or two I see something that scares me, I don't see it well or know why I am afraid of it, but I abruptly change directions. This now has me traveling downhill, a much more comfortable run. I can maintain this pace for a while. I quickly leap logs, avoiding rocks and other things that might trip me. I pause; I don't hear sounds of pur-suit behind me currently, but I know this is a false sense of se-curity. Once this race has begun, I know I cannot quit - my life depends on it. I can feel that. I decide it's best to change course again. I continue heading downhill but move a bit more to my left. This was the wrong move; I see a shimmering just ahead. I don't hesitate to see what it is because my instincts tell me to run in a different direction. As I change course, darting toward my right this time, I stumble down a small embankment.

At the bottom is a narrow creek. I leap across the stream but misjudge the distance. My foot catches on the other side. I go down hard; my ankle has twisted, and I feel a great deal of pain. I don't dare unlace my boot as I am hopeful the lacings will give my ankle support; I know I have to get up and run. I stand up, testing my ankle. No good, there is too much pain, there is no way I can run on this thing. I take in my surround-ings and I freeze. I've been here before. I know what is about to happen. In front of me, I see an odd-looking creature stepping out of the shadows. It is standing on two legs, the size of a large child, but looks nothing like a human. It seems to have hair on its head but the body is covered in large brown scales.

I jerk awake, sitting up quickly and completely disoriented. It takes a while for the realization to set in. I fell asleep while studying; my books are stacked neatly on my nightstand. Mom must have come in and done this, covering me up with my favorite blue heavy quilt as well. Willis pokes his head out from under the covers giving me an unhappy look complete with a small snarl for the disturbance. I look over at the clock: it is four in the morning. At least I have two more hours to sleep. I lay back down, dragging Willis up closer. I hug him tight and close my eyes.

After about ten minutes, I realize it's no good. I am so on edge from this latest installment of my nightmare. I refuse to call it a daydream any longer; it has gotten too dark and ominous. I toss and turn; I just can't get comfortable with the feeling of unease that has settled on me. I think about the dream again. How in the world would I ever end up alone on a densely wooded mountainside? I determine that I wouldn't, this is stupid, I need to let this go.

I try to think about plans for the weekend, but I keep coming back to that darn dream no matter what I try to think about. I toss and turn more. Willis finally gives up and goes to the very end of my bed to lay down, giving me a very disgruntled expression as he slips his head under the bottom of the quilt. I look at the clock again four forty-five. I have to get some sleep, or tomorrow is going to suck. I toss and turn some more. Still unable to sleep, I start reciting dates in my head from my European History notes. Certainly, this ought to bore me to sleep. It already did once this evening, right? Somewhere between the French Revolution and the outbreak of World War I, I finally fall asleep.

CHAPTER 3 THURSDAY

"All I want to do is go home and go to bed," I moan to Marnie at lunch Thursday.

"I feel ya, but we've got three more hours of school, then work tonight," she says, looking at me sympathetically. "Too much studying last night," She inquires.

"No, that stupid dream again," I answer. "I was so worked up over the dream I couldn't go back to sleep for the longest time. I started reciting dates for my European History test tomorrow, I don't know if they were right or not but it was boring enough I finally fell back asleep. I swear I think I'm going to fail that test."

"Rae, you've never failed anything in your life," she consoles.

"Well, there's a first time for everything," I counter.

"Somehow, I doubt that girl. Come on, let's get to class." She summons me to get up and follow her out of the cafeteria. I begrudgingly oblige, retrieving my bag from under the table before rising to follow her.

Marnie is driving today; since history ran over, she must wait on me to leave for work. We get to Browning's just in the nick of time.

"Sorry," I mutter to Marnie as she is grumbling about having to rush. I fumble once again with the lock on my locker.

Once open I shove my bag in, switch out my loafers for my smelly work sneakers, shove my jacket in the locker, then slam the combination lock closed a bit too harshly.

"Angry much," Marnie asks, looking at me questioningly.

"What, oh, no, sorry, I was distracted and hurrying, didn't notice how hard I closed that," I laugh.

"Well, no wonder those things don't like you; what's noodling on that brain of yours," she muses.

"Oh, I had that daydream again in study hall today, so ya know, nothing new. The frequency is getting much greater, between the daydreams and nightmares," I moan. "I'm stressed about school; Calculus WILL be the death of me, the usual." I finish in a huff.

"That's all it is, Rae. You're too worked up about school, college, life...boys," she adds with a sideways glance. "HERE," she screams. I jump, wondering why she is screaming before I see she is smiling, "I'll give you a new thought, start thinking about the Quarry, tomorrow is Friday!" She says with much enthusiasm, accompanied by Marnie's rendition of a happy dance.

"That, my friend, is just what I needed to hear!" I respond.

After an hour and a half at work, I come around the corner, freeze in my tracks. I turn back around, run behind the drink station, and, like the coward I am, hide. I set my tray down and hyperventilate for a good two minutes; Connor is sitting in my section. Oh my God, what am I going to say to him? Why is he here tonight of all nights? I am so tired; I'll probably mess up his order. I've been frazzled, my hair is ever the frizzier because of it, and these dark circles under my eyes are just so attractive. He has literally never even been in Browning's Burger

Palace before as far as I know, so why tonight?

"Rae, get your booty out there; you've got, uh, guests waiting," Marnie says with a wink.

"You did this, didn't you?" I accuse.

"He might have asked if you were working tonight, and I might have mentioned to Sam to seat him in your section if he came in," Marnie says guiltily. "Now you two will actually have to have a conversation. I expect details on our break!!" Then she sashays away with an air of arrogance to her.

"Could've done this on a day when I don't look like a three-year-old zombie," I mutter under my breath. Too late anyhow, she's long gone. I take a deep breath, concede to my fate, and walk out to my latest table. "Hey Connor, who's your date," I say, winking at his little sister. Where did this confidence come from? I can't believe I didn't just come over here spluttering about an order.

"Hi Rae, this is my sister Joanie. Joanie, this is Reagan. We go to school together." He says, looking at his little sister. I'm guessing she is between 12 and 14. She has the same red hair as Connor and an overly freckled face. I am a little jealous of how well she pulls it off. Her eyes are a deep blue like her brother's, compared to my crappy brown eyes, and her hair falls in silky sheets, unlike the frizz fest happening on my head.

"Oh, so your Reagan," she says with a sense of knowing. Hmm, so he's been talking about me to his sister. "OUCH," she gasps after he kicks her under the table. He apparently doesn't want me to know about it, even better.

"What can I get you guys today?" I ask, again with confidence I never knew existed within me.

"I'll just have a grilled chicken sandwich, fries, and a coke.

Joanie?" Connor responds.

"Um, Grilled chicken salad and water, please," she answers politely.

"I'll be right back with those drinks," I say, turn and slowly walk back to the computer to put in their order. Keep it together Rae, I tell myself as I enter their order and prepare their drinks. I fill their glasses, placing the tall red plastic cups on the heavy round tray.

I pick up the tray to head out to my table. As I am walk around the corner from the drink station, I somehow manage to trip. Down goes the tray, down goes the drinks, all in slow motion, ending with a loud clanging and me lying flat out on the floor. The typical clapping ensues as everyone in the restaurant laughs at my clumsiness. I just lie there for a minute, far too embarrassed to get up. Maybe I could just die right now; yes, that would definitely be best. Perhaps if I lay here long enough, everyone will finish and leave; then, I won't have to look Connor in the face after this catastrophe.

"Rae?" oh no, that sexy southern drawl is right beside me; maybe I should pretend I'm unconscious. No, that will only bring more unwanted attention. "Rae, uh, can I help you up?" Connor inquires.

I lean up on my elbows, placing my chin on my fists looking up at Connor from under my eyelashes. My apron is soaked from landing in the drinks. I don't even want to know what I look like right now. I am sure the front of me is not only wet but probably dirty to boot. I reach my hand up and allow Connor to help me up. "Thanks," I mutter, "who put that darn corner there," I add with an embarrassed chuckle.

"Do you want me to help you with that?" He asks, motioning to the mess at my feet.

"No, thank you, I've got it. I'll be over in a few with drinks that haven't been on the floor," I respond, going for a humorous tone, attempting to hide my utter embarrassment.

"No worries," he says, "take your time and uh maybe watch where you're going next time," he adds with a wink.

The rest of the shift passes in a blur. I manage to serve food and drinks for the rest of the evening without spilling a drop on my guests. I call that a win. I am however, totally lost in my fantasies of Connor, each more inappropriate than the last. I've barely ever kissed a guy before, where are these thoughts coming from? I really don't feel like my imagination is that good. Perhaps I've read one too many smut fiction novels on the internet. Well, I guess those hours were not wasted after all since they've given me fuel for Connor fantasies.

"OMG Rae, what the hell was that?" Marnie shouts when we are finally in the breakroom changing to go home.

"Oh, Mar, I made the biggest idiot out of myself. But apparently, it pays off. Two of my tables left me the biggest tips I've ever gotten. Perhaps I should orchestrate a fall every shift."

"They must've felt sorry for you." She says, laughing a bit too hard. "SO," she says purposefully, "tell me about your 'customers.'"

"What's there to tell? Your carefully orchestrated plan worked perfectly. So I embarrassed the hell out of myself, in doing so, managed to score not one but TWO forty-dollar tips. So...thanks," I respond.

"I'll take that gas money you've been offering now thank you," she says jokingly, "seriously though, what did you and Connor talk about?"

"Not much, just school. I think I talked to his sister more

than him. She asked me about my classes and plans for college. He told her before I could that I had a riding scholarship to Brooksburg in Texas. I found it interesting he was so well informed," I respond, looking at her accusatorily.

"Well, well, well, seems Mr. Tipton is not as oblivious all these months as we thought," she decides.

"More than likely my mom talks too much to his mom," I counter.

"Either way, he paid attention," she says with a wink. That is true, he could have dismissed the information and chose not to.

All I can do is smile while I change out my stinky sneakers for my comfy loafers, grab my purse, jacket, and shut my locker. It is not until we are halfway out the door that I realize I opened my locker for the first time ever with no trouble. Maybe Connor is good luck I muse to myself.

CHAPTER 4 FINALLY FRIDAY

I can't believe it is finally Friday, just two more hours until we get to leave this dreadful place and head out for weekend fun. Unfortunately, I have the two most boring hours of my class schedule left, Study Hall and European History. If history were first, I could skip study hall, but no, my luck just doesn't work that way.

I have that darn test in European History, so I pull out my notes to start studying. Like most things, as this final school year is winding down, it does little to hold my attention. I really don't care what happened in Europe in the 17 and 1800s. Should I care? Maybe, but as I do not plan to go into politics, history, law, or any such profession, why do I need to know?

I'm in the woods. This place smells good, like mountain air, clean and crisp with a hint of pine trees. But there is another odor here I don't recognize from my childhood, kind of acrid. The scent is out of place here, making me nervous. I start running through a dark forest. It is either early morning or dusk; it is hard to tell, but the muted light signals either the beginning or end of the day. My usually frizzy hair is a tattered mess and matted to my face with the sweat pouring down. Either it is hot outside, or I've been running hard to generate this fatigue. I decide I have been running for some time, I am worried, I am concerned about someone, though I am not sure who. I see shimmering in the air ahead of me alerting me I must change direction. Why is that shimmering so scary? I dart left, stumbling down a small embankment; jumping across the creek, my foot catches on a jagged rock and I go down.

I slowly rise and assess the damage; I have a lot of pain in my ankle though it seems stable. I look around and realize where I am. I know what is coming; today, I am waiting for the appearance of the strange man, or creature, or whatever it is that is waiting there. I stumble farther down the path, waiting for the nervous feeling, waiting to hear the footfall, but so far, it has not come. I turn to look all around. I know I am looking where the person was standing, or the thing as in the last daydream has appeared to me. This time, there is just a slight shimmering in the air, not really a person, or at least nothing substantial, a ghost maybe? I continue to stare at the space while the disturbance undulates but never really forms an identifiable shape.

Just then, a nasal buzzing draws my attention away from the scene, and I am back to sitting in study hall. This daydream wasn't overly different from the others. Still, it made an impression on me. I stand feeling utterly shaken and downright scared. Here, in this room, I can still feel the hairs standing up on the back of my neck. While I know it isn't real, it had an odd sense of familiarity and finality. I really hope I am just paranoid.

Mom often says she thinks there is a bit of clairvoyance in our family. She frequently has premonitions or precognition of certain events. It is not really fortune-telling, but just kind of like she knows what's going to happen in certain situations. I said it is only from being a mom and having seen it all by now. She claims it has been that way as long as she can remember. All I can say is I hope I am never in the situation I've been daydreaming about; it's very frightening.

Marnie says the only reason the daydreams are more frequent is I keep dwelling on them, making them recur. Adding to that I've got end of year stress and worry about the unknown moving into the college years. Of course, this is a very plausible explanation and I expect she has the right of it. After this weekend, I hope I am distracted enough to forget all about it; perhaps I'll start living out some of my steamier Connor daydreams.

The last bell finally rings or buzzes as it does in our school. I had just finished the final question on my test. I walk to the teacher's desk and hand it in. When I get back to my desk I hastily scoop up my books, shove them in my bag, and head to my locker. As usual, I fumble with my lock. You would think after four years at this school, with this same locker, I'd have figured it out by now, but no. Alas, I am destined to struggle until the last day. I console myself by saying they gave me a bum lock from the start; it's not my fault. Never mind, I can't open the lock at work either.

I ponder the latest changes in my daydream while I unceremoniously shove the last of my things into my locker. I feel a bit on edge from this newest installment of this mysterious, dreadful daydream, so I startle as I sense someone standing behind me. I whirl around and gasp a bit as I realize I'm standing just inches from Connor.

"So," he says then pauses, "Marnie told Isaac y'all will be at Quarry this weekend," Connor states with his amazingly delicious Southern drawl. You know, most people think a British accent is the sexiest accent, but I'll take a Southern Twang any time.

"That's the plan," I manage to squeak out, hardly able to speak with him standing so close. Deep breath Rae, deep breath, you can do this; seriously, he is just a person.

"Isaac, AJ, and I are heading up tomorrow. Maybe we'll see you there."

I find the courage I never knew I had and respond, "I'll save you a seat by the campfire." He gives me a great smile, tips his head, and walks off.

I stand there in stunned silence, staring after him; Marnie walks up while I am still trying to catch my breath. "Dude, are you alright? You're hyperventilating and look as though you've seen a ghost," she says knowingly.

"Connor just asked me if we'd be at the Quarry this weekend, and I was brave enough to say I'd save him a seat at the campfire," I exclaim, trying but failing, to keep my voice low. I hope he isn't lurking around the corner, or he just heard my desperate exclamation. I swear I am acting like a pre-teen just feeling the first twinges of hormones. I am off to college in a few months, why am I acting like this? I guess the answer is I haven't dated much and certainly have never been this attracted to anyone.

"Hmm, maybe there's hope for you two yet...you Gingers need to stick together," she says with a wink.

I get home from school eager to get out of town. Mom isn't home yet; in all likelihood, I won't see her before I leave. She usually works from home, but with whatever fiasco they are managing for their client, she has been working downtown for about a month. I know she hates the drive. Hopefully they will have things back on the rails soon and she can return to her telecommuting position. Though she hates the drive, I have heard her say it is not all bad; she feels like a grown-up when she has to dress up and go to town. She also likes having lunch away from the house with other adults.

Willis greets me at the door. He is usually asleep at this time; he must really need out. I go to the back of the house, letting him out on the back deck for a bit. Why not start relaxing now? I walk out with him, sliding into a chair at the table set on our deck, propping my feet up on an adjacent chair. The sun is bright. The weatherman was right it is getting warmer, by tomorrow afternoon it'll be shorts and short sleeves. I close my eyes, enjoying the feeling of warm sun on my face, breathing in the smell of the clean air that hints of Spring, and think of Connor. I wonder what sparked the sudden interest, or if the interest is not sudden, the bravery to act. Whatever or whoever it was, I am glad. I am not sure what school in Texas he is planning to attend. Perhaps it'll be close enough to mine, we can see each other. As my mind wanders aimlessly around Connor, I notice how good the warm sun feels on my face and arms. I can't help but drift off to sleep.

"Connor, what are you doing here? How, what happened," I gasp as we are finally able to talk. "Oh Rae, I am so sorry you are here. Are you okay? How hurt are you? I had hoped you guys would have made it out," Connor moans. "What is going on? Where are we" I ask with total desperation in my voice.

I am jerked back to reality by Willis barking at a bunny, taunting him from just outside the fence. What the heck was that? Connor looked horrible; we were in such a dark place. Why does this negativity have to be invading my best daydreams? Maybe it was the thought of school and going into the unknown. I have always had a tendency toward negativism and dramatics; perhaps I am dreading college? Ugh, now I've got goosebumps. That was a terrible daydream, absolutely awful.

I jump up, calling Willis over to me, "Let's go, buddy. That bunny looks meaner than you are; I've got to pack." Willis follows me inside, sitting patiently while I retrieve his treat from the top of the refrigerator. He gives me a shake, sits, rolls over, and "Bang" finishes with a performance of play dead. "Good job Willis, that was definitely worth a whole treat today," I tell him. After finishing his treat, Willis races to catch up with me on my way up the stairs. We turn the corner into my room; he jumps up on the bed, looking at me expectantly.

I begin the process of packing for the weekend. When I pull

out my duffle bag, Willis looks hopeful but gives me a pout, unsure if this is a trip he gets to go on. "Sorry, buddy, I'll dash your hopes now; it's a girls' weekend, no dogs allowed." He seems to understand because he buries himself under my quilt.

I start pulling clothes from my drawers; I really cannot decide what to pack. I would generally pack my rattier clothing for a camping trip, but Connor will be there this weekend. In the end, I settle for my new jeans, several well-fitted t-shirts, and my favorite hoodie. I debate a bit what to pack for sleeping, but since it's just Marnie and me in the tent, I settle for my warm but ratty sweatpants and thermal long sleeve shirt. I pack several extra pairs of socks; I hate when the dew gets my socks wet, leaving my feet cold and pruned. Then I throw in a couple pairs of shorts just in case.

An hour and a half later, after leaving a disgruntled Willis standing in the kitchen, we are in Marnie's SUV headed toward the weekend adventure. The feeling of pure relief grows with each mile we move away from town.

We roll down the windows and open the sunroof. Marnie syncs her favorite dance playlist to the radio, and we spend our trip rocking out to our favorite jams.

We're not too far away from the Quarry when I bring up my latest daydream. "So, I was hanging out outside with Willis when I got home from school. I must have drifted off while soaking in the sunshine," I begin hesitantly.

"Not this again, Rae, for the love of all that is holy, let it go," she exclaims impatiently.

"No, Mar, it's different. I was in this really dark place, but Connor was there, except he looked really beat up, I kept asking where we were, but all he said was how sad he was that I was there."

"Okay, I'll admit that it is weird. What were you thinking about before you drifted off?" Marnie inquires.

"Whether his school in Texas will be close to mine," I answered.

"That's it, you are unsure how school is going to go, you are nervous about the next part of your life, but you imagine Connor will be there to pull you through." She announces confidently.

"That certainly sounds amazing, but do you really think that is true?" I ask skeptically.

"What the hell else could it be child? Seriously, snap out of the gloom and doom. It is definitely scary moving away from home, and of course moving away from me! But this is going to be the best time in your life. Please stop imagining it as the end of the world," she finishes her tirade with a slight chuckle.

"I suppose you could be right," I concede.

"You know I am. When am I ever wrong?" she finishes with mock conceit in her voice.

"I can think of a..." I begin, but she shoots me a look that keeps me from finishing that sentence.

"So, where are we stopping for dinner?" She asks, ending the topic altogether.

After a quick trip through a fast-food drive-thru, we arrive at the Quarry just before sundown. Only a few sites have been rented, so we have our pick of location. After much debate, we settle on a site that is a few 'wheels' over from the bathrooms. Close enough to the other rented campsites, we are within earshot if you yell, far enough away it would be hard to eavesdrop on our conversations. However, we are an unfortunate distance to the bathroom on a poorly lit path, meaning a lot of squatting in the weeds. That's alright; we are farm girls, we can handle it. We get our blue and red two-person tent set up. There is not much space, mostly room for our sleeping bags in the middle and duffle bags around the edges.

The tent spaces are incredibly well planned. They have a sand base making them comfortable to sleep on, while there are anchors in the wood frames around the area to tie off, making for easy setup. We unroll our sleeping bags and arrange our things inside the tent. Marnie pulls out her blue tooth speaker to play some music while I start setting logs for a fire. Now that the fire is lit, the music is playing, we settle in for an evening of stargazing and girl talk.

CHAPTER 5 THE QUARRY

We both sleep in on Saturday, waking after nine o'clock in the morning. I sit up first with a feeling of giddiness, in anticipation of Connor coming later today. Marnie looks up at me, annoyed. "You're awfully perky this morning," she says with a bit of spite in her voice.

"Sorry, Mar, it's a glorious day, the sun is shining, the breeze is warm, and today is going to be a great day," I say with a smile.

"Kill me now" is all she responds, flipping dramatically to her side placing her pillow over her head.

I reach down and yank her pillow off her head, lean in placing kiss her on the cheek "rise and shine sleepyhead," I say, then duck quickly out of the tent before she can hit me.

After a visit to the weeds, I return and dress quickly. At the same time, Marnie moans about getting up before eleven o'clock on Saturday. The fire from last night is still hot, so I stoke up the flames to cook sausages for breakfast. They have a delightful restaurant at the Lodge, but we like to 'rough it' when we are camping. Once the sausages are cooked through, I crack a few eggs on the skillet over the fire. "Breakfast," I yell out to Marnie, who emerges slowly from the tent, looking less annoyed. "That smells amazing," she compliments before diving into her plate.

After we finish cleaning up breakfast, Marnie collects her assortment of research gear and heads out for a bit of research on rocks. I roll my eyes at her, but she definitely is on a mission. "Have fun," I call after her as she meanders down closer to the lake.

I know Marnie will be gone for a bit, so I grab my favorite trashy novel. I find a hammock strategically placed near our site and curl up for some recreational reading. I am reading a steamy romance scene between the lead guy and girl when I begin to drift off into a daydream of my own. My vision is sweet, not trashy, but a delicious invention of my mind.

Connor and I are sitting by the fire. It is dark and cold, so I lean in to get warmer. He slides his arm around me, hugging me even closer. After a while, he slips his hand down my side, just barely sliding underneath the hem of my shirt. I shudder a bit to feel his hand against my skin; he begins to gently rub small circles on my side with his thumb. I lean my head against his shoulder in complete contentment, gazing dreamily up in his deep blue eyes.

"Well, don't you look content?" That sexy Southern drawl brings me back to reality. Even better, the real thing. I realize I'm lying in the hammock with a shy smile plastered on my face and blush on my cheeks. Busted by the subject of my daydream himself!

"Hey guys," I recover, sitting up quickly, dropping my book onto the ground.

Connor reaches down, scooping it up. "I never really saw you as a trashy novel kind of gal," he says.

"We all have guilty pleasures," I admit sheepishly.

We stand there staring at each other awkwardly for a moment. Then Connor says, "well, I guess I ought to go help the guys set up."

"Where are you guys camping at?" I ask.

"Right next door," he winks, "we rented that platform tent right there; none of us had a tent large enough for all three of us." Then he saunters off to help his friends set up their camp.

Just after Connor heads back to their campsite, Marnie comes wandering up from the lake. "What's up Rae, why do you have that grin on your face," she asks.

"Oh, no reason," I say, nodding in the direction of the boys.

"Enough said, or, not said." She answers. She sets about organizing her tubes and samples, making an odd face every now and again. After an hour of shuffling tubes and rocks around, mixed in with many sighs and frowns, she finally throws her hands up in the air. "I don't get what I am doing wrong," she muses.

"What's up nerd, rocks misbehaving?" I ask.

"So, as you know, I've been taking samples out here for the past few years. Over the last few months, primarily starting around last August, the mineral content of the rocks and soil has drastically changed." She explains.

"Okay, so, there is a natural evolution to the Earth, right? I mean Ohio has salt mines under it because it used to be under an ocean." I console.

"Yes, there is, but if these numbers are right, it is happening way too fast, like something is leaching specific minerals from the soil." She lectures.

"Global warming?" I ask. To which she rolls her eyes. Marnie believes that while humans can and often do suck in their lackadaisical attitude toward our environment, certain evolutionary changes to Earth are expected. The last Ice Age did not end because of global warming; we weren't driving cars or participating in deforestation then.

"No, I have to be doing something wrong in my tests," she concludes. "I'll have to ask Mr. Thomas to take a look at school Monday."

"Dunno girlfriend" is all I can say.

Connor and AJ come striding over. "We're going bike riding on the trails if y'all are interested in joining us." AJ offers.

"Nope, didn't bring bikes, but we are about to each lunch if you guys are hungry before you go," I offer.

"I could definitely eat," AJ offers, "Isaac, get over here; Reagan and Marnie are going to feed us before we go."

"Rae," Connor corrects.

I smile a little too big as this correction. I set about cooking hamburger patties over the fire. At the same time, Marnie grabs the cooler from her car with the potato salad and hamburger fixings. Connor produces some paper plates and utensils from the boy's tent.

"Looks good, ladies," Isaac comments as he makes his way over.

After a quick meal, the boys head off to ride their bikes on the trails. Marnie and I tidy up the campsite. "Well," Marnie says, "They cleaned us out of food; I guess we're eating at the restaurant tonight."

"There certainly are worse things," I comment with a sly grin.

"True," she responds. "Come one, let's go lay down by the water and soak up some of this sunshine. I know spring probably isn't truly here yet, so let's take advantage of this while we can."

I cannot argue with that; I grab a blanket, book and follow in stride behind Marnie to the water's edge. There is a sandy beach at the edge of the lake where we lay out our blankets and stretch out for some sunbathing. We talk for a bit about school, college, and a little bit of everything else. "So, how much longer until Ethan comes home," Marnie inquires.

"Um, late next week, I think. Mom said he sounded stressed but was confident he would be back." I let her know.

"Well, things are looking up for you and Connor, perhaps maybe Ethan will finally realize I'm a girl and he's a boy," she muses.

Marnie grows quiet in her thoughts, so I go back to my book. Reading doesn't hold my attention for long and I once again drift off in my imagination. Connor stands up, grabbing my hand and pulling me to my feet. I willingly rise, following him down the path hand-in-hand. The warmth of his hand feels so good in mine. We get close to the lake when he slowly turns. I step in closer. He looks down at me, his eyes darker in the fading evening light. "Rae," he whispers. The sound of his voice saying my name sends a bazillion tremors up and down my spine, "I've always liked you." Oh, the words I've wanted to hear. "After watching my parents go through their divorce and living separated from part of my family, I've been apprehensive about being in a relationship with anyone," he continues. "But I know we're going to school close to each other next year, so there won't be that separation I feared. I feel now is the time to let you know."

I stare at him speechlessly, just a hint of a smile playing on my lips. Gazing into his eyes I feel I see the depths of his kind soul. He leans down, gently pressing his lips to mine. What starts out as a soft, gentle kiss builds. There is a palpable sense of urgency from both of our pent-up needs. His hands find their way to my neck. As the kiss continues, they slide ever so slowly down my neck, to my shoulders. The movement of his hands brings on a new wave of shivers I cannot control; butterflies begin doing somersaults in my stomach. He then draws his hand lightly...

"RAE," Marnie yells. "Are you listening to me?"

"Oops, sorry, different kind of daydream," I say, "one that

could potentially happen yet this weekend."

"Oh my," she snickers, "I thought it was getting hotter out here."

My only response is to blush.

"Anyhow," Marnie continues, "I was asking if you want to go up and get ready for dinner. We've been out here for hours; we must have both drifted off to sleep."

"Sure," I say, stretching, then rise scooping up my blanket and book on the way up.

Back at the campsite, we take turns getting dressed in the tent. It takes me a minute to decide what to wear. I settle on my new jeans, a fitted long sleeve T, and my new boots. When we are done, we turn to begin the walk up to the Lodge for dinner.

"Hey, girls wait up," AJ calls. "Give us twenty minutes and we'll head up to the Lodge with you. Seems we owe you guys dinner after you fed us lunch."

"I won't say no to that," Marnie chimes in.

Dinner is a lot of fun. The hostess sits us way in the back, I suppose thinking we'd be a rowdy group of teenagers. While we get a little loud at times, we are overall respectful and well behaved. I sit next to Connor, who scoots closer to me than the others. This does not go unnoticed by his buddies who give him approving grins.

Conversation flows smoothly during dinner discussing a little bit of everything including school, our families, and our plans for the future. The Pecan Crusted Grouper was absolutely divine, while Marnie's steak looked terrific. When the bill comes, Connor claims it for himself and pays the waitress. "Let us at least leave the tip," I protest.

"Nope, I've got that," AJ chimes in.

"Shall we go, ladies?" Isaac asks, rising.

Back at the campsite, the sun is setting. The boys take their turn stoking up the mutual fire, and bring out a set of corn hole boards. In the first round, Marnie and I played against Connor and AJ. They quickly slay us in no time flat. "There's no way that is 21," Marnie protests.

"Oh, sorry girls, but it is," AJ teases.

"Let's even this up," Connor suggests, "me and Rae against Marnie and Isaac."

"That works," I say, smiling shyly.

This game takes considerably longer, but thanks to Connor's excellent aim, we come out on top. He strides over giving me a high five, which I accept, despite my lack of contribution to the win.

"Alright! Time to break up this dream team," Marnie hollers, "this time Connor and I against Rae and AJ." As we start to split off, I begin to follow Marnie to the other end when she gives me a look and sends me to the side that Connor is standing on. "Oh," I say knowingly.

This round drags out even longer with a lot of teasing, razzing, and redoing. Finally, it is getting too dark to continue. "That's it," Connor announces, "we call it a draw." We all concede to calling it a tie; Isaac and AJ pick up the boards and bean bags to take to their tent.

The fire pits are surrounded by benches made from locally harvested wood. They are very scenic but not overly comfortable. Marnie heads back to our tent to get blankets to sit on while I stand awkwardly by the fire with Connor. Once she returns, I fold the blanket, wide enough for two.

"Want to join me?" I ask Connor shyly.

"Sure," Connor answers awkwardly. Geez, at our age, you

would think we would be better at this.

I sit hugging my arms around myself when Marnie returns from a second trip to the car, passing me a spiked seltzer her cousin Matt procured for us. "A little liquid courage for you," Marnie whispers.

"Thanks," I respond.

Just then, Isaac comes back, passing each of the boys a beer. The locals know underage drinking happens out here, but as long as you keep it quiet and within reason, most turn a blind eye. Occasionally someone makes a stink. This early in the year, we'll not likely see another person at our site.

"So, how was your day?" Connor asks, finally speaking to me. "No wallowing in spilled drinks or anything," he says with a chuckle.

"Hey now," I protest, "be nice." I can feel the blush of embarrassment blooming on my cheeks.

"Nothing to be embarrassed about. We all have our moments," he consoles me.

"Oh yeah, what's your most embarrassing moment," I ask, feeling the seltzer filling my veins with warmth and courage.

"Well, back in junior high, I was playing football at my school in Texas. I wasn't particularly good mind you, but that is what little boys did in my town, you played football. I finally got my chance to go out on the field; my mama was so proud. I bend over to start the play, and my pants split all the way front to back. Of course, I was wearing the most juvenile pair of underpants I owned that day. As I was bending over to start the play, I gave the whole bleachers a show of my underpants featuring a certain cartoon character. I never did live that one down. Even living here in Ohio, to this day when I talk to some of my 'friends' back home, they still greet me with an uh nickname." He tells me earnestly.

"Wow, that's tough. That must be why you came to Ohio with your mom, to get around that nickname." I joke with him.

"Yeah, that's why," he chuckles.

We join in the conversation with the others. Isaac tells us he is joining the Army after high school. He ships out to basic only two weeks after graduation. AJ is going to OSU to study engineering. "I'm heading back to Texas," says Connor, "I want to study Herd Management and Business, so I can run the family farm someday. There I'll be close enough I can see my sisters some on weekends."

"That's awesome," I say. "I didn't know those things were taught at college. I thought it was more of a passed down generation to generation type of career."

"Much of it is," Connor explains, "but there are so many developments in nutrition and genetics. I think there are things we can leverage to increase the value of our herd. And, while those farmers are good at doing business with each other, the feedstore and other basic suppliers, a business background could certainly improve negotiations with the buyers." I love the passion he has for the business and the animals. It gives me an even greater appreciation for him. Feeling this sense of warmth towards Connor, I lean in a bit closer. He slides nearer to me as well. I look up into those gorgeous blue eyes in wonder and just stare for a moment.

"So, Rae," AJ yells, interrupting our moment, "where are you headed after high school."

"Well," I say, shooting him an annoyed look, "I have signed to ride on the western equestrian team at the University of Brookburg in Texas. I am undecided about my major but leaning toward food science. I want to work on developing foods that you see on the shelf. My mom worked closely with food scientists for a while when consulting for a company. The work appealed to me. It is fast-paced and a lot of work, but I think I would really enjoy the science."

"That sounds interesting," AJ responds. "And really boring," he adds.

"To each his, or her, own." Connor defends me. I like that. "So, Marnie, how 'bout you? I'm going to guess you are going to study Geology."

"Actually, no, I am headed to IU on an academic scholarship. I am starting out in pre-med." Marnie returns haughtily. "We'll see how the first few years go, but my goal is to be an Obstetrician."

"Wow, that's cool," AJ answers.

"What are you doing after the Army Isaac," I ask.

"Not sure. I'll see what appeals to me. I think I'll get into mechanics or electronics," he answers.

I get up and wander back to the cooler in Marnie's car, getting another drink for Marnie and myself.

"Here ya go," I say, handing Marnie hers.

"Thanks," she answers.

CHAPTER 6 OCCURRENCE

I sit back down next to Connor, just a bit closer this time. I feel his arm slide around my waist, triggering tremors of anticipation along my skin. I lean into his side. This just might be heaven. He smells so good; the warmth from his side is seeping into every cell in my body. Marnie catches my eye and gives me a satisfied smile.

"So," Marnie interjects, "what do you boys do for fun?"

"We spend a lot of time out here biking on the trails," Isaac responds. "I like to run; I do track and cross country, so it is nice to stay in shape in between."

"Sure." Marnie answers.

"And of course, video games," Connor adds.

I look up at him, "I didn't have you pegged for the video game type."

"Well," he says with a smile, "I didn't have you pegged for the trashy novel type of gal," he winks at me.

"Alright, I'm going to have to make a trip into the weeds," I announce. I stand up, grabbing a napkin before heading to the weeds behind the tent. As I am just finishing up, I notice something move in the weeds to my right. I don't get a good look, but I know it looks like no animal I've seen before. I race back to the camp, barely having pulled my pants up.

"Okay, y'all, now I'm freaked out. I do NOT know what I just saw over there, but it was scary looking," I announce anxiously.

"You haven't had enough to drink to be hallucinating yet,

Rae," Marnie says with a bit of sarcasm.

"I'm telling you, whatever it was, does not belong in this region," I exclaim.

"Maybe it was Bigfoot," Isaac jokes.

I shoot him a nasty look, so Marnie asks, "fine, what did it look like?"

"It was some kind of animal, looked like a cross between that cartoon hedgehog and a gremlin, but was the size of a small child or adolescent," I answer, musing at my description.

"Gremlin?" questions Marnie "you must be a lightweight. Perhaps you need to lay off the beverages, girl."

"Dude, you know from that movie, with the thing that gets wet and multiples, then if you feed it after midnight, they turn evil, like that, the evil one," I respond.

"Oh, it's a Christmas movie..." Isaac interjects.

"THAT IS NOT A CHRISTMAS MOVIE," I exclaim with more than just a hint of irritation. It is not his fault. I have debated this on many occasions with my horse show friends and my brother. Of course, Ethan always took their side.

"Then why do they always play it at Christmas time?" asks AJ.

"Because it has snow in it, it is set at Christmas time, but it is NOT a Christmas movie," I say, exasperated.

"So, it is a Christmas Movie," Connor teases.

"No, evil things should not be present in Christmas movies," I say stubbornly, sticking my chin out, complete with a fake pout.

"But..." AJ starts but is cut off by an odd-looking man

staggering into our campsite. He looks as though he was just learning to walk. He had medium-length disheveled brown hair, greasy but in a purposeful way. He was clean-shaven, though he appeared to have significant amounts of dirt behind both of his ears. Despite the appearance of dirt on his neck, his clothing and face were exceptionally clean. His clothing was another sight itself; it was still early spring, so the evening was quite chilly. We had shorts on this afternoon, but it was way too cold for shorts now. But this guy was wearing cargo shorts with a sleeveless undershirt and flip flops.

"' Cuse me, Lodge, where?" he said in garbled English and a strange accent.

"Are you alright, sir?" Isaac asked, genuinely concerned.

"Lodge, where me show?" he simply responded, looking expectantly.

"If you follow the path up that hill, you won't miss it. In about 50 yards or so, you'll be able to see the lights from the building," Connor says, dismissing the strange man.

The man considers us for a moment, nods his head once, and continues staggering off in the direction Connor indicated. We all sit in stunned silence for a few moments, unsure of what to say, or if he has gone far enough he won't hear us talking about him.

"Definitely on drugs," Marnie finally says.

"Had to be, but how was he so clean? His clothes don't have a speck of dirt on them," I ask.

"Yeah, but did you see all that dirt down his neck, like behind his ears?" Marnie asks with a grimace on her face.

"Maybe," Connor muses, "his mama never taught him how to take a proper bath."

"So, what, he's never washed behind his ears his entire life."

AJ chokes out, laughing.

"Maybe it's a birthmark," I say kindly.

"On both sides," asks Marnie skeptically.

"I bet he's with a bachelor party at the Lodge or something. They got him all drugged up and took him Snipe hunting," at AJ's suggestion we all laugh. Of course, that is a very plausible explanation; who knows what they gave that poor guy? Hell, he's probably the groom.

This interruption caused all thoughts and discussion of whatever animal I saw in the weeds to be forgotten. The banter continues until late at night. Connor keeps his arm securely around me, making me feel happy inside. "Clouds are moving in," I observe, "I hope it doesn't rain tonight."

"Do you want another drink Rae," Connor asks, rising.

"Nope, I know my limits; I'm good. I will take a sports drink or water." I add.

Connor returns, passing the boys each another beer and handing me a red sports drink. "Thanks," I respond.

I sit sipping my drink for a while, just leaning into Connor's side when I start to yawn. "Well, it's getting late," I say, "I think I'm going to turn in." I look up at Connor, thinking he'll walk me to my tent. I am not disappointed; he rises and follows.

At the tent, I turn to look at him. "So, Rae," he says, "do you want to go out sometime?"

"Yes, please," I respond.

He leans down, gently placing his lips on mine. I feel the fire of anticipation racing through my lips down to my stomach, kicking up the butterflies like I've never felt before. The kiss deepens. I feel my lips naturally part, as do his. His hand wraps possessively around my back, pulling me in closer. My hand reaches up on its own accord, wrapping around his neck, while the other rests on his side. This goes on for an immeasurable time, though it was probably only a few minutes. When he pulls back, he looks deeply into my eyes. "Goodnight, Rae, pleasant dreams," and turns to head back to the rest of the gathering.

Seconds later, Marnie arrives, having clearly watched from a distance "Let's hear it," she demands.

"We kissed," I tell her, nearly fainting. "I have never been kissed like that before. I was fairly sure that my entire body had melted standing right here. He is so amazing."

"Wow, I am so excited for you two," Marnie says. "Isaac asked me if I wanted to go out next weekend."

"Oh?" I question. "And what did you say?"

"I said yes," she responds, "I mean, why not? As much as I like Ethan, he has barely shown a hint of interest. I don't have a thing for Isaac or anything, but certainly couldn't hurt to have some fun."

"I totally agree," I confirm, "then we can double date."

I drift off to sleep with a smile on my face and a mind full of Connor. I am awoken sometime later by the sensation of being wet. It takes a minute to register, but there seems to be a stream of water seeping into and flowing through our tent. At some point overnight, it not only rained, it deluged. "Marnie wake up, it's raining, and we're soaked," I yell at Marnie. She sits bolt upright as the realization of wetness sinks in. Fortunately, our bags are still dry. We change out of our wet clothes, careful not to kneel down on our soaked sleeping bags. "So, to the car?" I ask, wondering where on Earth we will spend the rest of the night until morning

She looks around. "Boys tent, they should have a few extra cots in there. It'll be way more comfortable than the car."

We run through the downpour to the platform tent the boys rented. We fling open the flap, AJ sits up quickly. "What's going on," he exclaims with evident alarm.

"Our tent flooded," Marnie explains, "can we sleep on your extra cots?"

"We only have one extra," says Isaac, "but you are welcome to it."

"Great, I'll snuggle with Rae for the rest of the night," Marnie says but doesn't sound like she thinks it's great at all. "At least there's only a few more hours left. Does anyone have an extra blanket by chance?"

"I do," Isaac offers, chucking a blanket in our direction.

I feel a hand wrap around mine. I then register the sensation of falling back as I am pulled down onto a cot. Looking back, I see Connor has pulled me down to his cot. He lifts the blanket and motions for me to lay beside him. Well, this escalated quickly. I think to myself. Thank you mother nature for being on my side.

"It's okay, Mar. I think I'll just sleep over here," I answer.

She gives me a wide-eyed are you out of your mind look, but thankfully doesn't say a thing. The cot size doesn't allow much room, so I have no choice but to lean back against Connor, fitting myself to the contours of his body. He smooths my hair down then protectively wraps his right arm around me; I snuggle in, resting my head on his left arm. I breathe in deep, savoring his scent, thinking I have absolutely died and gone to heaven.

He leans in and I feel his breath on my neck just behind my ear. I draw in a sharp breath with the sensation it brings. Slowly, I feel his lips move against me as he starts kissing the side of my neck ever so gently and quietly. I know he can feel the trembling this elicits from my body; I have goosebumps rising everywhere.

"Okay?" he asks shyly.

"Yes," I whisper back, quiet as a breath.

His hand moves from around my waist and ever so slowly begins to explore my body. He runs his hand along my arm, down my side and hip leaving a trail of goosebumps behind. He playfully nips at my ear for a moment then continues kissing my neck, shoulder, and collar bone. I roll towards him, and he raises up on one arm, thank God these cots don't creak. Leaning over me, he kisses me in earnest. I feel so warm all over. I never want this to stop. He leans up, just looking at me.

I am disappointed at this break in action; however, I am not sure I am ready for this.

"Rae, I really like you," he whispers.

"I feel the same," I respond shyly. I have to believe he will not take this any farther in a tent full of people. He leans in for another long kiss, then rolls me onto my side away from him. He slides one arm under my shirt and wraps it protectively around my stomach. I feel the fire in every part of my stomach where his skin touches mine.

He lays back down, again with his nose just behind my ear. He pulls me in closer. "I think we should sleep now," he whispers, a bit strained, but continues to gently kiss my neck a moment longer. He sighs quietly and leans back. When he stops, I settle contentedly against him. Eventually, I drift into the most peaceful, dreamless, restful sleep I've had in a long time.

"Wakey, wakey kids," Marnie says.

Oh, we must have slept in. I realize I am lying half across Connor with my head on his chest. I look up at Connor. He is awake, looking back at me. "Morn'n," he says with that voice that drives me crazy. "Morning," I reply. Ugh, my breath has to be horrible. I need to excuse myself to the bathroom.

"Um, I'm going to just make a visit to the bathroom," I announce, sitting up quickly.

Connor pulls me back down to him. "I don't think I'm ready to let go yet," he whispers quietly in my ear.

"I promise I'll be back," I respond, sitting up again. I blush slightly, remembering last night and wondering what the others in the tent heard, or at least suspected.

Marnie follows me to our tent to get our things before heading to the shower house. Once inside the questioning begins.

"OMG Rae, tell me everything," she demands. I tell her every detail of the night before reliving each moment in exquisite detail. As we talk, I feel the memory of the fire he left behind after his hands trailed along my skin. Then I have to ask.

"So, did you hear anything?" I ask, blushing.

"Nope, I honestly thought you two just went to sleep," is her response. "I was a little disappointed in you," she adds with a chuckle.

I take a scorching hot shower, taking time to try to condition the chaos out of my hair. Once finished, I brush my teeth and rinse thoroughly. I decide to braid my hair to keep it somewhat under control today and get dressed. Today is a lot warmer still, so I dress in shorts, a semi-cropped top in my favorite color teal, and my cutest strappy sandals. Once we're both dressed, we head back to our tent.

Everything in our tent is soaked, so we lay our sleeping bags, blankets, and some clothing that got wet over Marnie's car to dry. We leave the tent up and open to air out. We put our bags, which stayed miraculously dry, back in Marnie's car. As we close the hatch, the boys show up with donuts and juice.

After a quick breakfast, Connor says, "come walk with me."

"I would love nothing more, but I don't want to abandon Marnie," I respond, even I can hear the disappointment in my voice.

"I understand," Connor responds, squeezing me to him and kissing me gently on the forehead. "Until later then."

I about melt as I watch him walk away. I've waited a long time for this. Once Connor rejoins his group, the boys head off to do more biking on the trails. I watch longingly as Connor rides off with his friends. Once they are on the way, Marnie and I head down to the lake and take a long walk around, "Thanks for not ditching me Rae," Marnie says as we walk around the lake.

"No worries, we came to hang out and have girl time," I say with a smile. The trek to go all the way around the lake takes most of the morning. When we get back to camp, the boys have just gotten back as well. They help us fold up the tent and pack Marnie's car. Marnie and I whip up sandwiches and pass them around with cans of soda. The boys supply an assortment of chips to finish off the meal. We have a great time sitting around the remains of our campfire, talking about school and upcoming events. I, of course, sit as close as I can to Connor.

When we stand to leave and head back home, Connor takes my hand and pulls me into him. "You know, I don't even have your phone number Rae." He says with a smile.

"Hand me your phone," I offer. He obliges, immediately handing it to me. "Um, Connor, you've got to unlock it," I say passing his phone back to him. He whispers his code in my ear instead. Wow, that is impressive to give it up so quickly, must be nothing to hide here.

I unlock his phone, enter my number, take a quick selfie, assign the photo to my number adding my name complete with a heart emoji at the end. Then send myself a text, so I have his number. I snap a quick photo of him with my phone, and repeat the process of adding his picture to his number on my phone. This weekend could not have possibly gone any better if I'd planned every word and action.

CHAPTER 7 BACK TO REALITY

Monday is dull as expected after such a fantastic weekend, school drags on, and I have to work. Connor picks me up from Browning's around nine o'clock in the evening in his gray three-quarter-ton pickup truck. We head out to the barn to see Dixon. We haven't been dating long, like a day, so he needs to meet my most favorite boy in the world. When we arrive I see my trainer Janelle standing in the aisle talking on her phone. I wave as I make my way down the aisle. She gives me a bewildered look while motioning for me to come over.

She hangs up her phone, "Have you heard from Alyssa or Danielle lately?" she asks with obvious concern in her voice.

"No, I thought they were going abroad for a few weeks. Maybe they aren't back yet," I suggest.

"They should have been back last week," Janelle says, agitated. "Doc is coming out tomorrow, and I need to see if Alyssa wants Otis worked on before the spring series in Columbus. Her phone keeps saying not in range; she hasn't posted on social media in about 10 days. I am really getting concerned."

"Where exactly were they going?" I ask, Danielle told me once, but I forgot.

"Germany," Janelle answers.

My face falls, "Ethan was deployed over there a month or so ago. I have no idea what is going on though, he hasn't told us anything. I have heard on the news there is some sort of communications blackout over Europe and parts of Asia. All flights have been grounded because of this; perhaps they're just stuck over there off the grid. Have you tried calling Toni?"

Toni is Alyssa's mom; Alyssa recently graduated from med school; she still lives at home while completing her residency.

Janelle looks concerned with this as well, "No, she is traveling in Cozumel; it's her fifteenth wedding anniversary with Dennis." After a few minutes, she just sighs, "well, I guess they'll turn up. She'll just have to pay the farm call herself if she wants Otis injected."

"On a brighter note, Janelle this is Connor, Connor, my trainer Janelle. Janelle has been my trainer since I was a small fry." I introduce them.

Connor reaches his hand out, "pleasure to meet you ma'am, Rae speaks very highly of you."

"Nice to meet you as well, Connor. I might have heard a few things about you myself," she says with a smile.

Of course, I blush. "Okay then," I interject before she can say anything else; Janelle is known for saying whatever is on her mind regardless of how raunchy...or embarrassing for me. "Time for you to meet Dixon, so you know why you'll always be the number two boy in my life."

We move back the barn aisle to Dixon's stall, where he is happily munching on his hay. "Doc will hopefully release him to work tomorrow. I'm getting tired of being sidelined; they tried a newer drug to help heal his suspensory ligaments." I tell Connor.

"He's been very sound when I've been hand walking him," Janelle says, coming up behind us, "fingers crossed you two can go to Kentucky in three weeks."

"I hope so; I'm tired of being sidelined. At least I have college riding to look forward to in the fall. The qualifying period for worlds is almost over; I know I have to be on the bubble as much as we've missed. I've been too afraid to look lately." I say.

"I think you'll be fine; you had a great winter circuit." She says, then meanders back down the aisle, giving us privacy.

Connor walks into Dixon's stall and starts scratching his neck. Dixon absolutely approves, sticking his neck way up high, wiggling his upper lip in the air as though he is scratching another horse. Once he is done meeting Dixon, we step out of the stall, pausing to talk in the aisle. While standing there, I notice a few horses in the aisle are bucking in their stalls. "Hey, Janelle," I call up the barn aisle, "haven't you had these guys out in a while?"

"What, oh," she responds, walking back down the aisle to where we are. "They were all out today. They were nuts in the field. I had to bring them in. I was afraid they'd run through the fence. Most of these guys have been acting like this all day. Must be a weather change coming or something," she hypothesizes. "Though I've never seen the antics spread among this many at one time." She muses and then walks towards her apartment attached to the front of the barn.

"Night, Janelle," I call as I see her disappearing through the door.

"Night kids," she yells back, "nice to meet you, Connor."

"You as well ma'am," he calls back politely.

We leave the barn and walk out through the dark parking area to Connor's truck. "Well, I guess Dixon approves, you can hang around a bit longer," I tell Connor jokingly.

Just as we reach the truck Connor swings me around catching me in a big hug. "Girl, it's gonna be hard for you to get rid of me now," he says. He leans in, kissing me again. It starts off slow and innocent but builds into something more PG-13 than G rated. The parking lot at the barn is very dark, and Janelle has likely gone to bed after we left, so we keep going.

I can feel my need for him grow in intensity and wrap myself around him in a very non-PG fashion. We continue this make out sessions a bit longer. I begin to panic. "Connor, I am not quite sure I am ready for this," I stammer.

"No worries Rae, we don't have to go any farther" oh, does his southern drawl turn me on even more. We continue making out by the side of the truck a bit more PG. "Rae, I think I need to take you home now." He says breathlessly.

"Yes," I gasp, "that is probably a good idea." We stand there in silence, looking at each other for a few minutes before getting into the truck. As he starts driving, I build up the nerve to ask, "So, where'd you learn all those moves." I am only partially joking. I suspect he is not as virtuous as I. He has to have had a good deal of practice at this; no one can be naturally that good at making a girl melt.

"Yes, Rae, I've done it before, if that is what you want to know," he says, not at all embarrassed or sorry.

"That isn't exactly what I was asking, but good to know." I stay silent for a moment.

"I had a girl back in Texas; we continued to date over the summers I went home. Last summer, we thought we were old enough, had been together long enough to take it to the next step. I thought for sure she was the one. We made love, a lot, that summer," he says wistfully. "Then just after coming back up here, I got pictures sent to me from several different people showing her most decidedly in a relationship with another. I guess once she crossed the line nothing was off-limits." He mused. "That's why I didn't reach out to you sooner, ya know. When I was first attracted to you, I was with her, I was sure I had found my true love. Then after this summer, I was broken; we'd been together four years. Who knows," he muses, "maybe she dated others after I left the first time; I do know I was her first."

"Oh, I'm so sorry," I say, "that really sucks."

"Yeah, so, how about you, have you been with anyone?" He asks.

"I think you can guess the answer, but no. I've never been in a serious relationship before. I've dated a few guys, been kissed, gotten a bit handsy, but I've never had sex." I confess.

"I really like you Rae, I can see us being together for a long time, but I will never make you do anything you don't want to do," he promises. "I move a bit faster these days than I used to, having been in a serious relationship before, but we can take things at your pace."

"The problem is," I respond, "my body seems to want the things that I know I should not do," I say with a wink.

When we pull up in front of my house, I lean over and give him a kiss, "see you tomorrow," I say.

"Is Mar picking you up for school or am I," he asks.

"You are," I answer as I shut the door to head inside.

Mom is on the couch watching TV when I get in. "Wow Rae, you look a bit flushed. I thought you were just going to the barn." She says accusatorily.

"We did. Janelle will tell you we were there for a while," I hedge. "But we did hang out by his truck for a while before we drove home."

"Rae, I know you are responsible, but please don't make bad decisions now. You have your whole life to have sex." She says, very pointedly.

"MOM," I exclaim, "you know me better than that!"

"Do I?" She questions. "I have never seen you this serious about a boy before, and you've been dating for three days. I know you've liked him for a long time; I know his mom and I know he is a good kid, but cool your jets, girl, or I'll cool them for you."

"Mom, I promise, I won't ruin my future," I say with determination and a bit of slyness; I didn't promise I would not cross any line. "Come on, Willis," I summons my dog who is curled up beside my mom.

After a long hot shower, I climb into bed. I take a moment to text Marnie before I go to sleep. 'OMG, can't wait to talk tomorrow!!!!!!!' Is that enough exclamation points, I ask myself? If my mom reads my texts, I don't want to alert her she has more to be worried about. But I want to make sure Marnie understands the depth of the situation.

Just not sure when we will talk since Connor, Isaac, and AJ now eat lunch at our table. Michela is incredibly happy about this as she's had a crush on AJ for as long as I can remember. Still, he really doesn't show a bit of interest in her. Instead, I think he has a thing for Rachel. Oh, the drama of high school.

I drift off with a head full of Connor, and my dreams this night do not disappoint.

I wake Tuesday with a smile on my face. Between the actual events and dreams of last night, I'm happier than I think I have ever been. Connor picks me up early for school, helping me to be on time for once, he says. Just like he's known me my whole life. He has picked up fast food breakfast on the way. Smart man, there was no way I had time to eat this morning.

Once at school we go our separate ways to our classes. I get to lunch early, hoping to get some time to talk to Marnie but Connor is already at the table. I smile, grab my usual lunch of pizza, salad, and water, then head to the table.

"Do you ever eat anything else for lunch?" Connor inquires.

"Yuck, no, nothing else here is edible," I say.

"Take this noodle concoction," he says, holding up a forkful of mush, "I have no idea whatsoever is in this, but I think it tastes pretty good."

"You, my friend are much braver than I," I answer. "Yuck, how can he eat that stuff?"

Just then, Marnie and the others make it to the table. "Sorry," she says, looking at me knowingly, "Biochem ran over."

"That's alright," I answer, "Connor and I were just discussing the nutritional value of this mess the school provides for lunch."

"Maybe," Rachel says, "when you are a food scientist, you can tackle school lunches. Come up with a healthy, good-tasting, inexpensive alternative to whatever this is." She then holds up her fork full of mush. Isaac leans over, taking a big bite of the food off her fork.

"Yep, that's gross," he assesses, carefully unpacking his lunch he brought from home.

Lunch continues in much the same manner, with a lot of bantering back and forth. I get no chance to talk to Marnie. As we leave the cafeteria, I lean in, whispering to her, "Marnie, do you have anything going on in Calc today?"

"I don't think so." She says. Marnie has Calculus during my study hall period. "Why?" she asks.

"Meet me in the bathroom at 1:20," I suggest hopefully.

"Yep, that ought to work." She answers.

At 1:18 I head to the bathroom across from study hall; lucky for me, Marnie's class is just a few doors down. She is already in there; she nods toward the stalls indicating there is someone in here. We each go into a stall pretending to use the bathroom. We hear the other person leave and immediately dart out of our respective stalls.

"SPILL," she demands.

"OMG, Marnie last night got so hot, I thought for a minute Connor and I were about to do it in Janelle's driveway."

"RAE!" She shrieks a little too loud. "I know you've been crushing on Connor for two years, but you've only been dating for like three days. Don't you think it is a bit soon?"

"That is exactly what my mom said," I tell her.

"You told your mom?" She says, disbelieving.

"Not that," I tell her. "She just noticed my flushed face and demeanor when I got home last night. And yes, I think that, but holy crap, things get so hot so fast that I can't hardly control myself. He has such a magical way of touching me, I about come undone when he slides his hands over my skin."

"Enough, I am not sure I want to hear anymore," she says with a chuckle. "Well, just use protection, okay. Who knows what kind of gals he's dated in Texas." She urges.

"He told me last night he had sex with an ex-girlfriend down there, he thought they were going to get married, but she cheated on him not long after they had sex," I tell her.

"Oh man, that's rough," Marnie answers. "Just be careful, Rae; you've got a lot riding on your decisions for the next few months."

"I know." I say miserably, "I just don't know that I can make good choices."

"Do you need me to intervene? I can tag along everywhere you go." She laughs. "Well, if you decide to go all the way be prepared to spill the details," she threatens, then adds, "well maybe not all the details."

After school I meet Connor at his truck. I climb in the cab wishing his truck had a bench seat so I could slide over next to him. I settle for holding his hand resting on the console. He drives me home from school but only has time to kiss me quickly, explaining he has to help his mom move some furniture after school. I wonder if this is our mothers working together to keep us from having alone time. Whatever the cause, I muse, it's undoubtedly setting me up for a very dull evening. I make dinner to pass the time, meatloaf, baked potatoes, and a side of broccoli. Mom gets home about her usual time.

"MMM dinner smells good, no date tonight," she asks knowingly. Yep, they've definitely been working against us.

"No, Connor had to help his mom with something." I say, mentally adding 'as if you didn't know.' Mom helps me clean up dinner getting that done quickly. I head upstairs to do homework rather than sit and watch TV. The news has been terribly lacking in the information lately.

While reworking calculus problems I find myself daydreaming what it would be like if Connor and I did go all the way. I really don't know what to expect. I fall asleep with these thoughts in my mind, and once again my dreams this night do not disappoint.

CHAPTER 8 EARLY VISIT

Connor has to pick his sister from up school and Marnie is working, so I drive myself Wednesday. After being shuttled around by either Marnie or Connor the past few days, my rust bucket is a loud, uncomfortable mess. When I get home from school Wednesday, I see a familiar car in the driveway and my heart leaps out of my chest.

The 2019 gray sedan tells me my brother is home a bit early. I launch myself out of my car, not even thinking about shutting the door and hurtle toward the house. As I get close the front door swings open, and Ethan runs out to greet me; Willis jumping at his heels caught up in the excitement. It has only been about four months since I have seen my brother, not a terribly long time. Still, it was the angst of not knowing what was happening that triggers the sheer emotion of seeing him again. We embrace in a tight bear hug. I can't help but cry, cry from the happiness of him being home, cry from the sadness of the time we've been apart, cry from relief knowing he is alright and here in our home again. We stand there, hugging for what seems like an eternity. When I pull away, I see my tears have soaked the shoulder of his tan uniform shirt thoroughly.

"Sorry," I whisper, motioning to his shirt.

"Quite alright little sis. I am happy to see you too." He says gently.

"I thought you wouldn't be home until the end of the week?" I shriek, letting the excitement of him being home sink in.

"Well, we got to scoot early," is all he says.

"Really, that doesn't happen very often; what's going on over there?" I ask.

He hesitates and responds, "You're looking tired, Rae; what's up with the rat's nest on your head?" He playfully tussles my already hideously out of control hair.

Well, that's unusual; he's never dodged questions like that before. I play along for now, but I want to know what is going on. "Well, nothing new with the rat's nest, just worse than usual because I can't get my normal shampoo," I say with an appropriately hurt pout on my face.

"You know I'm just teasing, right?" he consoles, "I am so glad to be home and so happy to see you." As I look at him, I can see worry behind his smile. His eyes look as tired as mine, his never-ending smile I'm used to doesn't quite reach its normal heights.

My brother has always been the happy go lucky optimistic type. Even in the worst of times, he can find the silver lining and maintain that smile. Yet today, I can clearly see how hard it is for him.

"What's going on, Ethan?" I ask hesitantly.

"Nothing for you to worry about, sis. Where is mom? I was expecting her to be home?" He asks with another hint of worry.

"Well, we weren't expecting you for a few days if you recall, or I am sure she'd have a whole welcoming party for you. She's working downtown. They have a client working on a new product launch; the consumer input says they've got it wrong. So its the usual fire drills – multiple rounds of focus groups, product design meetings, you know, the usual." I casually respond, keeping an eye on his expression.

"Huh?" is all he says. I see a twitch near his eye as he looks down to check his watch.

Tired of the suspicion and oddness to our exchange, I change the subject. "So, how long do we have you for?" I ask.

This, however, has the opposite effect I was going for. The worry becomes even more clearly etched on his face. "I am not sure," he responds hesitantly "we'll just have to see how things go. But at least through the weekend, I think." Alright, something is up, I'll wait until mom gets home, but then he's going to have to spill the beans.

"Come on," he says, "let's get your books out of your car and close it up before it rains." I look up at the sky; the dark gray clouds are swirling angrily above. It looks as though it could rain at any moment. The smell of rain in the air suggests it is already raining somewhere nearby.

We get to my car, he grabs my backpack while I put the windows up and close the car door. We make our way back to the house, reaching the front door just as the rain starts to fall. I yell for Willis, who comes leaping around from the side of the house. Once we are inside, Willis immediately heads upstairs to his favorite place on my bed.

"So," I start at my latest attempt for a lighter subject, "Marnie was asking when you'd be home again." This at least has the response I was expecting, his eyes light up, and his smile widens a bit.

"Really, when do you expect Ms. Martina might plan to visit?" Ethan asks, trying to remain casual.

"Well, she's working tonight, so probably not until tomorrow." I let him know.

"Don't you guys usually work the same shifts?" He questions.

"Yea, but mom convinced me since I signed for my scholarship to reduce my hours and take a little time for myself. So, Mar's working and I am not." I say matter of fact.

"Mom's right you know, you only get one senior year. Well, most people, unless of course you're going to fail, then maybe you can do it again." He teases, jabbing me in the side.

"For your information, mister, I still have a 4.0 GPA; what was it you graduated with, like a 2?" I tease back.

"Nice try, smartypants, 3.4 thank you very much. The Air Force didn't seem to mind my lack of a 4.0." He retorts. "Anyhow, I think I have a hankering for a Double Palace Burger."

This makes me happy inside; perhaps he is finally going to cave and admit he likes Marnie. "Must take a lot to maintain those muscles," I say, poking him in the arm, realizing those muscles are pretty hard; somebody has definitely been working out. "Marnie will lose her mind when she sees you. Let me deposit my books in my room and I'll go with you. Maybe Connor can join us so you can meet him."

"Oh yes, the new boyfriend, sounds like a great night." He says with a genuine smile.

I run up to my room. Willis has already returned to his post on my bed, so I pet him quickly. I dump my books on my desk and shoot off a quick text to Connor. 'Hey, Ethan is in town early, join us at Burger Palace if you can.' It only takes a second for him to reply. 'Can't tonight, helping Joanie with her science fair project. I've blown her off several times already, can't do it again. Raincheck? Maybe I can come over tomorrow evening and meet Ethan officially.' My quick reply is 'sounds good.'

"You driving, or am I," Ethan asks.

"You better drive," I respond, "this old gas guzzler," I say, jerking my thumb towards my 2012 Forest Green SUV, "is on its last leg."

"I'll have to take a look this weekend." He offers.

As we ride along, I take a close look at Ethan. His hair is super short, as it has always been. He's got the same hair texture as me, so if he were to grow it out, he'd probably have an afro; he's not the big hair type. It is mostly auburn but has flecks of black, silver, and brown. Since joining the Air Force, his build is very muscular, much different from the overly skinny boy I knew him to be in high school. He has worry lines around his eyes and mouth now, but overall he still looks very young. He has also managed to pick up a nice tan somewhere. I am jealous of that; I am pale and fair-skinned as ever despite the sunbathing at the Quarry last weekend. Ethan senses my stare and interrupts my internal musing.

"So, is the famous Connor meeting us for dinner?" He questions.

"Nope, helping his sister with her science fair project," I respond sadly.

"Oh, a family man, you gotta like that." He says with a wink.

We ride in silence the rest of the short distance to Browning's.

When we get to Browning's, I see Marnie through the window, but she has yet to see us. Ethan is still in his fatigues so he's drawing a lot of attention. We walk into the restaurant but I don't see Marnie, she must have gone into the back. "A seat in Marnie's section, pu-lease," I tell Sam, the hostess, with a wink.

"Of course," she replies, giving Ethan a flattering look.

Okay, I concede, he must be handsome. Or maybe it's just the fatigues, who doesn't love a man in uniform. The uniform's light browns compliment his fair, yet somehow tanned skin tone and auburn hair nicely.

After we sit down, John, Ethan's high school buddy, saunters over. John will never leave this town, here he's somebody, the Mayor's son, permanent fixture working, or some might say hanging out chatting up the town, at the hardware store. Outside of this town, he'd be a nobody. I would be sad if he left. He's super helpful when you need a hand and absolutely hilarious; ambition is not for everyone. "What's happening, E" he almost shouts as he claps Ethan on the back, shaking his hand vigorously. "Dinner is on me tonight, as always, thank you for your service sir," he concludes.

After hearing the commotion in the restaurant, Marnie peeks around the corner. I catch her eye as she shrieks, drops an entire tray of drinks, and comes running over. She ran so fast I think she reached the table before the last of the red heavy plastic cups finished clanging against the floor. "MARNIE," I hear Mr. Browning yell, but he rounds the corner and sees Ethan there, a faint smile touches his lips. He then busies himself, cleaning up the drink mess.

She stops at the edge of our table, standing there speechless, staring down at Ethan. Her hair is as always perfect, today it is knotted in a bun at the back of her neck, her make-up flawless. Her apron is lopsided, indicating it has been a rough shift. Still, she has a massive smile for Ethan, standing there silently staring down at him.

"Hey, Marnie," Ethan says shyly.

"Well," John says abruptly, his loud voice breaking the tension, "I'll just head back to my table. E make sure you stopover at the hardware store before you head out again, won't you."

"Of course, John, I'll swing by tomorrow while Rae is in

school, it'll be good to catch up," Ethan responds.

"So, Marnie," Ethan begins, "how have you been?"

"Not too bad, keeping busy with school and work, I'm sure Rae has already filled you in on the excitement, or non-excitement, that is our life," she responds.

"Not really, we exchanged our greetings when I got a big hankering for a Double Palace Burger," Ethan teases, giving Marnie a wink. Maybe this will happen this century. I finally got my guy; Marnie should get hers.

"Well, let me get right on that," Marnie says, returning a giant smile.

Just then, Mr. Browning saunters up, "No need Mar, why don't you go on break? I'll get this. Ethan, dinner is on me tonight. Thank you for your service." Mr. Browning is a nice older man. He and his wife have owned this restaurant for as long as I can remember, one of the few hometown eateries to have survived the fast-food chain wars a few years back. The restaurant has a very dated seventies diner look, complete with red speckled vinyl seats, red laminate tables with ribbed silver aluminum trim around the edges. The look is straight out of the seventies. But he has maintained it well, the booths are clean, and the vinyl is in impeccable shape. I think the feeling here is one of the place's attractions.

He and his wife had one son who joined the Army in 1990 at the age of eighteen. I hear all he ever talked about was joining the Army and serving his country. He was killed a few years later in an IED explosion roadside in Iraq. Then just last year Mrs. Browning passed away after a long battle with cancer. So, he's a lonely old guy who has always had a soft spot for military folks and families; this reunion in his restaurant makes him happy.

"Thanks Mr. Browning, but John already said he's buying,"

Ethan counters loud enough to make sure John hears.

John looks over hearing his name and gives Mr. Browning a thumbs up confirming Ethan's assessment.

"Even better," Mr. Browning responds. "What else can I get you?"

"Besides that, Double Palace Burger, I'll have Saratoga Chips and a Strawberry Shake," Ethan responds.

"Anything for you, girls?" Mr. Browning asks.

"Just a soda and fries for me," Marnie respondents.

"Make that two," I agree.

Dinner at the Burger Palace is a celebratory affair with a lot of laughing and many smiles. We are seated right in the middle of the restaurant. The booth we are at is round, with a low back, so we have a good view of the whole restaurant, and, well, they have a good view of us. Many folks drop by throughout the evening to shake Ethan's hand, wishing him well, old friends, teachers, and even strangers alike. Marnie never really does go back to work; Mr. Browning goes about serving her tables whistling a tune low under his breath with a smile etched on his lips.

At about seven-thirty mom arrives. I secretly texted her earlier to let her know Ethan was home and where to find us. I know it probably killed her to finish her work, but she is nothing if not professional. "ETHAN," mom screams as she comes rushing in. "MOM," he yells back with just as much enthusiasm. They embrace hard, for a long time; mom doesn't cry like me, but you can tell she's very emotional. Once mom arrives, Marnie goes back to work, somewhat, trying to get her stations closed to leave on time despite her lack of effort all evening.

"You look tired," mom muses, looking at him.

"I could say the same about you," he responds.

The chatter continues a while longer. Around nine-thirty, Mr. Browning wanders over again, "sorry folks, I hate to do it, but we closed a half-hour ago. I've got to get this place closed up and get home. Missy is going to wonder where I am." Missy is Mr. Browning's calico cat he rescued from the shelter last year, his only companion at the moment, though Ms. Nester has been visiting the restaurant an awful lot lately. I am thinking she might be getting sweet on him. I know he would never re-marry at his stage in life, but some companionship for both of them would be nice.

"Yea, I've got school tomorrow and haven't gotten much time with my brother yet," I interject.

We all begrudgingly get up and head out, leaving Marnie behind to clear the table and finish work. "I'll see you in the morning Mar, I assume you're picking me up for school?" I question.

"You know I am," she responds with a smile.

CHAPTER 9 ETHAN'S VISIT

After getting home and letting Willis into the backyard, I join Ethan and mom at the kitchen table to catch up. I fill Ethan in on all the drama and goings-on of Southeast Lake High. Then mom takes her turn, filling him in on the drama she has been dealing with amongst the product team. Then lists out about a million things around the house that need to be addressed if he has time on his visit. Once she's done conveying her stories, she turns on Ethan.

"So, when did you get back, E?" She questions.

"Today," he answers.

"You got back to the US today?" she asks suspicioulsy.

"Well, no, we actually got back from Europe last week, but had to hang out for debrief meetings on the trip," he says, cautiously sensing where this is headed. "I was actually back on the base when I texted I was coming home for a visit."

"Oh, so is whatever the conflict is resolved?" She questions further.

"Our part is done," he hedges.

"What is up with the communications blackouts we keep hearing about on the news?" I add.

"Communication blackouts?" he questions, but is not convincing, he knows something.

"Come on, like you don't know. Spill it," I prod, with mom looking on intently.

"There were some issues while we were over there with

satellites," he says, "but I didn't realize it was a big enough deal it'd be on our news."

Neither mom nor I are buying this. The look on his face tells a different story. "Ethan, is this anything we need to be worried about here?" my mom presses.

"I don't think so," he says stoically.

"Think?" Mom continues, "so it could impact us here?"

"I honestly don't know, mom; it is all highly classified, and I cannot go into details," he says. "But," he adds, "I'd feel a lot better if you guys stick close to home for a while. If you would try to work from home rather than go downtown."

"Well, that doesn't give us much confidence, E," I say, bewildered.

"I am sure it is nothing, but still, no big trips, okay," he pleads. "How much longer will you be headed downtown every day?" he inquires apprehensively.

"About another week, maybe two. We've made great progress, but there are still some issues to be ironed out. The team is working hard." She says.

"Hmm, stay home as much as you can" is all he responds.

"Ethan, I've got a job to do and will go where is required. You're not giving me a whole lot to go on to stay home." She answers.

"I can't discuss it, mom, but please, as much as you can stay out of downtown." He begs.

"Alright, Rae, parties over, you've got school tomorrow, head on up to bed," mom instructs around midnight.

I go to the kitchen door calling Willis to come inside. He's already been out too long for his liking, but I was too engrossed in conversation with Ethan and forgot to let him in.

"Night guys," I mumble as Willis, and I head upstairs.

I've been in bed for about twenty minutes when I overhear a heated debate happening downstairs. I cannot make out every word, but it sounds as though mom is badgering Ethan for more information, but he is standing his ground. It really isn't fair. He is bound to not give away military secrets and knowledge, but why give us cryptic messages that make us worry? Eventually, I hear Ethan say goodnight angrily, ending the subject.

The rest of Ethan's visit flies by. During his visit, despite constant questioning, he won't tell us what is happening abroad. Connor makes it over Thursday evening. He and Ethan hitting it off immediately like old buddies, which is nice. Connor and Marnie spend much of Friday and Saturday at the house as well. It is nice having a house full of people again.

We have fun playing cards, staying up late telling stories about our childhood, trying to out embarrass each other, and watching slapstick comedies. Connor and I sit in the main service at Church Sunday with Ethan and our moms rather than attending Senior High Worship. The service is excellent, the music is on point, I leave feeling lifted and happy. The message is God's use of imperfect people in His perfect plan. God recognizes we aren't perfect but loves us anyway and has made a way back for those who accept Him. Mom leans over, whispering knowingly in my ear, "that does not give us an excuse to give into our whims." But I think to myself, there is forgiveness waiting if I do mess up.

After church Connor and Marnie come over for lunch but head home quickly to do homework and chores. Late Sunday afternoon, it is finally just Ethan, mom, and myself at the house, so he takes advantage of the quiet to work on my car. Ethan has just finished cleaning up from changing out a few belts when his phone rings. He steps outside to take the call, but I can tell it is his commanding officer from the initial interaction.

"You leaving us?" I question when he comes back in.

"Yep, sorry little sis, leave is over. I've gotta head back to base right away." He answers sadly.

"Everything okay?" I ask, sensing the tension in his demeanor.

"For now, if there's anything to worry about, I promise I'll take care of you guys," he says with spooky determination.

"When do you think you'll get to come back up again," I ask solemnly.

"Hopefully, I can be up on the weekends. I think we'll be home for a while." He says confidently. "Hey, I have to go right now, so tell Marnie I said bye, and I'll call her this week," he finishes.

"Of course," I answer.

Well, that's a good sign. Those two must have gotten more time in private than I realized while he was home. I was so absorbed with Connor I did not notice. At least neither one of them was ignored. Despite Connor and I spending every possible moment together, with Ethan in town, we have not been alone together very much. That, I think, is probably best. We have had plenty of kisses, but I haven't been forced to face a decision I am not sure I am ready to make. This uncertainty should be enough to tell me I am not ready, I know this, I don't need Marnie's constant reminder of this. But oh, when the heat turns up, it is hard to make that call.

Mom and I are both sad at Ethan's abrupt departure and feeling more than just a little stressed about what is or is not happening in the world. We decide to go out to dinner with the Tiptons to help ease the emptiness we feel in the house. I don't want to eat at the Burger Palace again, so we head to the neighboring town's steakhouse. They have the best steaks anywhere, I don't know what is in their seasoning, but I love the flavor, and the steaks are so tender they melt in your mouth. Dinner is a somewhat subdued, but overall a pleasant evening with many laughs; just what we needed.

Once dinner is finished, there is a debate about who is picking up the check; mom manages to snatch the bill right out of the waitresses hand before Connor's mom, Elaine, she keeps reminding me to call her, had a chance to get it. Elaine insists on leaving a tip. I am sure this gal just got the biggest tip of her life with Elaine making up for not getting a hold of the bill. After the tab is settled, we head out to the parking lot.

The night is quite chilly. Connor wraps his arm around me and pulls me along tight to his side. I feel warm in his embrace despite the chill of the March evening air. He walks me all the way to my mom's car, kissing me somewhat inappropriately since our moms are looking on. This goes on so long his mom has had enough and starts rapid-fire honking the horn, "let's go love bird, you've got school tomorrow." We step apart, moving to our respective cars.

When I get in, I see my mom is chuckling to herself. "Well," she says, "things seem to be getting along quite well."

I give her a sheepish grin and say, "definitely."

CHAPTER 10 EVERYTHING CHANGES

The next week flies by. I work Monday and head to the barn most other afternoons after school. Doc cleared us to start riding Dixon again and we are trying to prep for the show coming up in two weeks. There is a lot to be done. Connor comes with me Tuesday and Thursday, bringing Joanie along Thursday.

Joanie really seemed to enjoy the barn and is a natural riding. Janelle is still in a tizzy; all this week, she is still unable to connect with Alyssa or Danielle, or Toni for that matter. She concedes there is nothing else she can do, and 'surely, they'll resurface soon.' To top it off, she says the horses are all still acting like complete psychotic idiots.

Friday, I finally get a break; I don't have to work, and Dixon gets the day off. I am looking forward to a pleasant evening with Connor. Mom has finally wrapped up her project downtown and is having dinner with the team after they finish the day, which means Elaine will be joining them.

"Hey, baby," Connor greets me at lunch, "want to drive out to the Creamy Whip after school?"

"Yes," I exclaim excitedly, "I could really go for a treat."

"You and me both," he says under his breath a bit seductively. This causes me to eye him suspiciously, but I go on about my business. Lunch is the usual jovial affair at our table; even though Marnie broke off her date with Isaac amid her blossoming relationship with Ethan. The group that now assembles here gets along very well. There are plenty of laughs, everyone thoroughly enjoying the time together. It is always a disappointment when the buzzer sounds, and we have to go back to class.

Leaving the cafeteria, Marnie leans in whispering, "I've talked to Ethan every day this week," she is positively beaming.

"That is something, I've gotten a few generic texts, but that is all," I say, a little miffed by the lack of communication from my bother. "Is he still acting weird?" I inquire.

"Yea, he is definitely really stressed. He makes weird cryptic comments about being prepared, but I never get much more out of him," she answers.

"Hmm" is all I think to answer.

Once school lets out, the sky is a beautiful deep blue, complete with white fluffy clouds and a soft breeze that screams spring. Today, there is an odd smell on the breeze I can't put my finger on, it makes it not the same clean-smelling air I expect during spring. The scent seems like it should be familiar to me, but I can't place where I would have smelled it before.

Connor and I hop into my SUV and drive out to the neighboring town where my favorite ice cream shop is located. "That's weird, the radio doesn't seem to be working," I complain. I absolutely love music and have it going all the time. Connor begins fumbling with the radio controls, but he can't seem to get a station no matter what he does. Despite its age, my car has an excellent radio; Ethan bought it for me a few years back. It allows me to connect my phone via Bluetooth and play music. While I drive, Connor syncs my phone and cues up my favorite playlist.

We go through the drive-thru at the Creamy Whip. I order my usual Turtle Sundae in a Waffle Bowl, and Connor gets the chocolate-vanilla twist soft-serve cone. Once we are through, we head to a local park to finish our ice cream and enjoy the spring day.

"I don't feel like we've had any quality time together this week," Connor says with a pout as he finishes off the last of his ice cream cone, "you're always so busy."

"Yeah, sorry about that" I apologize, "things have even slowed down since I've cut back at work. I used to have to go ride Dixon at night after work."

"Wow, when did you study?" He questions.

"All hours of the night. It's been so nice since I signed for my scholarship, I can really back off the work schedule and breathe for a minute," I continue.

"Well," he says with a devious grin, "let me see if I can take that breath away beautiful."

He grabs me by the hand and we walk down a trail that starts just past the picnic tables. He has a certain air of excitement about him that is rubbing off on me, making me a bit giddy. It is early spring, so there are many people in the park, but mostly moms and kids hanging out on the playground. No one uses these trails very often since they put in a paved walking path toward the entrance. We have the place to ourselves back here. The trees are thick enough with branches to shield the trails from the central park all year, but now the leaves are sprouting as well, creating a thick barrier between the trail and picnic and play areas.

We walk back the trail until we are well out of sight of those enjoying the park, where we can barely hear the sounds of kids playing. This must be the place he was looking for; he abruptly stops, spins me around, pushing me against a tree, and kisses me passionately.

I pull back "it seems like you've been planning this for a while, Mr. Tipton," I say with a sly smile.

"Just since lunch," he admits.

He leans in, kissing me with passionate but gentle kisses, while I absolutely melt at his touch. His nose skims my jawline, leaving a trail of fire behind. I feel his breath move down my neck; I suck in a quick breath at the sensation this creates. This continues on for quite some time.

My mind is mush, my body is on fire, I really am not sure if I want this to go any further, but I am sure I will spontaneously combust if I stop this now. I am acting more on instinct and need than out of conscious thought. He continues kissing me, but he seems to sense my hesitation and pauses to look into my eyes. I see his question there, asking for permission to take this farther. I don't know what to say or do, so I grab his neck with both hands, to pull him into another passion-filled kiss.

Oh my, is this really going to happen here in the woods? I once again question what I am doing and I hesitate. Connor moves my hand to his back. He then slides his hands around my waist, and leans in for another kiss.

I am just about to give in and accept this will happen right here in the woods, when we hear a branch break in the woods off to our right, nowhere near a trail. We instantly freeze. I quickly remove my hands from Connor's body and readjust myself. We stand still looking in the direction of the noise for several minutes but see nothing.

"Perhaps we should go back to my house," I gasp breathlessly, "mom has dinner with the team to celebrate finishing the project. She won't be home for a couple hours."

"That sounds like a great plan," Connor agrees.

It takes me a minute before I can walk; Connor leans down, kissing me gently. "Are you sure this is what you want?" he asks gently.

"It's what I need now," I say, looking at him "kudos, sir, you accomplished your goal."

He laughs slightly, and we begin walking back down the path. We step out of the woods; my body is still absolutely trembling. Connor grabs my hand, rubbing gentle circles with his thumb.

I look back over my shoulder in the direction of the noise we heard and see an odd shimmering in the air. I decide it must be what little bit of the sunlight is not concealed by a haze now covering the sky playing off a puddle in the woods. But that doesn't quite seem right. Walking to my car, I look at the sky, which has changed drastically since we went into the woods, less than 20 minutes ago. "Wow, it's getting hazy," I comment. "Whatever that smell is, it's getting stronger too."

"Yeah, that's weird. It's not like we're expecting any weather, and the temperature has not changed that much. That smell is more pungent, but I have no clue how to even describe it, kind of acrid or sulfurous in a way," Connor comments.

It's a tense ride home. Connor drives, he drives well but with urgency. I place my hand on his leg, gently massaging his thigh. He occasionally looks at me like he is about to explode, then speeds up just a bit each time.

When we get back to the house, we see Ethan's car in the

driveway. Well, so much for quenching that fire. All thoughts of satisfying our teenage hormones are gone. Ethan doesn't even wait for us to get out of the car before he comes darting out of the house, meeting us in the front yard. "Thank God you're here," he says.

"What's up, E?" I ask, observing the apparent stress radiating from him.

"Where's mom?" Ethan asks.

"She's downtown again, I think this is the last day she has to be down there. She'll be excited your back, but she'll be late, they've got a dinner after work." I say, hoping the reason for his distress is not as serious as it appears.

"It's happening, Rae, it's happening here!" He says with so much urgency I can't help but feel on edge.

"Ethan, what are you talking about? What is happening here?" I ask, desperately trying to understand.

"The reason we were deployed to Europe, entire towns are being flattened with no warning, no obvious source. I've got to go find mom." He says, running into his car.

"Ethan, wait! What are you talking about? Just call mom." I say reasonably.

"Rae, haven't you noticed your phone doesn't work anymore. All communications have been jammed," he continues.

"I mean, I noticed the radio wasn't working in the car, but I thought that was just my car," I say, bewildered.

"Rae, all communication systems are down. There is no way for anyone to communicate with one another. Military bases across the country are under attack. Bases in Texas, Florida, California, Washington D.C., and Nevada have been destroyed. The cities of Washington, D.C., New York, Los Angeles and many others no longer exist, Rae. They've been completely leveled, the entire cities and everyone in them are gone. That haze you are seeing isn't weather. It's the aftermath of the destruction. If things continue on like we saw in Europe, this will continue across the country," he says rapidly.

"Our most top-secret secure communication channels remained functional until about two hours before I left the base, at which point they were breached. There is absolutely no way to communicate with anyone other than face-to-face. I don't know if any other towns or cities have been affected since the communication ended."

"Listen, Rae, stay here, collect what you can for food – focus on non-perishables, stuff that will keep; pack clothes and anything that you think of that might be helpful. I'm going to get mom and meet you back here. We're headed to my buddy Don's place in the mountains in Tennessee. Near where we used to stay as kids," Ethan finishes in a rush.

At the mention of Tennessee, my heart absolutely sinks, but I am not sure why. I've always loved it there. I am so bewildered by what he is saying. It is incomprehensible. "Ethan, if this is true," I start to say.

"Damn it, Rae, THIS. IS. HAPPENING." he screams, making each word a sentence, his voice becoming even louder on the last word.

"I was going to say, mom is working with Connor's mom, Elaine, please bring her home too." I whisper in a barely audible voice.

"I'll see what I can do," he mutters solemnly. Ethan jumps in his car and speeds away.

Connor and I stare at each other in silence for quite some time, completely dumbfounded. We slowly make our way into the house sitting at the kitchen table. "Connor what on earth do you think is happening. Obviously, something is going on, but do you think it as serious as Ethan says?" I ask.

"I don't know Rae, his story sounds preposterous to me, but he would have the inside knowledge the rest of us would not," he answers. "But then again, what explains the haze, the smell, the downed communications." He adds, thinking aloud. "Remember we couldn't get the radio in the car to work."

We sit in silence, staring at each other when the tension I feel bubbles up, and I cannot sit still any longer. "Connor, go get Joanie and meet me back here. See if you can find any news or any information at all. Ethan's story seems farfetched. There has to be some other explanation for what is happening, satellites down, solar flares or something. But let's be ready just in case this isn't some tall tale and the country really is under attack. I think it will make me feel better if we are at least prepared if something happens."

"None of this makes sense, Rae. I think we would certainly know, have gotten some indication if the country was under attack. There would have been some news story," he starts. I give him a look.

"There is no news right now," I counter.

"There'd be some sounds of war, right?" Connor protests.

"I don't know Connor; I've never seen Ethan like this. He is always so stable, we rely on him for consistency. Again, what about the haze and the smell? Where did that come from? Just go get Joanie and come back. You don't need to tell her what is up, tell her we're all going to the Burger Palace for dinner. If nothing is going on, no harm done, if there is, then we're together and as prepared as we can be." I say, trying to push down the anxiety I am feeling and remain calm.

At the end of this sentence, the lights in my house flicker several times. It appears as if the light is sucked from the bulbs but fights to return. We hear the sound of an explosion, I have no idea where it is centered, but the force of which is so strong the house literally shakes around us. We stare at each other in stunned silence across the kitchen for a minute, then run outside.

We look towards West where we believe the explosion occurred though we see nothing, no indication of where it came from. There is no smoke or fire in the sky. Within two minutes of the blast, the lights go out entirely around my neighborhood. "Go Connor, get Joanie, meet us back here."

Connor leaves the house running, he jumps in my SUV and speeds off. I run upstairs, grab a mishmash of warm and cold weather clothes, my lace-up riding boots, and gym shoes, stuffing them hastily in a bag. I run to mom's room and grab a similar assortment of clothing for her. I grab blankets, sleeping bags, a few beach towels, and washcloths from the hall closet. I drop these things by the door in the hallway. I then run to the laundry room, here I grab Willis' harness, leash, and a bag of dog food.

Back in the kitchen, I start filling cloth grocery sacks with non-perishable foods. I stuff one bag full of dried beans. Mom always keeps these on hand 'for emergencies,' she says they are full of protein, keep for a long time, and are portable. I continue bagging up items, adding canned veggies, boxed pasta, shelf-stable microwave meals, and canned soups. I look at the pile growing by the door, wondering how we'll transport all of this stuff. The power is out, and it is growing darker in the house.

I look at my phone in my hand mocking me with 'no service' displayed in the upper righthand corner. Now that the frenzy of collecting all these supplies has passed, I take a step back and slide down the wall in the foyer. I stare at the pile I've created on the floor. A very bewildered looking Willis comes to sit beside me, trembling and whimpering. I pick him up, squeezing him tight. Willis is obviously upset by the explosion and my odd behavior. "I don't know buddy. I don't know what is happening," I say, stroking his head. I am trying to console him while I'm totally falling apart on the inside. I lean my head back against the wall in the foyer, staring blankly out the window over the front door at the darkening sky.

Just when I think I will totally lose my mind Connor pushes through the front door with Joanie and Marnie right behind him. "I stopped at the diner and got Marnie. The power is out in the town too, so they closed earlier. I didn't tell her what was going on, just that she needed to come with me."

"Mar, where is your family?" I ask desperately.

"They took the girls to Lexington for the weekend to see my grandparents. They left last night and won't be back until late Sunday." Marnie says, looking questioningly at the pile I've created on the floor. "Rae, what the hell is going on. What was that explosion earlier? Why does it look like you've packed to leave forever?"

"I am not sure Mar, Ethan came home ranting about an invasion, entire military bases destroyed. Cities such as New York, LA, and D.C. leveled with nothing or no one left. It seemed super farfetched until we heard the explosion West of here. Ethan went to Downtown Cincinnati to try to find mom and Elaine. He said when he gets back, we're headed to Tennessee, a buddy of his has a place up in the mountains where we can hideout." I spew out extremely fast.

"Rae, that's crazy talk," Marnie protests. "Wouldn't there be something on the news about this? Wouldn't someone have called or texted? These types of stories blow up all over social media."

"Mar, look at your phone, there is zero service, no cell, no data, nothing. Turn on the T.V. or radio and there is no signal. I know for a fact the radio was out when we got out of school this afternoon. We were listening to music on my phone on the drive to the creamy whip. Ethan said even the most top-secret secure channels of communication the military uses have now been disrupted." I explain warily.

This exchange causes Joanie to cry, "Connor, where's mom?" she asks between sobs.

"Ethan went to look for her and Rae's mom, he'll find them," he says, looking absolutely devastated. Then corrects himself, "he'll do his best to find them."

"I don't understand what is happening," she moans, sinking into her brother's side.

"We don't know either, sweetie. Hopefully, Ethan is back soon, and we can figure this out." He consoles her, clearly distraught himself.

We all move into the living room, sinking down into the couch and loveseat. We sit in silence in the ever-darkening evening for a half-hour more, by now it has to be approaching eight o'clock. I can't help but notice it is getting dark much quicker than expected for this time of year. Typically, there would still be some remnants of the sunset highlighting the distant sky, or perhaps the city's lights reflecting the clouds.

We finally hear a car pull up outside. I run to the door and see Ethan's car with the windows shattered, himself covered in deep gashes. "Ethan, Oh My God," I scream, "what happened?"

He staggers out of his car, looks at me, and collapses on the grass in a heap of sobs. "Ethan," I shriek, terrified, "WHAT THE HELL HAS HAPPENED! ANSWER ME!"

He looks up at me with sorrow in his eyes I can't even comprehend. "I was too late, Rae. I was about 25 miles this side of the city limits. It's gone, Cincinnati is gone. I'm sorry, it's my fault. I should have told you guys when I was here. I should have told her why she shouldn't go into the city. I could have saved her. I really didn't think...it didn't seem like it was coming here. The commanders even thought we'd be okay, or at least have some warning since we saw what happened in Europe..." he trails off.

"No, no, no, no," I scream, "this seriously cannot be happening. These kinds of things don't really happen, they are made up in Hollywood." I protest, fighting the tears burning at the edges of my eyes.

"It is happening," he says, regaining some of his composure in the face of the horror we face, "and we've got to move, we've got to get on our way." He looks around and just now notices Marnie. "Oh, Marnie, thank God you are here." He runs to her and embraces her tightly. "We've got to go."

"Ethan, what if mom and Elaine weren't in the city? What if they were off-site somewhere?" I plead, praying to God mom was in Blue Ash or somewhere else today.

"Rae, the devastation goes pretty far North of the city. I'm not sure they'd be okay there either," he says, his voice full of defeat.

"This can't be happening," I sob, standing there staring at nothing.

"Come on, let's load this stuff in Rae's car and head south," he demands.

"What is happening? What are you talking about? What does this mean?" Joanie screams, the tears falling quickly down her face.

"Joanie, Mom was with Regan and Ethan's mom in the city when it exploded," Connor says, getting choked up but trying to remain strong. "She's gone, Joanie, moms gone," he whispers the last part, fighting off the break down that is coming.

Joanie becomes inconsolable, collapsing to the ground just beyond the porch. Connor sits down, pulling Joanie into his lap holding her tightly. Watching this, I feel more determined, "I'm not leaving, what if mom comes home." I protest. "We need to clean those cuts you've got, too; we should see if Aunt Lisa is working."

"Rae, we don't have time, I don't know how long it takes for people to start disappearing, but it's going to happen." Ethan fires back.

"Now, what are you talking about," I ask impatiently between sobs.

"There's no time Rae, I'll explain on the way, just get this stuff in the car." He spits back, getting angry now. About this time, we hear another very distant explosion. This new explosion coupled with Ethan's urgency in his words, we can't help but get up and move. I pull myself together, moving quickly. Ethan, Marnie, and I move the items I've collected from the house into the back of my SUV. Connor lifts Joanie from the ground and carries her to the car, placing her in the middle row. Her tears have quieted some, but she is still incomprehensible. Marnie climbs in and takes over consoling Joanie while Connor helps Ethan with a few more bags.

After the pile of items I have collected has been moved to the car, I make one last trip into the house. I collect basic toiletries I hadn't thought of before, soap, shampoo, and toothpaste. My next thought is about the gun safe upstairs. I run upstairs and remove my purple .380 my dad got me when I turned sixteen, and grab my dad's old 9mm. Then I load the range bag with all the ammo it can carry. I leave mom's 9mm and the shotgun behind in case mom does comes back. I relock the safe to keep out any looters or thieves. Before dad died, we loved to go to the range and target practice once or twice a week. It's been several years since I've shot a gun. I hope it comes back quickly.

Another thought comes to me and I head to the hall closet. I find a beach bag stored in the corner, loading it with whatever first aid supplies I can find. I stuff the bag full of alcohol, betadine, peroxide, an assortment of bandages, gauze, tape, and an elastic sports bandage. I didn't even think of collecting first aid supplies initially. However, at some point I've got to clean and bandage Ethan's cuts. It takes several trips to carry these additional items downstairs. On the last trip down, I see Ethan is returning to my SUV from his car with a couple duffle bags and several weapons.

"Where's Willis?" I ask.

"Rae, we're not bringing the dog. I know you love him, but he's a liability. We can't guarantee he won't bark if he sees something, and I have no idea what we are fighting here." Ethan protests.

"I AM NOT LEAVING WITHOUT WILLIS," I scream back

and run in the house, straight up the stairs, cut right and run into my room. Willis is hiding under the blankets on my bed, right where I'd expect him to be in a time of distress. Scooping him up, I tell him, "you come with us, buddy," and hug him close. I take one last look around, then I grab my favorite quilt off my bed too.

When I get back to the car Ethan in the driver's seat, Connor has claimed shotgun position holding a semi-automatic rifle. Marnie and Joanie have their arms wrapped around each other, crying in the middle row. "Ethan, what if mom comes back looking for us?" I ask in a whimper.

"Rae, she's not coming back." He says a bit frustrated but sympathetic and resigned.

"You don't know that. What if they got wind of what was happening somehow and got out before the explosion? We should at least leave a note telling her where we'll be, then she and Elaine can find us if they come back." I beg.

"That's not a bad idea, Ethan," Connor says, pleading in his voice, hoping beyond hope, I am sure that he can see his mother again.

"I don't know what we're fighting guys, I don't want to leave any roadmaps to where we are." Ethan protests.

"What if we leave a note with a clue to a location where the address is hidden?" Connor suggests. "The address will be hidden, and only someone who knows the clue will find it."

"That is not a bad idea, E, we can tell her our location can be found at our favorite place to swim in the mountains. She'll know right where that is, you said we're headed to East Tennessee, we can leave a message there." I beg.

"Fine, but we've wasted a lot of time. Get in there, get the message written, we need to be on the move. I don't know how much time we have. You have to understand this is serious," Ethan demands.

I hand Willis to Marnie and head back into the house. Despite Ethan's warning, I admit that I drag my feet; I am hoping that mom and Elaine show up before we go. It's been almost two hours since the explosion in Cincinnati, and it is pitch black outside. We've heard the sounds of several more very distant explosions, at which Ethan muttered "Dayton, or Columbus, maybe Louisville or Lexington" under his breath. After looking around the house one more time, I grab a photo album from the shelf with pictures of mom and dad and head to the car. When I get out of the house, the car is running, I climb in the backseat falling into Marnie's arms. Ethan immediately takes off; Marnie hands me Willis, who I clutch tight to my chest.

"Dig around in that bag and find the goggles for me," Ethan tells Connor.

After a minute of digging, Connor holds up a pair of goggles. "These?" he asks.

"Yes, night vision," Ethan explains, putting on the goggles and turning off the headlights of the car.

"Even if you have night vision Ethan, do you think it's safe to drive without headlights? No one else will see us either, particularly in this dark thing," I protest.

"That's the point. I don't know what is out there Rae, I certainly don't want to draw any attention to us as we go," he explains.

We ride in silence. I hold Willis tight and lean into Marnie, Joanie leaning against her other side. Though we are crying hard, we attempt to quiet our sobs. Tears are soaking our clothing and the dog. Fortunately, he doesn't protest but is content to be held tight and comforted. I finally sit up paying attention to my surroundings and am instantly confused. We should be on 275 or even 75 by now. Why are we on some backroad? "E, where are we going? I thought we were going to Tennessee," I ask quietly in between the remnants of my sobs.

"We are Rae, but we need to stay off the main roads and interstates. For one, I don't know how far this has gone, or if interstates are a target. Then, if others have gotten wind in any way, or are just scared of the explosions and are fleeing the cities, interstates are likely to be jammed. It will just make us sitting ducks." He explains.

"Where are we going exactly?" Connor asks.

"My buddy Don has a place in the mountains in East Tennessee, a self-sufficient off the grid kind of a place. It is well hidden by an outcropping of rock and camouflaging but provides a good vantage point to watch for miles around. There aren't any true roads into the place, but he said we should be able to drive most if not all the way to the cabin. He hasn't been up there in several years, so he is unsure if there will be trees down on the path. Another reason I wanted to take Rae's car it has four-wheel drive and good ground clearance." He explains. "He was going to try to locate his family in Mississippi and head there; he should meet us there in a day or so."

"How do we find the place, Ethan, if our GPS doesn't work?" I ask, completely heartbroken and terrified.

"Rae, seriously, I thought you were the smart one," he says with a hint of a chuckle, "you ever heard of a thing called a map?" Ethan says with an air of exasperation. He produces an old school paper atlas from the bag on the seat beside him.

"I'm scared Ethan. We most likely just lost our mother, and the world is coming to an unknown end. We have no idea what we'll find along the way," I finish this statement by screaming at the top of my lungs, "I AM NOT THINKING STRAIGHT."

"Ethan," Marnie whispers.

"Yes, Mar," he answers tenderly.

"My parents and sisters are in Lexington. Can we make a trip in to see if they are okay and bring them with us?" she asks sadly.

"If the city is still there Mar, we'll figure something out," he says sympathetically. She breaks out in more silent tears streaming down her face at his words.

We've been on the road just over an hour and a half so far, we just now crossed the Ohio river into Maysville, Kentucky. At least the bridge is still here, I think to myself. Joanie has now cried herself to sleep in my lap, Willis is curled up on her side, staying close to me. I lean into Marnie, who has her arm around my shoulder.

After riding in complete silence for another half-hour, Connor finally breaks the silence and tension we're all feeling. "Ethan man, what the hell is going on?" he asks.

CHAPTER 11 ETHAN'S TALE

"I've rehearsed this several times on the flight back from Europe, it doesn't sound any less crazy no matter what speech I give. Now that things are happening here I guess it sounds less weird, so here it goes." He begins.

"As you know, about a month and a half ago, we got deployed to Europe. We started in France. Going in, all we knew was there were 'disturbances,' and we would not be at a permanent base but rather keep moving day to day throughout Europe. Nothing prepared us for what we were about to see.

"We came in from the air, obviously. I was flying a personnel carrier, smaller than usual. We only had about 100 guys with us, mostly Army Rangers. We had a small fleet of fighter jets along-side. We came in from the Atlantic Ocean, flying over Bordeaux moving inland. We have been on maneuvers to France before, though there only once, I had expectations about how the landscape would look on approach. Coming in, something was definitely off. There were three or four fighters in the lead, I hear Dave come across the airwaves 'Commander, what the hell is going on here? What are we getting into?'; the Commander's only response was to 'go to radio silence, stay off the air.' Nothing prepared us for this. There were entire areas, hundreds or more miles around that were just vacant, black, charred looking ground. It was the most bizarre thing I'd ever seen.

"We landed at a make-shift compound at the base of the Pyrenees Mountains. Immediately we were whisked into the compound that was surrounded by enormous generators pulsing electricity constantly. Once seated in the makeshift briefing room, we heard a story straight out of a sci-fi horror movie.

"It had started just a week before our involvement. Entire towns with no warning were leveled completely, with no apparent source. It was like a nuclear bomb had been detonated. A wave of energy emanated, they believe, from the center of the town outward. The blast not just flattening but consuming everything and everyone in the blast zone, nothing left. When the first town fell outside of Paris, they labeled it some underground natural gas explosion. We heard about that one on our news stations. I am not sure if you remember, it wasn't a big deal over here.

"While it was certainly devastating to have so much death and destruction, these days, it doesn't leave much of an impression. But an entire town gone, along with everyone in it. However, within two days two more towns simultaneously were leveled in the same manner. At first, they called in the U.S. Geological Survey for assistance. Before they could even go wheels up, most of the European military bases and three more significant cities were gone, including Paris. Just after these next two towns fell, the entire country's communication systems were disabled, with no cell service, no data, no satellite, nothing. Not even the hackers had any sort of communication avenues.

"No one knows how, or the cause, but there was no flow of information in or out of France by obvious channels. Of course, the government had channels of communication that are much harder to jam, so at that time, they were still in communications with the White House and other nations' governments.

"No one knew what to do, when they went into towns after

the 'explosions,'" he uses air quotes "for lack of a better word, there was nothing there, literally nothing but charred dirt. It registered no radiation or evidence of any other known chemical. Nor could they find anything that served as a detonator or even accurately identify ground zero. They continued with the hypothesis the explosions work from some point in the middle outwards.

"Naturally, we're suspecting some sort of terrorism. We weren't sure what country can produce such a result. In the following days, we started to notice a pattern in the events. They'd begin in mid to large towns outside major cities, eventually enveloping the city. Moving west to east across the country.

"We determined what we expected to be the next target and the French Government began evacuating citizens as silently as possible. There was no way to warn people all at once since communications were down everywhere. Before they got more than a hundred out, all the surrounding towns and the city itself were gone. They lost many troops that day. We were flying some distance outside the town in sweeps to watch for any ground movement. We were using infrared technology to monitor the wooded areas, but we never saw anything. There was absolutely no indication of activity within or outside the city. The detonation in the town almost knocked us out of the sky. It was all we could do to maintain our planes with the disturbance to air currents. Had we been any closer to the city at that point, we would have crashed, no doubt about that.

"Next, the plan was to surround the area we suspected would be next, prevent movement in and out of the towns and city. The French Army, now joined by Swedish and Spanish troops, surrounded the towns. Many were lost when the towns exploded just like the others. Again, there was no movement in or out—no identifiable source.

"It was about this time we went back to neighboring small towns that were still standing to look for clues; anything to tell us what the hell was happening. There wasn't any noted radiation, but there was concern there had to be some sort of fall out that could affect the citizens. As the French government moved back into these towns, they were empty, completely empty. People were just gone, houses were left standing open, school lunches were still on the tables uneaten. There was no trace of the townspeople nor the troops left behind to protect the area.

"We'd been there for about a month when whatever it was finally jammed our most secretive and secure communications channels. Commander Jackson ordered us to get the hell out of there. We hadn't had any outside communication in three days when we took off over the Atlantic. We didn't know what to expect when we got back. We were relieved when we got over U.S. soil to see everything in tact. Whatever it is over there hadn't yet infected the U.S." Ethan pauses.

"If you had no way to communicate, how did you let mom know you were coming home?" I asked

"We were back on U.S. Soil when I called. We'd been back about a week, debriefing in Washington everything we did, and I suppose you could say didn't, see. I know the defense department was working on a plan, but we had no idea what we are fighting or where it even came from.

"Commander Jackson called us back last Sunday because they were starting to get indications of irregular electrical activity and intermittent communication jams. He was worried that would be the start of whatever was happening abroad.

Since Sunday, we've been in scramble mode, but it's hard to prepare for something when you have no clue what you are fighting. We moved a lot of planes, supplies, etc., off the base to other secure locations just in case, but it could have been nothing," He says with evident sadness.

He continues on, shaking his head slightly. "In Europe, we couldn't see, had no idea what we were fighting. We started bombing outside the cities that were decimated, hoping whatever it was, was still lurking, and we could take it out. Still, I think we just caused more civilian casualties than necessary. No matter what we did, the next city or large town was leveled. As it progressed, it happened within minutes of the town before. It was like there was a nuclear blast, but there was never an identifiable source.

"The devastation progressed across Europe, we saw Berlin fall ourselves from the air. We were hundreds of miles away; still, it appeared to have started in the center of the city and radiated outwards from what we could see. It took only seconds to devastate a radius of hundreds of miles around the city. Once it was complete, there was just nothing, literally nothing left, just charred dirt. No traces of a living person or being."

After his story, we sit in stunned silence. I am not sure how long we ride like that. No one knows what to say or do. Finally, Ethan breaks the silence. "Connor, I still feel like this road is too populated. Find us a way around to Lexington, will you."

Connor searches the map and spouts off several turns and road names. It's completely dark now, and I can't see out the window. Ethan's goggles do the job. He quickly spots the roads we need. "We're getting low on fuel," Ethan notes, "we'll hopefully pass a gas station soon."

"Let's hope they have power," Connor says doubtfully, "or at least a generator."

"Ethan, that reminds me. I have a question about something you experienced in Europe. Why the large power generators outside the mobile bases?" Connor inquires.

"Well, did you notice before the explosion in Cincinnati the power fluctuated wildly? They noticed that happening. They were hoping they could disrupt the power sources with the generators pulsing electricity rather than a steady flow preventing the explosions. The thought was it would keep the bases safe, but I am not sure if it did anything at all. If anything, I think it would have given them more power for the detonations.

"I honestly think we just moved around enough to prevent an attack. I never slept in the same place twice over there and sometimes even slept on the personnel carrier while someone else was flying." Ethan explains.

CHAPTER 12 THE JOURNEY

About twenty minutes down the road, we see the lights of a small town. We turn on the car's headlights, so we don't look suspicious. Coming into town we see an older Sunoco with the lights on. We pull up to the pump, an old-timer wearing a tattered ball cap and overalls with a sparse beard hiding the few teeth he has left saunters out. "Cash only kids," he says, eyeballing Ethan with the cuts all over his face and arms. "Credit card machines have been down since about lunch, can't get a single call out to get it fixed."

"No worries," Ethan chimes in, "I've got cash. Do you happen to sell fuel cans? My sister, our friends, and I are taking a tour of the back roads we used on travel as kids. Not sure how frequently we'll pass a gas station, and as you can imagine, this old beast is a gas guzzler. I am thinking maybe I can stock up a bit."

"Sure do, I think I've got four or five in there," he responds. He looks at the group of us even more suspiciously now, noticing our swollen red eyes and shattered expressions.

"Perfect. Rae, why don't you and Marnie go in and get a few cases of water, some snacks, and three or four fuel cans. Here's some cash, pay for those. I'll start filling the car and the cans, and then I'll be in the pay for the gas. Connor why don't you and Joanie take Willis for a walk? He probably needs the facilities." Ethan suggests.

Marnie and I head into the gas station. We take turns using the bathroom and gathering supplies. We each grab two cases of bottled water, a couple bags of chips, bags of donuts, and two fuel cans. It takes us a couple trips to get all of this to the car. Once Ethan is done pumping gas, he goes in to pays for the fuel. While inside he buys even more chips, candy, granola bars, and a few 12 packs of soda. Once reassembled, we head on our way.

"How far are we from Lexington" Marnie questions with anxious sadness in her voice.

"I'm thinking on these roads it'll be at least another hour or maybe two," Connor says consolingly, turning to give Marnie a sympathetic look.

"Please Ethan, hurry," Marnie pleads, bouncing in her seat with the anxiety she feels.

"I'm doing the best I can babe, I don't want to use the lights if I can avoid it. I have no idea what is out there. I want to stay as far from the interstates as possible. There's not a whole lot of choices," he responds.

Marnie buries her face in my shoulder and sobs uncontrollably. I feel bad for her. We have faced that our mother is likely gone and buried it deep in the face of what lies ahead of us. Not knowing about her parents and sisters is eating Marnie alive inside. Ethan pulls out his phone, syncs the blue tooth on the radio, and starts playing music. The familiar lyrics and rhymes do help ease the tension a bit. Marnie's sobs quiet as I sing along with the music softly in her ear. Music has always been that way to me, a balm or salve for a wound. Familiar sounds are comforting.

"Turn left up ahead Ethan," Connor instructs, and Ethan does what he is told.

"So, Connor," Ethan says, breaking the silence, "did Rae ever tell you she was a cheerleader in Junior High?"

"No, I don't believe I've heard about that," Connor responds a little too enthusiastically, "I bet that was cute."

"Yea..." Ethan begins, but I cut him off.

"Not this story again E, really," I complain. "Long story short, I had bad gas at a game and every time I jumped, I farted. Everyone in the front row was dying laughing at me. I quit after that game, never raising a pom-pom, ever, again! But at least I didn't end up with a nickname from it," I finish knowingly.

Everyone in the car starts laughing softly. Of course, I join in. It was a long time ago, and seriously what else can I do. The road is getting curvy, so Ethan pushes his goggles up his forehead, turns the lights on for a bit to better see where we are going. He doesn't like this and turns them off frequently. I feel like we are riding in a giant strobe light. "E, wouldn't be more of an alert for flashing lights to be traveling down the road," I ask.

"No," he says flatly, "I want them off as much as possible."

"We are nearing the farthest reaches of the outer suburbs of Lexington," Connor says.

"How far?" Ethan asks.

"Still at least 40 miles from the city center," Connor answers. I look at my phone. It is nearing eleven o'clock. This day is dragging on for an eternity it feels.

"Mar, where does your family live?" Ethan inquires.

"They're on the Southeast side. We'd be better to stay somewhere out here on this track until we are past the city," she whispers.

"Connor, is there any way we can get closer to the city but stay out of traffic?" Ethan pushes.

Connor spends a few minutes studying the map under the flashlight on his phone, then responds, "about two miles ahead, turn right."

Just then, something flashes overhead. It is a ball of light traveling about 75 feet above us and speeds along out of sight.

"What was that" I shriek? "Do you think it was a bomb?"

"No idea," Ethan mumbles, "but if whatever is behind this is showing themselves now, I am guessing they think they've won."

I shudder at his words as they ring true in my ear. A lot of work and planning had to go into this coordinated attack. No one, not one person got wind of it, saw something happening or something unusual? They have remained completely hidden until this point but now are beginning to show themselves. I don't have to wait to see Lexington to know what we'll find there.

We start getting closer, now we can see a void in the landscape, the place where Lexington used to be. Marnie begins sobbing harder, waking up Joanie.

"What's happening? Where are we?" Joanie questions in a sleepy tone.

"Just outside Lexington," Ethan whispers. She sits up and looks out the window. she shudders, and tears begin streaming silently down her face. It is dark out. You cannot see the devastation that happened here. But there is a void in the landscape. Where you'd expect to see lights, to see silhouettes of buildings, there is nothing there. "Mar, they might still be there outside of town. We don't know how long ago this happened, nor do I know how long once it happens, people start disappearing."

These words have the opposite effect sending Marnie into complete hysterics. "What if they're gone?" she sobs. I want to say welcome to the club, Ethan and I have now lost our entire family. But, expressing this frustration will not do either of us any good so I remain quiet, continuing to rub Marnie's back.

After seeing the landscape's void, we move to roads farther out from the city to work our way around to the suburb Marnie indicated. We stop about 10 miles outside the suburb parking on a vacant, used car lot. The power is out here so we wedge ourselves in between the cars for sale and remain hidden. Ethan parks between a full-size black SUV and a dark blue one-ton pick-up truck. My forest green beast looks like any other car on the lot between these two vehicles.

"Alright," Ethan says, "I'm going to take a different car to the neighborhood Marnie indicated. Connor, you stay here with the girls, keep watch, stay in the car as much as possible. Venture out only if you absolutely need to relieve yourself. Marnie, show me on the map where I need to go."

Marnie spends a few minutes getting acquainted with the map, then points to show Ethan where the family should be located. She highlights the best route into the neighborhood. I really do not like this. There is not a soul around on this side of town. It is eerily quiet. Nothing is stirring, not even a stray cat. Willis is whimpering quietly, though Joanie is holding him tight, stroking his head and neck. I cannot believe Ethan will find anyone, at least not alive.

He selects a dark inconspicuous sedan. The door is fortunately unlocked, so he just has to hotwire the car, and off he goes. All we can do is wait, all of us frozen in shock, horror, and anticipation. I cannot believe less than twelve hours ago, I was thinking Connor and I were about to have sex in a park. Now we've lost our families and are on the run for our lives from some unseen enemy. I just keep thinking to myself these things just do not happen, not here. Connor keeps pushing the button on his phone every so often to provide light in the car. It is comforting when we can see each other clearly.

"So, read any good books lately?" Marnie asks to break the silence. Her attempt falls flat; we continue to sit in silence.

It's been about twenty minutes when we hear something moving in the weeds to the left of our hiding place. Connor puts his fingers to his lips to give us the shh sign without making a sound and points for us to sink down into the seats. We do as we are told, listening closely. If anyone is paying close attention, they will see the condensation on the car windows and know someone is hiding inside. We will be found. None-the-less we are hardly breathing, trying to be as quiet as possible.

Then we hear talking, the voices have a strange accent that pulls at a memory in my mind, but I cannot quite figure it out. The language is nothing like I have heard before. It does not even sound like words, but more like humming at different lengths and tones. Marnie, Joanie, and I in the back seat just look at each other in shocked silence. My two companions are white as ghosts. The voices get louder as they come nearer to us. They seem to be just about to walk past the line of cars where we are hidden when they pause, causing my heart to sink. They speak a minute right outside our hiding place. Willis looks as though he wants to growl. Joanie manages to keep him distracted, scratching his belly, whispering ever so slightly in his ear.

I am glad he has never been much of a barker. They pause

their conversation but remain by the car for several more minutes. Finally, one of them speaks again, this time in heavily garbled accented English, "come none here find."

I almost gasp, but recover before any sound leaves my mouth. This speech reminds me of where I have heard this accent. Connor looks over the middle armrest at me in the back. He recognized it too. We both sit up slightly, peering over the dashboard at those walking away. It is all I can do to keep quiet. What I see terrifies me.

There, ahead of the car, are two figures walking. One appears to be a human man, the other is the size of a large child, looking a bit like an animal or gremlin as I once described. Connor turns to look at me in surprise. I turn to look at Marnie and see her mouth is hanging open. "The Quarry," she mouths with wide eyes. Yes, I saw a gremlin-like creature at the Quarry. We also encountered a very odd man who spoke similarly to this individual. In retrospect, the time at the Quarry was our first encounter with these invaders.

We remain still as can be, barely breathing. We make no sound for at least another twenty when Marnie finally breaks the silence with a whisper, "the Quarry, we saw one of those things at the quarry."

"How long have they been moving among us?" I whisper.

"They must travel in pairs like that, remember, I saw the creature in the weeds, and then an odd man like that came to the campsite," I whisper back.

"Why do you think the human-looking one showed himself to us?" Marnie wonders aloud.

"That is a good question. If they were planning a surprise attack, alerting anyone to their presence was not smart. Still, we certainly explained it away easily enough didn't we. I wonder how many more of these encounters have happened and people never knew, they explained it away like we did." I speculate.

"These bastards have been here that long," Connor quietly spits in disgust. "I should have shot them."

"No, we don't know how many more are here, could've brought a lot more of them down on us," I console him. "I wonder where Ethan is, how much longer he will be, I want to get out of here." At these words, Marnie begins to whimper. "Sorry, Mar, with who knows what going on around us, I really want to get somewhere I feel safe."

"Do you think they are far enough away? If Ethan comes back now, will they see him?" Connor wonders out loud.

Once again, we sit in silence. The tension making me crazy. I lean over the back seat and grab everyone a bottle of water and some chips. "I have to pee," I announce quietly, "but I am not about to get out of this car or head into the woods."

Marnie chuckles a little, "guess you'll just have to pee yourself."

"Good thing I've got a change of pants," I say, "but you don't," I tease.

As the silence drags on, I occasionally check the time on my phone. "Crap, my battery is running low," I comment.

"Not like your phone is useful for anything now," Connor says.

"We can tell time and listen to music," I counter.

"True," he concedes. He digs around in the console producing a port-a-power battery charger.

"Oh, I forgot that was in there, perfect," I exclaim, excited for at least one positive event today no matter how small and insignificant. "Ethan has been gone a little over an hour. It's been thirty minutes since those creatures left," I tell the group.

"I wonder how long he'll be gone. How long do we wait if he doesn't come back?" Marnie asks, looking petrified.

"Well, we don't know where we are going," I remind her. "I'm not leaving without my brother, he's all I have left."

We just look at each other, not knowing the answers to these questions. Joanie quietly sobs into Willis' side. He is good to have around. He'll help keep Joanie calm, I think. It has been about thirty more minutes, putting us just after twelve-thirty AM.

I think I am about to lose my mind for the nineteenth million time tonight. We hear the sound of a car on approach. Immediately we duck down below the seats as the car pulls up behind our hiding place. I chance a glance and see it is Ethan. "Guys, it's okay, it's Ethan," I whisper.

Even at these words, we still remain hidden a moment longer, too terrified to move. Finally, Marnie can't stand it popping up in her seat.

"Geez, you guys scared me, I thought you were gone," Ethan says conversationally. "Marnie, look who I found."

From behind Ethan steps, Marnie's six-year-old sister Marie, holding her two-year-old sister McKenzie and holding the hand of four-year-old Christy. The girls run to Marnie's arms, all sobbing hysterically.

"I hate to break up this reunion, but Ethan while you were gone, we had a visit from some 'creatures.' I'd really like to get the hell out of here," Connor says with a bit of panic coloring his voice.

"Where are my parents?" Marnie asks, still sobbing.

"Let's get on the road, and I'll tell you what I've learned, then you guys can tell me what you experienced," Ethan says.

"Ethan, please," Marnie begs.

"They weren't there, Mar; I'll tell you about it in the car." He reiterates, shoving her towards the open car door. We pile in while Ethan starts the car.

"Connor find a way into Tennessee staying as far away from large towns and interstates as you can," Ethan commands.

Connor studies the map quickly, using the flashlight from his phone, "go up to the next road and turn left," he says confidently.

"Okay. Marnie, it seems your parents have been taken somewhere, I don't know where or by what. But they survived the explosion. They were both still alive the last time your sisters saw them. We'll see what we can find out when we rendezvous with Don at the cabin. If we can figure out what is happening, we might find them and get them back."

"The girls were hiding in a basement closet, I almost didn't find them, but Marie recognized my voice when I was whispering their names. She came running out to me. Marie was able to mostly tell me the sequence of events that occurred in this area." Ethan continues, "The lights started flickering, then they heard the explosion in Lexington, the power went out completely soon after. Your parents surmised it was a transformer explosion, or maybe something larger like a substation.

"She's not sure how much longer it was, but based on how she described the light outside, I guess it was about two hours after the initial explosion. There was a loud commotion out on the street. Your dad went out, he looked down the street and saw men armed with small weapons forcing people out of their houses. He sent the girls and your mother to hide in the basement. The girls were in a closet next to a generator, so their sounds were probably muffled, which is why they didn't hear them. I am guessing from what Marie said they heard your mom crying and found her. She left quickly and easily, probably to keep them from finding the girls. She said she really had a hard time understanding what they were saying. They weren't speaking clearly.

"Following your lead back home Rae, I did leave a quick note behind that said the girls were now with Marnie, we were headed to a safe hideout. If it ever becomes safe, we'll head back to Ohio and meet them there." Ethan explains.

Marnie sobs quietly and chokes out, "they are still alive."

"Seems that way," Ethan says matter-of-factly. "But I want to get you guys hidden and safe as quickly as possible. We'll figure out a plan from there. Now, tell me about these 'creatures' you saw."

CHAPTER 13 WHAT WAS THAT

"This story goes back a bit longer than tonight," I begin. "When we were camping at the Quarry a few weeks ago, I went into the weeds to pee, and I saw some sort of creature. It was the size of a large child, brownish in color, stood on two legs, had hair on its head but appeared scaly over its body. I remember I told everyone I thought it looked like a combination of that video game character hedgehog, and a gremlin from that one movie. We all laughed and played it off. We'd barely finished that conversation when a really strange looking man staggered into the campsite. He didn't really seem to speak English. He had a strong weird accent that sounded somewhere between French and Middle Eastern. His words didn't even really make sense, but we gathered he was looking for the lodge, so we pointed him off in that direction."

"Oh, tell him about the ears," Marnie interjects.

"The guy was really clean-shaven, not a spec of dirt on him anywhere, but it looked like behind his ears was filthy with crusted dirt," I add. "We dismissed this as well, decided he was on something, probably with a bachelor party at the lodge and his buddies drug him out in the woods as a prank. We really didn't think anything of it, never giving it another thought after that moment in time."

"What does that have to do with tonight?" Ethan asks, confused.

"While you were gone, we heard movement in the woods." I start

"Turn right at the next crossroad," Connor instructs.

"We sank down in the seats. We were barely breathing we were so quiet. We heard what we thought were people talking after a bit, but there was a strange accent. At the time, I thought it was familiar but couldn't place it. They were speaking a language I couldn't understand a word of. When they got closer, it sounded like humming in different lengths and tones. They paused by the car, and I thought we were had. Eventually, they started walking away. Before they left, the one said something in the same fashion of garbled English as the guy spoke at the Quarry. When they were past the car, we peeked over the dash, we saw the same gremlinish creature I saw in the weeds at the Quarry, and what appeared to be a man walking away."

"Okay, that is creepy, so what do we think, it's aliens doing this?" Ethan says, trying to break the tension in the car, but it doesn't work. We are all too distraught by this day's events.

"I don't know. How many animals you know of walk on two legs and can speak in any language?" Marnie asks snidely from the back. She now occupies the third-row seat with her sisters huddled around her. We had to move many of the supplies to the middle with myself and Joanie. The rest remain in the trunk area in the back.

"Mar, there are blankets in the back, why don't you get them for your sisters." All three of her sisters are sobbing moderately quietly in the back seat. At least as quietly as a child is able when they try really hard. "We'll also probably need to find some diapers for Kenz somewhere."

As we ride along, one by one Marnie's sisters go to sleep, and finally Marnie as well. I try to sleep myself, but it is not happening. It is now creeping up on 4 in the morning. It is so dark out all I can see is black outside the windows. Ethan continues to drive with his goggles on and lights off. I will have to give him this; he was prepared.

"How's the gas holding up, Ethan?" I ask.

"We're going to need to find a place before long. Connor look for a small town near this path we are on that might have a gas station. We are far enough away from any larger cities we should be safe. And hopefully, they have power or a generator," Ethan responds.

"Looks like in about 10 miles we can turn right, it's called Bracken Ridge Road, there will be a couple of towns. The path takes us generally in the right direction, we won't have to backtrack at all to keep going south," he announces.

"That sounds good, let's just hope they are open in the middle of the night," Ethan mumbles, and we return to silence.

"More like this early in the morning," Connor corrects. "It's nearly four-thirty AM." Thirty-five minutes later, we pull up to a gas station in a small Kentucky town, the lights are dark and it appears to be closed. The town overall seems intact. There are no signs of damage. It seems that the houses are all closed up tight, there is a garbage truck picking up cans along the street.

"The town appears as if they don't even know the world is ending. The trash man is still working for crying out loud," Connor says. "What happened in Europe to the smaller towns? You said people disappeared around the larger towns and cities that were flattened, what about the smaller towns?"

"Don't know, while we were there, there were a few towns far up in the Mountains that were untouched. People there too were oblivious to what was happening around them. Though I don't know if it stayed that way or what eventually happened to them," he confesses.

We drive on to the next small town where we find a 24-hour quickie mart. We pull up to the pump, the sign reads cash only. "Rae, will you go in and get them to turn the pump on. Here's a hundred-dollar bill."

I take the money and head into the store. Behind the counter is an older man with a sparse patch of hair on the top of his head, a shaggy beard, and potbelly. I hand him money to turn the pump on, he eyes me suspiciously. I quickly turn away to peruse the shelves.

I grab a few medicinal items such as antacids, anti-diarrheal, and Ibuprofen that catch my eye. These will be good to have on hand. Then wandering along, I find diapers, picking up several packages of those. I return these items to the counter, add several candy bars, and a couple twelve packs of soda.

"Long trip ahead," the man behind the counter says questioningly.

"Yes, we're traveling with some friends to our old stomping grounds in Tennessee," I answer, somewhat following Ethan's lead from the last gas stop.

"Shouldn't you be on the highway?" he asks, "much faster."

"No," I answer, "we like taking the scenic backroads, that's how our parents brought us down here as kids," I reply casually. His questions are making me nervous.

"Whereabouts did you kids start out from?" he questions.

"We live in a rural town, far East of Cincinnati," I answer, trying to hedge.

"We're on generator power here. The power went out about four hours ago. Strange news coming out of the city, not sure what to believe," he hints.

"Oh?" I ask innocently.

"Talk of major power outages, even fires. Since yesterday morning, the credit card machines have been offline can't get a call out to get 'em fixed. My phone hasn't worked since yesterday afternoon as well, no internet, the satellite radio isn't working either," he continues.

"Really, I hadn't heard. We mostly listen to music from our phones in the car." I say, collecting my purchases and heading out the door, "we'll have to keep our eyes open for any signs of trouble." Leaving the store I see a stack of fuel cans in the corner. I know Ethan wanted to get more, to have extra gas on hand if we cannot buy more at any time, but with the car carrying more passengers now, there simply isn't room.

Once he is finished pumping gas, he starts to head into the store. "Store clerk's chatty, that one is," I warn him.

"Great," Ethan moans. He goes into to collect the change from the gas purchase.

When I get back in the car, Marnie is stirring, "where are we?" she asks sleepily.

"Somewhere in the middle of nowhere, Kentucky," Connor responds.

"Oh, how much longer until we're in Tennessee?" She asks.

"I have no idea on these roads. If we could run eighty on the highway, we'd already been there," he answers with a sigh. "But I agree with Ethan, it is safer to stay as far away from any areas you'd expect congestion." Marnie looks over at the girls sleeping with a sad smile, I know she is worried about her parents, but grateful the girls are now with her.

Joanie stirs in the seat beside me and shivers slightly, "Mar, can you hand me another blanket please" I ask quietly. Marnie hands me a heavy quilt I wrap tightly around Joanie, she instantly relaxes and falls back to deep sleep.

While in the store, Ethan buys more supplies, two more cases of water, more diapers for Kenz, a couple boxes of cereal, and is back out to the car quickly. "He was trying to get nosy," he says, speaking of the store clerk, "but I didn't give him a chance to converse," he says smugly.

"He's on a generator in there, said the power went out here four hours ago," I say, sharing the information I gained in my time with the chatty clerk.

"Four hours, huh? Well, he's still there, that's something," Ethan comments.

"Do you think he was one of them?" I ask, suddenly terrified.

"No, his English was perfectly backcountry Kentucky, he wouldn't have spoken that well based on what you've observed," Ethan consoles.

"True," I muse.

"It's nearing dawn, and Connor and I need some sleep," Ethan comments.

"Do you want me to drive for a while? I couldn't sleep if I wanted to," I offer.

"No, I think we need to find somewhere to hide out during the daylight hours. If we're the only ones traveling on the roads, we'll stand out like a sore thumb, even on the back roads," he answers.

We pull out of the gas station, driving along the same road for another ten miles, "turn left up here," Connor tells Ethan.

Just after rounding the corner, Ethan says, "this is perfect." However, the light is just beginning to break across the Eastern sky; without night vision goggles, we cannot see anything.

"What is perfect," I ask.

"A place to hide," he answers.

CHAPTER 14 A PLACE TO HIDE

As we get closer, in the dawning light, we can see a small run-down storage facility in the middle of nowhere. "This is perfect," I echo Ethan's sentiment. It appears it was abandoned long before the world came to an end. The gate is torn down and about half the units are open, their contents spilling out into the gravel parking lot, overrun by early spring weeds.

Ethan is already scouting out a hiding place while we approach the building. "There, we'll pull into that one and close the door. We can hide out during the daylight here unseen." He says, pointing to an open empty garage.

Just as the first rays of sunlight are crossing the horizon we slide the SUV into the garage space. Ethan puts the car in park, jumps out, and shuts the storage unit's overhead door. Connor and I climb warily out of the car while Ethan locks the overhead door from the inside. The unit is a pretty standard storage unit. It has gray cinder block walls, an overhead garage door that is bright orange inside and out, and an interior door that is bright orange.

"All this orange, I feel like I am in the cafeteria as school," I muse to no one in particular. My companions at least chuckle at this observation.

"Go Eagles," Marnie says without enthusiasm.

The entire group has now awoken. Kenzie is crying loudly in the back seat as a frantic Marnie tries to quiet her. "Here baby, have a pop tart," she offers. Kenz accepts, nibbling the corner of the treat, ending her sobs. "Mom never lets them have sugary breakfast," Marnie explains.

"Hey, whatever it takes to keep us undetected," I say. "Though we may regret it later," I add, thinking about a hyper two-year-old running around while we are trying to sleep.

The rest of our group hops out of the SUV, stretching. Willis is eager to run around the garage, stretching his legs, sniffing everything. He probably needs a good walk, but it is getting to be daylight now. Hopefully, he'll just find a corner somewhere. Ethan removes a pistol from his waistband and moves towards the orange walk through the door. He finds the door is unlocked; slowly he opens the door to peer into the hallway. Wearing his night-vision goggles, he looks both ways.

"The only signs of life I see are some rats," he announces stepping back into the unit, closing the door behind him.

There is a small skylight above showing that the day outside is brightening quickly. I point up at the skylight, "do you think that will be an issue?" I ask Ethan.

"Nah," he answers, "it's light outside and dark in here, no one will be able to see in, plus it allows us to get around in here without knocking into each other all day. I hope they all have these. Let's explore and see if we can find anything useful. Even if we just find some cushions to use for beds right now, that'd be useful."

He continues, "if you see any glass doors or windows, do not get near them, do not take any chances of being seen. Marnie, you stay with the girls and Joanie, try to keep them calm and quiet; keep Willis with you as well, he's a good distraction for the girls. Rae, you and Connor head down the hallway to the right. I'll go to the left."

Ethan walks back to the car; when he returns, he hands me

my .380, Connor dad's 9mm from the range bag, and a flash-light to aid us in our journey. He is still wearing his night-vision goggles. However, now it is getting light enough, he should not need them much longer. I let out a huge yawn, then nod in agreement. We set off our separate ways, Ethan to the left, Connor and I to the right.

The facility shows signs it has been abandoned for quite some time. The mustard carpet with purple diamonds is threadbare in many areas and heavily soiled in others. Many of the interior doors are hanging off their hinges, suggesting this place has already been scavenged. But, I tell myself, that that was a different day and time. I am sure whoever pilfered here was looking for things of value to sell, not basic needs such as cushions from a couch or essential children's clothing.

The first garage we explore is a bust housing only old wooden furniture and something that smells horrifically like a decaying animal. I would like to believe it is animal and not human. We quickly shut that door and move on. The next gar-age door is hanging off the hinges. Looking inside shows it is entirely empty. In the third, as soon as we crack the door open light comes spilling into the hallway suggesting the outer door is open. We don't go any farther. This is looking like a fu-tile exercise.

The fourth garage is more challenging to get into. The door seems to be locked or stuck. We are just about to give up when Connor manages to force the door open. I am glad we did. We have more luck in this unit. We find two shrink-wrapped couches; with some effort, we remove the plastic covering from the couches. The rodents have already made use of a few cushions. We ignore those but pull off the ones that appear to be intact. The fabric of these couches is exceptionally soft suede and will make a nice place to sleep. We set these outside the door in the hallway, carefully avoiding the horrifically stained patch right outside the door. We then continue exploring this unit.

As we continue exploring, we stumble upon a cache of weapons. The stash is mostly hunting gear. We find an excellent crossbow, several traditional bows, rifles, extra arrows, ammunition, and an assortment of hunting and pocketknives. "These are definitely coming with us," Connor states. "I wonder why no one made off with these already?" he adds questioningly.

"They were pretty buried over here. They probably didn't feel like they had time to look that closely, or they never made it into this unit," I surmise. "Wish we would've found those knives before we ripped through the plastic on those couches with our hands," I add with a bit of frustration.

We continue exploring this locker but find nothing more of use; mostly we see old knick-knacks, which may very well have had value at some point, but are useless now. Moving on to the fifth unit we once again have luck. We find children's clothing; some have been damaged by rodents, but there is plenty here. I think we can find a couple of extra outfits for Mar's sisters. I select an assortment of warm weather and cold-weather clothing in sizes I believe will fit the girls, then set these aside. There is also a stash of blankets in vacuum-sealed bags. We set the clothing and blankets outside the door in the hallway, making our way down to the next unit.

The next unit is quite interesting but useless. In this unit, we find several locked suitcases. Connor goes back to the previous locker, returning with a large hunting knife. He uses the knife to force the first case open. Inside we find an assortment of extremely embarrassing lingerie. He moves on to the next case to reveal even more inappropriate items. "I think we should take these to the cabin with us. We might need some entertainment," Connor suggests pulling out a feather boa and some unidentifiable item made of leather.

"Um no, we don't need entertainment that badly. And put that down, you don't know where, or on whom, that has been used." I answer sternly with a bit of blush touching my cheeks.

In total, we spend about an hour and a half searching the garages at this end of the building. We manage to find a few more cushions, additional clothing, and a few more hunting type knives. In the last locker, we find a single empty grocery cart. That is fortunate. It will make it much easier to collect our finds and make our wy back to our unit. We walk back up the hallway, collecting the items from outside the doors, placing them in the cart as we go. When we get back to our unit Ethan is back, trying to console a very distraught McKenzie.

"Marnie had to pee," Ethan explains, "she just woke up, but Mar should be right back."

"It's okay, Kenz," I say, "Marnie will be right back. I know you're scared, but you are safe here with us," I console her.

Marnie finally comes back through the door. "Oh, Kenzie girl what's wrong," she coos. At the sight of Marnie, McKenzie immediately calms. Ethan rises and announcing, "That grocery cart is great. I am going to go collect what I've found."

Ten minutes later, Ethan returns with several blankets, cushions, some cookware, and a cooler, the good kind that stays cold for days. That will really come in handy. We can buy meats along the way and have protein for a while. Before long, whatever is out there in storage will get warm and spoil, leaving protein options limited or non-existent.

"Someone should keep watch," Ethan announces. "Connor,

I'll take the first watch. I figure we've got around 10 hours of sunlight left, so I'll wake you in 5 hours if you are still sleeping, then I'll get some shut-eye."

"Sounds good," Connor agrees.

Marnie, Joanie, and the girls slept much of the night and are not tired. They sit on the other side of the car opposite where we are making a bed of cushions, inventing games to play. Many of these involve Willis, fortunately, a very willing participant. On our side, we arrange the cushions we've found into a large square bed, spreading the blankets out across the cushions.

"We're lucky it's still spring," Connor muses, "if it were summer, it would get scorching in here." Once the cushions and blankets are arranged, I slip down on the make-shift bed. Connor comes to lay beside me, pulling me close to him, wrapping his arms around me. It reminds me of that first night, I slept beside him at the Quarry. I sigh at the memory. Was that only two weeks ago? That can't be. How has so much changed in just this short time? Really if I think about it, in less than 18 hours. I snuggle my head deep into Connor's shoulder and feel the tears start. Though I sob quietly, Connor must feel the tears on his shirt. He leans his head down, pressing his lips to my forehead. We lay like this for a while until I have finally cried myself out and drift off to sleep.

The woods are darker than I remember. It's hard to see where I am going. I stumble along the path, but I know I am headed in the right direction. To my right, I hear a woman scream, I don't recognize the voice, but the cry is that of someone terrified. "No, no, please leave me, let me go," she screams. Crap, I think to myself, there's trouble in the area. It's so dark, it is hard to see. I frantically search around me, finally spotting the cave structure where the case is hidden. This will have to do; it'll be small but well hidden. I silently step toward the structure, lying on my side and curling into a tight ball to fit behind the crude covering we've made.

I am at a disadvantage, I won't see anyone coming until their shoes are under my nose. I lay silently, trying hard to not even breathe. It is going to be a long night, but I know I am trapped. This is my best hope at survival. I don't know how long I will have to stay silent before it is safe to move on. I worry the others will come looking for me when I don't return as expected and walk into a trap. This fear is creeping icily through my veins, and I think I am about to lose my mind. Laying there silently I hear a branch break near my hideout. I want to scream; instead, I bite down hard on my lip to hold in the terror. I taste a bit of blood in my mouth.

"Rae, Rae, wake up," Connor is whispering loudly while shaking me slightly.

"What, where am I?" I ask, sitting up disoriented, I hear Willis snarling quietly beside me.

"You had a bad dream; you were muttering and whimpering in your sleep," he explains.

Looking around realization settles in. We are in an old abandoned storage garage in nowhere Kentucky, my mom is most likely dead, and we are on the run for our lives from an unknown enemy. When I remember the horrors of the past day, the flood gates open once again. I start bawling like a child, "oh Connor," I sob. Connor holds me tight and once again lets me cry myself to sleep.

CHAPTER 15 LONG DAY

I wake in earnest, judging by the light it is sometime late afternoon or early evening, "what time is it?" I ask Connor.

"It's about four-thirty; Ethan has been asleep for about two hours now. He asked us to wake him around seven, so we can make our plan for getting on the road." Connor explains.

"Did you get enough sleep? I can take a watch if you need to sleep more. I know it couldn't have been restful sleeping next to me." I offer.

"I'm good Rae, though you look like you could use a bit more sleep," he responds.

"No, I don't think I can sleep anymore. How have the girls been doing?" I ask.

"Fairly well all things considered. None of them have slept since they slept much of the night. Hopefully, tonight is quiet and they can get some sleep on the drive." Connor tells me. "Willis should sleep well; the girls have kept him running, chasing water bottles and things all day. We had to stop for a while; he got so excited he started barking."

"Where's Joanie?" I ask.

"She took Willis across the hall to potty," he says, nodding towards the open door.

With nothing else to say we stare at the dreary gray concrete block walls in the garage. I start to feel antsy; the light outside the dirty skylight is beginning to fade. We've been in here quite some time, in our temporary hiding place that has the feel of a prison.

"What do you think we are going to find when we open the door?" I ask Connor.

"Well, I am hoping nothing. I believe it will look the same as when we came into this place," he muses.

"What do you think the towns along the journey will be like? Do you think they'll be abandoned? Will they know what is happening?" I wonder aloud.

"I don't know Rae," he says, placing his hand gently on the side of my face. "I really have no idea what to expect. Based on Ethan's observations in Europe, I am guessing it is going to be pretty desolate out there." He finishes in a very somber tone.

"Have you heard anything today while you've been awake?" I inquire.

"Not really, it sounded like a truck passed a couple hours ago, but it was muffled. I am not sure how close it came to the garage," he answers.

He reaches out, taking my hands, "pray with me, Rae, please," he asks.

I clasp my hands in his, bow my head, and close my eyes. "Father in Heaven," he begins somberly, "please watch over our loved ones who are still out there, give them the strength to endure and protect them from the harms of this new world. For those we love and those we have not met who have left us, Lord we pray they find their way home to you, to peace and comfort offered by your paradise. Lord, lay a path before us, guide us away from danger. Give us the strength to maintain our humanity and show love and charity to those in need in these uncertain and challenging times. But Lord, give us the wisdom to not fall prey to those wishing to do us harm. Protect us Lord and give us strength, in your son's name"

"Amen," we finish together.

"Thank you, I needed that," I say, "sometimes I forget the comfort God gives those who are willing to call upon him." And I feel a sense of peace; in this world, there will be trouble, but should we leave it, paradise awaits.

The pressure of sitting and doing nothing is getting to me. I cannot sit still any longer; I am about to go crazy. I get up, meandering about the garage, but nothing really catches my attention. I jump when my aimless wandering is interrupted by Joanie and Willis coming back through the door.

"I was about to come looking for you," Connor says, "where have you been?"

"Sorry, it took Willis a while to find the perfect place." She says. "I'm going to get him some food."

"Thanks, Joanie," I respond. "I have a full bag of dog food in there, but it's buried somewhere in the back," I answer.

While Joanie digs out the dog food, I wander over and start poking around in the car. I find a notepad and a pen; I collect these items and walk back over to sit by Connor. I begin sketching out random shapes on the page; this holds my attention for only a short time. I sigh heavily in frustration. Connor grabs my notebook and pen from me retruning it with a Tic Tac Toe board with a big 'X' in the middle spot.

I study the board and place an 'O' in the upper right corner. He responds by placing an 'X' in the top center box. I study the board a short time and go with an 'O' into the lower middle box, to which he responds with an 'X' in the right middle row. This forces me to place an 'O' in the left middle row. Next, he puts his 'X' in the upper left corner. My response is to place an

'O' in the lower right box. Well, it's a tie.

We laugh and he draws a new board to play again. We continue playing Tic Tac Toe for at least an hour, occasionally letting Joanie or Marnie take a turn. It is a fun way to pass the time, though when I play Connor, it usually ends in a tie. After the fifth tie in a row, I institute a new rule, you cannot start in the same box you did previously until you've used each square as a starting point; then you can start over again. After instituting this rule I manage to beat him twice but he gets the better of me four times.

"We need to find a deck of cards somewhere," I muse "we're probably going to have a lot of downtime to pass in the near future."

"Good plan, next gas stop we'll see if they have cards," Connor agrees.

"So, where exactly are we going to the bathroom?" I ask.

"There is an empty garage two doors down to the left. We've got some rags torn up in there for you girls to wipe with," Connor explains.

"Great, headed to the little girls' garage; be back in a jiffy," I say. I call Willis to go with me. Even though Joanie took him recently, I feel better with some company.

I quietly open the door to the hallway heading down to the door he instructed, Willis right beside me. Inside I find the rags Connor mentioned and pick a corner. After I finish, I discard the rag in the growing pile and turn to Willis, "buddy, this is your chance, go if you need to," I instruct. He sniffs around for a minute and manages to find a spot.

Once he is finished with his business, I begin to head out. While stepping away from the overhead garage door, I hear something outside. There is someone or something, outside the door. I stand perfectly still, listening intently, willing Willis to stay quiet. His big ears are piqued in the direction of the noise with his head turned to the side; so far, he is making no noise.

I listen hard and hear scraping against a door farther down the row. I manage to unlock my muscles, scoop up Willis before he can bark, and move towards the hallway. I quietly open the door, slowly look up and down the hallway. I do not hear or see anything. I cross the hall and dart back into our garage.

"Rae, what's wrong," Connor asks, my expression alerting him something amiss.

"I don't know, it could just be an animal. I was about to head back over here, I heard something outside. I listened for a minute and heard a scraping sound against another door down the row. It could have been an animal, but I am just not sure." I say.

"Ethan, man, wake up," Connor says, pushing Ethan.

"Is it seven already?" He asks.

"No, but close. Rae was using the bathroom and heard a noise outside. It could be nothing, but I feel like we need to be ready to defend ourselves or scoot in a hurry just in case," he explains.

Joanie, Marnie, and the girls gather around, staring at us in fear and horror.

"Girls, go ahead and get into the car. Rae, pack up everything we want to take with us into the car. Connor stand by the overhead door; I'll cover the walk-through door. If you hear anything, just give a signal, don't say a word."

Christy has started to cry at the stress of the situation. Marnie ushers her into the car, and we silently shut all the doors to muffle the noise. We stand in breathless silence for at least ten minutes when Connor quickly raises his arm, pointing to the overhead door. Ethan and I quietly run over to listen.

"I don't think we'll find anything useful here." We hear a male voice say, he sounds young. "Most of these are still locked, and we have no way to get in."

"Come on, it's getting dark; let's find somewhere to take shelter for the night." Another gruffer male voice agrees.

"I seen a house a bit back up that road," a female voice joins in, "maybe it's empty, or maybe who's ever it is will allow us a place to crash for the night."

We all remain quiet, but all breathe again, just a few humans, no reason to be scared. It sounds as if they are on the run, just like we are. We listen on a bit more.

"Did you see that?" the younger male gasps.

"What the hell was that?" The female voice responds.

"I don't know, let's get out of here." The gruffer male voice responds.

We all stare at each other, wondering what they saw that has them so spooked. As if hearing our thoughts, the woman says aloud, "I ain't never seen no plane that looks like that before."

"It looked like a giant silver bubble zipping through the sky. Wasn't flying very high neither." The younger male adds.

It sounds like the ball of light we saw zipping overhead last night. We hear their footsteps growing faint, I fall into Connor, resting my head on his shoulder. My nerves are fried. The stress of the last twenty-four hours, is that all it has been just twenty-four hours, has me crazed.

Connor stands me up right then lifts my chin to face him. He stares into my eyes, placing his hand affectionately on the side of my face, cupping my jaw. We stand like this for several minutes just staring into each other eyes. He then leans in quickly but gently, pressing his lips to mine. I breathe in a sigh of relief and comfort; with Connor by my side, I am strong enough to survive this.

The light outside the skylight has now faded completely. Ethan ventures into the hallway to get a look outside through an open garage door before we head out. He is gone for a short time; when he returns, he announces, "let's give it another half hour, and then I think we can hit the road."

We all sigh in relief; while this storage garage has given us safety and a bit of comfort throughout the day, we are ready to be free of here and on our way. Since my hasty packing job earlier in the evening left a mess without much room, we repack the car. Once things are carefully organized, there is quite a bit more room. We debate taking the cushions, but in the end, decide against it. They take up too much space since we hope to acquire more fuel and supplies along the way.

"Hey, I saw a car-top carrier in one of the units to the left," Ethan says, "let's grab that; it will give us more room to collect additional supplies along the way." Connor and Ethan disappear down the hall retrieve the carrier.

"Rae, I think I am going to go insane," Marnie confides when the boys are gone. Joanie is playing Tic Tac Toe with the girls in the back seat of the car.

"I know, but Marnie, you've got to stay strong for them.

They'll be asleep once we start moving; you can have a come part then. Hell, I might just join you." I console her. "I am so scared of what we are going to find out there. I feel stupid even saying this, but what if it really is aliens. How in the world do we fight that?" I continue.

"I don't know, that has me terrified. We generally know the limitations of humans; right, we have obvious capabilities and weaknesses. Aliens, who knows what we're facing. Like can they see better at night? Will they see us traveling? How do you kill them? Is there a weakness? I just keep coming back to what else could those creatures be that we've seen twice now?" Marnie says matter of fact, no emotion, just purely analyzing the situation.

"I don't know, I've never seen anything like it before. And what about the strange-looking men that we've seen in with the gremlins? What is that about?" I say with a shudder. "That language is something else altogether."

The boys return with the car top carrier after just a few minutes. With a bit of creative rigging, they manage to securely attach it to the top of my old SUV. We repack the car for a third time, moving whatever we won't need while traveling to the carrier, making room in the trunk for more scavenging. Before we go, we make a meal of canned fruit, granola bars, warm soda, and water.

While we are eating, Ethan and Connor study the atlas discussing the pros and cons of each route into Tennessee. They finally agree on a course comprised of what appears to be mostly of one lane winding back roads. This route will take us through a few medium-sized towns so we can look for more supplies. We all load up into the car while Ethan straps on his night-vision goggles. He slowly opens the garage door looking out into the night. After looking both ways several times, he declares it is safe to leave.

"I hope whatever these things are, they can't see at night any better than we can. Well, at least without these." He says, pointing to his goggles. "Away we go," he announces, and we pull out into the night.

Joanie occupies the back seat with Marnie's sisters. They've managed to bond during the day, which is nice because it'll give Marnie a much-needed break. Marnie and I sit in the middle row. Connor joins Ethan in the front, once again holding a semi-automatic rifle and an atlas by his side. Even though the boys have spent a great deal of time planning our route into Tennessee, we are unsure how long it will take to travel these backroads. We are hoping to make it to just north of Knoxville by morning, then we will just have to hide out one more day before making the short trip to Don's cabin.

CHAPTER 16 DETOUR

We've been on the road for an hour when we hit our first problem. Driving along a rural road, Ethan mutters, "Great, road construction signs." We continue on when about two miles later, he mutters, "Shit, road closed ahead."

"How much farther do we have on this road, Connor," he asks warily. Connor searches the map using the flashlight from his phone.

"Looks like another 2 miles," he answers.

"Well, that's no good, the road's closed 1 mile ahead," he says, slowing down, even more than the snail's pace we have already been traveling. "I'm going to approach slowly; if it is just a section of unfinished road, or if we can drive through the ditch around it, we'll proceed."

Once we get to the road closure, it is no good. It is a very wide, deep creek, and the bridge is entirely missing.

"Well, crap," Ethan says, defeated. There is no room to turn around, so he is forced to slowly back down the road until we pass a cornfield with an access drive. He slowly backs into the drive. "Connor, what's the best move from here," he asks.

"Unfortunately, I think we have to backtrack most of the way we've come," he says, clearly frustrated. "We need the darn maps app to keep this from happening; that happy gal would've told us an hour ago not to come this way." He says in frustration.

"No good dwelling on that," Ethan says pointedly, "we'll

just have to go back. Take a look at how this impacts the rest of the trip we've planned; figure out how we'll go from here."

We proceed almost an hour back in the wrong direction and turn down a different rural road. This road is a little wider so we can travel a bit faster. It also will take us through more towns, which may or may not be a good thing; that remains to be seen. Somewhere along this path we see two balls of light pass overhead, the same as last night.

"Geez," Ethan says, "those things fly low whatever they are."

"Drones, maybe?" Connor hypothesizes.

"I don't think so. They are traveling much too fast." Ethan counters.

I like that we are traveling in a dark vehicle with no headlights. It does help me to feel more secure. Hopefully, from the air craft's vantage point, they don't sense the movement below them in any way. However, If they spotlighted us, they would undoubtedly see us on this road.

"Do you think they can see us?" Marnie asks quietly with apparent fear in her voice.

"No, I think at the speed they are moving, they aren't searching but rather just getting from one place to another," Ethan says. "Makes me nervous to see them out and about."

"Well, they are using lights, so hopefully that means they can't see at night any better than we can," Marnie suggests.

"That's a good observation Mar, let's hope it is true," Ethan comments.

Connor syncs his phone to the radio, and we all relax a bit when the familiar sounds of our favorite country artist fill the car.

"I love this song," I announce and start singing along. "I've been walking this lonely road far too long; I feel the same old heartache coming on."

I smile, lean forward to Connor's seat and wrap my arms around him from behind and sing quietly to him, "I see you in my memories, but want to feel you in my arms."

Connor reaches up and squeezes my arms wrapped around his neck, singing along with me. We sing quietly so as not to wake the back row. The sounds from the car are not pretty. If we could sing at full volume, I am quite sure someone's ears might bleed. But it brings us relief from the tension we are all feeling.

"Headlights," Ethan announces, causing us to instantly fall silent. Ethan slows, pulling the car far off the road. "Thankfully it hasn't rained lately, so this yard is dry" he tucks the car behind a row of pine trees while waiting for the vehicle to pass.

It appears to be an ordinary sedan. With his night-vision goggles, he carefully watches the occupants. "They don't seem to have noticed us here. It is a man and a woman, looks to be a child in the backseat, but it could've just been an empty car seat," he tells us. We all instantly relax, but continue sitting a bit longer in the dark. Since the car had their headlights on it would have alerted anyone or anything watching there are people about. After a half-hour, maybe more, Ethan declares it is safe and pulls back onto the road.

"We are never going to make it to Tennessee at this pace," I whine.

"Sorry Rae, I am not taking chances. It sounds like Don's

place is well hidden and 'doomsday' prepped. I feel as though if we can get there safely, we'll be able to hide out for quite some time and formulate a plan," Ethan says.

"No, it's fine, just making an observation." I answer sullenly, "I'm glad you're here, making these decisions to keep us safe," I say, expressing my gratitude.

I lean back against the seat and rest my head against Marnie. It's another half hour when we approach a small town cloaked in total darkness. Ethan sees a small gas station on the corner. He stops on the road to watch the area before we approach it. After ten minutes, he announces that it's "all clear." He slowly rolls forward down the street, pulling into the station. There is no sign the store has any power, but gauges on the pump are backlit.

"Connor, see if you can get into the store, perhaps these are generator powered and you can to turn the pumps on." Ethan orders.

Connor grabs the 9mm from the console, steps out of the car cautiously approaching the store, disappearing quickly inside. A few minutes later the pump lights up and Ethan begins the fill the tank. Connor walks out of the store with several fuel cans.

"The doors broken, it has been looted, but there's plenty of water and food in there. I brought these out so you can fill these while I go back in for more supplies." He says.

"Wow, that didn't take long. I wonder how long it was after the power went out that the looting started," I wonder out loud.

"I'm going to guess not long," Connor answer sadly.

He makes several trips into the store returning with more

cases of water, diapers, canned foods, bags of donuts, sodas, and other odds and ends. He also picks up some essentials such as antacids, ibuprofen, bandages, and peroxide. He stuffs what he can into the car carrier, placing the rest in the back.

Ethan looks over the acquisitions, "good haul." He says.

"I feel bad taking this stuff, I'd leave some cash behind, but someone's already emptied the till, so I'd just be leaving it for a stranger." He says.

"I don't think there will be anyone to lay claim to it," I say sadly.

Ethan is just about done filling the fuel cans when Joanie stirs. "Connor, I need to go to the bathroom."

"Come with me, I'll take you inside," he says, "you can use a real toilet for a change."

"I'm in for that," I say, then Marnie and I join them.

When we enter the store, I am amazed at how much has already been taken. This gives me hope there are more people out there in hiding, safe from whatever it is taking over our world. Marnie goes first. After shining the light into the one-person bathroom she shrieks. Instinctively Connor sweeps her out of the way, aiming his pistol into the bathroom. "Just a rat," he mutters. "Marnie you've got to keep it together. We can't be making noise out here."

"Sorry, it was more when I registered the movement rather than it being rat that scared me," she apologizes.

"Totally get it, but we've got to be quiet," he sympathizes.

During this exchange the rodent runs from the bathroom. We then take turns using the facilities and return to the car without incident. While the boys finish loading up the now filled fuel cans, I take Willis for a quick walk, then we are back on the road.

"At this rate, we'll be lucky to make it to the Tennessee border by morning," Ethan comments.

"Great, that most likely means an extra day of hiding," Connor moans.

Joanie returns to the back seat, where Marnie's sisters have managed to remain sleeping through our stop, quickly going back to sleep herself. It's only about fifteen more minutes when I hear Marnie quietly snoring beside me. We continue slowly on our trek. It's nearing dawn and our best estimates have us still about 50 miles north of the Tennessee border. "We've got about an hour, then we'll need to be under cover," Ethan announces with the first hints of dawn on the horizon to our left.

"It'd be too much to ask to find another abandoned storage facility," Marine chimes in, "maybe with some futons or beds stored there."

"Dream on girl, but I thought you were sleeping," I say.

"I was, but I had a kink in my neck that woke me up," she says.

"We are looking for a place to hide for the day. Try to get more sleep because I am sure the girls will keep you up." I advise.

It's another twenty miles when we find a potential hideout. As luck would have it, it is not an abandoned storage facility but looks like an old truck garage that hasn't been used in quite some time. It is really starting to get light out, and we need to be undercover, so this will have to do. There is one door open showing us it is virtually empty inside. The windows are all high, so no one would be able to easily see inside. "Well," Ethan says, "it's as good a place as any." He pulls the car into the garage, slips out, then pulls the overhead door closed, locking it in place.

"It's not nearly as inconspicuous as the storage facility, but I've got to believe out here with nothing around for miles, no one will be searching this place for a while. We won't have the benefit of cushions today." Connor says.

Connor, Marnie, and I jump out of the car, joining Ethan in the garage. We pull the blankets out of the car, layering them to make as much of a bed as we can. Once again, Connor and I sleep first, while Ethan takes the first watch. He manages to find a ladder in the back of the shop and climbs up to look out the high windows. In the time it takes for us to prepare the bed, the girls have woken up ready to play; fortunately, Willis is happy to oblige. "I'm going to have to find some sleeping pills to give these rug rats during the day to keep them quiet," Marnie says grumpily.

I lay down on my left side while Connor lays behind me as before, pulling me close. His nose glides along my neck behind my ear, just like that first night at the Quarry. "Connor, please, we're supposed to be sleeping," I protest. "Besides, I haven't showered in like three days, I can't smell good."

"You smell just fine," he whispers, continuing his assault on my senses.

"Connor, please stop. I don't want this here, not now," I say.

"As you wish," he says with a smile on his face. He kisses me once more on my neck and pulls me close, leaving his right hand wrapped around my waist. I do have to say, I drift off to sleep with a smile on my face and a mind full of Connor. My dreams this day are much more pleasant than the day before. I sleep for hours, waking fully rested despite the horrifically uncomfortable floor. When I wake, Ethan is sleeping beside me, and Connor is up on the ladder looking out the windows.

I get up and wander closer to Connor, "What time is it?" I ask, the light suggesting I've slept all day.

"About 5," Connor tells me. I am surprised, I really have slept all day. It's going to suck when we get to the cabin if I have my days and nights mixed up. "Um, where are we going to the bathroom," I ask tentatively.

"Sorry, no privacy here; far corner on the other side of the car. We've arranged some old boxes to provide some privacy, but not much." He says, pointing to the corner. "We also found a working sink in that nook back there, no hot water, but we put a bar of soap and a towel back there if you want to clean up a bit."

"Great, you just keep your eyes out the window," I warn him, but I feel his eyes on me as I make my way across the garage. After I go to the bathroom, I find the sink. It is tucked nicely around a corner. In addition to the soap, they have discovered clean shop rags to use as washcloths. The water is cold, which is not pleasant in the chilly March air, but I go for it. I remove one article of clothing at a time and thoroughly wash.

The cold water leaves goosebumps all over my body, but the feeling of clean is worth it. I decide to go all the way, sticking my head under the sink, using the bar of soap, scrub my scalp. Ah, relief, this feels so much better. Once I am clean, I head back to the car, finding my leave-in conditioner and brush I packed back at the house. It takes quite a bit of effort, but I manage to comb through my hair, ripping out a large quantity in the process, but it is tangle-free at the moment. I braid my hair down my back to keep it that way. Once I finish, I make my way back over to where the girls are playing a game of duck duck goose.

"Don't you look better," Marnie says, nodding at my clean and freshly braided hair.

"Well, it was no hot shower, but yes, I feel so much better," I answer.

"I cleaned up earlier; that little sink, even with cold water, was pure bliss. I was able to get Kenzie's bottom cleaned up too. She was pretty gross from wearing a wet diaper the whole day mom and dad…" she pauses… "well, you know."

We both pause for a moment, reflecting on her sadness, but the girls do not allow us to wallow long, demanding our attention. Once someone is 'goosed,' they take off around the circle with Wilbur nipping their heels and yapping excitedly.

"Is it okay for him to be making so much noise?" I ask.

"We haven't seen any indication of a person, thing, or even any movement all day," Connor says, "I think it is harmless. And Rae, you do look fresh all cleaned up." I blush a bit at his assessment.

With this confidence, I relax and join the game. It is fun to play with the girls. I feel almost giddy playing along. We frequently have to remind them to play quietly so Ethan can sleep, but overall, they do a good job. The game gives them a sense of normalcy that helps keep them sane and wear them out a bit for the night of travel.

The sun is finally setting. It is almost time to wake Ethan. This has been an uneventful day, which is of course a good thing. This day passed easier than the first day, though I slept through most of it, which could be why. I do not know how

Ethan and Connor can stand it being on watch for five or six hours at a time. I would lose my mind. This thought has me scaling the ladder to just below where Connor is sitting at the top. I rest my head against his legs. I look up into his blue eyes and smile; he smiles down at me.

"Dreams a bit better today?" he asks.

Blushing, yet again, I say, "why yes, they were."

"Good, that was my goal."

"You devil," I say and rest my head against his legs; I ask, "what ya thinking about up here staring out these windows?"

"I am thinking about my dad, Shannon, and the girls."

"Oh," is all I can think to say, looking back up at him.

"They had no one to warn them to run. They are rural enough, both Dad and Shannon work the farm, so they had no reason to be near a town. But, eventually, you know they'll come searching. Will they know to take cover? We have an old shack way back on the farm. Nobody really knows it is there and it is fairly well hidden in a grove of trees. It once was the farmhouse, it is fairly equipped with a kitchen and two bedrooms, despite being a bit rustic. Back in the day, when we still had ranch hands, it served as a bunkhouse. I don't know if it is hidden well enough since we don't know how thorough these things are, but I am hoping they went there." He continues.

Listening to his words I feel selfish. I had not given one thought to the rest of Connor's family through this whole ordeal. Faced with the loss of my mom, the task ahead of us, I guess I just could not think about that as well. That is just an excuse though, I could have thought of them, I did not. This clearly is what keeps him up at night or during the day, as the case may be.

"I'm sorry Connor, I'll pray for their safety," is all I can think to say.

"Thanks," he whispers in response, distraught from thinking these thoughts out loud.

I rest my head against his legs, standing beneath him on the ladder while he rests his hand on my head, occasionally caressing my face. Finally, my legs tell me I need to move, sit, or do something different, so I make my way back down the ladder.

"Hey Rae, go ahead and wake Ethan, will you? It'll be time to go soon." Connor says as I walk away.

Once Ethan is up, we begin our preparations to depart the garage. There isn't much to reload at this stop. We carefully fold the blankets, collect the notebooks and colored pencils the girls found in my backpack. Then gather a few other things scattered about. Before we leave, we make a meal of unheated cans of baked beans, chips, bottled water, and for dessert, everybody gets a candy bar.

"We'll need to acquire some plasticware at the next stop," Marnie says, dumping a handful of beans into her hand and eating.

"Hopefully, we get to the cabin tonight," I say without much real hope.

"Doubtful, we didn't even make it to Tennessee last night. Still, about thirty miles shy," Ethan says, "looks like one more day of hiding out."

"Great," I moan.

Once the meal is finished, we return to the sink taking turns washing our hands; Marnie also thoroughly scrubs the baked bean residue from the girl's faces. We remove the garbage from the car, depositing empty soda cans, candy wrappers, chip bags, water bottles, and diapers in the same corner we used as a toilet. Ethan removes a fuel can from the back, topping off the car. I look at him questioningly.

"I don't know how far we'll have to go to find a town where we can get fuel. I have a feeling finding pumps operational will get few and far between. Plus, I'd like to just drive for a while without any stops." He answers.

"Makes sense," I say.

Once we've finally reloaded everything in the car, we are ready to depart.

"All aboard," Ethan calls, sounding like a conductor. This gets a chuckle from the girls as they pile in the back of my car. Ethan salutes each of them as they get in, and they, in turn, salute back with a small giggle. He is good at putting them at ease in this difficult time.

"He does have a way at putting them at ease," Marnie says, echoing my thought, looking wistfully at Ethan.

"The benefits of being a big brother," I respond.

CHAPTER 17 ARE WE
THERE YET

Once everyone is loaded into the car, Ethan scales the ladder looking out the high windows. He looks for quite some time, scanning all directions. Finally, he gives the 'all clear.' Connor unlocks and lifts the overhead door; he and Ethan climb in the car, and away we go. Tonight is smooth going. We have been on the road for a while when we all laugh at Willis, curled up in the back seat with the girls, snoring louder than an old man.

"How can they sleep with that racket," I ask, laughing.

"Oh, they can sleep through anything fortunately," Marnie responds.

About an hour later, we come into our first town. Same as the night before, Ethan stops at the edge of town and observes. He stares pointedly at a house to the right. "There's someone, or something stirring in that house," he says, pointing to the right. "It'd be hard for them to see us here, but not impossible." He continues staring for several more minutes and determines it to be a dog. "It's okay. It's just a big Husky," he informs us.

"I wonder if he can get out," I say, thinking out loud. "If not, he will die in there."

"We can't take a chance to let him out, Rae," Ethan says consolingly. "Besides, I am sure if there are no doors open, then this town hasn't been searched, and" he adds with a voice of sadness, "once it is, the doors will be open. Along that line of thinking, I think we should just roll through and not make any stops here. There are likely to be folks about; they might not take kindly to strangers traipsing through their town under the current circumstances."

A thought suddenly hits me that brings a new wave of tears to my eyes.

"What's wrong, Rae?" Marnie questions.

"I wonder if anyone let the horses out? They'll just starve to death if they are left trapped in their stalls," I sob.

"I am sure Janelle took care of that. If she were being forced from her home, she would have died before she left them trapped." Marnie consoles.

"But what if she didn't think it was going to be for long? What if she thought, leaving them in was the safest thing?"

"You can't think like that babe," Connor consoles "besides, this time of year, most of them were probably turned out anyhow."

"Not Dixon; he can't go outside." I sob even harder.

"I am sure he's taken care of Rae; you have to believe that. Janelle is not an idiot, and she loves those horses as much as you do." Connor says before abruptly turning to Ethan, changing the subject, "how's the fuel holding out?" Though the topic has changed, I continue sobbing in the backseat, wondering about the fate of my beloved Dixon.

"We're okay for now, but if we get into trouble, we still have several full cans back there, more than enough to get us to another town." He responds.

We roll through that town without incident. Ethan indicates in most of the houses, people are peeking out the windows. He thinks they can hear the car but do not necessarily see it in the dark. So, this town has not been searched. It is pretty rural; there is no stoplight, just one stop sign in the middle of town. The main street has only one gas station, a mom and pop type eatery, and about twenty houses. I catalog this in my mind. It's been three days since the attacks, this town is still standing.

"Where about are we, Ethan?" I ask.

"We crossed over into Tennessee about twenty minutes ago, but we are not near any town you'd recognize." Connor answers.

Sensing a declining mood in the car, Ethan cues up his playlist. Tonight, we hear a mishmash of country, pop, classic seventies, and eighties rock. The familiar lyrics and rhythms are once again soothing. Marnie is asleep with her head in my lap. I sing along quietly to the music while we ride along. Each of lost in our thoughts and worries.

It is once again slow moving along these backroads. We have been going for about two hours when we come across another town. This path has wound us closer to the interstate, so there are several gas stations, though most are entirely dark. Ethan stops at the edge of town, looking around. "I don't see a single person," he reports, rolling slowly forward, carefully searching around the streets looking for signs of life. He passes the first station since the pumps don't even have the typical backlights on. Just down the road, we come across a massive station, likely a truck stop. He stops, sitting for quite a while outside observing. "I can't decide, the backlights are on on the pumps suggesting we can easily fuel, but there are so many places in there someone can hide," he considers aloud. In the end, he decides it is worth the risk. This large store might have a lot of useful items. Pulling up Ethan announces, "we're okay, the doors are already smashed, so unless whoever looted this is still hiding in there, we should be good. I'd guess they are probably well on their way by now, so there should be no one around. Connor, you know the routine," he says.

Connor grabs the 9mm from the console and heads into the station. Moments later, the pump moves to 0000, and Ethan begins filling the car. While Ethan fills the car, Connor comes out carrying something large. "Look what I found; we can carry extra fuel this way." He announces, bringing out one of those racks that fits in the trailer hitch of a car to hold additional supplies.

"Perfect," Ethan says.

I wake Marnie so she can help scavenge for supplies. She and I go with Connor back into the store. Though people have clearly taken a lot from this store, they were focused on all the wrong things. The electronics display is thoroughly cleaned out, but the stack of coolers, fuel cans, and the like are untouched.

We make our way around the store and find the built-in refrigerators are still cold. They must also be on generator power. We go back to the front, grabbing a few foam coolers, we load up on frozen burger patties, hot dogs, frozen meals, and whatever meats we can find. With the car top carrier and now the hitch rack, we've got a bit more room. We grab a few more cases of water and some additional toiletries. Being a truck stop, this place has an excellent selection of soaps, shampoos, and other toiletries. At the last minute, I think to grab a couple packages of toilet paper.

We stop on our way out to the car to procure several large bags of ice from the coolers. These have been off for some time. The ice is somewhat melted into large chunks, but there is still some usable ice. We take the ice, break up some to put in with the meats we've scavenged, then place additional bags of ice in the high-end cooler we got from the first storage garage.

"I think we're about full guys," Ethan says. He has repositioned all of the fuel cans onto the hitch rack, though there is room for two or three more cans.

"I think there are a few more cans in there," Connor says, eyeing the empty space.

"Hurry in, grab them, but we'll fill them somewhere else. I feel like we are pressing our luck. We've been here so long already," he answers.

Connor races across the lot, returning with four cans, though only three will fit. We situate those on the rack and load up. Willis has just woken up, so I take him for a quick walk, it takes him a while to find the perfect place, but he finally relieves himself.

"With the time that took, I could have filled the extra fuel cans," Ethan complains.

I just stick my tongue out, jumping back in my seat. We all settle in and continue our journey. I feel good about the supplies we've gathered. This old thing sure can carry a lot. The addition of the car top carrier and the hitch rack have certainly helped.

"Maybe we can find an empty trailer somewhere," I say aloud, thinking about the months we might have to be in hiding.

"Nah," Ethan says, "I don't think it can get up the mountain. I don't think the road is paved and is likely to be a difficult trek even in this."

I give him a dejected look, "it is a good idea though. Perhaps once we get there, see what we are up against, we can find one and do a night of scavenging."

Marnie quickly falls back asleep, I soon follow. The night of cloak and dagger running in and out of the store, despite it seeming to be safe, still took a toll on my nerves. When I wake, it is nearing dawn; we've finally made it just to the west of Knoxville. Tomorrow, we will visit the park, leave the note for mom, and then make the final push to the cabin. The roads we will be forced to travel tomorrow will not be as rural, but we will do our best to stay hidden.

We start looking for a place to hide out for the day. The options are limited. It is just before dawn when we approach a gas station. The station itself is dark. Once again, the back-lights indicate they either have power or a generator. Ethan stops in the street outside the station peering in for several minutes before deeming it deserted.

After pulling up to a pump, Connor follows the established routine, takes the handgun from the console before heading into the store. A short time later, the pump clicks on, and Ethan begins pumping fuel. Connor is gone for quite some time but finally emerges, carrying a sack of groceries.

"It's pretty picked over in there, but I found a few things we can use, and I got Marnie's plasticware, no more baked beans from the hand." He says, smiling.

Just as Ethan is starting to fill the empty fuel cans we got from the last stop, we hear a gunshot off in the distance. For just a moment, everyone freezes, but then the boys jump into action. Connor closes and loads the fuel cans as Ethan places the handle back on the pump. The boys are in the car and rolling within seconds.

"What was that," I ask from the backseat.

"I don't know, but I don't want to find out. Someone is shooting not too far off in the distance. I don't think it was directed toward us, but they clearly think there is a reason to be afraid." Ethan answers. "We need to get undercover, but I am nervous to stop anywhere near here knowing they're shooting at something." He continues sweeping his vision from side to side out the windows.

Those of us awake are petrified; after a day and most of a night of peace, we almost forgot to be afraid. We travel in silence for ten minutes; the first rays of sunlight are emerging across the horizon. Ethan finally mutters, "no, we've got to get under cover, I am sure of that."

We have wound farther away from the interstate again. There seems to still be many people peering out the windows of houses, but that also means it is likely to be searched soon. Any place we stop, we are likely to run into someone, but at the same time, we need to be hidden before day ultimately rises.

"If they weren't shooting at us, does that mean whatever it is, is active at night?" I ask, suddenly more terrified.

"I don't know, Rae." Ethan mutters, "I wish I knew what we're up against. I just don't."

CHAPTER 18 FOUND

Another five minutes pass, and the sun begins to rise in earnest. Ethan finally spots a large barn in the middle of a field. There is a dirt road back to the barn, no house to be seen. Hopefully, whoever owns it won't see us go in and has no plans to visit during the day. It is not planting season yet, so really, they are not likely to have a reason to come into the barn. We pull back the drive. Ethan opens the sliding door pulling the car inside. There is a lot of stuff in this barn, providing a lot of potential hiding places.

The barn itself is a bit worn. The boards are spaced far apart, allowing light in, but also allowing anyone outside to see in. The loft is full of hay, probably 700 bales up there, that could provide a good hiding place. Below the loft is six horse stalls, not filled with animals but junk, something in there might be useful.

"Rae, Marnie, go up in that hayloft and make a fort. All sides should be closed in with hay. In the center, make a space that we can all fit. Make an opening of no more than two hay bales wide for us to get in and out. We should be able to replace the hay bales and be completely concealed inside. Leave a few small gaps here and there to see out if need be, small enough though we won't be seen unless someone is right there looking in. I'm going to look around and see if I can find anything to hide the car." Ethan instructs.

Marnie and I do as we are told, climbing a rickety old ladder to the loft. Fortunately it is still cool outside so it is not too hot up in the loft. I remember summers stacking hay in our barn when just climbing into the loft made you sweat. With the abundant supply of hay, we make a rather large hay fort in the middle of the loft. In the inside of the fort, we will be completely concealed from all sides. We return to the car retrieving blankets to create a bed towards the back of the fort. Ethan and Connor find several old painting tarps in one of the stalls; after pulling the car under a loft beside a large tractor, they use these tarps to conceal the car.

"Whoever is sleeping can go into the fort to sleep. We will stay down here as long as there is no trouble. That'll give the girls a chance to play and burn off some energy. If trouble arises, we'll head up to the fort, conceal the entrance with the hay bales and with any luck remain undetected." Ethan instructs us. "Connor, Rae, you two take the first snooze. I'll keep watch."

Connor and I climb into the loft, making our way into the hay fort. We are both exhausted, with a general feeling of unease after the gas station incident this morning. I think we are officially flipping our days and nights because even with a general feeling of nervousness we both fall asleep quickly.

It's pitch black, I cannot see anything. My body hurts so bad, I wish I could see where I am. I hear someone outside the door, instantly I tense in fear. I see one of them standing guard outside when a girl with a kind face walks in; she offers me water. My hands are bound. I cannot sit up on my own, so she helps me to a sitting position.

I jerk awake, sitting up completely disoriented. My sense of fear is only heightened when I hear scurrying footsteps approaching. The girls come diving into the fort with tears streaming down their faces, followed by Joanie, Marnie, then Ethan. Ethan quickly places the hay bales, so they block the entrance then looks at us with fear and sadness, motioning for us to not make a sound.

It is very dark; I can barely see his mouth move, but he appears to be mouthing "creatures." The girls are fighting the tears streaming down their faces and trying to remain silent as possible. Marnie is holding Kenz tight, cradling her gently in her arms, swinging her slowly from side to side. I am sure they are now reliving the night their parents were taken.

"Where's Willis," I mouth quietly.

Ethan just shrugs, looking sympathetically into my eyes. I bite down hard on my lip to fight the panic, threatening to make me scream, which will reveal us all. Connor wraps his arms around me, holding tight as I peer between the bales of hay. What if they find Willis? What if they hurt him? I don't think I can stand it?

We are peeking through holes in the hay fort when the barn door slides open. I start holding my breath and am trembling from head to toe. I am terrified we will be discovered or that Willis will be found, hurt or killed. We see five of the gremlin-ish creatures make their way into the barn. They enter speaking in their weird hums, each carrying a small silver weapon. They search the barn. They lift the tarp on the car but don't do more than a quick peek inside before putting the tarp back down. "No," one of them says.

I look back over at the girls. They look like they are about to lose it. Tears are falling like a river down their dirt-stained faces. I silently pray that they hold it together. Meanwhile, I am trying to keep my own breath from reaching hyperventilation. In my mind, I imagine every horrific scenario possible, us being kidnapped by these creatures, or killed, or who knows what. As if I think the panic can't get worse, one of the creatures climbs into the hayloft, and starts poking around.

None of us move a single muscle; holding our breath, trying so hard to not so much as shift our weight. The tension in our hiding place is palpable. Christy cannot stand it any longer, letting out a small whimper. This does not go unnoticed by the creature who begins quickly making his way toward us. All eyes of the creatures on the floor focus on the situation unfolding in the loft.

This is it; we're caught, I think to myself as terror takes over. Joanie reaches over, pulling Christy into a bear hug, placing a hand over her mouth. She appears to be cooing in her ear, so silently, I cannot even hear. Ethan and Connor silently move in front of us, pointing their weapons at the creature standing outside the fort. It comes over to the hay fort reaching its scaly hand out to move a bale of hay when Willis jumps from behind the hay fort snarling.

"That," one of the creatures on the floor says, pointing to where Willis stands. The creature in the loft looks at him questioningly, raises his small sliver weapon firing at Willis. I bite down hard on my lip until the blood flows freely, the tears fall like a silent river. I lean forward silently, looking at where he fired. Everything that was there is wholly obliterated. A large gaping hole now exists in the loft, opening to the stall below. Entire bales of hay, the floor of the loft, are just gone. It is similar to the devastation observed in the towns that were leveled.

I am fighting hard to keep it together and remain silent, but it is hard. Willis saved us but paid the ultimate price in the process. It is all I can do to keep my grieving silent. I fall into Connor, who holds me tight, helping to muffle my quiet sobs against his shirt. The girls, fortunately do not see what was happening in the barn. They are unaware our furry companion just saved us. I sob quietly into Connor's shirt; my mind is completely gone.

Shortly after this event, they must have decided there was nothing to see here and leave the barn. We sit still for at least a half-hour, maybe forty-five minutes. How ever long it is it feels like forever. It's all I can do to breathe between my silent sobs.

Ethan finally slips out of the hay fort looking all around the barn, peering through the large cracks in the boards. "They're gone," he whispers. "I want everyone to stay in this fort until dark. If you have to pee, slip into the loft behind the hay and go right back in, do you understand?" He finishes with a strong air of command in his voice. We all nod somberly.

Ethan climbs down the ladder; despite his order, I can't stand it. I run behind the hay pile, frantically searching for any sign of Willis. The longer I search, the more I lose hope. I am just about to give up when Ethan loudly whispers my name.

I peer down through the hole in the loft floor to the stall below, I see Willis. He was not hit but did fall when the floor disintegrated. He landed in a feed trough below with several flakes of hay from a broken bale covering him. Ethan gently lifts him and he lets out a small whimper of pain, but over-all seems fine. Ethan brings him to me in the loft. I slide back into the hay fort, clutching him tightly. "Oh, Willis," I cry, "I am never letting you out of my sight again. You could've been killed." Looking at him closer I see his leg looks odd. This must have been the whimper of pain. I think he has broken his leg.

Ethan returns to the loft, positioning himself as the look-out, peering through the boards' cracks. "Ethan," I call him over.

"What is it Rae," he asks.

"I think he broke his leg," I answer.

"Let see if we can find something small enough to splint it with. I saw some self-adhesive wraps in a stall down there. Maybe we can use those to stabilize the leg." He says. I know he learned necessary lifesaving skills as part of his Air Force training. Hopefully, he can apply these to a dog. He again descends the ladder returning with a small but bendable piece of thin aluminum, a kid's sock from the car, and the adhesive wraps.

He places the sock over Willis' leg, then bends and positions the aluminum to support the leg. Willis whimpers but remains relatively quiet, sensing the danger that still lurks in the area. Ethan then wraps the leg tightly to the aluminum with the self-adhesive wrap.

"That's all I know to do," Ethan says, "I am sure there are better ways to wrap it but I don't know. The poor guy will probably eventually get arthritis, but that is all I dare try."

"Thank you," I whisper through my tears. I lay down, resting my head on Connor's leg, clutching Willis tight to me, wishing I could give him something for the pain I am sure he is feeling in his leg. He licks my face letting me know he loves me.

"Connor, I want out of this barn," Joanie cries.

"We can't go now sweetie; we know they are in the area. They'd see us for sure." He says. "They've already searched here; it doesn't make sense for them to come back unless we give them a reason. And they didn't seem to search well when they were here, so that's something."

But I kind of agree with Joanie; I want out of here too. That was insanely close. I am so unnerved I cannot even think straight.

"Okay, I can't sleep now," Ethan says, "Connor, Rae, Marnie, you want to sleep?"

"I couldn't if I wanted to," I answer.

"Nope, me either," Marnie answers.

It is a long day; everyone is terrified into not moving. We remain in the hay fort for the remainder of the day. We give the girls paper and colored pencils from my backpack to occupy them, and they take turns consoling a distraught Willis. Marnie and I descend the ladder about midday to assemble a lunch of granola bars and water. After lunch, we have nothing to do but sit and stare at each other.

I feel like this day has lasted 48 hours. The sun is finally setting; soon, we will hopefully make the final push to the cabin. I hope it is as secluded, hidden, and disguised as Ethan says, or we do not stand a chance.

CHAPTER 19 THE FINAL PUSH

The trip has been exhausting. The near-miss today has us all frazzled; thankfully, we somehow remained undetected. The girls grew tired of holding Willis, so I clutch him tight to me. After thinking I had lost him forever, I can't seem to put him down. The sun has set, and we begin preparations to leave this horrible barn.

A trip that would typically take 5 hours has taken four days, and we have not even made it to our destination yet. Gearing up for the final push, or what we hope is the final push to the cabin, we make a meal of cereal, dried bananas, and water. Not very satisfying, but it quiets the rumble in our tummies, at least for now.

We once again empty the trash of spent water bottles, soda cans, candy wrappers, and chip bags from the car before we set out. Ethan peers through the cracks in the barn walls for quite a while before determining it is safe. We assume what has become our usual seats, Joanie and the girls in the back row, Marnie and I in the middle, and the boys in the front.

"We should try to go the back way into the park," Ethan says, "hopefully the bridge in the picnic area is still standing."

We travel in silence as the area landmarks become more recognizable. We continue to wind around until we find the familiar road into the park. We make our way toward the creek where we often swam as kids.

"Hey Ethan, should we really stop now? Or wait and come back later?" I ask, while we wind around toward the picnic area.

"I think it is safest now. The longer they have control, the more freely they will move about, the more it will restrict our movement." Ethan responds.

I nod in agreement. That makes a lot of sense. They are not trying to hide now, but the more of them there are out there, the more difficult it will be to leave a note. Although it makes me fear even more so if my mom is out there somewhere trying to get to us.

"The bridge is still there," Ethan says with relief as we round the last corner into the backside of the picnic grounds. We continue winding around to the place we will leave the note for mom.

I take several empty water bottles, write vague directions to the cabin, then seal them up tight. We don't give specific directions, so whoever finds them cannot get straight to the cabin. If it is mom, we'll see her coming and go get her. If it so someone else, they won't get close enough to cause any problems for us. I do not know if these notes will stay here or wash away if the river rises, but we have to try. I also know that mom is most likely gone; this is a wasted effort, and I pray it does not lead to our eventual demise.

Once we park on the familiar pull off Ethan announces, "the creek is already quite high. We will have to leave the notes up closer to the road." I get out of the car and start down the path towards the creek with the aid of the flashlight. I see the crooked forked tree we used to sit in as kids; this is perfect. In the center fork, there is a bit of hole worn into the tree. I drop one bottle in this hole. I wander parallel to this path, finding another hollowed-out tree; I place a second bottle within this tree. Finally, I put one simply on the ground, held in place by vines and roots. I know from being here as a kid, even during summer, not much foliage grows here, so while it might not be in plain sight, someone looking for it will be able to see the bottle hidden there.

I feel good once this task is done. It has been a long treacherous journey and I am ready for it to be over. I climb back into the car; tears are again streaming down my face as I think these are notes that will most likely never be found. At least not found by the one for whom they are intended. No one is going to come looking for them. My mom is gone from this world. Marnie hugs me close letting me cry into her shoulder while we go on our way.

"We've got to head toward Cosby," Ethan announces. "Unfortunately, the night is about over. The fastest way is to head straight through the park then through town. Once we get on the bypass, I think we can take some backroads over the mountain to Don's place."

Great, this is going to put us right out I the open. Fortunately, it is pitch black outside here at the base of the mountain. Hopefully, that is enough to keep us hidden. With no traffic on the roads and Ethan's familiarity with the path we are on, we make it out of the park faster than we ever have.

Passing the visitor's center I voice my thought's out loud, "Remember when mom used to make me go in there every year and take a picture with that stuffed bear." I say with a smile, but a tear slides silently down my face.

"Yep" is all Ethan can responds his voice breaking at the end of the single word.

We start towards town, it is eerie that there is no traffic, not a soul. The town is intact but silent, no lights, no signs of life. Ethan comments he can see movement in some of the hotels, humans hiding out. Not an exceptionally safe hiding place, they will likely be found. Still, there is probably food and water stored in there, so that is at least convenient until they are found.

We make our way through town without incident, now cruising three-twenty-one out toward Cosby. It is nearing dawn when Ethan asks, "Connor, we just passed Clear Springs Way. How much farther to the road I have marked on the Atlas?"

"Looks to be on the right about three and a half miles down," Connor comments. "But I don't see a road there."

"There's not really. It's the rangers' access road into the park; there will be a gate across the road. But it will get us to the path to the Cabin," he says.

Sure enough, about three and a half miles down, there is an access road with a pole across serving as a gate. Ethan pulls off the main road putting the car in park. He goes to the back and rummages around a bit, returning with bolt cutters. He uses these to cut through the chain holding the gate closed, swinging it open wide. Ethan climbs back into the driver's seat. "Alright kids, hold on, it's going to get bumpy."

He was not kidding. Even though he is moving slowly, it is a bumpy ride. The girls in the backseat wake up when they are all bounced off their seats to the floor. "Hey," Joanie protests, "what is going on?"

"We're almost there, Joan," Connor says, relief clear in his voice.

The access road winds up the mountain for several miles. In the light provided by the first rays of sunlight breaking through, I can see it goes farther up the mountain. But Ethan turns off before it ends, onto a path barely wide enough for the car.

"So, did they build this illegally in the park?" I ask Ethan.

"Not exactly; the property is not in the park. After the house was built, they let the main road to the cabin fall to disrepair, growing over with new trees and vegetation. Then, yes, they made an illegal access through the park so they could be 'off the grid.'" He explains. "No one has been up here in a year or so. I'm hoping the path is still clear, then we can drive all the way to the cabin. It has a full garage so we can hide the car inside."

"Does it matter?" I ask. "I mean, if they see the house, what differences does it make if there is a car there."

"Well, Don says the house is well camouflaged," Ethan explains, "not sure how they've done that. But he says if you don't know it is there and aren't looking for it, you won't see it. But a car would stick out, although this green beast might blend in with the trees."

"So, if you're standing right by the cabin, you won't see it? Seems a bit farfetched to me," I say a bit sarcastically.

"No, if you are right there, obviously, you'll see the house. But anyone scanning the mountain, from even a fairly short distance away, supposedly will not see it," Ethan explains.

We continue bouncing along in silence when we hit our first obstacle, a large tree across the path. Ethan and Connor have to work hard but eventually encourage the tree, which was halted by the flat path, to continue its trek down the side of the mountain. This setback cost us fifteen minutes, and the day is getting even brighter.

"How much longer?" Marnie asks, "it's getting awfully light

outside."

"I am not sure, I think we have a good bit to go, but we are pretty well hidden under cover of the trees here. Someone or something would literally have to be right along our path to see us. I'm hoping they're still concentrating on the towns at this point. If they ever even come out this far. They might stick closer to towns as long as there is nothing here to draw their attention. We have no idea what their ultimate goal is." He finishes rambling out his thoughts.

Rounding the next corner we come across a place where the path has washed away. It is not incredibly deep but is relatively wide; Ethan is concerned the car will bottom out and get stuck. I pass Willis back to the girls instructing them to stay in the car. Ethan, Connor, Marnie, and I begin searching for large trees or branches that are down we can use to fill the void in the path. This takes at least an hour, in the end we manage to construct a crude bridge that should prevent the car from bottoming out in the ditch.

We continue winding around the path for another forty-five minutes when Ethan announces we have arrived. Looking out the window, I think he has lost his mind. I see nothing. But after closer inspection, yes, there is something up ahead. Don was right; unless you know this was here, you would never see it just looking at the mountain.

The house is painted to match the woods that surround it. They have trees growing strategically around the house to provide additional concealment. The one side is windowed like you would expect of a chalet in this area, but the windows are covered in some sort of camouflage tinting that prevents the sun from reflecting off the surface. The tinting also blends well with the mountain behidn the cabin.

The back is built right up against the mountain allowing the camouflage used on the face to blend more fully. From this vantage point, it is hard to determine the structure's size, but it appears to be quite large. After we pull up just outside the house, Ethan jumps out and disappears around the side of the house. He returns moments later with a key he uses to open a large garage door I had not even noticed. We all remain in the car while he pulls inside, closes, and locks the overhead garage door. Since it is entirely dark in the garage, Ethan turns the headlights on so we can see to find our way into the house.

CHAPTER 20 THE CABIN

"Welcome home gang," he says, beckoning us out of the car.

"Is there anyone else here?" I ask apprehensively.

"No, Don said if any of his family came up here, there'd be a jeep or truck in the garage," Ethan explains. "All three keys were hidden behind the house, so no one has come yet."

Ethan uses the same key from the garage door to open the door into the house. The inside is rustic but nicely done, and massive. There will be plenty of room for all of us here.

The garage door opens into a medium-sized kitchen. It has an old wood-burning stove in the corner, I assume for heating, a gas stove and range for cooking, a newer looking microwave sits on the counter next to a toaster. There is a sizeable double-sided kitchen sink, so there must be running water here in some form. There is a large refrigerator across the room, but I wonder if and how it, the microwave, and toaster have power. The kitchen has a fair amount of stone counter space and a breakfast bar area that opens into a large, vaulted living room.

The cabin itself throughout has log walls, complimented nicely by wood plank flooring. The floors are covered every so often in warm tone throw rugs and carpets. After leaving the kitchen, just on the other side of the breakfast bar, we find a large dining table with eight chairs. The living room, just on the other side is spacious. There are three large couches in a U shape in the middle with two recliners at each end. In the corner sits an old-fashioned writing desk and chair. There is a

TV cabinet off to the side, holding a collection of books, board games, and puzzles. We continue making our way through the downstairs, we find two large bedrooms on the first floor, both equipped with large personal bathrooms.

"So, this place has running water?" Connor asks.

"Yes, it has a well. There are small solar panels and small wind turbines hidden around the mountainside that supply a modest amount of power. They didn't want large panels or turbines since they would stand out. Don says they can power the well and a few outlets always, and during spring and summer, typically power the whole house. They have a TV upstairs, not that there is anything to watch, but the kids can play video games," Ethan finishes.

We continue our exploration winding our way upstairs. Here we find five small but comfortable bedrooms. The first two rooms we encounter each have a queen bed and a tiny bathroom attached. The bathrooms hold a small one-person shower, sink, and toilet. The next bedroom has a full bed and a Jack and Jill bathroom connecting it to the next bedroom, which is equipped with a twin over full bunk bed. Finally, there is one more closet size bedroom with a twin bed and a small dresser.

"Well, I'll give them this; they've got plenty of places to sleep here," I say, longing to crawl into one of these beds and crash for days.

We head back downstairs and then continue on to the lowest level. Here we find the gas-powered water heater, which Ethan ignites, a storage closet, and three small closet-sized bedrooms, each with just a basic twin bed. These are mostly underground and do not have windows. There is also no bathroom down here, so I guess they don't get used often; hopefully, once Don's family arrives, we won't have to move down here.

We continue to explore the basement a bit more. We find a utility sink equipped with an old-fashioned washboard and clotheslines stretched across the space. We see a storage area with books and extra household items such as pots and pans in another corner. After our exploration is complete, we head upstairs.

"I think we should take the bedrooms upstairs for now," Ethan announces. "That way, Don and his family can have the master bedrooms on the first floor. Connor and Rae, you two take one of the queen rooms, Marnie, and I will take the other. Joanie can have that room with the full bed and be close to the girls who can take the bunk room on the other side."

"Should we unload the car?" I ask, I know this is no vacation, but thinking of all the times we moved into a chalet for a week, the first thing you do is get set up.

"No, it can wait. Right now, I think we all need some sleep. At least those of us that were up all night. Joanie, can you watch the girls downstairs while we get some rest? We won't sleep long; I'd like to get back to a normal sleep schedule as quickly as possible."

"Yes, can we keep Willis with us?" she asks, looking at me questioningly as I clutch my dog tightly.

"Yes," I answer, "just remember he is hurt and can't play like you're used to."

"Do you think I could shower before I go to bed," I ask?

"Rae, water is probably not hot yet. Why don't you get some sleep first," Ethan says.

"Fine," I answer gruffly.

We head up the stairs; Marnie and Ethan peel off to the first bedroom on the right; Connor and I go to the second straight across from the stairs. The bed has a wood frame that looks homemade. I do not have high expectations for the mattress, but after the last few nights, or I guess days, any bed is bound to feel good. I am pleasantly surprised when I pull aside the heavy green quilt and climb in, the mattress is absolute heaven. It is a firm mattress with a plush pillow top that I sink right into. Connor climbs in from the other side, sliding up behind me. He pulls me close to him and wraps his arms protectively around me.

"I could sleep like this for days," he says, lightly kissing my neck.

I turn and look at him, suddenly filled with a sadness I don't understand. He looks deep into my eyes and leans in to kiss me tenderly. His hand glides along my face then around my back, pulling me close. When he releases the kiss, I nestle my head down on his shoulder and let silent tears fall, eventually drifting off into a dreamless sleep.

I wake hours later to Connor kissing me awake, "time to rise and shine if we want to sleep tonight."

I smile up at him, "I think I can just sleep straight through." I notice that his eyes are red and swollen. He has cried sometime recently. It occurs to me that he has been so strong since this all began; he did not have time to process or mourn the loss of his mother. While Marnie, Joanie, and I blubbered in the back seat, he and Ethan held it together to convey us to safety. I touch his eye tenderly and place a soft kiss on his cheek but do not speak to his evident sorrow.

He takes a steadying breath, "that is a possibility, but

Ethan is cooking burgers downstairs," he answers. My stomach responds with a gurgle as the smells of cooking meat register in my mind.

"Yay," I scream and jump up quickly, "have we unloaded any of our bags yet? Just wondering if my toothbrush is inside?"

"Not yet. We'll work on that after we eat." He says.

I head into the bathroom quickly; I splash warm water on my face, and it feels incredible. I then grab a washcloth proceeding to wipe my neck and arms. Feeling refreshed, I head downstairs. Joanie, Christy, Marie, and Kenz enjoy plain hamburger patties, canned peas, and potato chips at the breakfast bar chattering excitedly about the morning fun. Apparently, they found several board games they all very much enjoyed. Also, they learned a few of Willis' tricks, such as 'Bang' and shake, offering him bits of potato chips as a reward.

Marnie and Connor are seated at the table, each with a plate of food. Ethan is in the kitchen, dishing up the last two plates.

"Smells good E," I say, accepting a plate and heading into the dining area. I sit next to Connor. He immediately jumps up and goes to the refrigerator returning with a cold bottle of water.

"Wow, it's working?" I question.

"Yeah," Ethan answers, "it's been fairly windy I believe, and the sun is peeking through the haze fairly strongly."

"Nice." I answer enthusiastically.

"Why don't they have a big generator up here?" I ask Ethan.

"Well, I think they do, but they try to conserve the fuel for the water heater, stove, and heating in the winter. They have several full-size fuel tanks buried outside, but since the official road up here no longer exists, refilling those in bulk would be impossible. Hence, they use it as sparingly as possible." Ethan explains.

"Wow, these guys thought of everything. Why did they feel the need to create such a place? Don't get me wrong, I am glad they did." I ask.

"Sometime in the late nineties early two thousands doomsday prepping was a thing, everybody was preparing for the end of the world. There were shows and books about zombies and various apocalyptic scenarios that really got under peoples' skin, making them worry. Couple that with the all-out political unrest in the country at the time and people were scared.

"The family always liked nature and the mountains, so they created this getaway. While they were building, they paid attention to the details making it as self-sustaining as possible and as hidden as they could make it. It is recorded with the county to exist here, but without an electric meter or water meter, there is no need for anyone to ever check on it. Then once the road grew over, no one even remembers it is here. They've enjoyed a lot of time up here as a family. It has mostly served as a vacation retreat, until now." Ethan tells us.

"The backside of the property we came in on is actually part of the national park, so there would never be any houses behind here. They own pretty much the whole mountain down to the main road and a good distance on the other side. That has kept any houses from popping up anywhere near here. Hopefully, to these invaders, there is nothing here but woods." He continues.

"Well, I'm glad they did a good job," Marnie says.

"So, what's our plan now," Connor asks.

"We'll definitely sit tight and wait for Don and his family to get here. In the meantime, we need to start cataloging all we've noticed so far. What we know to be true about these invaders, it will help us plan. We need to stay inside; any movement outside could alert someone we are here. We'll observe what we can from here. From the upstairs windows, you can see all the way into the nearby towns with these binoculars," he says. He points binoculars on the table I had not yet noticed. "Don has a set on him as well. With the park at the back of the house, there won't be much to see there. The view on the front is relatively unobstructed other than a few trees planted strategically around the house."

"I'm not sure sitting still is what I need right now," I say, "if I have downtime, I am just going to go crazy thinking about all that has happened."

"You're going to have to face it sometime, sis; the sooner you do, the quicker you'll be able to move forward," Ethan says, not unfeeling but matter-of-fact. He is good at compartmentalizing. Part of his Air
Force training, there is a part of you to mourn, but you must move through it to face the task at hand. I wonder if in the future he will regret not mourning more now, in the present.

"I wish I could face it all as bravely as you. I just can't," I say, tearing up again.

"It's not bravery Rae, it's need. It's what we have to do," he answers.

Seeing the tone the conversation is taking, Connor takes this opportunity to redirect. "Willis will need to go out during the day; what do we do about that?" he asks. Like Ethan, Connor is very tactical in thinking. He's been so strong and brave that I tend to forget he lost his mom also.

"I think if we just take him out the back, through the garage by the mountainside, we should be fine. We should observe the area first before heading out," Ethan informs us. He has clearly thought this through already.

"You have to admit E, he's been a nice distraction for the girls," I say, defending my choice to bring him with us.

"Yea, yea," he says, not entirely willing to agree, having the dog is a good thing, "that remains to be seen, doesn't it?"

"He saved us back in that barn," I add a bit defensively, shuddering at the memory.

"That he did," Ethan concedes.

Ethan and Marnie brought just enough in from the car to fix lunch, so once our late lunch is over, we unload the rest of the car. It takes a while to get everything in but gives us a chance to inventory our food and supplies. We've got enough here for a month or a bit more if we are careful. Hopefully, Don's family will bring additional supplies as well.

What we don't have a lot of are diapers for Kenz. We'll have to figure something out there. Once the unloading is done, it is still early evening, and no one is hungry yet after our late lunch. I peruse the books on the shelf and curl up on the couch with a cheesy romance novel. Since we have power now, I charge my phone, I can play games on here later. The girls are happily coloring, but I wonder how we will keep them entertained through the indeterminable amount of time ahead, locked inside in this quite comfortable prison. Connor comes over next to me, scooping me into his lap, and hums thought-lessly as he stares out the windows rubbing gentle circles on my shoulder.

I read for a while but stop to look at Connor. "What are you thinking about," I ask.

"Sorry, I'm not attentive," he says with that delicious southern drawl, "I was thinking about my dad and the girls."

"You know I don't think you've ever told me their names," I say.

"Oh, they are Kiera, she is 6, and Myra is 4," he answers.

"I like those names," I respond.

"I just worry. I wonder if they are safe. I can't imagine why any of them would've been in a big city, but if they were...I can't think about that. But even still, they are very rural. How long do they have before those things come searching? Did they make it to the shack?" He says, troubled.

I lean up and kiss him gently on the lips. I want to take his pain away, but it is hard facing the same pain of my own. Ethan is here with me, but I've probably lost my last surviving parent. It's hard to face, even if I am an adult. I lean back down, resting my head on his chest, and continue reading as he stares contemplatively out the window.

After a few chapters, I become restless, so I begin to wander the cabin. It is a very nicely built cabin. Though made for concealment and safety, it has comfort. The beds, the couches, and chairs are all quite comfortable. The house is spacious. The girls have found plenty of activities to occupy their time today. "I'm going to take a shower," I announce frustrated, heading up the stairs.

I have to admit, a hot shower is more than I ever expected

at the end of the world, not that I think I really ever thought about the end of the world before. I go to the bathroom off our bedroom and find it well-stocked with soap and shampoo. I even discover new toothbrushes in the packaging; these folks have thought of everything.

I hop in the shower. The hot water feels good. I've always thought a gas water heater is so much warmer than an electric water heater. After I lather up I give in to my misery. I sit down on the floor and once again cry. I grieve for my mother, I grieve for Dixon, for Janelle, for my lost future, I grieve for Connor's family I have never met and his mother. I allow myself to wallow, to feel all the emotions I have bottled up over the last few days of our dangerous trek. The water is starting to cool. I think I've used more than my fair share of hot water. I hastily rinse, quickly shave using the razor I found stocked in this bathroom, rinse once more, and exit the shower.

Upon leaving the bathroom, I feel much better. It felt good to allow myself to feel the emotions bottling inside me, to finally let go when no one was watching. When I come to the bedroom, I am pleasantly surprised to find Connor has brought my bag to the room. I find clean underwear and clothing. I dress in a pair of figure-hugging stretch pants and a tight fitted t-shirt. In my mind, I have another anxiety I have bottled up I plan to release tonight.

CHAPTER 21 NEEDS

I dress quickly then head downstairs; the sun is gone from the sky with just a few rays of light left. Ethan is moving about the house lighting dim blue lanterns. The lights provide dim light, enough to allow us to move about unencumbered, but should not be visible from outside the tinted windows.

"How does Spaghetti sound to everyone," I ask.

"Yay!" chimes in Christy, "I love spaghetti."

"My too," echoes McKenzie.

"Well, that settles it," I say, making my way to the kitchen to fix a meal of spaghetti. "Um, Ethan, how do I work a gas stove?" I ask, having never done this before.

"Geez sis," he exclaims, "you're useless."

"Yeah, yeah, I know," I answer.

He comes over to light the stove, in the meantime I fill a pot with water. We did not bring sauce with us, but I did see some earlier in a cupboard. Not sure how old it is, but we'll give it a try anyhow. I wish we had cheese to top it off, but I will just be grateful we have food I tell myself.

"Um, Rae, you paying attention," Ethan asks, noticing my mind wandering.

"What, oh yeah, turn it up to here and simply push the button" I repeat what he said, not even realizing I was listening.

Dinner is quite fun despite our situation. We tell stories

and jokes. Marnie's sisters have settled right in here; the benefit of being young and pliable. Connor helps me clean up dinner, while Marnie takes her sisters upstairs to bathe. Once dinner is cleaned up, Connor, Ethan, and I gather around the large dining room table while Joanie goes up to take a shower in our room.

"We've got to start cataloging what we've observed," Ethan announces, sitting at the head of the table.

"Do we really have to do this tonight?" I ask perturbed.

"Yes, if we wait, we might forget important details, or embellish other details. It is important to get this right." He says.

"Why, what difference does it make, our world has ended," I shout a bit too loud, letting out the emotion that has welled inside me all day. "It's not likely a group of teenagers is going to take down an entire alien invasion."

"The world as we know it, yes, but we are still here. We need to formulate a plan. First and foremost, our plan will keep us all here, alive, and preferably together." He says not necessarily upset by my words but determined to make an impression. "Then, if we are fortunate enough, we'll find a way to end this. Do I really think this small group of adolescents can take on a full-scale invasion? No, I do no; but I do think we will find others out there. I think we can work with others to form some kind of a coordinated attack and take our world back." By the end of this speech, he is yelling. Clearly, I've upset him.

I shrink back into my chair. I am so exhausted emotionally, I just do not even know what to say, so I shut my mouth and just listen for a while.

"So," Ethan continues, "let's make a list of what we know. I'll start. Major cities and virtually all military bases are destroyed along with all who are in them."

"Yeah, like mom." I blurt out without thinking. Thankfully, Ethan glazes over my self-pity.

"Based on Marnie's sisters' experience and what I observed in Europe." He continues, "sometime after the attacks on the cities/bases, those remaining are abducted."

Frustration has built in me to a whole new level. "YOU WERE HOME," I scream, "you came home after you knew what was happening and didn't tell us. You could have saved her. You could have told her not to go into the city." I scream, breaking down into full hysterics. I immediately regret my outburst; Ethan's face crumples in pain like I have never known.

Connor comes to console me, but I do not deserve it. I know there was nothing he could have said or done. I know he was bound by his role, not to speak. There was no way he would know it would continue here. But at the same time, I am frustrated. How could he have been home and at least not told her not to go to the city? Certainly, she could have finished her work from the house. Connor pulls me to his lap and hugs me close. I look up and see him give Ethan a look of pure sympathy. This infuriates me, but I do not say a word. I sit, stiff in Connor's embrace and fume.

"I couldn't, Rae, I tried, I gave all the clues I could, but I couldn't," Ethan whispers, clearly in pain.

At that moment, Marnie comes downstairs, "What the hell is going on here?" she says in a loud whisper. "I just put the girls down, Joanie is her room, please don't disturb them. Ethan, are you okay?" She runs to him.

I can't take it. I break free of Connor's arms and run up

to my new room. I curl into a ball there on the comfortable mattress and once again become a sobbing mess. It is not long until Connor joins me in the room. He sits on the bed, resting his back against the rough-hewn headboard staring at the ceiling. "Rae, you're not being fair," he says. "He couldn't tell you, even if he could, would you have believed such a story? With the evidence right in front of us, we didn't believe at first. Would your mom have changed a thing? She was a professional with a job to do, she would have done it. He lost his mom too Rae. He is in pain just the same as you, dumping your pain on him won't make it go away."

Why does Connor have to be so strong, knowing that just like me, he lost his mom and has no idea what has happened to his father and sisters? I just sob harder. I know I caused my brother, my only remaining family member, so much pain by my words, but I am not ready to forgive him. He saw this devastation before it came to our country, he could not have stopped it, but he could have stopped her.

I cry a bit longer before the sobs finally subside. Connor gently rubs my back and starts singing softly. The man cannot carry a tune in a bucket. I chuckle silently to myself, but his gesture is welcome. The light has completely faded out of the tinted windows. I finally look up at him, "will you excuse me a moment?" I ask.

"Of course," he answers.

I get up and move to the bathroom. I spend a few moments staring at myself in the mirror. I have never thought of myself as a person who causes others pain, and I am ashamed. Ethan lost his mother too. It is not just me; I know that I should not have to remind myself so often. I turn on the cold water. After soaking the washcloth, I push the cold compress against my face, focusing on my eyes. Once I feel like my face has somewhat recovered, I brush my teeth thoroughly, use the bathroom, thankful to have toilet paper again, then head back to the bedroom.

Connor is looking so handsome in the blue light as he leans up against the headboard of the bed. "Feeling better," he asks.

"Yes, I am sorry," I answer.

"Rae, it's okay. No one is prepared to deal with what we've faced, but I do think tomorrow you owe Ethan an apology." He says gently.

"Yes, I already regret my words," I say.

I lay on the bed, curling myself around Connor and resting my head on his shoulder. I have already decided, and I am determined tonight is the night, I need this. I need to feel human; I need to feel close to him, I need the release what we started five days ago. I finally look up, staring intently into his blue eyes. After several minutes he leans down and kisses me gently. We kiss like this, soft, tender for several minutes when make my intentions clear.

"Rae, we don't have to do this tonight," he says.

"I need this," I tell him urgently.

"Just think about it," he advises.

Oh, I have thought about it, I have thought about it all day, and this is happening. The world has ended. Being good does not matter. Scholarships do not matter. Abstaining from life does not matter. Working your ass off for things no longer matters. None of it matters. We have now, we have this moment only, and I will make the most of it.

"Rae," he moans, but now it is my turn to make him crazy. I do not hesitate. I roll, pushing him back on the bed, kissing him relentlessly.

"Rae, are you sure?" he questions.

"Yes, please," I moan back quietly in response.

"As you wish," he says.

When we are finished, he lifts his head and kisses me; the pure emotion of this kiss might overwhelm me. He embraces me tightly, then lies beside me.

"I love you, Rae," he whispers.

"I love you Connor, I love you so much," I answer.

I lay my head on his shoulder, inhaling his scent. I think I should feel ashamed, sad, as though I have lost something, but I do not. I feel nothing but happiness and closeness to Connor. We lay still for quite some time, each of us lost in our own thoughts. After a while, I get up and use the bathroom. Returning to the room, I am not ashamed as I thought I would be. As the world ends, so does it seem shame ends. I stand at the edge of the bed looking down at Connor for the first time taking in all of him.

He pulls me to him on the bed, kissing me gently and deeply. "Rae," he says, "I love you so much, I never have, I promise you, ever, felt like this."

I lay with my head on his shoulder. He carefully pulls the blankets up around us; we lie still, saying nothing, enjoying the moment. I finally get up, pull on a ratty T-shirt. I head downstairs, finding a disgruntled Willis lying by himself on the couch. I scoop him up and return to our room. Connor has redressed in clean boxers, now holding the covers up for me to join him.

"We get to sleep with the dog, yay" he says with mock enthusiasm.

"Of course," I respond. I lay across Connor with my head on his shoulder; Willis curls up against my back contentedly.

With this peace I now surround myself with, I succumb to exhaustion drifting into a dreamless sleep.

CHAPTER 22 THE FIRST DAYS

When I wake, it is morning. Connor is hanging off the far side of the bed with Willis now claiming a large portion of his side of the bed. The dog is even sleeping with his head on Connor's pillow. I chuckle at the sight before me, pick up Willis to move him aside, he growls at me in what I imagine he believes is a mean snarl. I gently roll Connor back to his position. He opens his eyes slowly, "Hey you," he says softly, "I certainly hope Willis had enough room last night."

"About that, sorry he is a bit of a bed hog," I answer, "If you lay your leg across him he will get mad and move." I lean in, giving him a long kiss, then rise and head to the bathroom. After a quick shower, I brush my teeth, slap my hair in a ponytail, and head to the bedroom to dress. Connor has already left the room and seems to have taken Willis with him. I dress quickly and head downstairs.

"MMM Bacon, where'd we steal that from?" I question.

"The last stop in town before we headed up the mountain," Ethan tells me looking a bit gruff.

"Ethan, about last night. I am sorry, I know it is not an excuse. We've all lived the same life the past few days, but I just couldn't anymore. The exhaustion, the emotion, it overcame me, and I am sorry. I had no right to say those things; I love you, I know you've done all you can for us, and I can never express to you how grateful I am." I say honestly.

"I know, Rae, it's okay. I get it. You just touched a nerve. Don't you think I already have those same thoughts," he says with a bit of anger, still coloring his tone.

Connor breaks in, "Ethan, it wouldn't have done any good. No one would have believed your story until we faced it. Hell, we didn't believe even with the evidence in front of our eyes at first."

"He's right," Marnie chimes in, "I would have never believed a word of it. I still don't know if I do. I keep waiting to wake up from some ridiculous dream."

"Where are girls?" I ask, noticing they aren't in the room.

"They needed a change of scenery already. God help us, they're in the basement with Joanie playing hide and seek," Marnie explains.

"Well, that's not creepy at all, hiding in a completely dark basement," I say, "not sure that's where I'd play hide and seek."

"They've got every lantern down there. It's lit up like a sunny day at the beach," she chuckles, "but there are still plenty of places to hide. There's a lot of stuff down there."

"So, what's on the agenda for today, more moping around, moving from chair to chair, and sleeping?" I ask, trying to be humorous but failing miserably.

"I want to spend some time upstairs observing what we can see around us. If nothing else get the lay of the land, then we can tell if anything changes." Ethan explains.

I make a breakfast of the remaining slices of bacon and a granola bar, accompanied by a soda we procured along the way...breakfast of champions. The boys head upstairs with the binoculars while Marnie and I pull up chairs along the windows and look out.

"What day is it, Mar?" I ask.

"Not entirely sure," she answers. "We left on Friday, we drove four nights, we've been here one night, Wednesday I'd say."

"Hmm. I'd have to work today." I muse.

"I could go for a Double Palace burger and a visit from Ms. Nester right about now," Marnie laughs.

"So, I guess I'll never find out how I did on that European History test. We were supposed to get that back on Monday," I say with an air of sadness.

"What do you think is happening to my parents?" Marnie asks.

"I don't know Mar, perhaps we'll be able to observe something up here. But I have to assume and be hopeful as remote as we are, we won't see anything." I answer. "I imagine, unfortunately, we'll have to venture out to get a lay of the land and understand what is happening. If we can figure out where they take people, what they are doing, then we can formulate a plan to get them back."

"I just can't help but worry, I am afraid they're dead," she moans.

"I know sweetie, you've got to stay strong for the girls. They look to you for how to react to this craziness." I say. "I'm here for you, though; you can fall apart on me any time. Want to know a secret?"

"What?" she asks.

"Connor and I did it last night," I say excitedly.

"YOU DID WHAT?" Marnie shrieks a bit too loud. We sit in silence for a moment making sure no one is coming to check on us.

"Yep, we came close in the park the day everything happened. We are on the way back to the house to, you know, when Ethan was already there. Yesterday I decided I'd had enough of being good, of sacrificing fun for the future. The future doesn't matter anymore, does it? Scholarships don't matter, grades don't matter, being good doesn't matter. I think of all that mom missed in terms of having friends and having fun. The hours she worked so I could chase my dreams, the miles she drove, it was worthless, all of it meaningless. So, I decided, I want this experience, I want to be that close to Connor, and I went for it." I say

"Okay, first, you know your mom loved every minute of that right. She loved that you seamlessly assumed her dreams as your own, and they were truly your own, you didn't do it for her. She loved every mile driven; she loved every success and failure. She would never have traded a minute of it for anything. She was so proud of you, Rae. And second, what the hell, did you use protection?"

"Nope, didn't even think about it," I answer.

"Rae, this is not the time to be getting pregnant. The world has ended in case you haven't noticed." Marnie says, again a bit too loudly.

"We're fine. I'm super early in my cycle. But point taken, we'll definitely be more careful in the future." I concede.

"How was it?" She asks.

"AMAZING, never in my life could I have imagined it like that," I say.

"Wow, just wow." She says. "Ethan and I have kissed, gotten a little handsy, but that is all. I do love sleeping with his arms around me. It brings comfort I don't think I'd find otherwise in these times. That is until the girls get scared and I have to go to them. I ended up sleeping in their room from sometime around one o'clock on."

"Bummer. Do you think they'll settle in?" I ask.

"Not sure, they've had a traumatic experience. Not only did they lose their parents, they saw them taken, and then they were nearly taken themselves. That is a lot to deal with at any age, let alone at their ages." She says. "Joanie is a blessing, being a tweener she is enough of an authority to keep them in line but young enough to be able to play on their level. I don't think I could do this without her," She finishes.

"I worry about her; she's been so quiet through all of this. She's never known her dad, and she lost her mom with mine. Connor had been crying when we woke up yesterday. I know he is anxious about his dad and sisters in Texas, but what can he do? There is no way to get in touch with them," I say.

"Wait, Joanie and Connor don't have the same dad?" she asks.

"Nope, the red hair comes from his mom's side. She had a brief relationship after the divorce from his dad that produced Joanie. I guess the guy didn't want to be a dad and split," I answer.

"Wow, that is tough. At least she has Connor," Marnie says.

"Yes." We stare out the windows in silence.

The day passes at a moderate pace, better than I had hoped. We find one of the master bedrooms on the first floor has a large TV and a good selection of DVDs. Marnie and I spend the day laying on the king-size bed, Willis curled up between us, watching musicals and comedies. It was just the lift we needed.

At lunchtime we make a meal of ground beef, mixed up with macaroni, green beans, and corn. The boys surface long enough to eat, then return to their post as lookout. Once lunch is cleaned up, Marnie and I head back to the TV. Joanie and the girls go upstairs this time to 'play spy' with Ethan and Connor. I think the girls play spy; Joanie takes a nap. After clearing it with the boys, I take Willis out between movies around 4. The air is clearing, the sun is shining more brightly, that is at least a good thing.

For dinner, we simply reheat lunch leftovers making it an easy meal. Once dinner is cleaned up, we play cards at the table with the girls. Playing go fish is a fun mindless way to pass the time. The dull blue lantern light makes cheating easy. I'm fairly certain that Christy was hoarding cards. Finally, the girls are getting sleepy, Marnie takes them up to put them to bed. Joanie follows to get a shower and go to bed herself.

"I'll be up to tuck you in a bit Joanie," Connor calls behind her.

"Yeah, yeah, I'm fine. I've got the munchkins to keep me company," she calls back down the stairs after him.

"So, what'd you guys learn today?" I ask timidly.

"Not a lot. There was some movement at the base of the mountain towards town, right where we came through. We couldn't tell if it was the gremlin-like creatures or not. There is an odd area over that way," he says, pointing to the South, "where the woods are oddly thinned. It's nothing like the devastation of a lost city but certainly is not as full as you'd expect. We're kind of focusing on that area." Ethan reports.

"We did see some wildlife, so if anyone knows how to hunt, we'll have fresh meat," Connor reports.

"What of it Texas boy, don't you know how to hunt?" I tease.

"It has been a long time since I've hunted. I've been in Ohio the past three hunting seasons, never could get momma interested," he says with an air of sadness.

"I want to make a log," Ethan interrupts our banter, "of all we know so far. It is easy as time passes to miss some details or embellish others."

"Okay. Well, we know we saw the creature at the Quarry,

going on, geez, three weeks ago now," I say.

"They don't speak English well at all and have a distinct accent," Connor adds.

"Then, of course, the experience you had in Europe," I add.

"That is already well documented," Ethan responds.

"Yea, at a base that no longer exists," I say.

"No, I have my own record here," Ethan answers holding up his notebook. In the dull blue light, the notebook appears to be half full of writing. "Okay, so we've seen no sign of them moving about at night," he says.

"Other than those balls of lights shooting over," I correct.

"True. And the gunshot we heard near dawn could have been a sign of their presence," he adds.

"It was night when they walked through the used car lot," I add.

"We know from Marnie's sisters' experience, it was about two hours after the explosion in Lexington before they came to the house," Connor interjects.

"In that instance, what they saw was what appeared to be men forcing people from their homes with small silver guns," Ethan adds.

"But we don't know where they took them or for what purpose," I say.

"What else can we say we know?" Ethan asks.

"Those silver things absolutely obliterate to nothing whatever they shoot at," Connor adds, "the hay they hit became nothing, similar to the cities they destroy."

"They don't seem terribly smart, either. Any human would have known we were in that barn. Would have searched the car, looked closer at the hay." I say.

"True, we were lucky at that point, they were not so attentive," Marnie says, coming down the stairs.

"And in the car at the car lot, the car's windows were the only ones in the lot with condensation on them, but they didn't look in the car even though they were standing right beside it," I add.

"That's at least something," Connors says.

"But how can something that unobservant conquer an entire planet," Ethan muses.

"Unless somewhere else is the brains behind the operation," Connor suggests.

"So what, terrorism using mutant gremlin minions?" Marnie asks with a chuckle despite trying to be serious.

"Who knows," Ethan says, staring off into space, becoming lost in his thoughts.

When no one comes up with anything to add, I decide it is bedtime, "I'm going to take a shower, the hot water should be recovered by now."

CHAPTER 23 AWKWARD

I step out of the shower and bundle up in a beach towel I brought from home, wrapping a second towel around my hair. I head into the bedroom, unsure what to wear to bed, I finally settle for my ratty T-shirt and bike shorts.Willis has already centered himself in the center of the bed.

"Willis," I say, "you're going to have to learn to share with Connor." As if he understands English, he gives me one of his supposed to be fierce but utterly adorable snarls. "Nice try buddy, but you've got to share."

I brush out my hair, braid it down my back, then climb under the covers. I've replaced the green quilt on the bed with my favorite heavy blue quilt I brought from home. I lay on my left side, facing away from the bathroom, with Willis tucked in against my stomach. Moments later, Connor emerges from the bathroom. Already dressed in boxers, he slides under the blankets and wraps his arms protectively around me. His nose skims along my neck. He kisses my neck, my ear, and neck again, but his hands remain still tight around my waist. "Goodnight, beautiful," he quietly whispers in my ear, "I love you."

"Goodnight, handsome," I tell him. I drift off into a peaceful sleep.

"Where is this place?" I ask, so weak I can hardly stand, my body is in a great deal of pain; the ice-cold water I am laying in is both painful and soothing.

"We're in an underground camp the shifters have created," the man is telling me. Rick, I think he said his name is Rick.

"Why do they have us here?" I ask. "What will they do to us?"

"Don't worry about that right now, for now, we need to make you strong again."

"I feel so miserable." I moan in a soft whisper. That is all I can manage.

"I know," he says, "that is part of their process, everyone here has been through it, though I have to say, you had it worse than any we've seen. Now Reagan," he continues.

I look up at him, startled "how...how do you know my name" I stammer out.

"I do know your name," he says, then he leans in under the guise of washing my wounds to whisper quietly in my ear, protecting our conversation from the creature guarding us. "There is someone here that knows you. In a stroke of luck, you will be in our cell with this person. I know this because they chose me to clean you up. They rarely deviate from their routines."

It's him, I think, is it Don, did they really catch Don? He really is okay, well as okay as you could be here.

"But I have to warn you," he says fiercely in his whisper, "do not show any familiarity when they are around. We are guarded well enough by their barriers; they typically disappear for the entire night. It will be safe to speak then but showing familiarity in front of them will only cause you both trouble. Do you understand?" He asks, the warning on his face is real. I give a weak nod in response.

I jerk up out of my sleep feeling completely panicked.

"What is it?" Connor asks, instantly worried and scanning the room for trouble.

"Bad dream again. I was in some underground camp or

prison the creatures created. I was injured and starving," I say, trying to shake off the chills left behind from the terrible dream.

"You're okay Rae, I am sure it is just the nerves and pressure of the situation we're facing," Connor says, consoling me. "You're safe, I've got you and will not let anything happen to you."

Connor squeezes me tight to him, then gently presses his lips to my temple. I do feel instantly calmed, though my breathing has yet to return to normal. I roll towards him, looking deep into his eyes in the blue lantern light. I see trouble behind his eyes, is it the fear my dream instilled in both of us, or is it something more?

Pure emotion takes over my actions. I reach up, grabbing his neck, pulling him into me, crushing my lips to his. He kisses me back with passion, moving his hands up from my waist, wrapping behind my neck. I roll to my back, and he rolls, so his weight is upon me. We continue to kiss, covered in this embrace. When we are lying still after he speaks first, "I didn't mean for that to happen again, I think we should have waited, we used this situation as an excuse, we shouldn't have crossed that line."

"Connor none of that matters anymore. The world has ended, life has ended. There are no more scholarships, no more futures. All we have is now," I say, voicing the frustrations that led me to cross the line in the first place.

"We have eternity. Beyond this world, we face one judge, what do we say then?" he asks.

"That we're human, that we're scared and make mistakes," I say. "You were certainly willing to have sex with me before all of this happened," I say accusatorily.

He has no response; he just looks at me. "Connor, I love you.

You are my other half. There is no doubt in my mind that God created you for me and me for you. Had the world continued as it was supposed to, it would have been you and me forever. Now you have no choice. There is no one else," I add, attempting to lighten the situation with humor.

"Rae, this is not a joking matter," he says earnestly. "I was sure I was going to marry Alicia."

Interesting, I think I've never heard her name before this. "Yeah, well, that didn't stop you in Janelle's driveway, or at the park after school," I say, getting really annoyed. "What is it now that you suddenly think this is a bad idea?"

"It's just, with all that is happening," he says slowly. "I started thinking about what happens if we die. What legacy will I leave behind? What will I say when I face my final judge," he says.

"I don't know Connor; perhaps that is something you should have thought about before you started driving me mad in the park," I spit out, getting angry now. "I love you; you are the one for me, the ONLY" I stress "one I've been with or will be with. There is no church to be married in, no future to promise. I do not regret it." I say. I get up, storming out of the bedroom to the bathroom.

While I clean up, washing my face in the sink, all I can think is what the hell, the nerve of him. I brush my teeth, use the toilet, and head back out into the room. Connor is still in bed, staring blankly at the ceiling. I dress quickly, call to Willis, who is sleeping on a pillow on the floor to follow. Once he meets me at the door, I scoop him up, heading across the hall to descend the stairs. What a weird turn last night took.

Once I get downstairs I realize it is still quite early. Though the sun is rising, no one is stirring yet. I quietly take Willis into the garage, slowly opening the door against the mountainside, letting him wander out to pee. I never leave the garage. As soon as he is done, I drag him back inside.

I head to the kitchen. After searching the refrigerator, I do not find much. Turning to the coolers, I find sausage links. I start the range and begin heating a pan. Once I have the sausages sizzling on the skillet, I rummage through the cabinets finding cereal and donuts we procured along the way. I laugh humorlessly at this meal I am preparing; what a combination.

The smell of cooking sausages makes its way upstairs, slowly bring people out of their slumber. Marnie descends the stairs first. Seeing the look on my face, she rushes to me, "Rae?" she questions, "what's up?"

Before I can answer, Ethan and Joanie come traipsing down the stairs as well.

"Smells good, Rae," Ethan says.

"Well, today's breakfast is a doozy," I say, "sausage, donuts, and dry cereal."

"Way to sell it, Rae," Marnie laughs.

Eventually, all the inhabitants emerge for breakfast. The girls are a bit cranky this morning, crabbing about the sausage and that the donuts aren't chocolate.

"What's up with them?" I ask Marnie.

"NONE of them," she says, stressing the 'none' "slept much last night. I see naps in their future," she says with a sigh. "Don't get me wrong, I am grateful they are here and safe, but geez."

"I get it," I say.

"Marnie and I will take first watch upstairs today; I think she needs a break from the girls," Ethan announces. "Joanie, can you keep an eye on the girls?"

"Sure," Joanie announces, sounding a bit annoyed but willing.

"Okay, after lunch Reagan and Connor can take watch," he finishes.

Great a morning with grumpy, I think to myself. Marnie and Ethan head upstairs and I busy myself cleaning up breakfast. At the same time, Connor wanders to the windows to look outside unseeingly. Once breakfast is cleaned up, I really have nothing to do to occupy my time, so I join the girls working a puzzle at the table. Once I arrive, Joanie gets up and retreats to the couch with a book. We're going to need to find some sort of routine for these girls before they make everyone crazy. Sitting at the table I grab a pen and paper to start sketching out a schedule to keep the girls occupied. Once complete, I set this aside, I will propose it to Marnie when she and Ethan return.

"I'm going upstairs," I announce, so Joanie knows she'll need to keep watch after the girls. I make my way to the bedroom where Ethan and Marnie are keeping watch, knocking before entering. Marnie sleeping quietly on the bed while Ethan trains his binoculars on the valley below.

"I'm starting to see a lot of activity to the south near that thin spot," he says. "But just more of what we know, the gremlin looking creatures, and the odd-looking humans." Ethan hands me the binoculars. For a moment, I peer down on the space in question, seeing the same as his assessment.

"Has Connor been up here?" I ask.

"No, why, did you two have a fight?" Ethan asks.

"Not really, he's just being really weird," I answer. "What's the activity been like around here? Can I take Willis for a walk?"

"That should be fine," Ethan says. "I've seen no activity anywhere near here, and no one seems to be looking this way either. They are focused on whatever is happening over there," he finishes pointing at the area of interest to the South.

"Cool," I mumble, walking away. I briefly consider waking Marnie to come with me so I can unload about Connor's strange behavior. I quickly decide to let her rest. She did look exhausted this morning.

CHAPTER 24 DISCOVERY

I wander downstairs, pick Willis up off the couch, putting on his harness and leash. He is excited as he limps along toward the door. I head out through the garage, grateful for the fresh air that hits me when I step through the door into the sunlight. Here, sandwiched between the back of the house and the mountain, there is little chance of being seen unless someone was actually back here with me, in which case we'd be caught anyway. I let Willis wander along slowly as he searches for the perfect place to relieve himself.

I stop just before reaching the outcropping of rock that protects the Southeast corner of the house from being seen. I lean back against the mountainside but instead find myself falling backward. I stifle a scream as I fall. I land hard on my backside in a dark cave-like tunnel. I sit frozen, taking a moment to orient myself to what has happened.

From the light filtering in, I can see an opening in the rock hidden by vines and a dark green mesh. Given the camouflage, I am assuming Don's family created this, whatever it is. Rising, I turn on the flashlight on my phone. Taking a few steps forward, I see a crude ladder anchored in the mountain in front of me. I tether Willis to the end of the ladder and start climbing. I climb for what seems like forever, though I am sure it is only a minute or two when I come to a bit of a platform carved within the rock. This too is encased carefully in green netting and vines looking like any other part of the mountain. Anyone behind the mesh would not be visible below. From here, you have a three-hundred-and-sixty-degree view of the surrounding areas. I spend a few minutes getting my bearings, realizing that I have trouble locating the cabin even from here. They did an excellent job hiding that place. Still, I can just make out the cabin below after orienting myself to the direction I am facing.

I look around one final time before beginning my descent. I need to get back before anyone misses me or Willis starts barking. Going down seems to go much faster. I am eager to get inside and tell Ethan about this find. I reach the bottom. After untying Willis, I head back in through the garage.

When I enter the living room, everyone is assembled there looking anxious.

"Where have you been?" Ethan questions angrily, "we were about to send out a search party."

"Sorry, hadn't realized I had been gone that long, but come see what I've found," I say enthusiastically.

I hand Willis off to Joanie then Connor, Ethan and Marnie follow me back out of the house to the opening hidden in the side of the mountain. "Don's family must have made this," I say, pushing aside the netting so they can see inside. I lead the way in; once inside, I ascend the ladder emerging again in the hidden watchtower above. Slowly, one by one, they join me there.

"Wow," Marnie says, "this view is spectacular."

"This is a great vantage point," Ethan remarks, "I assumed by watchtower Don meant the upstairs windows. I had no idea they actually created a watchtower. As long as the weather cooperates, we'll take watch up here from now on."

After spending a little more time looking around, we head back down the ladder to have lunch. We make a quick lunch of canned vegetables and burger patties. Connor produces a second pair of binoculars he discovered in the basement during his aimless wandering this morning. When we are done, I leave Marnie to take a turn cleaning up the dishes while

Connor and I head out the back to the watchtower. Once at the top, I lay on my stomach, looking to the South. You get a slightly different view from this angle. However, you still cannot see any identifiable compound or camp to understand why the creatures are congregating in that area.

Connor moves around a bit, taking time looking in all directions. The silence between us is prolonged and awkward. What is with him, I wonder. Finally, Connor comes to lay beside me training his binoculars to the same place.

"Rae, I'm sorry. I know I'm acting like a jerk. I used to think of myself as so mature and grown, but I am not. Throughout this whole experience, I have been a mess inside. I worry about my family, I cry silently for my mother, I don't trust anything I am feeling..." he trails off.

"Connor it's okay. None of us were prepared to deal with this. How could we be? We've all lost so much in such a short time. We have no real path forward; we are safe for the moment, but what happens when the food runs low." I say. "I totally get it, but please, rely on me, don't push me away."

"I am so worried about my family...Whoa, did you see that?" he says, urgently pointing to the South.

"Yes, what was that? I thought that was one of the creatures." I say.

"They're shapeshifters," he says warily; when he says Shifter, it triggers something in my mind, a memory I can't quite put my finger on. I feel like I should already know that is what they are called.

"Shapeshifters?" I ask.

"Yeah, in science fiction, something that can assume a different shape or form. Did you see that shimmer? Another one just did it." He exclaims in wonder.

"They are definitely not from this world," I say, watching. We continue silently watching, holding our breath even though they are nowhere near us or the least bit interested in us. Then, where one of the gremlin-like creatures is standing, an odd shimmering is undulating in the air for maybe 30 seconds or less. Once it stops, in the same place, there stands one of the odd-looking guys we've seen accompanying the creatures. Connor and I turn to stare at each other in horror.

"That is creepy," is all I can think to say.

Connor trades me the ordinary binoculars he has for the high-powered binoculars Ethan brought from the base. He spends time studying the creatures below. "I don't think that is dirt behind their ears. It seems like some sort of remnant of their original form," he says.

The trio of shifters heads off toward the town below. "Search mission, you think?" I ask Conor.

"Not sure. I wonder if Ethan has seen anything like this?" I speculate.

"Certainly, he would have told us if he had," Connor says with confidence.

We continue our watch focused on the area to the South. There is little activity for several hours. One of them occasionally comes out from behind the trees to wander about. The day begins to fade to evening, we see the trio returning with two completely terrified looking humans walking in front of them. They have those silver weapons pointed toward them as they walk along. The couple seems to be a middle-aged man and woman. They continue on into a small cluster of trees then disappear from sight.

"I just don't understand where they are going. They always disappear behind that cluster of trees." Connor says, irritated.

"It would make sense," I add, "if beyond there was evidence

of anything, but it is so thin you'd see some sort of camp or compound."

We are silent as we focus on the place where they disappeared. We do not see any others emerge throughout the time we are there. Finally, it is really starting to get dark. We need to make our way back down to the cabin before we can't find our way. It is not hard, but I imagine trying to scale the ladder in total darkness will be difficult. Moving from my position, I realize I have remained still far too long, every part of my body aches. "Ouch," I say, stretching, "I guess we should have moved a bit more today." I look over. Connor nods while rubbing his back.

We descend the stairs in silence, both absorbed in our thoughts around what we've just witnessed. We have a lot to add to the log tonight. We find the garage door effortlessly even though night has fallen. Before stepping through, I take a long look at the stars above.

"Thought you two fell asleep up there," Marnie says with a wink as we make our way into the kitchen.

"No, but we do have some significant discoveries to add to the journal tonight," I say in return. "Today we saw..." but I trail off as Joanie, Marie, Christy and Kenz emerge from the basement, "later," I finish.

Just then, Ethan comes down the stairs running his hands through his wet hair. "I thought I'd get my shower in earlier before all the hot water is gone," he announces.

"Smart," I say.

"You guys see anything interesting today?" He asks.

"Yeah, we've got quite a few interesting observations to add to the journal tonight," Connor says.

"What did you see?" Marie asks as we suspected, paying a

bit too much attention to the conversation.

Connor sneaks up behind her, taking her by surprise, scooping her off her feet "we saw bears," he says.

"Really?" Christy asks.

"Sure did," he says, lying smoothly.

"Well, you're just in time. Dinner is ready, I make no promises, but it's the best I can do with what we have," Marnie says.

We sit down to an odd meal. Marnie has somehow fashioned a pie out of bread, rehydrated dried beans, and some random vegetables.

"This really isn't half bad Marnie, kudos to you," I say, actually enjoying the meal immensely.

"Thanks," she says, "sometimes you just have to get creative. By the way, I found this," she adds, holding up the schedule I made earlier for the girls. "Pure genius, I think giving them some routine and structure will help them settle in a bit better. We can take turns making up the worksheets for the school portion."

"Thanks, a moment of inspiration in desperation," I say.

After the meal is finished, the boys take the lead on cleaning up dinner while Marnie and I set up for a quick game of Go Fish with the girls. After a few rounds, Marnie announces bath time for the girls. Before heading upstairs she says, "save the details until I return," looking at us menacingly.

While we wait for Marnie's return Connor, Ethan, and I start a game of Twenty-One. None of us are hardly paying attention to what we are doing or how the game is going. Soon, after setting a world record for speed of a bath, Marnie returns down the stairs. "Alright, spill it. What did you guys see up there today?" She demands.

"They're shapeshifters," Connor blurts out.

"What, they're what? That isn't possible," Marnie protests hastily.

"No, it's true. We were both watching from the tower down to the South, where they congregate. We saw a trio of the creatures standing there. There was an odd shimmering in the air it lasted about thirty seconds each. Then standing in the exact space was what appeared to be a human," Connor explains.

"They have to be aliens," I add, "there is no way they've existed somewhere on this planet."

"Wouldn't the military or NASA or someone have noticed if we were being invaded? Like, they had to come in on some kind of spaceships, right?" Marnie questions looking at Ethan now for a response.

"In theory, but who knows what kind of technology they have. They are capable of destroying entire cities, leaving no trace of the city or inhabitants behind. We saw their little guns do something similar on a much smaller scale in the barn. Maybe those little balls of light planes can somehow go undetected on the radar, or they found a weak link, some sort of hole in the observation between satellites," he muses.

"We know they can take down our communications completely. Perhaps they can do a similar temporary jam when entering the atmosphere. There are a lot of ways around, unfortunately. A bit of chatter occurred a few years ago about odd occurrences, strange lights, and radar disturbances. Still, no one ever made anything out of it. Like I said, this was a few years back, so I don't think it is related to these creatures, but you can see the system isn't perfect." Ethan finishes his dissertation with a sigh.

"I guess," Marnie responds.

"We also saw them capture two humans," I add. "A man and

a woman, they got to that strange cluster of trees before the forest thins and disappeared. Even from that vantage point, I still can't make out any kind of a camp or compound or anything to explain where they go."

"We'll have to keep our eyes peeled and see if we can see any sign of those two in the future. It might be interesting to note in our log," Connor adds.

"Yea," Ethan adds absently. "Marnie, let's head up to bed. You should get some sleep before the girls start having bad dreams again."

"That's probably a good idea, night guys." She says, giving me an unsure look. We never did get a chance today to discuss the issues Connor and I are facing.

I look over at Connor, looking once again unseeingly through the windows into the dark night. I sigh, not knowing where we stand. Getting up, I walk over to the couch and pick up Willis, "I'm going to let him out quickly before heading up to bed." I announce.

"K" is the only response I get.

I take Willis through the garage, once again allowing him to go out but not leaving the building myself. As soon as he's done I drag him back inside by his leash and harness, locking the door behind me. When I get back in the kitchen, Connor has already gone upstairs. Well, alrighty then, I think to myself. I dim the lanterns, so they are barely burning, pick Willis up and head up the stairs. "I wonder how long your leg needs to heal," I say absently to Willis, "people I think are usually 4-6 weeks, I've heard. It's going to be a long couple of weeks if I have to keep dragging your butt up and down the stairs." He just looks at me expectantly with that sweet face. I kiss his forehead and hold him tight, "I am so glad you are here, buddy. I couldn't do this without you."

When I get to our room, Connor is in the shower already. I change into my ratty t-shirt and remove my pants. I climb under my quilt, curling up on my side, holding Willis tight to me. I am starting to drift off to sleep when Connor comes in from the shower. He doesn't say anything but slides into bed behind me, wrapping his arms protectively around me. He kisses me softly then whispers, "I love you, Rae, good night" before leaning his head back to his pillow.

"I love you too, Connor, please, never shut me out. I want to be here for you," I answer.

He says nothing but squeezes me even tighter. I decide he'll open up when he is ready. I drift off to sleep.

The next morning Connor seems to be in a better mood when we wake. I find I am laying across his chest with my head on his shoulder. He is looking down at me with those piercing blue eyes. "Morn'n," he greets me, "sleep well?"

"Yes," I say, "it was very nice, no bad dreams."

"Good."

"And you?" I ask.

"Can't complain. It was a nice night." At the end of this statement, he leans down, kissing me with great urgency and passion. The kiss is not long, but it is very satisfying.

"Thank you," I say, "I needed that." I lean in, kissing him once on the lips, then get up and head into the shower. Once I'm clean, I step out of the shower, head into the bedroom, and dress for the day. My hair is so unmanageable with the randomness of the shampoos and conditioners we have here I give up and slap it into a ponytail once again today.

When I get downstairs, everyone is at the table eating dry cereal. "Yummy," I say, looking at the selection of cereal boxes on the table. I reach down, picking a box at random, and begin munching. "So, what's the schedule for today?" I ask.

"Rae, I thought you and I could take first watch," Ethan announces. "Marnie is going to work on getting the girls on that schedule you created. They lasted a bit longer last night but still had fits overnight. Then after lunch, Connor and I can take the second watch."

"You sure you want to be up there twice?" I ask.

"Yea, I really want to see if I can get a handle on what is going on down there." He says, but personally, I think he just wants to get away from Marnie's sisters for the day. They were a handful yesterday.

Since there isn't much to clean up from breakfast, Ethan and I quickly pack a backpack with water and granola bars, then head out through the garage to the back of the house. Ethan looks out the door and listens for a few minutes before declaring it safe to move ahead.

We walk along behind the house, climb the dark ladder to emerge at the top of the tower. The view from here really is spectacular.

We set up similar to the approach Connor and I took yesterday. I lay on my stomach, watching the South while Ethan moves about looking in all directions. "Ethan," I whisper loudly. "Come here. Some are coming out of that cluster."

As we watch, three emerge from the cluster of trees, two creatures, and one looking human. "The human-looking one has the marks behind its ears," Ethan notes.

"Connor thinks that is some leftover remnant of the shift," I say quietly. Though we are far enough away we could probably yell and not be detected, somehow, I cannot bring myself to do more than a whisper.

From behind them come three more people. "Hey," Ethan

says, "I think those are humans. They don't have the lines behind the ears."

"Really?" I question, my binoculars are not quite powerful enough to see that much detail.

We continue watching when we see a silver ball zoom across the sky, slowing down and dropping to the ground in front of them.

"They look terrified," Ethan says, commenting on the situation. From the aircraft, what we assume is a shifter emerges. It walks to stand in front of the three humans assembled there, two men and one woman. It looks them over intently. He has words with the creatures standing around, then points to two of them. The two he pointed at, one man and one woman, are led back into the cluster of trees. There is a struggle as they force the remaining man toward the aircraft. Finally, one touches the back of his head with some sort of metal rod, he freezes and is lifted into the aircraft.

"What the hell did they just do to him?" I ask Ethan.

"I don't know, those metal rods must produce a shock or something that paralyzed his central nervous system or something," he says.

We continue watching, the three shifters remain outside the trees, the one affecting a human appearance shimmers into nothingness and reappears as a creature once again. Ethan drops his binoculars. Looking at me, he says, "I didn't think you were joking, but until you see it yourself..." he trails off.

"By far, the craziest thing I've ever seen," I say.

There is not much activity after that, though we watch way past the lunch switch. At what we guess to be one or two in the afternoon, we head back down for lunch. Inside the house, it is obvious Marnie was anxious "there you two are. I was getting worried."

"Sorry Mar," Ethan says, "got caught up in watching. I saw the shift. These things are somehow able to take multiple forms. We'll have to be careful to watch closely to see if there are any other forms they take." He says the last part as though he is just thinking out loud to himself.

"Where are the girls?" I ask.

"They're having quiet time in their room; it was on your schedule, and it is brilliant." She says with a smile.

"I agree," says Joanie from the couch. I had not even noticed her lying there.

"Joanie, seriously, thank you for all your help and all you are doing." Marnie says honestly, "you are truly keeping me sane."

"Don't mention it," she says with an air of attitude "what else do I have to do right now."

None of us are quite sure what to say, so we just move on from the conversation. "Connor, have you eaten yet?" I ask.

"Yes," he answers me, then turns to address Ethan. "I'm ready to head up whenever you had a chance to eat."

"Sounds good," Ethan says through a mouthful of another Marnie casserole creation. That girl has cooking skills.

Connor stands staring out the window again. I walk up, wrapping my hands around his waist, resting my head against his back. "Whatcha thinking about over here," I ask, knowing I may not want to know the answer.

"Just thinking about where these things came from, and why they chose our planet," he says.

Okay, not quite what I was expecting him to say, but indeed a reasonable thought. I swing around to face him from the front, staring into his deep blue eyes. I lean up and kiss his lips. At first, he is a bit rigid but then kisses me back. We kiss several times when Joanie clears her throat "ugh guys get a room," she jokes.

"Ready, Connor?" Ethan asks.

"Yep, just let me disentangle myself from your sister," he jokes, leaning in to give me one more kiss. Okay, things are looking better here.

Once Connor and Ethan head up to the watchtower, I go to the kitchen to help Marnie clean up. "So," Marnie starts, "what's up with you two love birds?" she asks.

"I wish I knew. The first full night here we had an amazing night," I whisper, wanting to keep this conversation from Joanie's ears. "The second night when he came to bed, we just snuggled and fell asleep, no big deal. I had a horrible dream that night. I was captured by those creatures. They kept me in an underground cavern and tortured me. There was a guy there, I don't remember what he said his name was, Randy maybe, I don't know. Anyhow, I digress from the real issue." I say all of this very quickly without even taking a breath. "Anyhow, I woke up so emotional, when he kissed me, instincts took over, and we did it again in the middle of the night. I wake up the next morning, and he says it is a mistake we never should have done it in the first place. He didn't want it to happen again." I finish looking at Marnie, exasperated. "Yesterday, up on the tower, he apologized, told me that he's just stressed, worried about his family in Texas, and just not managing it well. I, of course, understand, but I need him too right now. Am I selfish?"

"I don't think so, but I think you'll have to be patient. He talked about his family in Texas a lot today while you were on lookout." Marnie says.

"I'm terrified he is going to go off to try to find them," I say, voicing the fear that has been gnawing at me for a few days now.

"That's crazy. How would he ever even find them." Marnie says, dismissing the thought, "besides, Joanie is here. He can't leave the one living family member he knows he has."

"Yeah, I keep holding on to that thought," I say.

We busy ourselves around the cabin cleaning, reorganizing the food in the cabinets, refrigerator, and coolers, inventorying what we have to plan meals. We need to be strategic to make our food last as long as possible, so no one has to go on a mission to find more. Connor and Ethan return at dusk, indicating that the rest of the day was quiet and nothing to report. After a quick meal of spaghetti, we begin our nightly ritual of cards with the girls.

CHAPTER 25 THE MITCHELLS

We've been at the cabin four days now. While starting our game in the blue lantern light, we hear a vehicle coming up the mountainside. It is entirely dark outside but just recently became that dark. We dim the one blue lantern we have burning at the table where we sit. We assume it is not the enemies we observed earlier today since whoever it is, is driving a car. We have yet to see them drive, but we don't want to invite any dangers strangers may pose if they stumble upon this place. The cabin is so well camouflaged they would have to literally run into it to see it this late at night. "I am sure it is just Don or his family," Ethan says, trying to calm us, "I'd have thought he'd be here before now."

It takes a good twenty minutes, but we finally hear the garage door open. Ethan, confident it is his friend, turns the blue lantern light back up, so we are visible when he enters this room. A few minutes later, the door to the garage goes down. Don will have seen our car in the garage already, so he knows we are here. The door between the kitchen and garage opens, "Ethan?" we hear a deep booming voice ask.

"Don," Ethan sighs in relief, "I assumed that would be you but wasn't sure." Ethan rises, meeting Don in the kitchen. They shake hands and briefly engage in a one-armed embrace clapping each other on the back. Behind Don steps an older woman, probably the same age as my mom would be.

"Where's the rest of the family?" Ethan asks Don cautiously.

"They were in the city. Dad had taken Tash and Ralph to the orthodontist of all things," he says sadly, his booming voice quieting slightly. "When I got there, the neighborhood was intact. I got mama out, it took some persuasive convincing but we headed back this way."

"That's too bad man," Ethan responds, "mom was in Downtown Cincinnati as well. Her last day she had to work down there too."

"I see you found at least a few," Don responds, nodding to the group of us huddled around the dining table.

"Yes, this is my sister Reagan. Most people call her Rae, her boyfriend Connor, and his sister Joanie. Their mom was working with ours in the same office building. And this here is Martina." Says Ethan. The way he says her name I know he is expecting what happens next.

"Oh, this is the infamous Marnie," says Don knowingly. "Girl, you are all he ever talks about," he continues causing both Ethan and Marnie blush.

"And who are these little rug rats?" Don inquires, looking at Marnie's sisters.

"These are Marnie's sisters Marie, Christy, and McKenzie," Ethan finishes the introductions. "Marnie's parents were taken in Lexington. Her sisters were able to hide in a closet undetected. Marie told us the story of mostly what happened there. I'll share more details sometime when they are asleep," he finishes.

"Well, y'all are most welcome here. I'm Major LeDonatello Mitchell, Army Rangers, well if there was an Army anymore," he introduces himself. "This is my mama, Dr. LeWanda Mitchell. She thought it'd be cute to name all us kids 'Le' something since that is how her name starts. I think she had a thing for Renaissance artists too because I'm LeDonatello and my brother was LeRaphael, they don't even fit together. I used to get slapped by my daddy so often for suggesting that's why she named us the way she did. Anyhow, I prefer to be called Don." He finishes his long-winded introduction.

I like him instantly, totally understanding why Ethan was drawn to him as a friend. He is a down to earth kind of guy with an infectious personality. He is not bad to look at either, I add to myself. His skin is perfectly smooth, like dark chocolate. His army buzz cut perfectly accentuates his sharp facial features, strong jawline and cheekbones. He is obviously a bit older than us, guessing he's in his late twenties maybe. "We'd have been here yesterday, but I saw all sorts of strange things out there. I decided to lay low yesterday during the day in a house on Knoxville's outskirts. The neighborhood had been ransacked, there wasn't a soul around."

"Hello," I say, rising to cross the room and shake his hand.

"Ma'am," he says in return greeting, reminding me so much of the way Connor greets someone new. Don's southern drawl is very muted from years in the service, away from his home in the South.

Then I address his mom, "Hello Dr. Mitchell, it is nice to meet you, thank you for sharing your home with us," I say.

"Call me Wanda dear," she says sweetly, "I am just glad to have the house full. It makes my heart happy." She has a few tears in her eyes as she speaks. Wanda is much shorter than her son but incredibly attractive. Like her son, she has well defined facial features. She is a bit plump in her short stature but well proportioned, her dark black hair shows signs of graying around her temples, but her face is youthful.

"A doctor, wow, that's handy to have at the end of the world," Ethan asserts.

"Oh, sweetie, I won't be much help to you. I'm a retired veterinarian," she answers.

"OH!" I shriek, making everyone jump a little, "after you've had a chance to get settled will you take a look at Willis' leg? He hurt it when we had an unfortunate run-in with some... shifters," I finish.

"Shifters?" Don questions.

"Later," Ethan says, looking pointedly at the girls staring on intently at the greeting.

"Oh sure," Don responds.

"Who is Willis?" Wanda asks.

"My Boston Terrier. He fell a long distance; I think his leg is broken," I explain. "We have him bandaged, for now. Get settled. It will keep until you've had a chance to rest." As if on cue, Willis comes limping around the girls, excitedly greeting Wanda and Don.

"Well, aren't you the cutest thing," she says, "I'm glad we've got at least one friend here."

"Don't you have any pets at home?" I ask.

"No, Tash and Ralph were about to graduate high school. After our last dog passed of old age, we decided not to get another, so Denver and I could do some traveling." She explains, with evident sadness in her voice and expression. Don walks over to his mom and rubs her back in a consoling manner.

"Well," Ethan breaks in, "there's some leftover Spaghetti in the fridge, and the water is hot if you want showers. We've also got bottled water and sodas loaded in the fridge."

"I could go for a diet soda, please, Don," Wanda tells her son, moving over toward the couch.

"We've moved in upstairs," Ethan explains, "so you guys can have the master rooms downstairs."

"That's nice," Wanda responds, "my arthritis is getting a bit bad, not having to climb those stairs every day will be a blessing."

Wanda makes her way over to the couch. Once she is seated, Willis attempts to jump into her lap. Christy lifts him up, placing him next to Wanda. The girls return to their game of Go Fish while the 'grown-ups' retire to the living room surrounding Don and Wanda on the couch.

"How was your trip besides having to lay low today?" Ethan inquires.

"Was rather uneventful. We traveled mostly back roads steering clear of any high traffic or populated areas. Until late day before yesterday, the smaller towns were intact. Nobody even seemed to know anything was going on; this was in extremely rural places, though," Don explains. "Then, about mid-day day before yesterday, the towns we vistied were empty. The people were all just gone, just like in Europe."

"Yeah, our trek down took us through more populated areas. The towns that weren't decimated in explosions were empty after about the first night. I think we passed through a few places that were rural enough that still had people in them." Ethan explains.

"Strange things I saw out there," Don hints.

"Yeah, once the girls go to bed we'll tell you about what we've learned so far," Ethan says.

While this conversation has been going on Wanda has unwrapped Willis' leg. After a careful examination she says, "good news is I don't think it is broken. I think he just sustained a nasty knock. We can take the metal out of the brace but probably makes sense to leave it wrapped with the sticky wrap a few more days."

"Thank you," I say, "this dog has been by my side for 6 years now, we've shared a lot, and he means the world to me. I thought for sure when it happened, he was gone. But miraculously he survived."

"He is a good-looking dog," Wanda adds.

The chatter continues smoothly as the night continues; finally, it is time for the girls to go to bed. Marnie once again makes us promise not to start the 'grown-up' talk until she returns. Don heads over to a cabinet we had not yet explored. He pulls out a bottle of whiskey and offers to make us all a cocktail. Though I have never had hard liquor before, I find the whiskey and soda go down pretty easily.

"Take it easy there, Rae," Don chuckles as I take a big swig of my drink, "that's probably a little stronger than you are used to."

"Sure," I respond, taking a much smaller sip next time.

When Marnie finally returns, we all move to the dining table. Ethan pulls out his notebook to record any new information Don has to share and accurately share what we have learned over the past week. Wow, it's only been a week. That is so hard to believe as much as things have changed.

"They're shapeshifters," Ethan says bluntly, "we're hypothesizing extraterrestrial."

"Excuse me, did you say shapeshifters?" Wanda asks.

"Yes, Rae, start with your story. We'll tell you all we've seen and recorded until now. Then you can fill in any gaps with what you've observed." Ethan continues clinically. "Did you share with your mom what we experienced in Europe Don?"

"Sure did. It was the only way I was going to get her out of that darn house. We saw the destruction in Jackson as well, drove past there on our way out of town." Wanda shutters at her son's assessment, clearly disturbed by the images in her mind.

"Go ahead, Rae," Ethan encourages.

After relaying the events of our time at the Quarry, Don's only response is "creepy."

"Once the explosions started, I got home to get the family, and we started our trek South. I was super conservative in our path..." Ethan starts.

"You, overly cautious?" Don says with mock surprise, "no way, man," he says with a chuckle.

"Hey, I got us here safe, though we did have one close encounter." He pauses, "anyhow, as I was saying before, I was rudely interrupted. The first night was relatively uneventful. We were traveling down a back road somewhere in Kentucky when a large ball of light flew overhead. It was like no airplane we'd ever seen and was only flying about seventy-five feet above us. We camped out during the day but heard people talking outside our hideout; they saw two more fly over then. The next night of travel was mixed. We found some towns abandoned, some populated.

"That next night towns were largely still populated, but we were very rural. We stopped at a gas station near dawn and heard someone fire a shot off in the distance. That day our hideout was visited by the creatures like Rae described. They weren't terribly detailed in their search but were clearly looking for people. One of the girls let out a scared squeak and they heard us. That is when Willis got hurt. He jumped from behind a bale of hay. They assumed it was him that made the squeak. They pulled out some silver gun-type device, where they fired was totally obliterated. A lot like the towns and cities there was nothing left. Fortunately, Willis must have ducked behind the hay before they fired. Still, he did fall into a feed trough in the stall below where the floor was gone."

"Oh man, that was close," Don exclaims

"You have no idea; we had a hard time keeping the girls quiet. Which brings us to, on the way down we stopped in Lexington." Ethan continues his story without interruption until finishing up with our trek up here. "So, we finally got down here and have been observing every day. There is a spot to the South where the woods are thinned. There seems to be a great deal of activity around that area," Ethan continues.

"Man, that close?" Don asks.

"Not super close, but yea, they aren't far. That's when we saw the shift with our own eyes. Yesterday when Connor and Rae watched, they saw a trio of creatures come out of the trees. One by one, they changed. There was a shimmering in the air for about thirty seconds then where it stood, there was a human-looking person. Though there are brown stripes along their necks, behind their ears, we're guessing some remanent of the change." Ethan finishes.

"Man, that's crazy. How is this even possible?" Don asks.

"How is it possible that all over the world entire cities are leveled with nothing and no one left?" Ethan counters. "This brings us back to the notion of extraterrestrials. Yesterday, we saw them capture two humans. Today, an 'aircraft' landed just outside the cluster of trees down there, one person was forced on the aircraft; the others were escorted back into the clump of trees and whatever is there."

"As hard as we look, we cannot see any kind of a camp or compound of any sort," I add.

"I think that is the gist of our experience so far. Given the lack of effort or perception in their searches and general behaviors we've seen, we don't think they are too incredibly smart. Still, someone somewhere has to be pulling the strings," Ethan finishes.

"What did you guys see on your way in?" Connor asks.

"Not much different than your experience. The longer we were on the road, the more deserted towns we came across.

We saw a lot of those silver balls fly overhead," Don tells us.

"Did you travel during the day?" Marnie asks.

"Until yesterday, yes," Don answers. "Yesterday, we started seeing some odd things. A few times I thought I saw that shimmering you were talking about. I decided the risk to travel during the day was too great, so we laid low," he finishes.

We all sit in silence for a while. Don breaks the silence musing out loud, "shapeshifters, I have got to see this for myself."

"Tomorrow you and I can take the first watch in the tower. By the way, this place is amazing; you guys thought of everything." Ethan adds.

"Thank you son," Wanda says, "Denver was a planner. This is something we worked on for many years. It certainly didn't happen right away."

"It's perfect," Marnie says, giving Wanda a soft smile.

"Well kids, I sure am tired from our journey. Don, don't forget to unload the car, get that meat in here before it gets hot," Wanda says, rising to head to bed.

"What do ya think, Don?" Ethan says, "what do we do?"

"I don't think we know enough at this point. Let's observe a few more days, see what else we can figure out. For instance, they've taken many people; where do they have them all? You've seen them congregating around a specific area but see no camp. We saw no signs of activity on our way here." Don says. "Where are they all?"

"Very good questions," Ethan answers. After sitting in silence for a few minutes he continues "Mar you ready to get some shut-eye, the girls are likely to be up at least some overnight," Ethan says, rising.

"Yep. Goodnight guys," Marnie says.

"Night Mar," I answer.

"Don, do you need any help unloading the car," Connor asks.

"Nah, I've got it. I've gotten a bit of sleep today, so I'm not feeling too bad. You kids go on to bed," he dismisses us.

Connor grabs my hand, and we head up to our bedroom, hand-in-hand. I am apprehensive heading upstairs, not knowing what version of Connor I will get tonight, but I vow to myself to be patient. I know he is suffering inside. Once inside our room, he gently closes the door while I go sit on the edge of the bed. He turns to stare at me momentarily, before making his way over to the bed. He places his hands on each side of me, then leans in for a passion-filled kiss. I am encouraged. I get the happy Connor I am used to tonight.

Cautiously I wrap my hand around his neck, running my fingers up through his hair. He leans me back on the bed, laying over me, continuing to kiss me passionately. "I love you, Rae. I'm sorry I've been acting so terrible," he whispers in my ear.

"Connor, it's okay. None of us were prepared for any of this" I console, "I love you so much."

We lose ourselves in each other. He continues looking deep into my eyes before gently resting his body on mine, protectively wrapping his arms around me. He breaks for a moment to pull the blankets up around us, which is how we fall asleep. I encased in his arms.

My peaceful sleep is interrupted by a scratching at the door a short time later. I move to the door, allowing Willis to come in. I sleep through the night with no nightmares. When I wake the next morning, I am apprehensive about how Connor will react to last night. I am pleasantly surprised when I look up to see him smiling down at me. "Good morning," I say tentatively.

CHAPTER 26 TIME PASSES

"Morn'n," he says with his delicious southern drawl. Then leans down to kiss me gently. I sigh, nestling my head down against his shoulder, breathing in his scent. Despite my contentment, I cannot ignore my body for long, forcing me to get up to use the bathroom. When I return, Connor is dressing, then sits on the bed to wait for me. I dress quickly, and we head down to breakfast together.

When we get downstairs, Wanda is already up fixing breakfast for the group. She and Don brought bacon and eggs with them, along with fresh potatoes. Once breakfast is complete, we wait for everyone to assemble before eating.

"Wanda, this is amazing," Joanie comments between mouthfuls.

"Yes, not sure how you turn ordinary breakfast into something so extraordinary," Connor comments.

"Oh, it's nothing, just happy to be able to do something normal," she says wistfully.

"Well, we certainly appreciate," I add.

"Mmm, Hmm," Ethan agrees around a mouth full of fried potato.

Once everyone has had a chance to fill their bellies, it is time to get down to business. "What's the plan today?" I ask tentatively.

"Don and I will take first watch," Ethan announces. "Then after lunch Rae, you and Connor can take a turn."

"Sounds good," Connor says.

"I'll be teaching the girls school," Marnie says with a sigh. It has to be tough, becoming a mom to three young girls overnight. She doesn't complain, but I know the responsibility is wearing on her.

"You're doing a good job," I say to Marnie sympathetically. "I know it's hard."

"Thanks, Rae. Perhaps you can be a guest lecturer today," she says sarcastically.

"Sure, I'll take a spin this morning," I say playfully.

The morning passes quickly. I busy myself helping Wanda around the cabin. There are many things she wants to clean and reorganize with all of us here. She and Don managed to bring quite a bit of groceries with them. We are running low on bottled water, though, so I spend some time boiling the well water, letting it cool, and filling empty bottles.

I do take a turn with the girls. Relieving Marnie for a bit. I read them stories, and work on letters with Christy and Kenz. I think she is grateful for just a few minutes to go stand outside behind the house and breathe a bit of fresh air; it gets tiresome being cooped up inside so much.

The boys come down for lunch in the afternoon, "nothing new to report," Don announces as they settle in at the table.

Lunch is simple, sandwiches made with lunchmeat they were able to procure early in their trip, kept cold in coolers along the way. They got the bread from a small store at the base of the mountain. They reported that store had not yet been looted, making a decent, close, place to get supplies, for a while anyway.

"We are going to need some more self-sustaining ways to feed ourselves," Don points out.

"You mean like getting chickens?" I ask.

"Well, chickens would be nice, but they'll be hard to hide for long," Don says, laughing at me a bit.

"Or a garden," Joanie suggests.

"Garden would be good. We did grow some vegetables one year behind the watchtower. It's actually pretty flat right around there and gets good sun. There aren't trees, but a garden looks just like any other vegetation on the mountain," Wanda says.

"Next time we have a need to make a supply run, we'll have to look for seeds," Ethan says.

"We might have some sealed up in the basement," Wanda says, "I'll look later on today."

"Well, I suppose Connor and I will head up to the tower," I say, beckoning Connor to me. "Willis was just out about an hour ago, so he should be good for a while," I tell Ethan.

"K," he answers.

Connor and I head out the back, hand-in-hand. After ascending the ladder, we sit together under the net, looking down on the mountain below. "Looks like someone has set up camp over there," I say, pointing a bit to the Northwest. "I wonder where they are traveling to, and if they'll make it?" I wonder out loud. The family reminds me of Marnie's family; a mom, dad, and two little girls about the same age as Marie and Christy.

"It looks like the activity today is far to the South of them. Hopefully, they remain undetected. But if they keep on their same path, they'll run straight to them." I say somberly.

Connor looks sad as he looks down on the family. I wonder if he is thinking about his dad and sisters in Texas. I reach up placing my hand consolingly on his face, then lean up to kiss him tenderly. He looks down on me with great sadness, finally leaning down to rest his head against my shoulder.

The day passes uneventfully. We spend a great deal of time watching the family in the valley. Grateful, it seems the shifter's activity remains far to the South of them. I wish there were some way to tell them to change their course, but there is not, not without jeopardizing our whole camp. The sun starts to fade and it appears the family will remain undetected. We are just preparing to head down for dinner when movement in that area catches my eye. "Connor," I gasp.

We train our binoculars on the family; we see a shifter in the form of a man walking into their campsite. There is no opportunity for this family to run. He points his silver weapon at them, where they all now stand petrified. A dozen more shifters in various states, gremlin or human, emerge from the woods surrounding the family.

"Where were they?" I whisper to Connor. Even though there is no way they could hear us from this distance, I can't help but whisper under stress I feel for this family.

"I don't know Rae; I didn't see a single one of them," he says. "We're going to have to pay better attention to see if we can figure out how they are hiding so well." He says stress plain on his face.

It is getting dark, making it hard to follow the progress of the group through the woods. Though we can see when they finally march the family into the cluster of trees. We stare at each other in silence. We are just about to leave when an aircraft comes swooshing down, landing just outside the cluster of trees. The woman and two girls are led back out of the compound, loaded onto the aircraft, which immediately takes off.

"Where do you think they are taking them?" I gasp, panicking for this family that has been separated.

"I don't know," Connor says again with concern etched

across his face.

"How do they communicate so fast to get an aircraft here? Where did it come from? How does it move so fast?" I voice my concerns filling my head.

"We'll definitely want to discuss this tonight," Connor says, stress still evident in his voice. I wonder if his mind has traveled to Texas, to his family there. If he sees a similar situation in his head where his dad is separated from the girls. But what will he do? If they were taken, he'd never find them. If he tried to go to them, chances are he'd just lead the shifters straight to them. Still somewhat frightened by what we've seen, we stand still a while longer before descending the hidden ladder.

CHAPTER 27 GETTING WORRIED

"You guys look a bit spooked," Don comments when we come walking through the door into the kitchen. Most everyone is assembled in the kitchen while Wanda prepares the evening meal.

"We have a report to give tonight," Connor states in a very matter of fact tone.

"What happened?" Marnie questions.

"Where are the girls?" I ask.

"In the basement again, Wanda gave them some chores down there. They are entertained, for now," Marnie says.

"We saw a family set up camp off to the west. It appeared they were not going to be discovered, but Shifters emerged from nowhere. We'd been watching the area all day and never saw a thing. Once it revealed itself, aiming it's weapon at the family, a dozen or more stepped out of the woods around them." I explain.

"Man, it was strange. We didn't see a single one out there," Connor says, stressing this point.

"Anyhow, they marched them through the woods to that weird cluster of trees. They were only there a few minutes when an aircraft sped in. The mom and girls were forced on the aircraft and whisked away." I say, the sadness I feel for the family creeping into my voice.

"Were you watching the area around the family or just staring directly at the family?" Don asks.

"Around the family," Connor says, a bit defensive.

"My other question now is how did they communicate with the aircraft so fast? It took a bit of time obviously for them to get across the valley to the cluster of trees. But then it was only a few minutes for the aircraft to arrive." I wonder out loud.

"That is a good and disturbing question," Ethan mummers.

We sit up late this night; Don mixes cocktails, and we play cards well into the night. Finally, I can't keep my eyes open any longer. "That's it," I announce, "I'm heading up to bed."

"You're just tired of losing," Don says with a snicker.

"You got me. Seriously, I want to be able to keep my eyes open tomorrow if I take a watch," I counter.

"I'll be right up," Connor calls after me. I turn, giving him a small smile.

Willis follows me up the stairs. I change quickly and snuggle down in my bed. Willis curls up against my side, and I begin thinking about the past week. I think about how much life has changed, how much we've lost, though we've gained a new family. Don and Wanda are amazing, taking us in, taking care of us. I don't feel like crying every second of every day, though, the sadness of loss often creeps up on me. I think about the invaders who have taken over our world, wondering if we'll ever get our planet back.

I've been up here a while and Connor still hasn't come upstairs. I finally drift off to sleep stroking Willis' head.

When I wake the next morning, Connor is sound asleep beside me. I look down on him with a smile. I debate waking him with a kiss but decide to let him sleep. He obviously stayed up later than I last night. I slip silently from the bed and head into take a shower. When I return, he is still sleeping, though Willis is now curled up under his arm. "Traitor," I whisper to Willis as I head out of the room.

When I get downstairs, Wanda and Don are locked in a heated debate in the kitchen. "Good morning Rae," she breaks in when she sees me coming down the stairs.

"Good morning. What's going on down here?" I ask apprehensively but trying to remain casual.

"Oh, not much. We're just working on some breakfast," Wanda answers casually.

"What can I do to help?" I ask.

"Well, if you don't mind you can get to work on some scrambled eggs," she suggests.

I work on the eggs while Wanda hums to herself, scurrying about the kitchen. Before long, we have a restaurant-quality breakfast for the gang. While we were cooking, most everyone came downstairs, though Connor is still seemingly asleep.

"I guess I'll go wake up Connor," I announce.

Wanda, Don, and Ethan glance at each other after this comment and it does not go unnoticed by me. "What?" I ask sharply.

"Connor drank a bit much last night. Let him be," Wanda says gently.

"Really?" I question.

"He's having a tough time with things," Ethan says softly.

"Why doesn't he confide in me?" I question, hurt by the fact he confided in the larger group but not me.

"He doesn't want to burden or worry you," Don answers.

"Just let him be, sweetie. He'll come down when he's

ready," Wanda says kindly.

I fix my plate, making my way over to the table slowly. I stare longingly at the stairs waiting for Connor to emerge. As a group, we have just finished breakfast when Connor comes staggering down the steps. He pauses when he realizes we are all staring at him intently. He looks at each one of us in turn before continuing his descent of the stairs.

"Good morning, y'all," he says.

"Morning," I say, a bit of hurt coloring my voice.

Since I am standing at the kitchen counter, I fix him a plate, motioning for him to take a seat at the table. "Thanks Rae, this looks good," he comments.

"Reagan made the eggs," Wanda announces proudly.

"Did she," he says, trying too hard to be casual. "So, what's the plan for today?" Connor asks between bites of food.

"Don and I are headed up to keep watch this morning," Ethan announces, "then you and Rae can take the afternoon shift."

"Alright," he says with no emotion to his voice.

The day passes slowly at first. I spend some time reading a book, but it does little to hold my interest. I watch out the windows, trying to envision what is happening in the world beyond the woods. This just depresses me.

After a while of aimless wondering, Wanda enlists my help with laundry downstairs, showing me how to use the old-fashioned washboard. I decide I will help Marnie out by doing the girls' laundry, now that I know how to use the washboard.

Once the laundry is hanging up in the basement, we make our way up to start lunch.

"Anything I can do to help you ladies?" Connor asks.

"Thank you, but we've got it," Wanda answers sweetly.

"You look better," I say, giving him a smile.

He returns a warm smile, "Thank you. A good shower does amazing things."

Wanda teaches me how to make a pie crust using simple ingredients we have in the cabin. We combine this with beans we brought from home and canned vegetables to make a lunch casserole. Don and Ethan return just after we take the pie out of the oven.

"Well?" Marnie asks, coming down the stairs.

"Nothing happening out there. Mornings seem particularly quiet," Don answers.

After a quick lunch, Connor and I head up the tower to keep watch. We sit in silence for quite some time, but I can't stand it anymore. "What's going on, Connor?" I ask pointedly.

He walks over to where I am sitting, sits down behind me, and then wraps his arms around me. "Nothing, I'm just trying to process all that has happened. I still worry so much about dad and the girls. Joanie seems to be adjusting well here. I try to be grateful that she is here and safe." He finishes softly.

"Connor, I get it, but there's nothing we can do. It's too risky to travel to Texas. That's a lot of land to cover, and a lot of open land at that." I say, almost begging him to see reason. "Certainly we can formulate a plan as a group. Somehow find others, but for now, we have to stay here."

"I know that Rae, I just wish I knew what was happening to them." He says, then kisses me gently behind my ear. "Rae, I love you so much," he whispers, squeezing me tight.

The next few days pass slowly. Connor switches between happy go lucky and mopey. I feel bad for him, I know it has to be challenging, but it is not like there's anything we can do now. We just don't know enough about these invaders to formulate any kind of plan. I support him any way I can. I listen when he voices his concerns. I try to remind him of the life we have here, of his sister, who has no one left but him.

CHAPTER 28 SHATTERED

We've been at the cabin for about a week and a half, the mood is very subdued. After breakfast, Don and Ethan head up to keep watch. There has been little news to report over the past week, but we still feel like we need to know more. Even just to head into town to find diapers for Kenz, we feel like we just cannot see them well enough. You stare at an area for a while and see nothing; next thing you know, there are several of them. Seeing this makes us feel we aren't prepared enough to venture out for any reason.

I sit on the couch to read for a while when Connor approaches me. His expression is distraught. He doesn't say much, just sits next to me, pulling me into his lap. He hums a familiar tune while rubbing small circles on my arm with his thumb. He abruptly stops the motion of his thumb and stares down at me intently.

"What's up, Connor?" I ask, very apprehensively.

"Rae, I've decided to go to Texas," he blurts out, "I can't stand not knowing what's happened to dad and the girls. Seeing that family caught last week is really weighing on me," Connor says, the stress plain on his face. I knew this is what he had been brooding over for days, I knew this was coming, but I can't face it.

"Connor, please don't go," I beg, "please stay with me. You probably won't even be able to find them. It's not worth the risk Connor. There is a lot of distance to cover. There aren't the winding hidden back roads to travel on like we did to find our way here."

"Rae, I have to. I can't stand it anymore." He says, pain clearly etched in his face.

"What about me? NO! What about Joanie? She has no one Connor, no one. Are you going to just leave her here?" I beg as the tears beging falling.

"I know she is safe, though. I know you guys will protect her, who is there to protect the rest of my family," he says.

"Yes, but what about her?" I ask. "She lost her mom too, Connor. She has no one but you. You're just going to leave her behind."

"I know you guys will take care of her. Please Rae, you know I love you; you know I don't want to leave you, but it is eating me alive inside." He begs for my understanding.

"They have your dad Connor. Joanie has no one." I beg a bit of venom in my voice.

"But she has you. I promise Rae, I will get them, and I'll be back. I'll come back here with them. I have to try." He continues to plead for my understanding.

"You'll never make it" I cry harder. "I have had dreams, premonitions, Connor, you're going to get caught," I say.

"Those are just your fears Rae, I'm going to be fine. We've learned a lot over the last week and a half. I'll travel at night like we did before. I'll stay well hidden." He says. "I know I can do this; I know I'll be fine."

"Connor, please, please, don't go. We are missing seeing them out there all the time," I beg as the tears flood down my face.

"I'll travel at night. They aren't active at night." He says confidently.

"We don't know that for sure," I sob.

"I'm sorry Rae, I have to do this." He says.

"Why? Why do you have to do this?" I say, becoming completely hysterical.

"It is just what I have to do. I can't stand not knowing," he continues to beg for my understanding.

"But you're just putting the not knowing off on us, Connor," I say, getting angry.

"No, I'll be fine. I'm going to head out tonight." He finishes quietly.

"TONIGHT!" I shriek. "You are not the person I thought you were. That person would never leave Joanie like this," I say with venom. I jump off his lap, scoop up Willis, head upstairs, slamming and locking the door to my room.

I spend the rest of the day locked in my room, sobbing on and off. Willis eventually goes to stand by the door. He needs to go out. I simply let him out and lock myself back in my room. Once Ethan and Don return, Ethan knocks on my door, "Rae, come down for lunch."

"I'm not hungry," I reply grumpily.

"Please come down," He pushes. But I just ignore him.

When day fades into evening, there is another knock on the door. "Rae," Connor says, "Rae, please let me in. I don't want to leave like this. We need to talk."

"No," I say, stubbornly holding on to my anger.

"Please Rae," he begs. I return his pleas with silence.

Once night falls, there is one more tentative knock on the door. "Rae, I'm leaving. Please open the door." I really want to hold on to my anger, but conscience will not let me. I slowly make my way over, opening the door just after he turned to go down the stairs. "Thank you," he says, tears in his eyes.

"Please, Connor, please don't do this. You'll never be able to find them if you even make it to Texas." I beg. "Please stay here, stay here with Joanie, stay here with me. Don and Ethan will figure something out. They'll figure out a way to get to them." My voice trailing off at the end. "Please…"

"I'm sorry, Rae. I love you so much, but I can't stay, I've got to go look for them. If I can't find them or even if they won't come back with me once I know, I promise, I promise," he stresses, "I'll come back to you." He begs my understanding.

"I Love you Connor; God be with you," I whisper. I lean in, kiss him passionately, and walk away. I head back into my room, gently closing and locking the door. I lay on the bed, crying silently to myself until I finally fall asleep. Sometime later I hear a soft knock on the door, "Rae," Marnie calls in, "Rae, do you want to talk?"

"No," I say back, just loud enough for her to hear.

"Do you want a shoulder to cry on?" she asks.

"No, thanks Mar, I just want to be alone," I answer back.

"Well, if you change your mind, I don't care what time it is, wake me up, okay? We saved you some dinner; it is in the fridge." She adds.

"Thanks," I whisper hoarsely.

I lay staring at the ceiling, thinking through the past month. I start with the flirting at school, the night at the Quarry, at Janelle's, the weekend at my house, the trip to get down here, and the time spent together here. I think to myself; I never really knew him. I gave myself to him, without knowing the real Connor. I am so disappointed, disappointed in me, my actions, disappointed in him. I think about Joanie. How is she going to handle this? How could he possibly do this to her? Whether she has us or not, he is her brother, her only known living relative.

I sigh in frustration. My mind goes blank. As the night passes, I stare unseeingly at the ceiling. My thoughts are so jumbled I think of no one thing. Finally, somewhere in chaos, I drift off to sleep.

The next morning, I do not bother with a shower. All I do is add a pair of shorts to my ratty t-shirt and head downstairs.

"Breakfast was hours ago, baby girl, have some cereal," Wanda says, sympathetically. She pours cereal into a bowl, then goes to the refrigerator, retrieves a gallon of milk, comes back over pouring over my cereal.

"Where'd we get milk," I ask without feeling.

"Ethan and Don drove down the mountain last night. Don't look like that it was late. There had been no activity for quite some time. Anyhow, the little store down there, the coolers are on generator power. I can't imagine they'll be running much longer; I am sure they've got to be about out of fuel. But they stocked up on milk, eggs, and meat while they were there. Got Kenz more diapers too." Wanda explains.

"Where is everybody?" I ask tentatively.

"Joanie's up in bed hasn't come down yet. Marnie and the girls are in the basement having gym class. The boys are up at the watchtower." She explains.

"Huh" is my only reply. I finish my breakfast, walk to the sink, wash, dry my bowl, then put it away. I move to a chair in front of the large windows and simply stare outside. I contemplate our situation, feeling loss more significant than I have felt yet. After spending most of the morning like this, I head over and lay down on the couch. Once again staring at nothing, I fall asleep. I awake early evening to the sounds of chatter.

"How long has she been asleep?" I hear Ethan ask.

"Since before lunch," Wanda comments.

"Rae, wake up," Ethan shouts, shoving my shoulder.

"No," I answer nastily.

"Rae, it's dinner time, get up," he demands.

"FINE!" I shout angrily.

"Reagan," he says sternly. I just roll my eyes and head to the dining room table.

After dinner, I don't wait around for the usual card games. I simply stand, leaving my plate on the table, and head straight upstairs. I take a long hot shower, spending a great deal of time just standing under the flow of water; using far more than my share of hot water. Having not really even cleaned myself I leave the shower and dress. And this is how the next four days of my life pass. On the fourth day, Marnie wakes me up around nine in the morning. "Rae, get your ass out of bed. It's time to stop feeling sorry for yourself and start pulling your weight around here."

I just stare at her uncomprehendingly. "Seriously, Rae, GET UP," she shouts unapologetically. "The shower is running. March your happy self in there and get cleaned up. After breakfast, you and Ethan are taking the first watch."

I roll over, slowly rise out of bed, and stomp off to the shower. Today I spend time actually washing and conditioning my hair, shaving my unkempt legs. I do actually feel better when I emerge clean. I notice it is sunny outside, so I dress for warmer weather, braid my hair back out of my face, then head downstairs. I guess it must be April now. The days should be getting warmer. It's been almost a week since I've been out of the cabin, so I am not entirely sure what to expect outside.

When I come down to breakfast, Ethan has already eaten and is packing a satchel with water and snacks for the day. I walk to the breakfast bar, where there are bacon and eggs on a plate waiting for me. "Thank you, Wanda," I say sheepishly.

I know my behavior has been beyond disgraceful the past few days.

"No worries, sweetie, good to see you up and dressed," she says with kindness I don't deserve.

"Alright Ethan, let's do this," I say after wolfing down my meal.

We head out the back and up the secret ladder to the watchtower above. Once on top, I ask. "So, what have we learned in the last few days?"

"More of the same. We've seen them chase a few more groups of people. It's always the same thing, more of a herding practice. As prey runs, the shifters show themselves redirecting the person or group until they run into a whole pack of them. It's weird how they are stationed throughout the mountain, but somehow they make it work." He says clinically.

"That is weird; any more air traffic?" I ask.

"Yes, after they bring in new humans, whether they chased them across the mountain or if they found them elsewhere, some or all of them are flown away from here," he explains.

"Have you seen any sign of Connor among them?" I ask tentatively.

"No," he answers, but I can't tell if he is telling the truth.

"Don and I drove him down into town. He found an inconspicuous car and headed out," Ethan says matter of fact.

"I can't believe he left Joanie," I say, voicing the anger that has been nagging at me for days.

"I know Rae, it was really crappy of him," Ethan consoles.

"Not the person I thought he was," I say, trying to stifle the sobs I feel building.

"Rae, that's not true. We have all been given more to deal with in the past month than imaginable. Everyone is equipped to deal with things differently. Connor was putting too much pressure on himself to act on the situation. He didn't know how or what to do, so that was his only avenue for action." Ethan says.

"Perhaps," I say, not willing to forgive him. "Or perhaps his action could have just been keeping his sister safe."

When our shift is nearly ending, I voice the other thought nagging at me, "Ethan, what are we doing up here? Are we really learning anything? Are we going to take some action or just watch forever" I ask.

"First and foremost, we're here to keep watch on the cabin. We need to know if any activities are bringing them closer to us. The second is to understand as much about them as we can so we can formulate a plan should one of us be taken; or, to be able to coordinate an attack." He says.

When our turn on the tower is over, we head down the ladder back to the house. A late lunch of sandwiches is waiting for us, which I gladly accept. Having finally eaten a good breakfast, my stomach is now registering how much I've neglected it over the past few days. While I eat lunch, Marie and Christy come into the room, look at me, and then immediately turn on their heels and head back upstairs. Huh, wonder what that was all about.

CHAPTER 29 NO,SHAME STILL EXISTS

"One more," I tell Don as he's passing around the cocktails.

"Reagan, I think you've had enough young lady," Wanda says sternly.

"Just one more Mama Wanda, it's not like I have to get up for school in the morning," I protest.

"You've just been going through a lot of alcohol the past few days, I don't want you to get dependent," she says.

"Well, here's the good news, it's the end of the world, and we're almost out. So unless I'm going to go scavenging for alcohol, I think I have a stopping point in my near future," I say with sarcasm.

"I know you've been through a lot, and I know you miss him, but you really can't do this. Tomorrow I am locking this stuff up." She says firmly.

"Guess I'll just drink more tonight then," I say, getting angry. Who is she to tell me what I can and can't do? I suppose it is her house, but she is not my mother. I don't have a mother anymore.

"REAGAN," Ethan shouts, "stop being so disrespectful." This does sober me up a bit. Ethan rarely yells at me. He typically allows me to wallow in my misery. I must have really crossed the line now.

"I am sorry Mrs. Mitchell," I say, abashed, "I don't know what has come over me. I just can't..." I trail off, fighting back the tears that are threatening to come.

Ever since Connor left, I have given in to the misery of everything that has happened. Marnie's sisters don't even come near me anymore. It has been seven days since he left. I wonder if he has made it to Texas yet. No, I know he has not made it yet. It'd be a two-day trip under normal conditions. I'm guessing now, it will be at least a week, probably two to get there. Then he'll have to convince his dad and stepmom to uproot the girls, making a perilous trip back across the country to Tennessee. I seriously doubt he will get them back here.

Regardless, it'll be at least a month. He promised, he promised, if they wouldn't come back with him, once he knew their fate, he'd return to me. I just don't know. And what happens when they won't come? I try hard not to think about this anymore.

"It's okay Rae, I get it, but we've all lost everything. It is not just you. I also know we all handle things the only way we can. I forgive you girl, but remember to respect your elders." She says soothingly but with a firm tone. "Now, I've had enough of this day. I am going to bed." She announces, getting up to cross the room.

"Goodnight," I respond, along with Marnie, Don, and Ethan.

"I think I'm off to bed too," Ethan announces, looking pointedly at Marnie. The girls have managed to sleep well the last few nights. Marnie and Ethan have been able to sleep the night through together.

"That's my cue. Good night you two." She says, looking at Don and me.

"How 'bout that drink," I say once they've climbed the stairs.

"Coming right up," Don answers, filling my glass and handing it back. "I am sorry about my momma Rae. She is old school. However, she's softened since the world ended; I'd have gotten my face slapped if I'd have talked like that to her." He says with a chuckle.

"I know he left because the worry was eating at him, but now he's just placed that worry on Joanie and me. Joanie shouldn't have to deal with his selfish choices. Does he really think he can find them?"

"Rae, I know it's hard," he says, coming over to sit beside me on the couch, wrapping an arm consolingly around me. "But you two have only been dating for a month or two. It is his family," he says. "He had to go find them."

"New topic," I announce, "dwelling on this will only make me crazier. So, you have a woman out there somewhere? You've been quite silent on the topic."

"Um, no," he says with a quiet laugh. "I've had plenty of girlfriends," he says, looking at me meaningfully. "All around the globe, I've never found anyone I connect with on a permanent level."

"Oh. Well, you're young, you've got time." I say absently.

"Not much chance of finding her now, not like the local bars are a hopping place." He says with a wink.

"No, I guess not," I answer. "How much longer did you have left in the Army?" I ask, redirecting the conversation again.

"Just re-upped for another two years right before all this happened," he answers.

"Any plans after the Army?" I ask.

"Hadn't gotten there yet. That's why I re-enlisted. Want another?" He asks.

"What would your mama say after just chewing me out for having this many already?" I say with a chuckle. "But yes, please."

He stands, picking up my cup he then heads to the kitchen. When he returns, he places a full cup in front of me on the table. "Want to sit out on the deck? It's cloudy tonight with absolutely no light. No one will see us."

"That sounds amazing," I answer. We stand, silently moving across the room, and head out the door to the small deck facing the valley below. We sit in the two wooden chairs made from locally harvested trees. They are nice because they blend in with the background, but they aren't terribly comfortable. It is nice being outside. "Oh, Katydids," I say a bit too loud.

"Shh, Rae, you might wake the neighbors," Don says with a silent chuckle.

"Sorry, I get excited whenever I hear Katydids. They remind me of vacations down here with the family when I was a kid. My mom would get super excited too. She said it reminded her of vacations down here with her family as a kid." I explain.

"That's so cool. What a tradition to continue," he says.

"Yeah, I am grateful they instilled a love of this life. By this life I mean clean mountain air, starry nights, though there are no stars tonight. The simple things like the sound of Katydids while playing cards on the deck as a family. It is certainly memories to last a lifetime. I'm grateful I've got them." I say, the conversation making me sad again. I swiftly down my most recent cocktail.

"Hey Rae, slow down, or my mama will beat my butt tomorrow," Don interjects.

I respond by taking his cup and taking a big swig. "I know I will regret it in the morning, but for one night, I don't want to feel anymore," I say. "It's cowardly, I know it is. But I just need to get away from the pain, from the thoughts in my head."

"Say no more. I've got a great hangover remedy I'll share with you in the morning." He says, rising to refill both our cups.

Once he returns, we sit on the deck in silence for quite some time, just listening to the night noises around us. Finally, it registers I am getting mosquito bites. "I'm going to need to go in," I pout, "I've got more mosquito bites than skin right now."

Once we go back into the living room, lit by the blue lantern light, Don turns, asking, "one more, or are you going to bed."

"One more, I think. Please though no matter what I say after this, do not bring me another. There are no hospitals around if I have alcohol poisoning," I slur.

I plop back down on the couch, waiting for my next beverage to arrive. Don returns, sitting next to me on the sofa. "Cheers," he says, "to spending the end of the world with the best possible people."

"Cheers," I say with a giggle, leaning back into the couch.

Don puts his arm around my shoulders and we both stare out into the night. "I am sorry you are suffering," he says, "I understand why he left, but I don't know how he did it."

"Please, let's not talk about it," I beg. Even drunk, I can't stomach the conversation.

"You don't think it would help?" He asks.

"No," I say. I turn and look deep into Don's eyes. I stare for a long time, not sure what I am looking for, but continue searching. After a while, he leans in, placing his lips gently to mine. At first, I freeze, unable to process what is happening. But my muddled mind cannot make heads or tails of the situation. In the end, I welcome the distraction.

I kiss him back with urgency. I love the feel of his lips on mine, the heat his body gives off. I reach my hand up to caress the back of his neck and draw him in closer. His hands wind their way around my back, pulling me to his body. Our kissing intensifies.

Quickly, catching me by surprise, he stands, lifting me off the couch, cradling me in his arms. He carries me to his room, gently closing the door behind him. My muddled mind registers I should not want this, but the part of me that needs freedom from constant pain does not care. Made brave by the alcohol, I allow this.

He gently sets me on the bed. Standing in front of me, he stares deep into my eyes while he removes his shirt. Once his shirt is gone, he leans over me and begins kissing me again.

Things most definitely get out of hand. My mind is mush. Between the alcohol and the full release of emotion, I cannot think. When we are done, I pass out next to Don. Sometime in the middle of the night I jerk awake, nausea overtaking me. I run to the bathroom just in time as the night's indulgence makes a reappearance. I am in there for quite some time. When I feel as though there cannot possibly be anything left in my system, I rinse my mouth out and head back to the bedroom.

It takes me a minute to realize where I am, and even worse, what I've done. I see Don stretched out across the bed. Oh God, please forgive me, I think to myself as coherency sets in. I wander around the room in the dull blue lantern light gathering my clothes. Once I am dressed, I head out to the kitchen. In the refrigerator, I find sports drinks and bottles of water. I take one of each and head up to my room.

Willis is waiting for me in my bed, clearly unhappy about my absence. "Sorry, buddy," I mutter, "you have no idea how sorry I am," I say. I lay in bed, sipping my drinks, totally consumed in misery. If I thought I was miserable before, it has nothing on how I feel now.

I cheated on Connor, I did it with a man I barely know who is much older than me. I betrayed my best friend, who is out there risking his life to find his family. I am a horrible person. I remember thinking after Connor and I had sex the first time that shame ended when the world ended. I guess that is not true after all. I feel shame like I never have even imagined possible. I wallow in this guilt and misery, the tears start falling. I cannot believe what I have done.

I remember, when I was younger I sat in 'grown-up' church upstairs with my parents. The message was about God's laws are not to make our lives miserable but to protect us from ourselves. To keep us from making mistakes that might seem like fun or enjoyable at the time, but later will haunt us. He couldn't have been more right tonight. This is one of those times. If I hadn't overdone it on the alcohol, I would have never had gone too far with Don. If I hadn't done these things with Don, I would not feel this misery now.

I spare a moment to think about Pastor John. I wonder how he is; I wonder if he and his family are safe. Once these thoughts have passed, all I can think is please God forgive me and take away the pain of what I've done. Somewhere in these silent prayers I find oblivion again.

Once I wake, it is late morning, or maybe early afternoon. Getting sick in the middle of the night and drinking the sports drink really helped. I don't feel half bad despite myself. That is until I remember what happened last night. I lay in bed a while longer, not sure how to face my own treachery. Once I decide I have to get up, I make my way to the shower. After a long, relatively cold shower, I emerge and dress.

I head downstairs, sure that the group below is already judging me for my attitude and drinking last night. When I get down the stairs, Marnie is the only one in the kitchen. "How are you feeling?" she asks with an air of superiority. I do not need this right now.

"Not too bad," I say, "I yacked last night, drank a sports drink and some water, so just a bit of a headache." I make my way to the cabinet and remove the ibuprofen. I grab a water from the fridge and down all four pills in one swallow. "Where is everybody?" I ask.

"Ethan and Don went up to the watchtower, Joanie and the girls took Willis for a walk along the mountain, the boys said it was eerily quiet out so that would be fine. Wanda is in the basement, washing clothes, I believe. What time did you finally go to bed last night?" Marnie finishes.

"Oh, Marnie, I did something terrible," I say, the tears starting to run down my face.

She looks me in the eye for a moment, "you didn't," she says accusatorially. I break down into full-fledged hysterics. The tears falling like a waterfall. Marnie rushes to me, embracing me. Pulling my head to her shoulder, she strokes my hair and lets me cry myself out. "Rae, it'll be okay. I just can't believe you would do that."

"I was so drunk," I sob, "I was so upset over Connor, I just didn't want to feel anymore. Clearly, neither of us were making good decisions."

"Clearly," she says. "Will you tell Connor when he gets back."

I look at my friend, dumbfounded. 'Gets back,' I think to myself; he's not coming back. I have resigned myself to this fact, he will never make it to Texas. If he does, he will not make it back. There are more and more of these things out there each week. It is only going to get worse. "Mar, he's not coming back. There is no way for him to make it there and back. There's too many of them."

"You don't know that," she says optimistically, "maybe there are some remnants of the army somewhere making plans. Maybe they'll conquer these idiots, and we'll be able to move about freely."

I stare at her blankly. Where is this child-like optimism coming from? There is no army hiding somewhere. She should know this; she is sleeping with my brother for crying out loud. I hope he isn't pumping her full of this false hope. "What makes you say that?" I ask.

"Wishful thinking, but Rae, the point is, you don't know. You can never know how all of this will turn out." She answers.

I manage to pull myself together, not a second too late as Wanda comes upstairs. "Towels are hanging out to dry." She announces proudly, "well, in to dry," she finishes. Then she looks at me in earnest, "oh sweetie, you didn't stop drinking when I told you to, did you?" she asks knowingly.

"No," I say, filled with shame.

"Well, let me fix you up a meal that'll make you feel better," she says, moving into the kitchen. She then busies herself in the kitchen while Marnie and I sit at the breakfast bar observing. Just as she sets a plate of the most delicious smelling casserole in front of me, the boys emerge from the watchtower, the girls and Willis in tow.

I meet Don's eyes almost instantly. After a moment of awkward staring, we both quickly look away. Ethan does not miss the exchange; I feel his eyes bore into me. When I turn I see him staring at me with the most patronizing look I've ever seen. Fortunately, Wanda was busy in the kitchen, missing this entire silent exchange. Marnie comes to the rescue drawing the attention away from me, "so, what did you boys see up there?" She asks.

"Not much," Ethan answers, "it's pretty quiet out there. We saw a few of them congregating around that sparse area to the south. They seemed fired up over something but never strayed from the area."

"I wonder what's over there?" I voice, trying to seem nonchalant.

"Who knows, we'll continue to keep watch on that area," Don answers, trying too hard to make everything seem normal.

"Willis," I say, and he comes running to me. He's much happier since Wanda deemed him healed. With his splint now removed entirely, he runs about freely unencumbered and loves it. He finds it much easier to traverse the stairs chasing the girls throughout the day. I can say this, they keep him tired. When it is time for bed, he crashes hard.

Lunch is amazing. I am still in awe at what Wanda finds to make out of the limited ingredients we have here in the cabin. But each day, she amazes us with something else absolutely fantastic.

"If this ever ends, you've got to open a restaurant, Wanda, we can call it Wanda's Apocalypse Café," I say, laughing. "I seriously don't know how you do it."

"Oh, it's nothing, family recipes we've kept on hand from generation to generation, including the substitutions to make it work. If Don here ever finds himself a girl, I'll share the secrets with her," she says, giving Don a wink. "The meat supply won't last long; it won't be long we'll be out of protein."

"We brought our stash of dried beans. That'll give us at least some," I say.

"Your mom was a smart woman; I wish I could have met her," Wanda says with an air of sadness. "Maybe you boys could take one of those bows up there with you and do some hunting," she suggests.

"Funny thing is mom, we haven't seen much, if any, wildlife in the last few days. It's like they are in hiding," Don reports.

Once everyone is done eating, Marnie and I insist on cleaning up. With the meal in my stomach and ibuprofen ridding me of my headache, I don't feel half bad. Marnie and I make quick work of clean up. Even with no dishwasher up here, we can clean the plates in no time.

"We're getting low on dish soap," I say to no one in particular.

"There are a few other things we could use, too," Ethan notes, "we might have to make another trip to town soon."

"Rae," I jump when Don says my name, "want to head up to the tower with me to take the second watch?"

I look at Marnie, unsure of what to say. Why does he want me to go up there alone? Does he think we'll be an item now? Heck, does he even remember what we did last night? I know I will have to face him sometime, "sure," I answer quietly. Wanda gives her son a searching look at my tone, but in the end, dismisses whatever inclination she was feeling.

We climb the hidden staircase in silence. After a half-hour, Don finally breaks the awkward silence. "Rae, I am sorry. Last night never should have happened. I took advantage of a situation..."

"No, Don," I cut him off. "It is my fault. I was so caught up in my own misery, I allowed it to happen. Hell, I wanted it to happen. I wanted to not feel anything, to feel something. I wanted to be gone from this space and time. If anyone is to blame, it is me," I say, hanging my head in shame.

"Rae, please don't do that. I should have been a better friend. I should have taken care of you, not take advantage of you. I am so sorry." He says.

"Me too," I answer, "so what do we do?"

"I'd like to say we pretend it didn't happen, but we both are adults, and we know it did happen. So, I say we admit our mistakes, we ask forgiveness, and we continue being friends who support one another," he answers.

"I'll do my best," I say, "though it's bound to be awkward."

"Why does it have to be awkward?" he asks.

"Well, for starters, you've seen me naked," I answer.

"That's just skin, Rae. We've all got it," he says, winking at me. I have to admit he has a way of putting me at ease.

The rest of the afternoon is pleasant. Don is a gentle soul that soothes my nerves with his mindless chatter. We talk about school, careers, families, movies, music, and books. Time passes swiftly. Before we know it, night has fallen. We silently make our way back down the hidden staircase to the cabin. Once inside, we smell Wanda has made yet another fantastic meal.

After dinner, we play cards with the girls as usual. Kenz is actually starting to get it, playing along for real. It is comforting to see her growing; that she is learning in this environment. The girls really have adapted well, they miss being able to play outside at will, but Willis helps them stay active. Nightly games are over, and Marnie takes the girls up to bed. Once Marnie has the girls in bed, we begin our nightly debrief.

"So," Ethan begins, "what did we learn today?"

"You know, after what, two or three, or whatever it's been, weeks, you start this conversation the same way every night." I joke. "What are we doing with this information? How do we use it to regain our world?"

"Don't know yet Rae, right now, we're learning all we can until we find some weak link or way to take them down." Ethan answers.

"Well," Don interrupts, "we didn't see anything out there today. It was eerily quiet, not even activity around their hub."

"Yeah, I thought that too. I wonder what that means. Do you think they've moved on from there?" Ethan asks.

"Dunno, I don't know how we know. I guess we keep watching." Don responds.

"Well, this was productive," I say, annoyed. "I didn't sleep well last night; I'm going to bed."

"Night Rae," I hear in a chorus from the table.

"Night guys," I answer.

I head up to bed, calling Willis with me. Heading to bed, no longer having the distraction of my friends, my shame of the former night swallows me. I begin crying before I've climbed the last stair. I am in full-blown hysterics by the time I get to my room. I curl up on the bed, Willis curled against my stomach, and cry myself to sleep.

We head out on an ordinary run to town. It's unnecessary at this point, but we need toilet paper and a few odds and ends. We haven't seen any activity in this area in quite some time, it seems like the time to go. Don and I are making our way down the familiar path, a trek we've made several times now. It is evening but not yet dark, we can still easily see around us, it will be dark when we return. We are moving through the trees with ease. We are just about to the base of the mountain when something seems off. The hairs on the back of my neck prick up. We freeze. I turn to look back at Don. As I turn, I register the shimmering to my left. Oh no, "run," I mouth to Don silently.

We are too far from any of our hidden hideouts; we'll have to find a temporary place. I follow Don through a web of branches into a thicket of berry bushes. We settle in and we hear their odd communications all around us. We are surrounded. We're doomed. There is no way out of this. Once they start a search, they don't quit.

I am comforted knowing that as a group, we've discussed this repeatedly, what happens if someone is caught. We don't waste our lives. Someone has to walk away from this, if at all possible. Someone must continue for our families, for our race, for our world. I look over at Don and mouth, "I'm sorry." He pulls me into a giant bear hug, holding my hand and squeezing it tight. He mouths, "the count of three," holding up three fingers. I nod solemnly. He holds up one finger, then two, then off we go, the game that will only end with our capture or death once it has begun.

I jump, sitting up quickly in my bed. Looking around I am confused until the dull blue light and other surroundings register. Just another dream, I need Connor here to kiss me, to make it all better so I can drift into a peaceful sleep once again. But there is no one here to comfort me. I'll have to get through this myself. These thoughts opne the flood gates once again. I don't cry myself to sleep this time, but eventually stop crying, lying awake for hours.

Once morning dawns, I am exhausted. I slowly make my way to the bathroom, where I take a somewhat cold shower. The shower does little to make me feel awake. But at least it helped with the puffiness around my eyes. When I come out to dress Willis is already gone. The girls must have come got him when they heard me in the shower. That is good; he'll have needed to go out.

"Diapers," I hear coming down the stairs. "Kenzie is getting low on diapers," Marnie is saying.

"I really think it's best if we get her potty trained. It's going to be hard to find diapers before long. I'll add it to the list for this trip, but let's start on getting her used to using the toilet."

"I think you're right," Marnie says, "I didn't want to push it on her too quickly once we got here; she was dealing with so much. Now she really is getting along good these days."

"Well, good morning Rae, you slept late," Wanda greets me.

"Sorry, another bad dream last night. I had trouble falling back to sleep after," I say, punctuating that statement with a yawn.

"Oh, sweetie, want to talk about it?" She asks motherly.

"Nothing too different from the ordinary. Don and I were on a run for supplies; out of nowhere, there were shifters everywhere." I say, giving a shiver as I re-live the terror I felt.

"Oh, Rae," Marnie says, not realizing my dreams have a way of coming true "that's awful. I am sure it is the uncertainty we are all feeling. It's been so quiet the last few days, it's unnerving."

"Yea, I hope that is all it is," I say miserably.

"The boys up on watch?" I ask.

"Yep, they went up about two hours ago," Joanie chimes in. I hadn't even noticed her on the couch. She's been so quiet since Connor left. I walk over, sitting down next to her.

"How are you doing?" I ask.

"I'm here, so, I suppose that is something," she answers with a voice way too old for her young body.

"I'm sorry, sweetie," I say, "we're here for you, you know

that, right? Anything you need."

"I know," thank you. "I'm just so angry. How could he?" she says, voicing her frustrations with just a hint of the tears trying to fall.

"I don't know. I guess unless we are him, we don't know what he was thinking or feeling." I answer, trying to be strong but echoing her anger.

I spend the late morning reading a book from Wanda's collection. I will say this, she is well stocked, books from every genre imaginable. I drift off mid-morning while reading. I must sleep for a while. When I wake up, the boys are coming down for lunch.

"Morning," I mumble as I wake from my sleep.

"You sleeping Rae?" Don asks, feigning shock.

"Sorry, bad dreams last night, with no one there to console me, I had trouble going back to sleep," I say, irritated.

"Oh, sorry," he mutters.

"What's for lunch?" Ethan asks, sniffing the air appreciatively.

"Casserole again," Wanda answers, "though before long we'll be down to plain canned vegetables," she says, hinting at the need for someone to make a run to town.

"Yeah, I guess we'll have to get on that soon," Ethan says.

CHAPTER 30 AND LIFE GOES ON

After a hearty lunch, Ethan and I make our way up to the watchtower. Marnie hasn't been out of the house lately; she plays school with the girls during the day, and I think she's getting frustrated. "I think tomorrow I'll take the afternoon shift with girls so Marnie can get out of the house," I tell Ethan as we climb the ladder.

"She would LOVE that," he says.

"It's got to be tough, eighteen, and a mom to three, incredibly young girls, I can't imagine. Well, I guess I can imagine I'm living it with her, but they aren't ultimately my responsibility," I say.

The afternoon passes slowly, not much activity, but late afternoon things change. "Ethan, get over here," I whisper loudly.

"What is it?" he asks.

"I think they are chasing someone," I answer.

We hold our breath watching the chase taking place below. It is difficult to see, given the woods are very thick in some areas. It appears to be a group of three teenagers, two boys and a girl. We watch from our vantage point, we can watch the course the chase takes even if we can't see every step. Shifters are placed across the mountainside. As one appears to the trio, they change the path running into another, shifting their trek again. This continues, but we can see the eventual outcome and wish we could warn them somehow. Each shift that changes their course pushes them closer to a cluster of shifters who have positioned themselves a bit farther down the mountain. It appears for a moment they might get out of it, the direction they've moved to seems to be free, but then suddenly there is the shimmer.

"Whoa" Ethan exclaims, "where did that one come from?"

"I don't know, I didn't see it there either. Do you think they are taking on other forms now? We've only ever seen the gremlin-like creatures and the human look-a-likes."

The course they change to takes them straight into the rattlesnake pit. They freeze when they are instantly surrounded by shifters with their silver weapons trained on the trio. Through these military-grade binoculars I can see the terror on their faces. The girl is sobbing. I wish there were some way we could help; there just isn't, not without jeopardizing everyone hidden here.

"Well," I say, "that was something."

"They seemed like they've been so quiet lately; I wonder if we are just missing them?" he speculates.

"I don't know. I think we're going to need to be more careful," I say. "We really need to see what they're shifting into so we can keep better watch."

"Definitely," Ethan echoes.

The afternoon gives way to evening and we still see no evidence of the shifters around the mountainside. It is eerily quiet, but we now question whether this is an accurate assessment or not. This certainly puts a damper on going into town to gather supplies if we can't be sure of what they are or the shape they are taking. Once night falls and it's too dark to see anything, we make our way down the ladder, quietly heading back into the house.

"You guys are late," Marnie says, "dinner was an hour ago."

"Sorry Mar, we've got an update to give tonight, though,"

he says, looking meaningfully at the girls. He walks over to the table, "what have you rug rats been into today?"

"We make cafts Efan" Christy says, showing Ethan a collage of pictures she cut from a magazine.

"Very nice," Ethan responds indulgently.

Ethan and I find our plates on top of the stove covered in foil, then sit at the bar eating, discussing the day in low whispers. Just as we are finishing, Don comes up from the basement.

"Where've you been," I ask accusatorily.

"Helping my mama with laundry, thank you very much. What kept you two out so late?" he asks in return.

"Later," Ethan says a bit too sternly.

"Oh," he responds.

After Marnie has the kids in bed, we gather around for our nightly debrief. I'd love to say planning sessions, but there is no planning happening here. We still have no clue how to move forward. If only we could figure out what is through that thicket of trees. If we could know what is happening behind there.

"Okay, let's have it," Don says once we are all seated.

"There's nothing too dramatic to tell," Ethan starts.

"I don't know, I thought it was pretty traumatic," I say.

Ethan shoots me a dirty look and continues. "When we were observing today, we witnessed them chase and capture a trio of teenagers. The odd thing is, just observing we didn't think there were any about, that is the scary part. They must be taking on different shapes, maybe even trees for all we know. Once they started the chase, you could follow their path. From the start, they were herding them as we've seen before. A shifter would show themselves to them; they'd change course until they ran right into a group of them armed and ready. For the most part, we could see the shifters before they appeared to the group, but there was one shift, neither of us could see before it happened, had no idea it was there until the shimmer was there."

"Well, that is something," Wanda says, clearly disturbed by the tale.

"We're going to have to be more vigilant in our observations, particularly if we are going to try to make a trip into town," Don says. "You really couldn't see them before?"

"Well, we weren't looking in the exact places necessarily until we could see the path it would take." Ethan says, "but no, generally we had no idea they were out there."

"Shit," Don mutters under his breath.

"So maybe," Marnie voices, "if you are being chased the best approach is to run through the shifter rather than changing course."

"You might be on to something," Ethan agrees.

We all sit in silence for quite some time. Don gets up, fixing himself a drink. "Anyone want one?" he asks.

"I'm good," I say firmly. Wanda gives me a pleased smile.

The chatter continues for several hours, but it is all speculation, which is hurting my head. "I'm headed up to bed," I announce. I call Willis to me and climb the stairs; I startle a bit when I open my door and see someone in my bed. "Joanie," I say, "are you okay?"

Joanie sits up "can I sleep with you? I have bad dreams too."

"Of course," I answer, "we'll find a way to get through the night together."

I head over to the bed, putting an arm around Joanie. Willis, sensing both of our needs, lies between us, and together we drift off to a peaceful sleep. In the morning, I wake early once again, feeling refreshed. Joanie is still sleeping; I leave Willis in bed with her and go into the bathroom for my morning rinse. Once clean, I head out; Joanie is gone. I'm guessing she went to get dressed. I dress, call Willis and head downstairs.

As usual, Wanda is already up doling out breakfast to the girls. Don and Marnie are at the breakfast bar as well. Joanie hasn't come down yet.

"Joanie slept with you last night?" Marnie questions.

"Yes, she was already in my bed when I went up to my room. I guess she's been having bad dreams too," I say.

"I went to check on the girls, and she wasn't in there. I freaked out. I started to go to wake you and noticed there were two people in your bed." Marnie explains.

"Where's Ethan?" I ask.

"Sleeping," Marnie says, "he decided we needed some night surveillance, so he went up the tower last night."

"Huh. That's probably actually a good idea," I say. "Who's taking the first watch today? I would take the girls so you could get outside a bit, but I was figuring you'd be with Ethan. Do you want Don and I to take the first watch, you and Ethan can have the second?"

"That's fine," Marnie answers, a little sullen.

"OR," Don says in his big booming voice, running up behind the girls grabbing the trio in a great big bear hug, "I'll teach the rug rats today, and you two girls take watch."

"Uncle Don, Uncle Don," the girls join in a chorus chanting.

"Well, I guess that's settled," Wanda says with a chuckle.

"Thank You!" Marnie mouths wordlessly.

Once we've finished breakfast, we gather up a few water bottles, a couple snacks and head out the back. We silently slip along the mountainside to the hidden ladder. Once we reach our destination, Marnie takes in a deep breath of fresh air, sighing it out.

"God, it is nice getting out of the cabin for a bit. Don't get me wrong, I am grateful, beyond grateful for the refuge, but man. I keep thinking about bringing the girls up here sometime. I just worry about Christy and Kenz on the ladder." She says.

"Maybe bring Marie up," I suggest. "Though they are so used to being together all the time now, not sure how separating them would go."

"Yeah, that is a consideration," she concedes.

The morning passes, we diligently stare to the South. Occasionally we do catch sight of a shift we wouldn't have previously noticed.

"They are still pretty well concentrated around that cluster of trees," I observe out loud.

A while later movement catches my eye. "Hey Mar, there's a group of people coming out of the cluster of trees there. Do you see them?" I say excitedly.

"How do you know they're people?" she asks.

"They don't have the line on their necks. Here look through these binoculars," I say, handing her the military-grade binoculars Ethan or Don brought from the base.

"Oh," she says as realization sets in.

"How many are there?" I ask.

"Two, three, four, five; looks like there are five," she answers.

"They're well-guarded, look at that group. How many guards do they have?" I ask.

"At least, what, fifteen that we can see," she answers.

We watch as the sullen group of fragile humans slowly make their way away from the cluster of trees, eventually disappearing from our range of vision. We just look at each other, "What do you think?" I ask Marnie.

"No clue. Let's stay up here a bit longer. We'll see if anybody, shifter or human returns," she suggests.

"You just don't want to go back inside," I accuse.

"Got me, but no, I am seriously curious at this point. This seems like a lot more activity than we've seen in a long time." She answers.

"True."

We pass the time talking about anything and everything. Her relationship with Ethan has now gone all the way. Though, this development is a bit more recent than I thought it would have been. They are both delighted with their relationship, which is nice. We talk about my night with Don. We haven't really had a chance to discuss it since then. I confess I still feel awful about it. I can't believe I betrayed Connor that way, even though I doubt I will ever see him again. It was just too soon. I do admit it was utterly amazing. Finally, we sit in silence, out of new topics for conversation; we are just about to give up and head down for a late lunch when movement catches my eye again to the west.

"Mar, look that way," I say, pointing where I saw the movement. "How long has it been?" I ask.

"Maybe three, four hours, I'm not totally sure. I haven't bothered charging my phone or watch in days." She answers.

"Yeah, me either," I agree.

Watching we see the group that left earlier returning on the same path they went out on. Now the humans are ladened with bags. "Let me see those," I say reaching for the better binoculars.

She willingly hands them over, "here go."

"It's food. They were on a food mission," I say, "I see canned goods through that plastic bag," I tell her, pointing to the guy in the front.

"I wonder who the food is for, the humans or the aliens," Marnie is wondering out loud.

"How would we know?" I say sadly.

We make our way back down the ladder, slipping into the cabin through the back door.

"Anything new today?" Wanda asks as we make our way into the kitchen.

"We saw five humans emerge from the trees with about fifteen guards. They came back a while later laden with grocery sacks of food." Marnie reports.

"Hmm, I guess they have to eat," Wanda ponders aloud.

"Yeah, but for us? Or them?" I pose my question again.

"Maybe both?" She questions.

CHAPTER 31 INTRUDER

We've been in the cabin now for about three months. Life has settled into a routine we are all comfortable with. I have finally stopped looking for Connor to return. He's either been caught or is dead, or I allow myself to suppose, found his family, and they won't allow his return. I have my doubts though.

We've witnessed some odd and some gruesome events over the past few months. On several occasions, we observed a human carrying the broken remains of other humans, in varying states of decomposition, out from the compound. They don't go far, disposing of them in the woods. Those days are particularly hard. On another particularly tough day, we saw a Shifter shoot a human with their shiny silver weapons. There was nothing left of the man after the weapon was discharged; he simply was no longer there. It's been at least a month since we've seen them catch or bring in anyone new, so that is at least something to be positive about.

We've also noticed they've established a routine, so we have somewhat learned what to expect from their activities. Every fourth day all activity is restricted to around their compound's opening near the cluster of trees. On this day, only two or three shifters even emerge from their compound, wherever it actually is. On the sixth of the day of the cycle, the emaciated defeated looking humans emerge for a scavenging run. Occasionally, aircraft fly in, shifters come and go, and sometimes move a human in or out. These activities usually occur on days one and three in the ten-day cycle.

"I want to shoot one of them," Don says one night after dinner.

"Yeah, but if we fire off a shot from here, we'll alert them to our presence," I say.

"We'd have to move far away from here," he says, agreeing with my assessment.

"But then once they know you are there, how do you get back?" Joanie questions. Joanie has matured a lot over the past three months, too much for her young body. She celebrated her 14th birthday sometime in the last month. While we know the approximate month, none of us know the day anymore. Since there is no cell service, once our phones died, they don't set to the appropriate day or time when we charge them. She has moved on from her sorrow to become a strong member of our group. She takes turns on watch, helps with planning supply runs. She also continues to lend a hand with the girls giving Marnie a break.

"You'd have to have a hiding place set up to lay low," Don says, having obviously thought this through. "We know they are inactive near the middle of the week or at least every fourth-ish day. On an inactive day, we'll go up and prepare a hideout. Then once they are active again, we'll shoot from there. We'll lay low for a day or so, then head back this way."

"I don't know, it still feels risky," Ethan voices concern.

"With the way things echo off the mountains, they'll never know exactly where it came from anyhow," Don disagrees. "AND!" he says, his voice booming with enthusiasm, "I brought a silencer from the base for my long-range rifle."

"I don't know," Ethan continues dismissing the thought.

"Damn it, Ethan, we've got to figure out if bullets can kill these assholes; otherwise, how will we make a plan?" Don counters.

"I'll go with you," I volunteer. "Quiet day should be in about two days; we'll go prepare the hideout. Just because it is there doesn't mean we have to do anything. Actually, it might be nice to make a few of these around the mountain, could provide a place to lay low if we are ever being chased on a supply run."

"See, now this girl is thinking," Don says, giving me an appreciative smile.

Two days later, we are confident it is a quiet day with little or no shifter activity. We wake early to begin the trek across the ridge to the other side of the mountain, encasing the valley below. It is hot outside; we think we are into July now. Not expecting trouble today, I dress for the heat, wearing shorts and a sleeveless cropped tank top. Don emerges dressed for war, wearing his Army issued cargo pants and a fitted tan T. I find myself staring at him longingly in his uniform.

"Ready red?" Don asks, catching me in my stare, looking back questioningly.

"I was born ready. Let's do this," I answer, recovering from a juicy daydream I was developing.

"I'll be in the watchtower. I'll let out a loud whistle if I see trouble," Ethan promises.

"There won't be trouble today," Don assures him.

"You don't know that," Ethan argues.

"I do, first we've never seen them as high up on the mountain as we'll be traveling; second, it's a rest day, I'm telling you we've got this." Don assures him, then adds, "We'll keep to the thickest parts of the woods."

"Still," Ethan mutters, clearly unhappy with our choice.

I walk up, kissing my brother on the cheek. "We'll be fine, Ethan. We've made all our runs so far on this rest day. This isn't even as dangerous since we're staying up on the ridge of the mountain."

Don, Ethan, and I pick up our packs from the garage on our way out the back. We each carry several backpacks with various supplies. After leaving through the mountainside garage door, we make our way out behind the cabin to the hidden ladder. Don and I will leave from behind the watchtower; we can travel parallel to the valley across the ridge from there. The weather today is perfect for our trip. The sky is a clear blue with a few puffy clouds, despite the heat, the humidity is rather low. There is the scent of pine and Mountain Laurel filling the air. Once up the ladder, we check in on Wanda's garden, which is looking quite nice "your mom will have fresh vegetables soon, that'll make her happy," I observe.

"Yeah, if we could only find something other than canned meats," he says.

"Maybe we'll happen across a deer on our trek," I say optimistically.

"Doubtful, we haven't seen any wildlife in months," Ethan interjects.

"Alrighty, mister negative," I say, sticking my tongue out at him.

"Take care of my sister Don" he threatens, adding a meaningful look. He then shoves one of the extra packs he carried up the ladder roughly into Don's hand.

"You know I love her too, E." Don counters, which earns him a nasty look from Ethan, so he adds, "she might as well be my sister too."

"Yeah, I know," Ethan says, a bit spiteful. He's been very consumed with Marnie lately; Don and I have become quite close in the intervening time. I think it bothers him.

After this awkward exchange, we arrange all of our supplies and turn toward the path into the woods. Once we've made our way farther up the path, Don and I slip into easy conversation. Don is so easy to be around. There is rarely a lapse in conversation between us.

"What's with E?" he asks.

"Oh, I think he is jealous of how close we've become. Don't worry about it, I am glad," I say, "I was afraid after, well you know, it would be awkward."

"You can say it, Rae, we're adults, we had a wild night of drunken debauchery," he says with a chuckle.

I laugh out loud at the way he says this.

"Shh, Rae, let's not go disturbing the neighbors. I am quite certain we are safe but let's not add unnecessary risk mmm K" he says, rolling his eyes at me. "Although it is nice to hear you laugh."

"Sorry, just the way you said that," I smile.

It takes us several hours to trek around the mountain's ridge to the place Don has in mind. "I think here," he says, stopping and dropping his backpacks.

I look around; the place does seem perfect. There is sapling tree coverage here, this will provide coverage down low, but you can still get a clear view of the valley below. The angle does put us at a disadvantage since we can't directly see where we believe is their compound's opening. Despite that limitation, this should work well.

We brought a mishmash of supplies with us, not knowing exactly what we would need. After a couple hours of work, Don has constructed a crude hideout built of rocks, trees, ferns, and extra green mesh he had at the cabin. The bulk of the shelter is made using a natural cave formation in the ridge. We just had to construct a closure that is solid enough to not give us away. "Nice work," I say, patting Don on the back.

"Thanks for being the guard," he says.

He lays on his stomach, pointing his rifle into the valley below. "This will be perfect," he mumbles. "I can fire, observe for a short time, then solidly hide away. I'll bring some supplies so I can hide out a day or two if needed."

I stand resting my hand on the pistol strapped to my side, keeping watch. While I survey the valley, I hear two things simultaneously that cause my heart to sink. I hear a loud whistle echoing around the valley and a twig break behind us. I spin around, not hesitating to draw my pistol and aim at the intruder. I see a blonde man standing there, aiming what looks to be an automatic rifle right at me. He is tall and skinny but looks as though he's not been roughing it too badly. His blonde hair is kept buzzed on the sides with a shock of curls on top. He has a very boyishly handsome face, complete with piercing blue eyes. I can see there are no marks behind his ears, so I know he is human.

"Move away from that rifle," he commands of Don with a voice full of authority. Don freezes. "NOW," he says more sternly. Don does as instructed, leaving the rifle on the ground and standing, facing the valley, with his hands in the air. "Now, drop that pistol, sweetheart," he says to me.

Crap, I am not good at split-second decisions. "Do it, Rae," Don whispers to me. I set my pistol down on the ground, returning upright with my hands in the air. I mentally wonder if Ethan's rifle can reach this far.

"You," he says to Don, "turn around now."

I chance a glance at Don; he doesn't seem overly concerned but more curious. I wonder if he knows this person is human because of their speech pattern and thinks that he can either take him or negotiate with him once he's face-to-face. He looks at me, question evident in his expression. He turns slowly, then drops his hands. "Damn it, Todd," he says, "you scared the shit out of me," he says, laughing.

"You two know each other?" I ask with annoyance in my voice, dropping my hands.

"Sorry," says the man Don called Todd, laughing. "I see a black guy and redhead out here in the mountains. I can only assume it was you and a relative of Ethan's."

He approaches the man, shakes hands, and then give each other an awkward one-armed hug slapping each other on the back.

"What the hell are you two doing out here? I figured I'd make it to your cabin tomorrow," Todd says.

"You're not that far," Don explains. "We are out here creating a hiding spot; I want to shoot these bastards and see what happens."

"Hmm, what bastards would those be?" Todd questions.

"These alien pieces of shit that invaded our world," Don says.

"That's what I thought but didn't want to be the one to say it in case I was actually crazy and not seeing what I thought I was out there," Todd says.

"Um, hi, hate to break up this reunion here, but what the actual fuck is happening?" I finally interject.

"Sorry, Rae," Don says, "This is my buddy, Todd. He was heading to Georgia to look for his family then meeting us at the cabin." He finishes moving over to wrap an arm around my shoulders, almost possessively as he eyes Todd. I'm going to guess Todd is a player

"Um, okay, anyone else we are expecting?" I ask.

"Well, one or two more I suppose. When it went this long and no one else showed up, I assumed it would just be us," Don explains. "We're done here. Let's head back to the cabin. I'm sure Ethan was glad to see you."

"See me already?" Todd inquires.

"Did you hear that whistle? That was Ethan keeping watch," Don explains.

"Well, as usual, he sucks at his job. I was on you before he saw me," Todd gasps laughing.

"Well, the shifters aren't that clever," Don says defensively.

"So, Todd," I say, "where about are you from?"

"Macon, Georgia," he says.

"And what branch of the military did you represent?" I follow up.

"Army Rangers," he says, "your brother is the only fly boy among this group, though he's handy to have around."

"Yeah," Don adds, "there's some aircraft hidden not far from here if we need to make a fast getaway."

"Really?" I ask, this is new information to me I had not heard before.

"Don't get any ideas, Red. We aren't headed on vacation," Todd says.

"Todd," I say pointedly, causing him to look my way, "don't be a dick."

"Ouch, I like this one, Don," Todd says.

Don looks at him sharply, "Todd," he pauses for effect, "don't be a dick."

I'm not really sure how I feel about Todd. But he hangs out with E and Don, so he can't be too bad; perhaps he is just trying to make an impression. We walk in silence for a while when Todd asks apprehensively, "so, who all is at the cabin?" What he really wants to know is who made it, who didn't.

"Me and Momma," Don starts, "Rae here and Ethan. Ethan found Martina, her three little sisters, who were somewhere else, but they miraculously were found."

"That's got to be a story," Todd says.

"Yes, we debrief every evening. We'll fill you in, and that is it." Don finishes. "What about you? What's your story?"

"No one was there by the time I got there. The neighborhood was ransacked. I stayed for about a month, looking for them, but nothing." Todd says sadly. "Then took me at least another month or so to make it up here on foot, but I didn't really know where else to go."

"That's too bad, man, I'm sorry," Don consoles.

"What about Bud and Thomas?" Todd inquires.

"Not here. It's been just us for about three months now," Don explains.

We continue in silence for the rest of the trek back to the cabin. My trip out with Don was much more fun, just he and I bantering back and forth. The uncomfortable silence with Todd in tow makes the trip feel twice as long. Finally, we get back to the landing behind the watchtower when Ethan comes running, "Damn Todd, you're a sight for sore eyes."

"Yes, I usually am. How the hell are you?" Todd asks Ethan.

"Well, I've been better," Ethan says.

"I hear the girlfriend made it; things not going well?" Todd asks pointedly.

"Get your mind out of the damn gutter boy," Ethan says a bit angrily. "You gotta watch this one Rae, he's a bit...um... yeah," he finishes.

"You were a bit late up there with your whistle today. I had them," Todd says.

"No, actually I had you way before. I was attempting to distract Rae long enough that she didn't shoot your ass when you surprised them," Ethan says.

"Uh-huh," Todd says.

"Let's go you two," Don says.

Yeah, I've decided I definitely do not like Todd, way too cocky for my taste. We make our way down the ladder, slipping in the backside of the cabin as usual. When we get inside Wanda has already made dinner, Marnie, Joanie, and the girls have gathered around the dinner table.

"Well, who is this?" Wanda asks.

"My buddy Todd" Don answers, "made his way back up from Macon, Georgia, to help us out here."

"Welcome, Todd," Wanda says, "pull up a seat and help yourself to some dinner."

"Ma'am, thank you," Todd says. Okay, well, he can be polite if he tries.

Once dinner is finished, Marnie whisks the girls off to bath and bed while the rest of us gather to tell Todd all we've learned so far. His reaction is much the same as others at the notion of shifters. "I haven't seen that," Todd says.

"Just wait, we'll take you up on the tower tomorrow; you can witness the whole thing. They should be pretty active tomorrow." Ethan says.

"What did you see out there?" Don asks.

"Not much, man. I traveled at night and laid low as much as I could. Like I said before, the neighborhood was ransacked, everyone was gone. I hung out in the house for about a month. I had food and supplies there. But it was obvious I wasn't going to find them on my own. So, I decided to head back up here and see if you guys had any better luck." Todd explains. "I thought I saw some bizarre creatures out there, all brown and scaly, but decided I just imagined things."

"No, that is their natural form we think," I say.

"Ew" is his only response.

We sit around the table a while that night. We learn that Todd is the youngest of 5 boys; that must be where the salty attitude comes from. I suppose he's had to fight his whole way through life. His mom lived with his oldest brother, his brother's wife, and their grandmother. His brother and sister-in-law had just welcomed a baby girl before all of this happened. Todd was about to take leave to go home to meet her for the first time. He finishes his story with evident sadness.

There is finally a break in the chatter; Todd looks up, pointing at Joanie, "what's her story," Todd asks.

"This is my friend's sister, Joanie," I say defensively. "Their mom died in the city with ours. He went off to Texas to look for his dad and sisters," I finish, trying to stay very matter of fact, but even I hear the sadness in my voice. Todd does a double-take but thankfully manages to not say anything obnoxious.

"Well Todd, we are a bit low on bedrooms. There is a bedroom with a full bed available upstairs since Joanie moved in with Rae, but it is attached to the bunkroom with the rug rats. Or, there is a room up there with a twin bed, but you still have to share a bathroom with the rug rats." Don says. "The only other options are a few tiny rooms in the basement with twin beds, but no bathrooms down there."

"I don't take up much room, but I'm no vampire. So, I'll take the twin room upstairs," Todd answers.

"Well, bed-time for me, it's been a long day; I got more exercise today than I have in months," I announce. Joanie immediately gets up to follow.

"Good night all," she says a bit timidly.

"Night kids," Ethan calls.

CHAPTER 32 EXPERIMENT

It is awkward over the next few days adjusting to an extra person in the cabin, especially someone with such a strong personality, but we manage. He actually becomes like a big brother to Joanie, which makes me smile. I just hope he remembers how young she is, though he's relatively young himself, only nineteen.

It's been about ten days since we created our hideout on the opposite ridge; Don is anxious to try shooting the aliens to see what happens. He decides to take a sleeping bag, some food, and head over today, the day they are inactive. He will set up today, spend the night in the cave hideout to take aim the next morning. He plans to spend two nights in hiding, making sure he puts plenty of time between the attack on the aliens and when he makes his way back to the cabin. Neither Wanda nor I are particularly fond of this, but his mind is made up. Just before dusk, he packs up his supplies and heads to the hideout. We are all anxious for the next day.

Sleep is difficult this night; I worry about Don up on the mountain by himself. Part of me wonders if he is thinking of me, unsure why I want this, but I know that I do. Once morning comes, we are all apprehensive. We are not only concerned about Don's safety but anxious if this experiment will lead to our discovery. We also wonder if our bullets are effective against these invaders. A lot is riding on today.

After a quick breakfast of cereal, we sit in silence while the sun finishes rising to the sky. We have a general idea of where he will be targeting; after a scuffle over binoculars, we each take up various observation points. I head up to the watchtower with Ethan; Marnie, Todd, Joanie, and Wanda take up the watch from the cabin's upstairs windows.

We've been up at the watchtower for about an hour when the shifters become active. We have our binoculars trained on the target area. We do not hear the shot when it happens; the silencer is successful at blocking the sound. We see a Shifter fall to the ground, an apparent head wound. Ethan and I embrace at the sight of the shifter down. The shifter's companions do not look for the source. Instead, they stare at the shifter on the ground with curiosity. Despite ample opportunity, Don does not take another shot. At this point, they don't appear to know what has happened, and we aren't ready to begin a full-on war.

I am just about to look away when I see activity around the fallen shifter. It stands; the wound in the head is no longer visible. It looks questioningly at the shifter next to it, then aims, firing his silver weapon at that shifter. The shifter in question is obliterated, nothing left, just like the hay in the loft, the human we saw shot months ago, and all the major cities and military bases worldwide.

I turn to stare at Ethan in misery. "So, they can only be killed by their own weapons?" I ask miserably.

"I don't know, it would appear that way. I wonder if Don was watching that or if he had already ducked into hiding?" Ethan speculates.

After the shifter shoots his companion, it appears an argument ensues. The shifters turn, looking about them, though their suspicion never travels farther than their immediate surroundings. Well, we already know they aren't too smart.

Ethan and I continue our watch the rest of the morning, though nothing changes. We are about to head down when a noise alerts us that there is activity behind us; we both spin around quickly, hands on our pistols. Out from behind a tree steps Don.

"Didn't seem like they suspected anyone as high up as me, so I thought it would be safe to come back around," he says.

"We didn't even see you traveling around," I say, "but we were watching the shifters, not you."

"That was something, wasn't it? I thought for sure it was going to work. Seems only those devices they have can eliminate those things," Don says sadly.

"Yeah, that certainly puts a damper on things," Ethan says, "though it looks like if need be, it would slow them down, give someone a chance to get away."

The three of us head down the hidden ladder together. When we enter the cabin, the mood is very subdued; everyone's face holds the same look of defeat. "Don," Wanda says with relief, "I am so happy you're back, but I thought you were going to lay low until at least tomorrow?"

"Their suspicion never traveled up this high, so I felt confident making my way back here," Don explains to the group.

No one goes back up to the watchtower after lunch; we sit around the table, staring at nothing in particular. "Well," Ethan breaks the silence, "we know it will at least slow them down if we are being chased," reiterating his earlier thought.

"We really need to get our hands on some of those weapons; see if we can figure out what they are or how they work," Todd says wistfully.

"Well, to do that, we'd have to get awfully close," Don says. "Not sure how we'd be able to do it and get back out again."

"I wonder if now we know more about what we are facing, we can find more clues in the cities, at the site of detonation?" Ethan thinks out loud.

"No way," I interject. "There is no cover, nothing left, no way to hide."

"We could get close, go on their rest day," Todd offers.

"We don't know they all have a rest day or what day it is. We only know what happens with these idiots here in our little valley. There's got to be thousands upon thousands of them out there." I protest, not at all happy with the direction this conversation is going.

"That's true. We really need more observation points." Don ponders.

"Where will we get more observation points without leaving here?" Marnie questions.

"That's just it. We'd have to leave," Ethan says.

"We don't have to decide now guys, just something to consider," Don says. "We know enough to keep safe here, we know we can travel safely at night, they are generally inactive after 11PM, and they have one day a week they aren't active at all."

"Man, I wish I knew what technology they're using in those guns," Todd fumes.

"Dude, it's probably not even from this planet," Ethan counters.

"Probably not," he concedes.

Ethan pulls out his notebook, adding in the findings of today's experiment. Eventually, one by one, we rise from the table and meander about the cabin. Wanda is humming away in the kitchen, Marnie has gone back to teach the girls, the boys each flop down on the couch brooding in silence. Willis makes his way over to Don, curling up beside him. I make my way into the kitchen to help Wanda with dinner.

"We're going to need a supply run soon," Wanda says when

I enter the kitchen. "It'd be too good to be true to find a deep freezer filled with meat somewhere."

I give a small laugh as I set to peeling potatoes. We've got to use these; they're pretty old and won't make it another week. "Last time out, we didn't find any meat. If those chickens are still at the farm, perhaps we can get eggs. Maybe snag a few chickens. I'm guessing we can figure out how to clean and cook 'em." I muse.

"That'd be something," Wanda says with a laugh. "But I'd doubt you'd get chickens caught without making a hell of a ruckus."

CHAPTER 33 THE UNFORESEEN DANGER

Supplies are getting low; we can't put off a run any longer. Once again, Don and I will make the trek down the mountain. On the day of the run, despite the heat of summer settling around us, I am dressed in jeans. If we get into trouble, the jeans will provide some protection for my legs running through the forest. I grab my purple .380 stuffing it into the waistband of my pants, then cram a sheathed hunting knife through my belt. I do wear a short-sleeved shirt, it is just too hot for long sleeves.

I make my way downstairs, where I see Don slinging the strap of an automatic rifle around his neck. Don accepts a pair of night-vision goggles from Ethan. Though no one says it out loud, we only take one pair with us when we go out so, if we don't make it back, those left behind will still have two pair on hand.

It's just after midnight when we set out. The shifters have been inactive for over an hour now, we feel confident in leaving. Since we need a good run we are taking the jeep; as long as the road remains intact, we can get down the mountain and into town a lot faster. As much as we are hoping to find meat, the likelihood of doing so is long past. After over three months of no electricity, even if generators are still running the meat has gone rancid by now. Wanda's assessment of finding a deep freezer somewhere is the best shot at finding a good protein source.

"Maybe a restaurant," I muse out loud as Don and I bump along in the jeep down the path.

"What's that?" he questions.

"I was just thinking about finding some protein. Maybe if we found a restaurant that had a natural gas line fed generator and a deep freezer, we could find some meat," I say.

"Keep dreaming, girl," he says. "I think we're on the lookout for more beans. That stash your momma had going has lasted a long time."

"Let's just make sure we don't forget toilet paper this time, 'eh. My butt is raw from using paper towels the past week." I joke.

"Too much information there, Rae," he says playfully. Then adds, "But yes ma'am, toilet paper is at the top of my list; well, behind life-sustaining supplies that is," adding a quick wink in my direction.

We make it down the mountain without incident and pull onto the access road. "What are you feeling on the main road, left or right?" Don inquires.

"Left, right feels like it is taking us too close to the shifters," I say.

When we get to the main road, we turn left, and head towards town. It takes a few minutes before we are back into an area of town with houses, stores, and restaurants. While the homes along the way stand wide open, restaurants and stores are closed up reasonably tight. Many have broken glass, indicating people have broken in, but the doors are shut.

"Let's check out the grocery up there on the right," Don suggests.

"Don't you feel like that place is a bit conspicuous?" I hedge.

"It'll be fast. We can fill the jeep pretty darn quick and get back before daylight even dawns," Don counters.

"I suppose," I concede.

After about ten minutes, we pull up outside the grocery. The store is situated beside a mountain; there is a small road that winds around between the grocery and the mountain to the back of the store. On the opposite side of the mountain is the main road into town. In the far reaches of the lot, there are several groves of trees. We park here, in the back of the lot under the concealment of the trees, watching the store.

After about forty-five minutes, Don declares there is no movement anywhere; he pulls the jeep into the space between the store and the mountain to keep it hidden. We each grab our weapons and cautiously make our way to the store. We find a side door near the back that is propped open; this allows us to enter the store from the side by the mountain and not walk out in front of the store, risking someone seeing us.

"Let's stick together," Don says, "I still think this is the right call, but now that we're going in, I am nervous."

"Great," I answer, "I count on you to be the confident one."

Entering the store I am immediately struck by the smell of decay. The smell of rotting meat and vegetables is almost too overwhelming to stand. I pull my shirt up over my nose, moving forward. We enter into a storeroom where food and supplies are stored in boxes on pallets.

I touch Don's shoulder then point to a case of toilet paper, "all packed up for us and ready to go."

He gives me a thumbs-up and we proceed into the store. Many of the security lights still provide a weak light; the batteries are not quite dead yet. We head to the front, grabbing a grocery cart each. The store is somewhat picked over, but there is still plenty of good food here. We avoid the store's outside aisles; the produce, bakery, meat, and dairy are no longer edible. We head through the center aisles. Here we do well, flats of canned vegetables and soups, potato chips, crackers, cookies, cereal, flour, and other baking goods. We do find non-refrigerated kinds of milk, such as coconut milk and almond milk.

"Mom can use this in her baking," Don notes.

Soon our carts are heaped and cannot hold another item. We make our way back out to the jeep. Don stands at the door watching outside for several minutes before declaring it safe to proceed. We head to the jeep and unload the first round of groceries. I run back inside, grabbing the case of toilet paper, and adding it to the mix.

"I think we can get a bit more," Don whispers.

"Agree, let's stuff it full; I don't want to come back again any time soon."

We head back to the baking aisle, adding sugar, cooking oil, chocolate chips, pumpkin, cherry, and apple pie filling. We add some premixed pancake, bread, and muffin mixes. We load up on dried beans, filling an entire cart, taking all left in the aisle. We finish filling Don's cart with more soups, vegetables, and canned meats. "Mama will find a way to make these taste good," Don says, looking disdainfully at a can of potted meat.

We head out to the jeep once more, standing at the door for a moment, Don surveys the lot, once again deeming it clear, we proceed to the jeep. The items we grabbed this round do not entirely fill the jeep; stuffing the bags of beans in tiny spaces allows us to make one more trip inside.

This time we focus specifically on canned goods and shelf-stable meals that include meat of some kind. I hold up a shelf-stable package of bacon, Don gives the thumbs up, so I pick up several boxes. I wander farther down the aisle when I come across the jerky section. "Oh!" I say out loud. Then gather as many packages of pork, chicken, and beef jerky as my cart will handle. We wander the aisles once more, grabbing a full case of paper towels.

"Where on Earth are we going to put that?" Don inquires.

"What if we find some rope? Then we could tie the toilet paper and the towels to the top. That'd give us a bit more room; we could stock up on more toiletries," I suggest.

"Good thinking Red," he says appreciatively. "Next time we need to bring the hitch rack," he adds thoughtfully.

We visit the hardware section finding rope, then make our way back out of the store a third time. It takes some time to reorganize all the supplies, but we manage, creating more space. "What do you think?" I ask Don, "I kind of feel like we've been here too long already and are pushing our luck."

"Yeah, but if we fill up now, we can head back and not have to make a run for a while." He answers.

"Fine," I say begrudgingly, I know he is right, but man, I want to be out of here; there's just a bad feeling in my gut.

We enter the store one final time, hitting the personal care aisle, stocking up on shampoo, conditioner, soap, toothpaste, and girl's items. Then we make our way to the pharmacy area and load up on over-the-counter medicines of all sorts. The actual pharmacy has been broken into already. Don slides through the window, returning with bottles of antibiotics. "You won't find any narcotic painkillers in there, but the useful stuff is still there," he says, climbing back out the window.

We grab dish soap, coffee, and powdered creamer as an afterthought on our way to the exit. Finally, we are done in this store, we make our last trip out the side. We just finished loading the last of the shampoo into the car and closed the hatch when we hear a gun cock behind us. We both spin around automatically, having our guns drawn on the person standing before us.

"Well, well, what do we have here," a sinister male voice says.

"Friend, I think you just need to move on," Don says, "we don't want any trouble."

"Hear that Joe," the man says, laughing, "they don't want any trouble. Thing is, I want that jeep you've loaded up with all those supplies."

"That's not going to happen, sir," Don answers, cautiously sliding closer to me. My eyes have adjusted to the darkness, so I can see fairly well, but so can they. Don has the night vision goggles on, so he has the best view.

"Oh, I think it is," says the man stepping closer to Don. He makes his way closer, and we hear the sound of approach behind us. Neither of us has dropped our weapons; they are both still pointed at the sneering man in front of us. Though my gun is drawn, I am trembling violently, trying to process the situation.

We can give them the jeep, and he would probably just drive away. If we give up the jeep, it will suck carrying one little bag each of groceries back up the mountain to the cabin. Having to walk will likely take us the better part of the night and day, risking detection by the aliens. I'd really rather keep our jeep loaded with supplies. Don, once again, casually slides one step closer to me.

"Put your guns down. We've got you surrounded," says the man.

"I only heard one other set of footsteps," he whispers silently in my ear. More loudly, he says, "that's fine, but I guarantee if someone fires on us, you will die before we both fall. Not to mention if you fire that weapon, you are likely to draw a dozen or more aliens to us."

"Aliens?" He questions.

"Yes, don't you and Joe pay attention to what is happening around you?" Don asks snarkily.

I see the man look behind us questioningly at the person back there.

The man, whether meaning to do so or doing so unconsciously, has moved toward us. "I'm going to lunge on our friend here," Don whispers in my ear, "as soon as I move, spin around and hold your weapon on Joe. These guys are typical bullies, all talk, want something without having to work for it. As soon as they are both neutralized, we go."

It's a tense standoff, lasting several more minutes. The man takes another half step towards us. Don takes advantage of the movement and lunges forward, instantly grabbing the man's gun and pointing it upwards. Before he has finished this move, I spin around and train my weapon on Joe. I am taken aback by the sight before me; Joe is just a child, about 10 or 12, standing there, trembling like me. I hear the sounds of struggle behind me, but I don't dare turn around. Even facing this child, I don't know if he's used that weapon before.

Distracted by trying to keep my eyes on Joe and listening to the struggle behind me, I do not notice a third person emerge from the other side of the jeep until it is too late. Suddenly, my pistol is knocked from my hand, and I am being spun around. I feel a knife pressed sharply to my neck. Someone, I believe a female based on size, is holding tight to my hair, pulling my head back with one hand, the other pressing a long blade against my skin. Don, distracted by the sounds of my struggle, loses concentration, and the man gets the upper hand, punching him in the face and shoving him backward. Don recovers quickly, aiming his rifle at the man. They are once again locked in a stare down, weapons drawn on each other. The man cautiously moves over next to where I stand, held by the woman.

"Now," he says, "drop the weapon, or Linda here will end her."

Rather than being more scared, as I felt facing a 10-year-old, I really did not want to shoot, I gain confidence. I am sure it is just the adrenaline pumping through my system, but she doesn't feel particularly strong; I think I can take her. I take deep slow calming breaths trying to determine how to get out of this situation without losing our jeep and supplies. And most importantly, not losing my life.

The man next to me holding the gun is a concern, but I know if I can neutralize the woman, Don can quickly get the gun away from the man during the struggle. I stare intently into Don's eyes, trying to convey my thoughts. He looks at me questioningly, then gives a slight nod as if he understands.

"What'll it be, boy?" the man asks menacingly.

I blink purposefully, slow, and over-animated, one, two, take a deep breath, three. I throw my arms up behind me while spinning, grabbing the woman by the hair. She quickly drops her knife but not before causing a somewhat large but superficial gash in my neck. Though a bit distracted by the pain, and sensation of blood seeping down my neck, I manage to keep my focus. Pulling her face down and smashing it into my knee.

The man distracted by my action is caught off guard when Don barrels into him from the side. I don't even give Joe a second thought and grab my pistol from the ground pointing it at the woman who is now disarmed, clutching her nose. I was right; she is a fragile-looking woman, almost sickly. I almost feel sorry for her, well, if she hadn't just held a knife to my throat. "You bitch," she spits out, "you broke my nose."

I don't even dignify this with a response. While I hold the woman at gunpoint, the struggle between Don and the man continues. I hear Don yell, "Rae, start the jeep." I move around to the driver's side, keeping my pistol pointed in the direction of Joe and Linda. Stepping inside, I start the jeep. A minute later I hear a hard blow as Don yells, "Army Rangers asshole," then the passenger door opens, and Don climbs in.

"Go," Don yells. I do not hesitate; I gun it, swerving to avoid hitting Joe, standing dumbfounded in the middle of the drive. Well, at least it doesn't seem like he's used that rifle before, that is something. I don't go far; Don is the one with the night vision goggles. I can't really see where I am going. When I feel we've traveled far enough to be out of range of the family, I find a small side street and pull off to switch Don places.

"Are you okay?" Don asks, looking concernedly at my neck.

"Yeah, it is superficial, probably looks worse than it is," I say, wincing as I touch the area on my neck. Don digs around in the glove box producing a rather clean looking shop rag; I accept and push against the wound across my neck.

"Look," Don says quickly, pointing straight ahead. Though he didn't sound alarmed, I swiftly turn my head terrified of what we must now be facing. However, in front of us is a park store, stocked with propane cylinders. "Those might come in handy if the gas ever runs low; we can use them for the stove or water heater. We should make a point to grab a few every time we're down here," Don says.

"Lord, I hope we are not hold up there so long all of your propane tanks empty," I say miserably. When we get out to switch places, we move to the display, break the lock, and remove two tanks. Don takes the tanks back to the jeep, working to secure them to the roof with the cases of toilet paper and packages paper towels. I close the display, trying to make it look as though it is still locked.

I climb back in the jeep, "take me home," I moan to Don.

"Not one for adventure, Rae?" He asks.

"No," I sigh back, repositioning the towel over my neck where the knife cut my skin, "I've had enough for one night."

The trip back to the cabin passes in a blur. Before I know it, we are pulling the jeep into the garage. We will wait until morning to unload the groceries.

"Don? Rae? Is that you?" we hear Ethan whisper as we make our way into the kitchen.

"Yes, it's us," I say back quietly.

"I didn't expect you guys back so quickly," Ethan hints.

"No trouble, well, nothing we couldn't handle. We just hit a grocery that was still well-stocked." Don answers.

"What trouble?" Ethan inquires.

"Tomorrow, it is nothing that will follow us here. Right now, I want my bed," Don says.

"Ditto," I answer. I try to slip past Ethan, he grabs my hand, pulling the towel from my neck.

"Rae?" he questions with evident concern. "What the hell happened?"

"We ran into a couple of bullies trying to take our jeep," Don explains. "But your sister is a badass, and we handled it perfectly well. We'll talk more about it tomorrow; right now, I want to sleep. The adrenaline rush is over, and I am exhausted."

It is close to dawn when I make my way up to my bedroom. I go to the bathroom and retrieve a clean washcloth to hold to my neck. I change out my bloody shirt for a clean one, then fall blissfully into my bed. I am asleep within seconds. An hour or so later, I hear Joanie rise, but I just roll over and go back to sleep.

Marnie comes in around lunch, "Wakey, Wakey," she sings cheerfully. My response is to throw a pillow at her.

"Why are you so cheery?" I ask.

"Why be grumpy," she says, "that doesn't help anyone."

"Fair point," I concede. "Is Don up yet?"

"Just got up," she answers.

"Todd and Ethan on a watch?"

"Nope," she answers, "Todd and Joanie are on watch."

"Who's teaching the girls?" I wonder aloud.

"Wanda," she answers. "Ethan is sleeping. He kept watch most of the night. He came back in just before you guys got back."

"So why aren't you waking him up?" I question dejectedly.

"I tried. He threw a book at me," she says with a wink.

"I'll remember that next time, hard objects make you leave!" I answer with a smile.

Sitting up allows Marnie to see the carnage on my neck, "Rae, what the hell?" she shrieks.

"We ran into a bit of trouble in town, but we're fine. It looks worse than it is. We'll talk about it downstairs," I say blowing her off.

She stares at me open mouthed for a moment then leaves the room. Once Marnie leaves, I take my shower and dress for the day. I find some gauze and bandage tape in the bathroom and bandage my neck. It looks awful, and I know will draw a lot of attention, but the wound is still seeping slightly. When I get downstairs, everyone is busy unpacking the supplies from the night before.

"You guys had a good run," Wanda says appreciatively,

grabbing a bottle of water before heading back to the girls' school lesson.

"I'm sure Don told you already, we hit the grocery store on the way into town. The smell of rotting food about made me puke when we went in, definitely no working freezers there." I say with a sigh.

"That is too bad," Wanda says earnestly. "Rae," she says reaching cautiously up to my neck.

"It's nothing, we ran into a bit of trouble with some bullies in town, we'll talk about it later. Right now, I am starving." I say.

I sit down to a bowl of cereal in almond milk, which is surprisingly good. I am finishing up when Ethan comes sleepily, plodding down the stairs. "Morn'n guys," he says with the sounds of sleep still in his voice. "So, what the hell happened last night?" he asks directly.

"Nothing we couldn't handle," Don assures. "We just ran into other refugees. Some guy thought he, his sickly-looking wife and his 10-year-old kid could take Rae and me. He wanted the jeep and all the supplies we'd loaded into it."

"You didn't hurt the kid, did you?" Marnie asks, concerned.

"Of course not. But I did have to kick his dad's ass right in front of him," he says. "Then, the woman, who I assume is his mom was holding a knife to Rae's throat." I hear a collective gasp in the room at this revelation. "So, he also saw Rae smash her face, so he may be a bit scarred from that event."

"Hmm, that could definitely be a big problem going forward," Ethan ponders, "do you think we should send larger groups on the raids?"

"No," Don answers firmly. "What if the shifters caught us? Then that'd be three or four of us instead of two. We do not waste our lives that way. Which brings me to my next point of conversation. If God forbid, one or more of us do not make it back from scavenging, the rest do not waste their lives. You do not seek revenge. You do not make your presence known. You buck up and continue. Is that clear?"

"That is hard to stomach, but I think you're right," Ethan agrees. When he finishes this statement, Marnie runs over, wrapping her arms around Ethan.

"Ethan, you have to promise me you'll never go out," she says in a whimper.

"I can't do that, Mar. We all have a role to play here. If that is what is required of me, I will do it. Besides, you'd lay the risk always on Rae and Don?" Ethan challenges.

"Not that I'd want to. I've just lost so much already," she trails off.

I stare at my friend, dumbfounded. "Glad to know the past thirteen years of friendship have been important to you, Mar," I say, stung by her comments.

"No Rae, I didn't mean," she begins.

"Whatever, Marnie, just save it," I snarl back at her and sulk off to the living room.

A few minutes later, Don takes a break from putting supplies away to come to sit beside me. "I don't think she meant anything by it, Rae. She's simply scared," Don says sympathetically.

"Yeah, well, I've lost my mom and my boyfriend. At least her parents are probably still alive out there. What, were we friends the past years just because she liked Ethan?" I say, still feeling the sting of her comment.

"You know that's not true. Ethan says you guys have been friends since kindergarten. Hopefully, she wasn't crushing on him already at that age," he says with a smile.

"Stop being practical. I'm tired and cranky. I don't want to be logical," I say, sliding back to lean against Don.

"I am sorry you are suffering, Rae. If you ever want to talk, I'm here for you," he says with a warm smile.

"Thanks Don. I am curious?"

"What about?" he questions.

"What do you think about Todd and Joanie up on lookout together? She's just fourteen, you know," I say.

"I think he's harmless. I think he sees her as a baby sister to protect. He never had a sister, you know," Don reassures me.

"I suppose," I say snuggling into Don's side, resting my head against him and drift off once more.

CHAPTER 34 A
PATTERN TO LIFE

Life in the cabin has been harmonious. We each have a role to play and everyone seems content. The monotony can wear on us, but we manage to get by. Don and I generally volunteer for any runs that need made. We've been out quite a bit lately as a group we've discoverd we need supplies other than just the basic food and care items. Don and I have gotten good at these trips; we react well to each other with unspoken communication.

Don and I are on watch today, tomorrow we plan to make a run for supplies. The girls just keep growing and need clothing. They need clothing for now, the summer months, but will also need warm weather clothing as fall approaches.

"Did you see that?" I ask Don pointing over to the west. A little higher up on the mountain than usual, I saw a shimmering.

"Yeah, can you see what it shifted into?" he asks troubled.

"No," I say equally concerned. "I saw the shimmer; I didn't see anything before the shift and now I can't see anything that it is complete."

"Wait," Don says, "it just moved. It's still there, still scaly but is now the same color as the surroundings."

"Great, so they are chameleons now too?" I say with a gasp. "You're right though, now that you've said that I can see it."

"At least we know how we are missing them," he answers.

After making this observation I continue scanning the mountain side. "Over there to the left," I say.

"Good eyes Rae," Don says appreciatively. "At least we know what we are looking for now. Though if they are blending into the background that well, I don't know how we'll ever see them all."

"That is troubling," I add.

Our nightly debriefs have gotten shorter. We get new information so infrequently now, but at least this will make for news tonight. The rest of our watch goes with no other incidents. We do manage to spot the shifters across the mountain we previously had not noticed. Though this is of little comfort; it takes a lot of effort to spot them, in an emergency situation they will be difficult to see.

Dawn rises the next morning. I wake and take my normal shower, braiding my hair tightly, then wrapping it in a bun. Since the run-in at the grocery store, I keep my hair wound tightly on runs so there is nothing for anyone to grab. I dress in my usual jeans, and short sleeves. My pistol is secured in my waistband. I stare at it for a moment, wishing we could do some target practice. I haven't fired my gun in years, but the noise might attract the shifters. Once dressed, Don and I head out on foot down the mountain. The aliens have been off their schedule a bit these past few weeks, but today can be generally counted on as a day rest day for them.

"I wonder why," I muse out loud.

"Why what, baby girl?" Don asks.

"Why the change in routine. It's been what, five, or five and a half months? They haven't deviated from the schedule hardly at all. All of a sudden, they're all over the place on any day." I say.

"Not sure. It is definitely troubling. It is good we can count on today to be quiet. As long as we kept our days straight," he says with a wink. It is early in the day. We left right after breakfast, knowing the trek down the mountain will take about two hours, then several hours of searching the houses, followed by three or so hours back up the mountain. It will definitely be a long day.

We follow the jeep trail to the ranger's road, then walk a short distance to the houses. In the August heat, is it August, I am not entirely sure; I am sweating buckets by the time we get down there. "Maybe we should check a house with a pool," I joke. "We could cool off."

"What are we going to do Red, go skinny dipping?" Don says, raising his eyebrows at the thought.

"Why not?" I ask, "you've already seen me naked." I add a wink.

"That is true," he answers a bit maniacally.

"Come on Romeo, we've got a job to do," I say, bringing his focus back to the task at hand. We slip through the trees close to the road keeping our eyes open for a house. A sub-division would be great, more opportunities to find what we need, clothes. Marnie and I need summer clothes as well, we're washing the same three or four things every few days. Trouble is, where we are we aren't likely to find subdivisions, just vacation rentals which won't be stocked with clothing.

We travel about a mile down the road before finding a cluster of houses. We watch the street for a half-hour before determining it is safe. Once we are sure there is no movement, we proceed. The first house is a bust, must have been a single male. Don does find some items he can use, nothing for the girls, Marnie, or myself.

We look around outside before moving to the next house. In this house there are four bedrooms upstairs. This house had multiple children. Two rooms are designed in girl themes, while a third is in boy colors.

We enter the master bedroom making our way to the oversized closet. Here we find plenty of clothes for Marnie and me. I see a large duffle bag on the shelf and stuff it as full as I can get of summer clothing. Then I find another small bag throwing in a few hoodies that'll be nice to have around in the fall months. Once we are done here, we head to the first girl's room. Here we find clothes that will fit Kenz for a while. We choose a selection of basics to get her through, adding to a duffle bag Don found in the boy's room.

"What do you think happened to the family?" I ask Don sadly.

"Who knows. The doors were standing open like the house had been searched, but maybe they left before? Or maybe it is a vacation house, and they weren't even here," he says hopefully.

We spend a great deal of time in the house; it looks as though we'll find all we need – and can carry, here. That is definitely a spot of luck.

We finish stuffing our finds into various bags we've found and walk down the stairs. Stepping into the kitchen we freeze dead in our tracks. Standing at the cupboard is a filthy, disheveled, emaciated man. He is thin in the extreme; his clothes are dirty and torn, and his hair is longer, almost dreadlocked in places. What is most frightening are the scars, so many scars all over his body. He looks at us with a start, then places one finger to his lips and points out the window. The sight out the window causes terror to seize my body. Outside is a guard detail. They are scavenging. This is not their typical scavenge day, what is going on, they shouldn't be scavenging for six more days.

We plaster ourselves to the wall beside the refrigerator out of sight of the shifters outside. Then the man begins muttering under his breath. It is barely audible, so I am assuming these things hear really well.

"Two hours, going to be about two hours before we get back. I need to get back to my wife. They keep our wives, so they know we'll come back and not cause trouble. Be at least two hours," he mutters again, looking at us very pointedly. "Nothing here doesn't look like I will find anything. This is where we get food. We don't get much, but eat what we find," he continues muttering.

He reminds me of someone who is mentally handicap you see muttering to themselves at a bus stop, but I know he is trying to give us information. I wish I could ask questions, but don't want to risk adding a different voice. If the shifters can hear that well, they'll certainly notice the difference. Don begins to open his mouth to speak when the man shoots him a sharp look, shaking his head, he points to his ear then outside.

"More coming, we've been getting ready for some alien event, haven't gotten enough to eat, too busy preparing. The damn king of them is here in Tennessee. Who'd have thought that" he continues. "They'll kill you if you even look at them wrong, or if you look at the crystal, what's with that stupid sparkly thing. Total control, they have total control of us, cannot even move if they don't want us to. Most of them are dumber than a bag of hammers, most of them are. The king though, he's the brains."

"YOU," we hear a shout from the outside. He jumps a bit, then starts to make his way to the door, once more giving us a meaningful look. "Two hours, usually out here about two hours, then maybe two hours to get back. I hate being gone that long." And disappears out the door. We hear him speak more clearly to the guard confirming the muttering was for our benefit, "Nothing in there we can use. It's been picked over." After he finishes his sentence, the guard doesn't even spare a second glance and they continue walking down to the next house.

I finally let out a breath I didn't even realize I was holding. Don sets down his bags, and I follow his lead setting the duffles on the floor. He then points to the floor, then to the stairs. He crouches down into a crawling position. I follow suit and we slink our way along the floor to the stairs, staying below the windows' view.

We silently scale the stairs to the master bedroom where we close and lock the door. Don continues crawling to the window to peer out the corner. He points to the house next door then holds up seven fingers. He leans back against the wall, tipping his head to the ceiling and closing his eyes. This will be a long three hours. I crawl over to Don and sit in his lap, curling myself against him for comfort. He wraps his arms protectively around me, resting his lips against the top of my head. "We'll be okay," he murmurs quietly, "we'll just have to lay low for a bit."

I realize I am silently sobbing when I feel his wet shirt against my face. I lean up, "I'm sorry," I whisper, pointing to his shirt.

"It's okay," he whispers back, "that was too close for comfort."

We remain silent for at least another half hour. I continue resting my head against Don, him wrapping his arms around me in comfort. He looks up, then whispers more loudly, "they're a few houses down across the street now. Damn, that was close."

"What do you make of what that man said?" I ask.

"He was definitely trying to give us information. Not sure what to do with it. I gathered that only partnered folks go on raids. They separate them to ensure compliance on the part on the part of the searcher." He says.

"What about more coming and 'stupid alien event'" I ask, "that cannot be good."

"No, but I'm fixating on the 'damn king' here in Tennessee," he says. "We always suspected someone else pulling the strings, he confirmed that."

I shake my head slightly leaning back into Don. "How are we going to pass three hours," I muse.

"Oh, I've got an idea," he answers with a sly grin.

"NO!" I answer sternly but laughing quietly.

"I was only kidding Rae," he says defensively.

"Were you though?" I ask smiling back up at him. Our eyes lock in that moment, I feel tingles down my spine and butterflies in my stomach. We gaze into each other's eyes, he leans down gently kissing my lips. His kiss is warm and tender, filled with so much emotion.

He pulls away, continuing to look into my eyes "I really like you Rae. You are so smart, and brave; you are someone I could see spending forever with. I know you still aren't over Connor leaving, I understand. I don't want to take advantage of your vulnerabilities."

"And that, is one of the many things I love about you. You are chivalrous, your mama raised you right," I say. Then I lean up, kissing him gently on the lips. Once we pull apart, I lean back into his chest resting my head against him. "Tell me about your family," I suggest as a way to pass time. We spend hours talking about anything and everything in the fading daylight. Finally, it is dark outside.

"So, do you think it is safe?" I ask.

"As safe as it is going to be, I think we can go," he says, lacking confidence.

We cautiously make our way back down the stairs. Don pulls out a set of night vision goggles and surveys the ground floor. Suddenly he sweeps his hand across me, pushing me against the wall. "What?" I gasp in a whisper.

"Movement over there," he whispers back pointing toward the kitchen. We stand rigid against the wall not making a sound. "Just a cat," he sighs out in relief, "we're okay."

I just want this trip to be over, to be back in the cabin with our family. We stop, pick up our bags and head out the back door. Once again, at the doorframe Don stops looking carefully around before motioning me out with him. The moon is out, filtering down through cloud cover making it bright enough to see just in front of us, but not far ahead. Don takes the lead, draping one bag over his arm, allowing him to entwine his fingers with mine. We travel about an hour up the mountain when the burden becomes too much.

"Let's stash this bag here, it has more fall type clothing in it. I can come back down this far on their next rest day and grab it," I suggest.

"Do you think it will rain between now and then?" He questions.

"Does it matter?" I ask, "we can wash the clothes."

"Okay, but let's be sure it's well hidden. I don't want to give anything away about our presence here," Don concedes.

We travel a little farther up the mountain when he sees a small cave like structure, stowing the bag inside, we cover the opening with branches and leaves.

"It will also be fairly protected from the weather in there as well," I comment admiring Don's handiwork.

"Yep, and we're making really good time, we're only about

forty-five minutes from the cabin I expect. It'll just take an hour and a half to get back here, retrieve the bag and return to the cabin," Don says confidently.

"Great, just an hour and a half in no man's land," I whine, but grateful to have the load lightened.

"Better than going all the way into town," he says to comfort me.

"True." I reply. He reaches down, once again taking my hand in his as we continue our walk back up the path. We make the rest of the trip back to the cabin without issue. When we open the door we are met with a chorus of relieved sighs and "Oh, thank God."

"We saw the scavenging detail go out, it was too late to warn you," Joanie says, tears in her eyes.

"When you weren't back when we expected we started to get even more worried than we already were," Wanda adds rushing over to hug her son. He gives her a solid one-armed hug but keeps his fingers entwined within mine. This does not go unnoticed by anyone; they all look at us questioningly.

"Well, they were at the house we were in," Don begins. "We came down the stairs and stood face-to-face with a horrifically thin, dirty man. He warned us, placed a finger to his lips and pointed outside. Then he began muttering under his breath. He was feeding us information in a way it didn't sound like he was talking to anyone."

"What?" Marnie shrieks, "oh my God that was so close. I am so glad you guys are okay."

"What kind of info did he share?" Todd questions. "Do we finally know where they go?"

"No," he starts. "We ascertained they are typically on scavenges for about two hours. They send people who are coupled, keeping one back at the compound, sending the other out. He said this is how they keep them in check when they are out. He said something about they have total control, cannot even move if the aliens don't want them to."

"That's crazy," Joanie says.

"Yeah, but is anything out of the realm of possibility at this point?" Don asks. "He said the 'damn alien king is right here in Tennessee'. He is the one 'pulling the strings.'"

"What?" Ethan asks astounded.

"That is what he said," Don says getting annoyed at the interruptions. "He said the schedule is messed up because they are preparing for an alien event. That they were expecting a lot more of them."

"Wow, that is a lot of information," Ethan comments. "Anything else?"

"The only other things were that they'll kill you if you look at them wrong, and something about if you look at the crystal, they will kill you for looking at it." Don finishes.

"That's creepy," I say out loud remember the conversation, "what in the world can that be about?"

"Clearly whatever 'the crystal' is, is quite important to them," Don answers.

"The way he acted to; Don was about to speak, but the man stopped him pointing to his ear then outside. I think these things might hear really well," I add.

"This is certainly the most information we've had yet," Ethan says thoughtfully.

"That poor man," I say, feeling bad for him, "was covered in scars. They looked fairly recent. I wish there were some way we could have helped him. I am just grateful he didn't give us away."

"He didn't want us captured, he's rooting for the rebels," Don says with evident sadness.

"Well, it's been a long stressful day," Ethan says standing up and stretching. "I'm headed up to bed, we can debrief more tomorrow on how this impacts us, if at all."

"Night E," we say.

Slowly everyone moves off to bed. I notice Todd give Joanie a long hug before she heads up to bed. He sits down on the couch with us after she's gone.

"So what's going on there," I ask pointedly. I feel responsible for Joanie, even though she is not my sister, and her brother left me without a second thought.

"Nothing nefarious Rae, I promise," Todd says a bit defensively. "I do like her very much. She is a very smart, amazing young woman." I give him a hard look at young. "Yeah Rae, I know she is young. Nothing physical is happening, I've vowed to myself to be there for her, support her. She is really still struggling with Connor's betrayal." I flinch at the mention of his name. "Which brings up," he continues, "what's with you two?"

"We're dating," Don says confidently. I give him a small smile at this assessment.

"Really now, does big brother know this," Todd asks.

"Oh, I think big brother knows a lot more about Rae and me than you do," Don says, making me blush. I turn to stare at him, certainly he didn't tell him about that one night so long ago. "We've found we are very compatible," Don finishes.

I give his hand a squeeze, then reach up giving him a peck on the lips. "I'm headed to bed gentleman. It has been one hell of a day."

"Night baby," Don says, giving my hand a squeeze.

CHAPTER 35 NEW REALITY

The next several weeks pass without much excitement. We've decreased our time in the watchtower. We feel like we learned more from our one encounter with the man from the scavenging detail than we did in five or so months of watching. Obviously, we aren't going to count on meetings like that one to provide information consistently, but watching hasn't offered much. We do spend a few hours a day watching to understand where they are and if their activities create a threat for us. We also watch more closely ahead of a scavenging mission, but otherwise, we've dropped the constant surveillance.

Late one night Don and I are watching movies in his room when we hear the outer garage door open. Startled, we both jump up grabbing our weapons and head into the kitchen.

"Who could it be?" I whisper.

"They used a key so I can only assume it is Bud and Thomas, but I can't know for sure," Don whispers back.

Hearing the noise, Ethan tiptoes stealthily down the stairs, holding his Air Force issued pistol. He looks at us in the dull blue lantern light pointing at the door. Don nods as we watch.

Slowly the door to the kitchen opens. The newcomers, anticipating the welcome on the other side enter with their arms in the air. "It's us," they whisper.

"Oh thank God," Don says. "We'd given up hope of ever seeing you two again."

"Just took us a while," the male voice responds.

Don relaxes his pose, moving over to hug the two newcomers. "Bud, Thomas, this is my girlfriend Reagan, who also happens to be this loser's sister," motioning to Ethan, slinking around the corner.

"Ethan," the other says with evident relief.

"Boys," he says, "excellent to see you. What the hell took you so long?"

"Well, we set off together as you know. We had to go to both Indiana and Pennsylvania, looking for our families. Though sadly we found neither," he says.

"Rae, this is Bud," he says, pointing to a man with spiky brown hair and green eyes. "And this is Thomas," he says, pointing to a man with dark, almost black hair, freckles, and dark brown eyes.

"Welcome," I say. "Guessing you guys are army since my brother seems to be the only pilot around," I say, offering each of them a handshake.

"Yes, ma'am, we're the bad asses of the Army," Thomas answers.

"Well guys," Don continues, "It is certainly late. For tonight it is probably best if you guys take the couches; we'll sort out the bedroom situation in the morning."

"That's fine" Bud answers, "though I'd love a few minutes in a real bathroom before nodding off."

"Sure, use the bathroom in there," Don says, pointing towards his room.

"Thanks," Bud answers, he and Thomas head off towards Don's room.

"Um so, they're together," Don says.

"Yeah, I kind of gathered that," I respond, "well, good for

them, they were able to stay together so far."

Bud and Thomas disappear into the bathroom for a while. Goodness knows the last time they had toilet paper or a shower. They return refreshed, though in the same tattered clothing they arrived in.

"Well, you two look a little better," I comment when they reappear.

"Sorry, it's been a tough journey," Bud says.

"Do you guys need a meal before we all head to bed?" I ask.

"No, we found some food at a house outside of town before we headed up here." Thomas answers.

"Cool," I answer just as Don returns from his bedroom with extra blankets and pillows.

"This will do for the rest of tonight," Don comments.

"Thanks," they answer in unison.

"So, who else is here?" Bud asks questioningly.

"Todd made it a few months ago," Ethan states matter of fact.

"Really?" Thomas asks.

"Yes, but he arrived alone," Don adds.

"Oh that baby girl," Bud adds with sadness.

"Obviously, Ethan made it. He brought Rae here, her friend Marnie," Don gets out before being cut off.

"Oh yay, he found Martina," Thomas exclaims with excitement. Man, these two are exuberant.

"Yes," Ethan chimes in, "her three small sisters are here as well, though her parents were captured. Mom, along with Rae's friend Joanie's mom, were in the city when it was destroyed. Joanie is upstairs too."

"Wow, you've got a houseful," Bud notes.

"Yes," Don says, "my mama is here as well. She occupies the other bedroom on this floor. She'll be up before any of us in the morning. So, when she shrieks seeing y'all on the couch, just tell her who you are; all will be right with the world. She will be excited to have a few more to take care of," he finishes with a silent laugh.

"Speaking of Joanie," I break-in, "I should get upstairs to her. Nice to meet you, Bud, Thomas. Night Don," I finish slipping over and giving him a kiss on the lips. While I disappear up the stairs I hear one of them say, "Oh, you have got to tell us about how that happened," to which Ethan responds, "I'd rather not hear about it." I laugh to myself entering my room to call it a night.

The next morning all the boys are up on the watchtower, so I fill Marnie in on the newcomers that arrived during the night.

"Wait," she says, "they're together, together?"

"Yeah, why?" I ask

"Eww." She answers.

"Seriously Mar," I say "to each their own. It won't bother us any. Besides, they are a hoot."

"Yeah, but how do I explain that to the girls?" She asks.

"Why do you have to tell them anything, it's not like they'll have sex in front of them," I counter. "Or tell them when two people love each other they are together, no matter whether you agree or disagree, it is none of your damn business." I add pointedly.

"Yeah, but it's not..." she trails off.

"Again, what difference does it make to you? You're not the one engaging in the, um, activities. God commands us to love everyone regardless of their differences." I say, a bit put off by my friend's behavior.

We had gay friends at school, but I guess we didn't have to live with them. "Besides, I am sure if you ask them nicely, and not like a squeamish prude, they will refrain from all activities in front of the girls. The rest of us do."

"Yeah, you're right. I guess it just caught me a bit off guard," she says. "I never planned on playing mom to three little girls. Conversations like this were ones I never though I'd encounter."

The next few days are tough. Bud and Thomas are both helpful but have larger than life personalities. After being used to the quiet day-to-day of the group assembled here, it is feeling a bit claustrophobic. Tomorrow should be a rest day for the aliens, so I decide I'm going to trek down the mountain to get the bag we stashed a few weeks ago.

"Do you want me to go with you Rae?" Don asks concerned.

"No," I answer. "We never see them this far up the mountain and it should be a rest day. I just want some time alone; we don't get that around here."

"Okay, we'll go up the watchtower," Ethan counters.

"Seriously boys, I'll be fine," I argue.

The next morning I get up early, grabbing a breakfast of a granola bar and water. Don once again tries to convince me to allow him to accompany me. "Nope, I've got this, be back in about two hours."

I am in no hurry as I make my way down the mountain, this journey won't take long and is relatively safe. I keep my hand on my pistol just in case. It takes about forty-five minutes to find the cave structure where we hid the bag. I am feeling much better by now. Having had time to think, daydream, and ponder life by myself. When I reach into the cave to retrieve the bag I hear a woman scream to my right, I don't recognize the voice, but the cry is that of someone terrified. "No, no, please leave me, let me go," she screams.

Crap, there's trouble in the area. I frantically cram myself into the cave where the bag was hidden, lying on my side. I then work to silently pull the branches and leaves back over the opening.

I am at a disadvantage, I won't see anyone coming until their shoes are under my nose. I lay silently, trying hard to not even breathe. It is going to be a long day, but I know I am trapped. This is my best hope at survival. I don't know how long I will have to stay silent before it is safe to move on. I work hard to slow my racing heart beat and quiest myu breathing.

I worry the others will come looking for me when I don't return as expected, walking into a trap. This fear is creeping icily through my veins, and I think I am about to lose my mind. I hear a branch break near my hideout. I want to scream, instead I bite down hard on my lip to hold in the terror. I taste a bit of blood in my mouth.

They are obviously moving about the area but none of them turn their attention to where I am hidden. I lay with silent tears of fear falling down my face. I tell myself I will never venture out by myself again, claustrophobic or not. This little cave is much smaller than the cabin. It is fortunate I am alone, only one person can fit in here.

Eventually it grows quiet, I no longer hear the sounds of searching but I don't dare move. I am even more upset by the fact they have ventured this far up on the mountain; we've never seen them this high before. Hopefully, it was just the woman camping that caught their attention and this will not become a routine thing.

The day fades into night, I am wondering if it is safe to move when I hear silent footsteps. These steps are of someone trying to remain undetected, but I do not dare show myself not knowing if it is a friend or a stranger. Then I hear my name whispered silently, it is Don.

"Thank God," I murmur emerging from the cave.

"We saw the whole thing from the watchtower, you did just right," Don says hugging me tightly.

"Ugh, get me home will you," I say.

"Of course," he says but gives me a long kiss first.

"What happened to the woman?" I ask.

"She had a campfire going, which is what alerted those idiots to her presence. They took her back to their compound, then she was flown away in one of their aircraft." He says.

"Oh," is all I can think to say.

Back at the cabin everyone is relieved when I return. "Sorry guys," I say sheepishly.

"No worries, girl," Thomas says running over to hug me. "It did seem like a perfect day to make that trip; we are all just glad you're okay."

"Plus if there had been two of you, you couldn't have hidden in that cave," Bud adds.

"Thank you," I say.

CHAPTER 36 DEJA VU

As summer begins to fade into fall we are no nearer a solution than when this whole thing started. Life in the cabin has once again settled down, flawlessly absorbing our latest additions into the fold. Bud and Thomas are hilarious and have proven to be quite helpful around the house and in planning. They share the burden of making scavenging runs as needed, which takes some pressure off Don and me.

Don and I have moved into his room together. Joanie is happy for us and has settled down enough since Connor's departure she is able to sleep well on her own. I do suspect, whether anything inappropriate is happening or not, Todd spends many nights in there with her. She swears he just comforts her, I trust her, but am concerned again about her youth.

After being largely unpredictable for the past several months, the shifters have resumed somewhat of a schedule again. That is a good thing, we are going to need a good supply run soon. A good portion of the road washed away recently in a horrid summer storm, we won't be able to take the jeep, so that means multiple runs over the coming weeks. None of us are thrilled about this notion but it is what has to be done.

One day, in what I believe to be late September Don blurts out, "Rae and I will go ahead and go, Bud and Thomas made the last trip. It's been tranquil out there again, so now seems like it is the time to go. Rather than waiting until later when the need is greater, but the danger is also potentially greater."

Of everyone in the cabin, the four of us are unfortunately the natural choices to make these trips. Ethan is a born leader; he needs to stay home and keep the group safe. Marnie needs to stay and keep her sisters calm. Wanda is older, and while not to be discounted, she is decidedly slower. Joanie is out; she just mentally isn't up to the challenge. With Joanie's dependence on Todd since Connor left, she cannot lose another anchor in her life. So, that leaves Bud, Thomas, Don and me to take the risks and make the raids. Any one of us can do it alone, but we all agree, the way we've seen them operate, it is better to have two, so you can split them up.

"We'll go just before sunset," Don explains, "that way we can observe before we go, making sure there is no movement out there. Hopefully then we can make good time while there is still some light."

"That works for me," I say a bit apprehensively, the way I always feel before one of these treks. "I'm going to take a nap, so I'm well-rested," I announce to the group making my way absently to the bedroom Don and I share.

Once in my room, I find it hard to relax and fall asleep, I always do ahead of one of these trips. But, I manage in time. It's good that I do because the trips' stress always takes a toll on me, and I need to function.

Once I wake, I dress for travel. I put on a pair of jeans, even though it is still hot outside in a late Indian Summer. I choose a short sleeve but heavy shirt that will provide protection from sticks and thorn bushes to my torso. It is still just too hot for long sleeves. I finish by lacing up my ankle-high riding boots. This time we aren't going that far. A few houses down the mountain at the edge of the park are still relatively well-stocked with food and will provide what we need today.

"Well, shall we," I say to Don. Even though we've made these trips often and have gotten exceptionally good, it is still nerve-wracking

"Let's hit it, little lady," he responds.

"I'm going to head up to the observation tower," Ethan announces.

"Awesome, with any luck, we'll see you in five or six hours," I say, heading out the door along the backside of the mountain.

Don and I are making our way down the familiar path, it is evening, but there is still plenty of light. We are making great time, and pause to inspect the road where it washed away over the summer. We discuss the pros and cons of how we can fix the road to get the jeep down.

Moving on down the mountain we can still see, but it will be dark when we return. Our eyes adjust easily as evening falls, and we can move through the trees with ease. We are nearing the target area, the houses on the edge of the park, when something feels off. I slow my pace when I feel the hairs on the back of my neck prick up. Turning to look at Don, I register the shimmering to my left, almost like I knew it would be there. 'RUN' I mouth wordlessly to Don. He takes off, and I follow.

There are none of our hidden hideouts down this far on the mountain. We're going to have to improvise—Don darts through a wall of branches, into a thicket of berry bushes. I settle in beside him, covered in scrapes from the thorns. We sit, silently hoping we've lost them. We hear them calling in their werid speech of hums while we crouch in the thicket of berry bushes. It doesn't take long before we're surrounded.

We're doomed. There is no way out of this. Once they start a search, they don't quit. I am comforted knowing that as a group we've discussed this, what happens if someone is caught. We don't waste our lives. Someone has to walk away from this, if at all possible. Someone must continue for our families, for our race, for our world. I look over at Don and mouth, "I'm sorry." He pulls me into a giant bear hug then kisses me passionately, holding my hand and squeezing it tight. He mouths "the count of three," holding up three fingers.

I solemnly nod my head. He holds up one finger, then two, then off we go; the game that will only end with our capture or death once it has begun.

As I run, I am grateful these things are not as fast as humans. It's the sheer number of them that is the problem. Once on your trail they chase you into another grouping. That is how you are caught, that and those hideous weapons they have. I know these things, so I am on alert for the first sign of a shift in front of me. I also know, no matter how many twists and turns I make, eventually I will mess up, running straight into one of their groupings. I dart behind a tree and see shimmering in front of me indicating a creature shifting. I duck low behind a thicket of berry bushes and change directions before the shift is complete. Don flawlessly follows in my footsteps, already anticipating the need to change direction. It's several steps before we once again sense pursuit behind us.

We've been running for several minutes when I see the shimmer again. At this point, I break left, Don goes right. We've had this planned as well. We think we'll have a better chance individually if we divide their group. I travel uphill temporarily but see a shifter already formed in front of me. He raises the silver weapon. I tuck and roll down a hill and push my pace a bit faster. I am continually searching for a place to hide. If I can get far enough ahead of them, I could duck in somewhere. Maybe they'd leave. As I continue no such place appears before me.

I am running downhill when I see the shimmer again. I turn back right and continue uphill a bit. It occurs to me I am leading them back in the direction of the cabin, this won't do. I quickly make a sharp left and head downhill again. Immediately I know this was the wrong move; I see three creatures in front of me. They've just completed their shift, not having yet raised their weapons, so I run through their line continuing downhill.

I am faster. It takes them a moment to orient once the shift is complete to continue along the path. I do not sense pursuit behind me and wonder if I've lost them. If I continue as I have, I will make noise, allowing them to follow me. If I try to hide here thinking if I've lost them, they might find me. I stop for only seconds to ponder these two options when I hear them crashing through the woods. Off I go continuing along the same downhill path.

My mind suddenly registers I am running to that void in the landscape where we assume they have their camp. This is not good. I've got to move the other direction, but away from the cabin. I shift to my left and continue downhill but now moving to the north instead of the south. I've been going for a while now, and my lungs burn with the effort.

I think of Don. I wonder if he is having better luck than I. Perhaps he did find a reliable hiding place. I just hope he led them away from the cabin. If they continue searching, they might find the cabin instead. Distracted by these thoughts it takes a minute to register the shimmering ahead of me. This time, I dart past it, then snake back uphill a bit, determined not to lead them back to the cabin.

I've been running for at least 20 minutes, maybe longer. I won't be able to go much longer, but as long as they are on my trail, they move farther away from my family in the cabin. The shifters only know there were two of us, and from what we've been able to observe, they don't stay back to search for more. They chase what they can see. I think of Don, kind, strong, determined, but proud and belligerent, all the things that made him a great Army Ranger.

I begged him if he were ever captured to not fight, to be submissive, and have a chance to escape someday, but I know better. He won't be caught; he will be killed if he is cornered. I will with all my heart that he can escape, finding a path clear of the shifters to run away. This distraction makes me clumsy, jumping a small creek, my foot catches on a jagged rock on the other side. I stumble, twisting my ankle hard. My boots don't allow my ankle to flex as it needs to causing my ankle to bend in unnatural angles. It takes me a minute to stand and regain my balance. I listen but do not hear anyone behind me. This itself seems strange.

Taking in my surroundings makes my insides go cold; that foreboding sense of Deja Vu takes over my body. I've been here so many times in the past year in my mind. I know how this is going to go. Can I run? I don't think so, not on this leg. I listen for the footfall, and the twig snap I know is coming.

Just then, I feel the hairs on the back of my neck stand up and I hear it. I turn around to face the thing or person behind me, not exactly sure what to expect. In my daydreams or nightmares, I never got past the shimmer of a recently changed shifter. When I turn the shifter is becoming human, which explains the fuzzy appearance in my daydreams.

In the time it takes me to blink, a handsome man steps from the shadows, though I know the truth, this is no man. It's a shifter, and I am caught. If there is one, there are many more lurking, hidden behind, or maybe pretending to be trees for all I know.

I see the weapon in his hand pointed at me. I don't know exactly what those weapons are, but I've seen what they can do, "Come with me won't you?" he says in frighteningly good English but the same odd accent. He says it like a question, though I know I have no choice.

I step forward with a sense of dread enveloping me. I've never seen the inside of their compound, just the emaciated, broken humans who come and go on scavenging runs. I take a few tentative steps forward and a dozen or more shifters emerge from the trees completely surrounding me. I ran right into their trap.

Some step out as humans, some in what we believe to be their natural gremlinish alien form, all brandishing those same silver weapons. I fight hard as the tears threaten to fall down my face, the panic threatening to paralyze me. I pray silently that Don has better luck than I and can find his way far away from here. No tears won't help any of us now, so I pray for my loved ones. God, please let Don have gotten out. Please don't let my presence here alert them to others. Keep Marnie, Ethan, Joanie, Wanda, Todd, Bud, Thomas, and the girls safe. Then I hesitantly step forward into the unknown.

EPILOGUE

Today's detail was easy, making for a better day than most here, but the best part was the note. I never thought I would feel happy ever again, let alone in this place but today I did. I often reach my hand in my pocket, feeling the note is still there, so I know it is real and I did not dream it. I always like it when I get assigned to the scavenging detail. It is nerve-wracking because they separate couples when we do this. They know we would never leave each other, so it is hard being away from Missy. But I get to be outside, not having to continually dig a new cavern or space. Today we visited the neighborhood where my mom had lived.

I was unable to go into the house. I was glad. What if they perished hiding in that closet? I would be unable to go on if I found their emaciated bodies there. Ted searched the house instead; the smile on his face when he emerged told me that the girls were not there in any form. Well, that is something, but where are they? What happened to them? They are way too young to be out on their own, Marie being the oldest at six. This worry has kept me going but is also eating me alive inside.

His sacks are loaded with canned goods; I told him where to find the cache. While we travel he works his way closer to me; it takes about twenty or thirty minutes before he is close to me. Once near, under the guise of passing me a sack, he hands me something else, a piece of paper it seems. I wonder what it could be; maybe he found a loose photograph or some other memorabilia. I do not dare look at it now under the watchful eyes of these warriors. I will wait until we are back in the underground compound. I am dying inside to see what he has passed me.

It is a long, taxing day. We are not allowed to speak to each other while out of our cell, so I cannot ask Ted what he found. Finally, the sun begins to set, we are heading back to the underground compound with the food we have been able to scavenge. Food taken from these houses sustains us slaves in these alien compounds. When this supply runs out, I do not know what will happen to us and how we will eat.

I have come to learn there are cavernous compounds such as this all across our country. Many of those imprisoned here have family members that were shuttled off to other regions. They do not know what has happened to them. Is it possible the girls were caught separately from us? That they are enduring these unimaginable horrors we experience here, but somewhere else, alone? That thought terrorizes me always, and I shudder. Ted notices the shudder and gives me a consoling look.

Based on the tick marks we make on our cell walls it has been nearly six months since we were imprisoned and left the girls hiding in the house. Not to mention, I have no clue about our eldest daughter Martina. Was she killed in an explosion? Was she captured after the blast in the raids? If she was caught, is anyone with her she knows and can trust? What happened to her best friend, Rae? Are they together? I am distracted by these thoughts as we make our way back to the compound, making the time passes quickly.

Finally, we are back in the cavern, locked behind the invisible barriers in our cell. I am fortunate enough that not only did my wife stay here, in this compound with me, but she is in the same cell group as I am. Once the forcefields have been re-established around us, we are released from the immobilization that accompanies the forcefield's opening. That is when the aliens all disappear into their respective spaces again; I can finally reach into my pocket to see what Ted had passed me earlier. My eyes instantly dissolve into tears. I stare at the note with relief swelling through my body. Missy, concerned with what I have, rushes over and looks at the note.

"Oh, thank God," she whispers, "Ethan is taking care of all of our girls. They are safe." My wife and I embrace tightly. I know Ethan is a good and smart soldier; he'll have a safe place to hide them. I know they are not in some alien prison camp somewhere. They have not had to endure the torture and abuse we have faced. They will not be scarred for the remainder of their lives by having to suffer what we've gone through here.

I re-read the note:

'Frank/Missy, I really hope you get a chance to read this note. I had some, not much, warning what was about to happen. I was able to rescue Marnie and Rae. While on our way to a friend's safe house, we stopped to get you but were too late. I did find the girls. They were still hiding in the closet, but Marie recognized my voice. I am taking them with us to Tennessee. When, or I guess if, it is ever safe, we will meet you back in Ohio. In the meantime, God be with you. All my love, Ethan.'

Even if I die tomorrow, I can die at peace knowing my girls are safe.

After giving us a few minutes to process alone, Ted walks over and claps me on the back. "I wasn't completely sure what I was reading in that note, but I was fairly sure it was something you would want to see," he says.

"Yes," I whisper, still somewhat choked up. "My eldest

daughter Marnie, her best friend's brother is in the Air Force, and elite squadron. Well, was in the Air Force, I guess there is no more Air Force at this point. He and Marnie, and his sister Reagan, rescued the girls that night and have them in hiding somewhere."

"Well, that is good news," Ted answers, his face full of solemn happiness. Ted's family was captured. His wife and son were sent to another compound somewhere shortly after arriving here before he was even marked. He does not know where they are but knows that they are likely enduring the same tortures we have had to face here. I hug him, knowing the pain he must be feeling inside. "I pray," I say, "you will see them whole, again one day."

BOOK 2 - ENSLAVED

Prologue: Rick

Coming January 2021

From the footsteps coming down the stairs it sounds like they have caught some other poor soul. That poor person does not know what a difficult and painful week they are in for. I am sure he or she is appropriately terrified. We all exchange glances with one another in anticipation of seeing the doomed soul coming down the steps.

We finally catch sight, it is a beautiful girl. Beside me my cell mate starts to jump up from his sitting position; I reach over clamping my hand down hard on his shoulder holding him in place. If he knows her, showing interest now will only cause more trouble for the both of them. I shoot him a warning look, and see tears filling his eyes. "It's her," he mouths breathlessly.

"Get a hold of yourself, showing familiarity to her now will only cause you both trouble" I warn in stern whisper. The look on his face is of utter pain and misery "man I am so sorry" is all I can say. I watch as the trembling girl is ushered down the tunnel to a holding cell at the end. The next four days will be the absolute worst of her existence. Of course, each of us has certainly endured enough torture labeled punishment since we've been here, but it has never been as bad as the first days physically, when they break you completely.

The day they murdered Tasha and Sam were mentally the most anguish I know I have ever felt in my life, a year and a half later I still wake up crying for them. But I know they are safe now; these things cannot hurt them any longer. That is the only comfort I can take from this situation. If I could have taken my life that day, I would have, they were my reason to continue here, but the aliens even have control over that too.

Just as they are shutting the door, he moans out her name; it echoes around the room. I am certain they don't know where it came from or even the word that was spoken, but I shoot him a dark warning look not to do it again. Once the girl is locked in the cell and the aliens have dispersed to their respective rooms my friend breaks into hopeless silent tears. "I really hoped she'd have stayed hidden, what was she doing out?" he sobs quietly.

It has been about two hours since she was locked in the cell and had her hands bound. A shifter removes her from the cell, it must be inspection time. I clamp my hand hard on my friend's arm to keep him still; I give him another look of warning to be quiet. He is absolutely trembling in rage as he sees her stumble along with the hood over her head, receiving smacks of punishment from not being able to keep up. She is gone for a time, but they return her to her cell; that is a good sign, she is staying here. At least he'll be able to know her fate, at this point though, I am not sure what is worse knowing or not knowing.

The week is miserable, I spend most of my time consoling my friend when we are not working. He has been punished often this week for slacking at his tasks. He has more welts and burn marks from the electric prod they use to punish on his arms than unblemished skin. We are currently tasked with digging out another room, they must be expecting another batch of these assholes. More of them coming here, how will they ever be defeated if they keep shipping in more from who knows where.

Time passes, the girl has been in her cell for around five days now with nothing but water. This is the longest we have seen them keep anyone isolated. She must have put up a hell of a fight before they got her down here. Carrie gave her water yesterday, she said she is alive but just barely. She has never seen someone get so weak before. She tried to console her earning herself a beating for it, but she says she is not sorry, someone had to give the girl hope so she would continue holding on.

We agreed not to tell her he is here, knowing this before she learned the ropes would cause them both trouble. On the sixth day the leader, Tadako, emerges again, this is it, though this will be the most painful day of her life to date, at least the isolation ends.

Several of us are on hand to restrain our cellmate once the screaming begins; it will be all he can do to not get himself killed. They are very rough with the girl while she is still in her holding cell. She is punished more than anyone I have seen yet, which is ridiculous seeing as how she cannot even stand on her own. The door is shut, my friend is bracing himself for what is to come. The door is reopened after Tadako leaves and she is led to the room. My friend whimpers her name seeing her lead by, but fortunately says no more.

I have been in that room twice, once when I was marked and once when it was my duty to remove those who died in the process. They do not remove them often, only when the presence grows large enough to impede their work. It is a horrifically disgusting task, the bodies in varying states of decay.

It does not take long for the screaming to start; my friend is lost in his agony. We do not have to restrain him as we had prepared for, he is immobilized by the sounds of torture coming from that room. He falls to his knees his face buried in his hands. Carrie is there, wrapping a consoling arm around him.

The screaming abruptly stops, faster than usual. He looks up at me, completely dead behind his blank eyes. We are all holding our breath for several minutes more, when one of them emerges carrying her limp body. "She must still be alive if they have removed her themselves, she has just passed out" I console him. Well good for her, she passed out a lot faster than most. It was probably from the starvation more than pain. Whatever the cause, she had less to endure. The shifter returns to the holding cell and uncaringly drops her on the floor. Ouch, that will leave a bruise.

The next morning Bruko, the exceptionally dumb, mean, smelly one is looking around the room at the various cells. He then walks over to our cell and presses the button to release the forcefield holding us. We are all instantly paralyzed. He looks at each of us in turn and moves to me, pressing the device in his hand against the disc implanted behind my ear, releasing me from the immobilization. "You" he grunts.

I am unsure of what task I have been chosen for, so I am feeling a bit apprehensive. I do not have to worry long, I am led to the holding cell where the girl is located. This is a stroke of luck, she will be imprisoned in our cell. She will find some comfort here and they will be together. I am thankful it didn't choose him for this task, I don't think he could have handled it. The cell opens and I see the blood-soaked emaciated shell of the girl laying pitifully on the floor. I work to choke back tears of my own. In this instance I can speak to her without punishment, so I take advantage to try to put her at ease after all she has endured.

"Hi there" I say gently to her, "my name is Rick, I'm going to take you to a room to get cleaned up. I am sorry you won't have privacy; I think they do that on purpose. We need to get the blood off you and apply ointment to your marks.

Once we're done there, you will get some food. Don't expect your stomach to tolerate much, you've been without food for around five days now. I will try to be gentle and speak to you as much as I can get away with along the way, but if I am ignoring you it is not out of cruelty, it is to keep us both safe. Do you understand?" I finish.

She looks up weakly, through distant eyes that I don't think can even focus on me, and gives a small nod.

Made in the USA
Monee, IL
02 February 2021